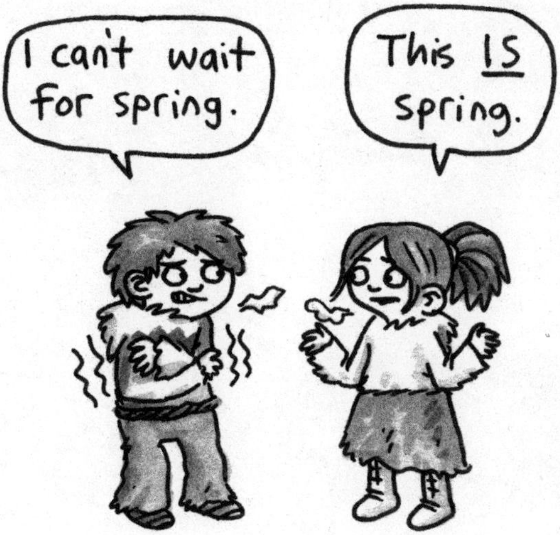
I can't wait for spring.
This IS spring.

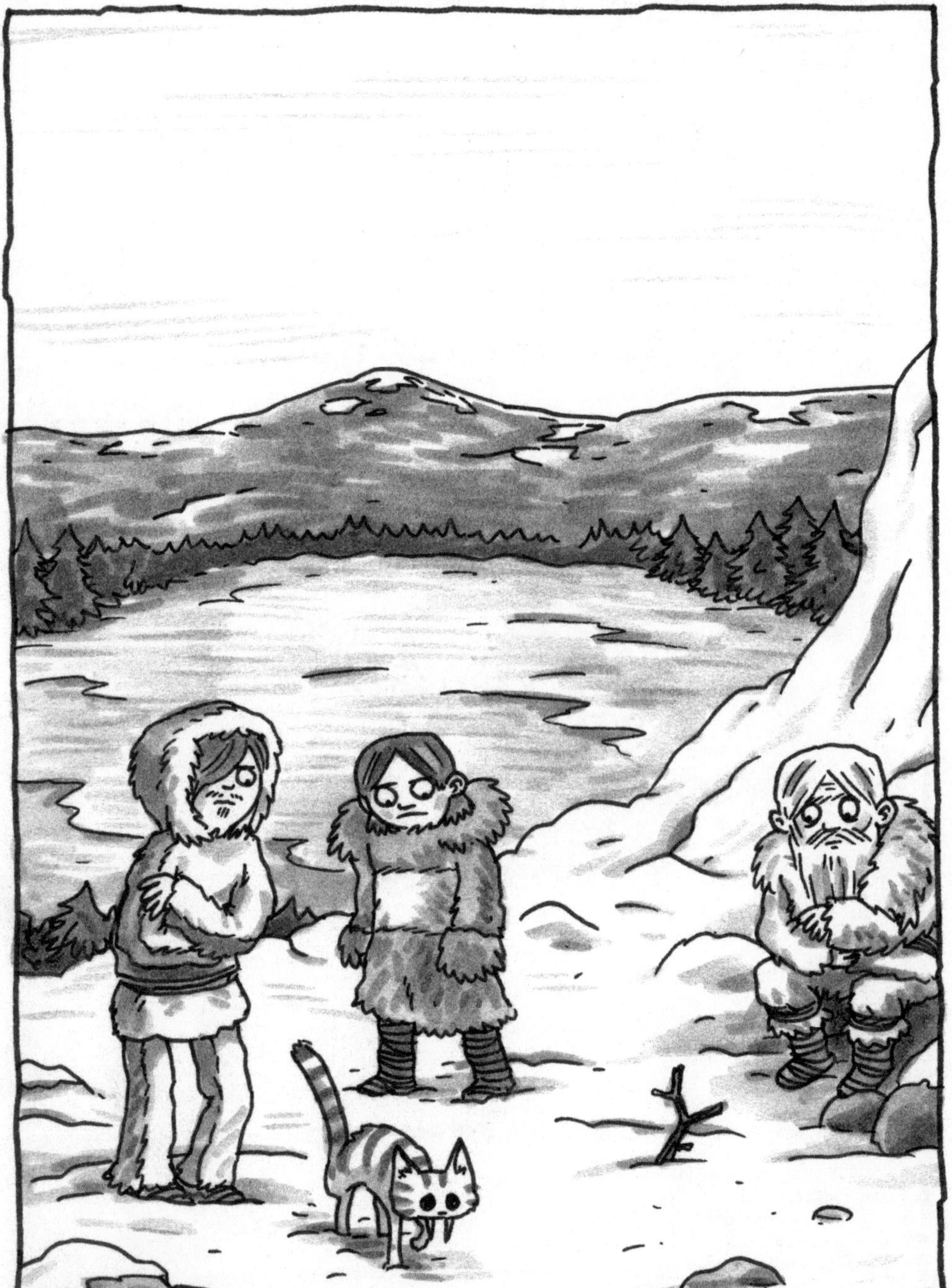

LUCY & ANDY NEANDERTHAL
THE STONE COLD AGE

Jeffrey Brown

CROWN BOOKS
for YOUNG READERS
New York

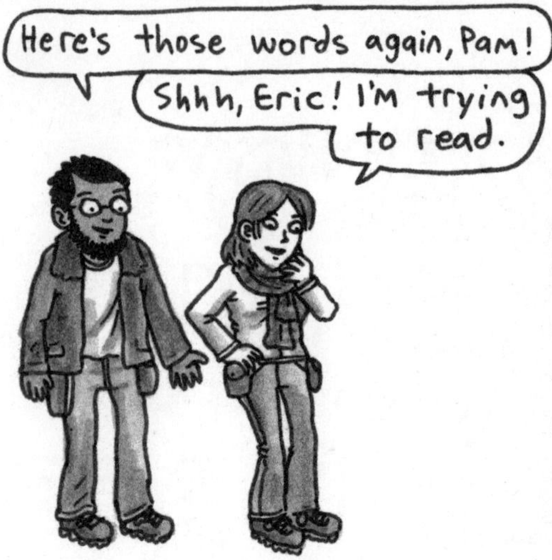
Here's those words again, Pam!
Shhh, Eric! I'm trying to read.

Thank you to my family, friends, publishers, and readers for all of their supports. Thanks also to Marc, Phoebe, and everyone at RH for making this book happen. And special thanks to Kevin Lee for giving me the nudge that led to the idea for this series.

For his expert assistance, grateful acknowledgement to Jonathan S. Mitchell, PhD, Evolutionary Biology, and member of the Geological Society of America, Socioty of Vertebrate Paleontology, and Society for the Study of Evolution.

 Published in the United States by Crown Books for Young Readers, an imprint of Random House Children's Books, a division of Penguin Random House LLC, New York.

Crown and the colophon are registered trademarks of Penguin Random House LLC.

Visit us on the Web! randomhousekids.com

Educators and librarians, for a variety of teaching tools, visit us at RHTeachersLibrarians.com

Library of Congress Cataloging-in-Publication Data is available upon request.
ISBN 978-0-385-38838-2 (trade) — ISBN 978-0-385-38840-5 (lib. bdg.) — ISBN 978-0-385-38839-9 (ebook)

Printed in the United States of America
10 9 8 7 6 5 4 3 2 1
First Edition

Random House Children's Books supports the First Amendment and celebrates the right to read.

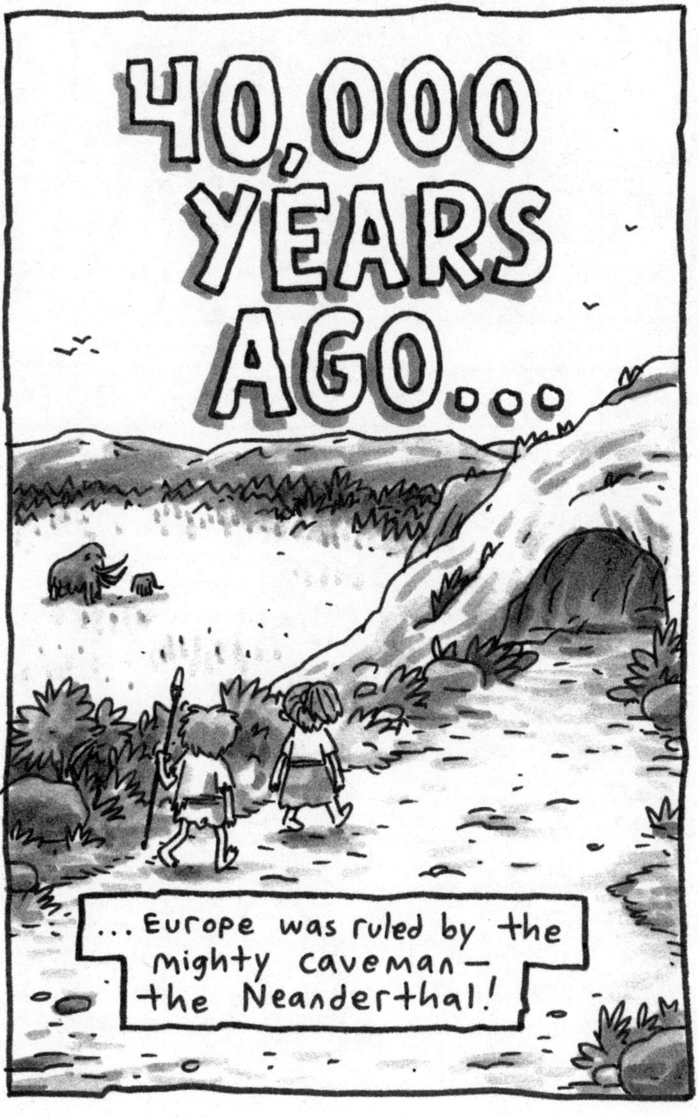
40,000 YEARS AGO...
...Europe was ruled by the mighty caveman—the Neanderthal!

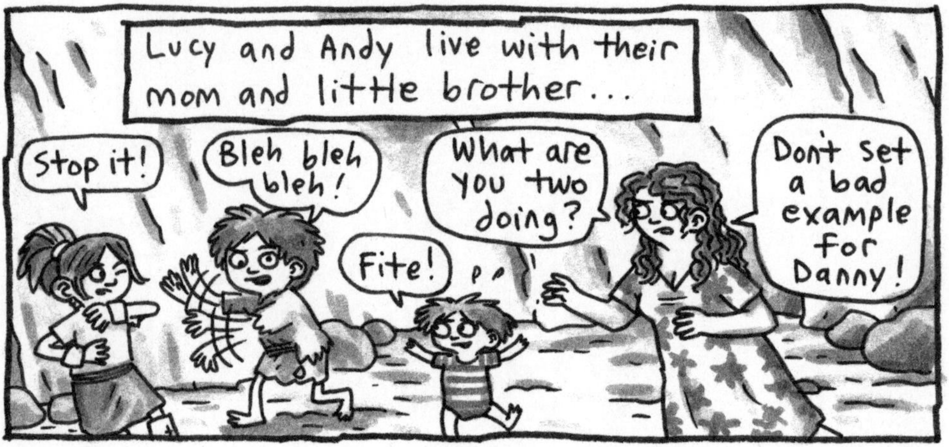
Lucy and Andy live with their mom and little brother...
Stop it!
Bleh bleh bleh!
Fite!
What are you two doing?
Don't set a bad example for Danny!

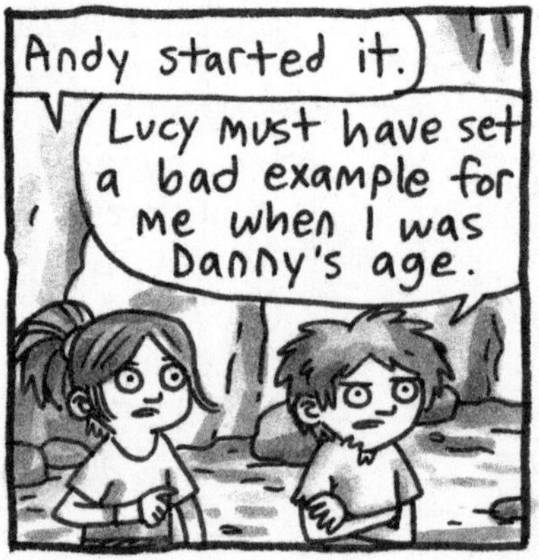
Andy started it.
Lucy must have set a bad example for me when I was Danny's age.

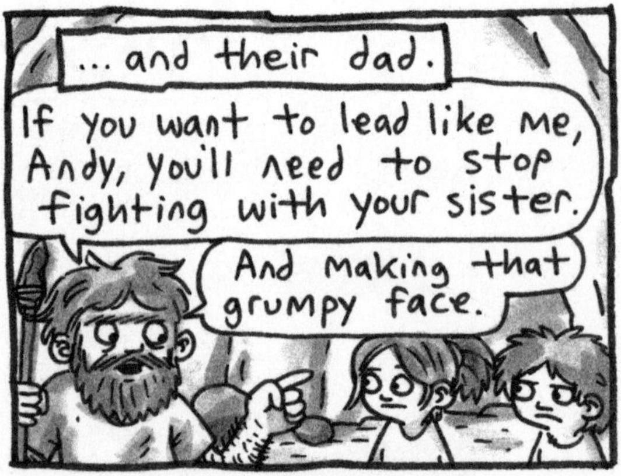
...and their dad.
If you want to lead like me, Andy, you'll need to stop fighting with your sister.
And making that grumpy face.

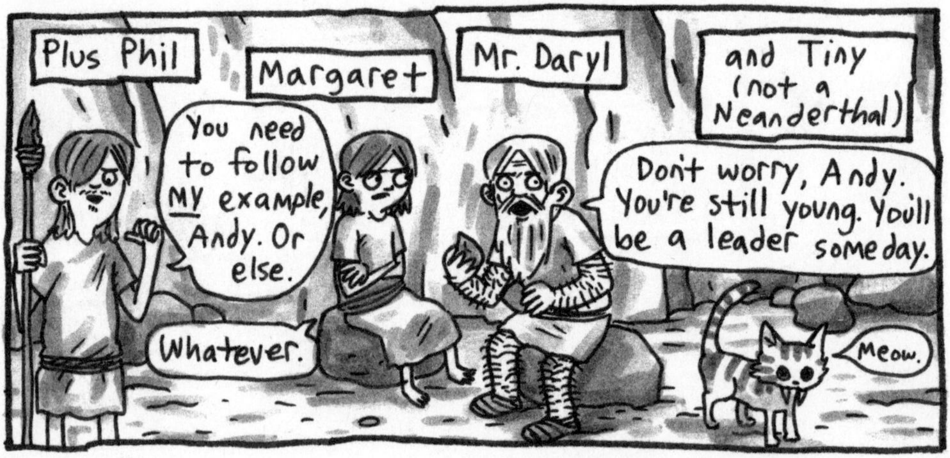
Plus Phil
Margaret
You need to follow MY example, Andy. Or else.
Whatever.
Mr. Daryl
Don't worry, Andy. You're still young. You'll be a leader someday.
and Tiny (not a Neanderthal)
Meow.

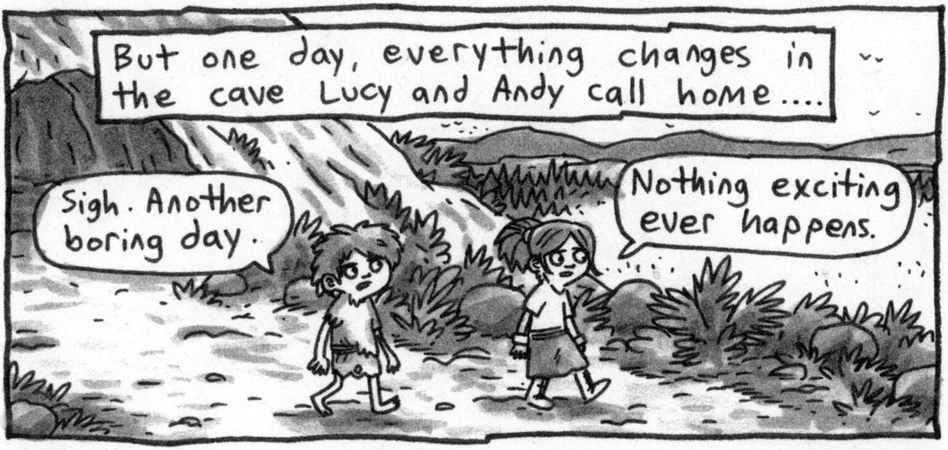
But one day, everything changes in the cave Lucy and Andy call home....
Sigh. Another boring day.
Nothing exciting ever happens.

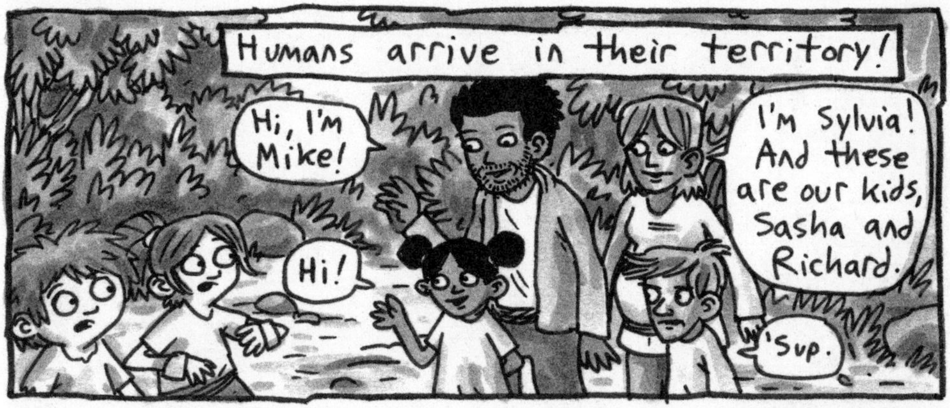
Humans arrive in their territory!
Hi, I'm Mike!
Hi!
I'm Sylvia! And these are our kids, Sasha and Richard.
'Sup.

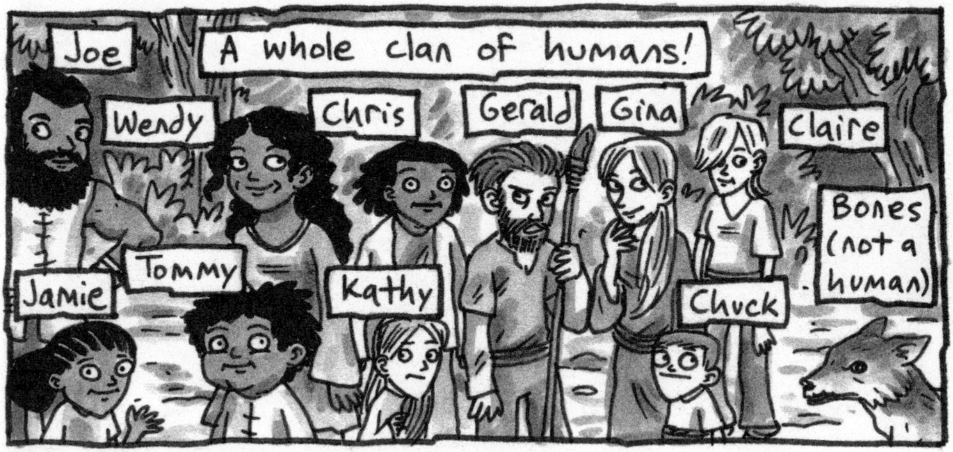
Joe
A whole clan of humans!
Wendy
Chris
Gerald
Gina
Claire
Bones (not a human)
Tommy
Jamie
Kathy
Chuck

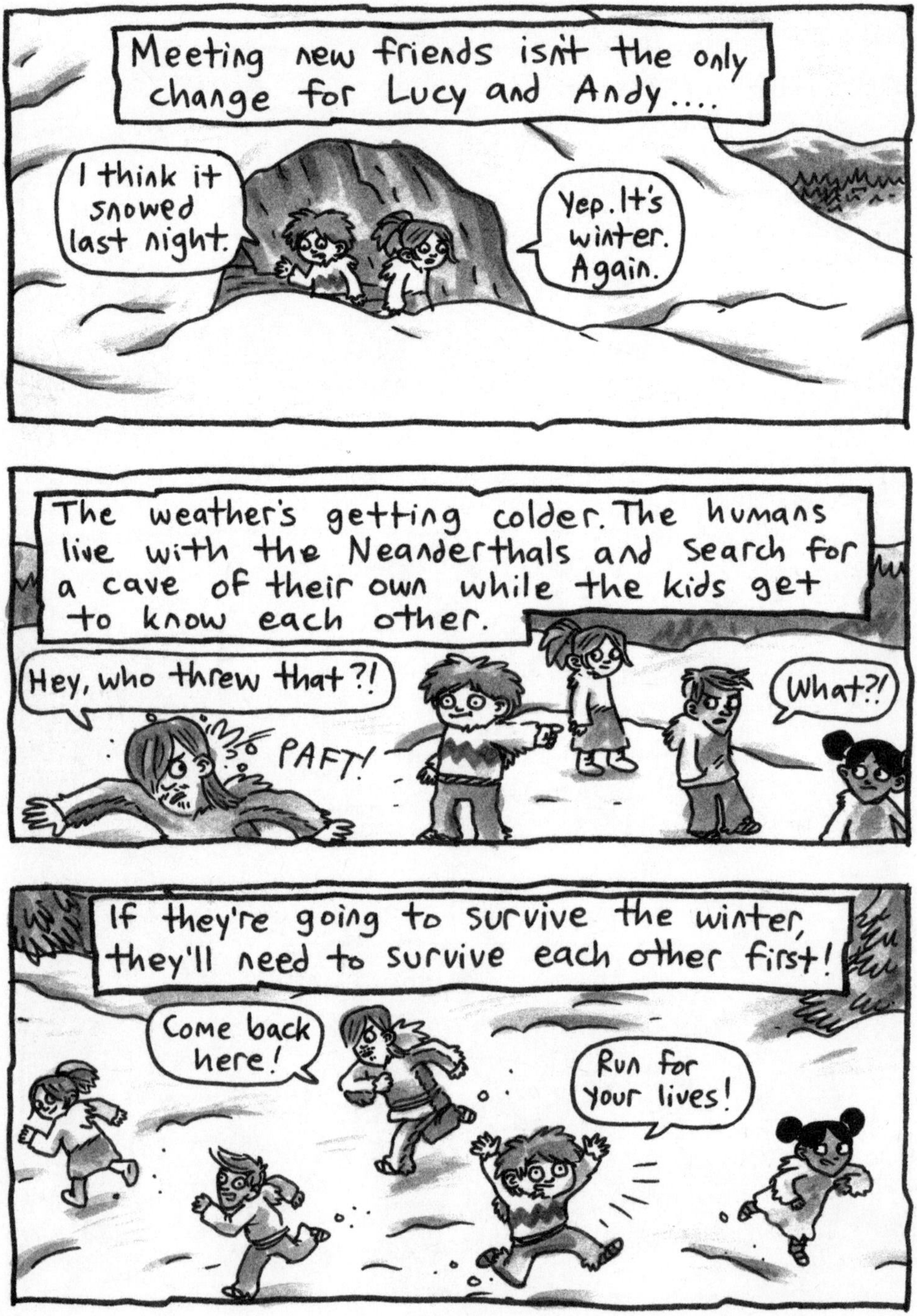
Meeting new friends isn't the only change for Lucy and Andy....
I think it snowed last night.
Yep. It's winter. Again.
The weather's getting colder. The humans live with the Neanderthals and search for a cave of their own while the kids get to know each other.
Hey, who threw that?!
PAFT!
What?!
If they're going to survive the winter, they'll need to survive each other first!
Come back here!
Run for your lives!

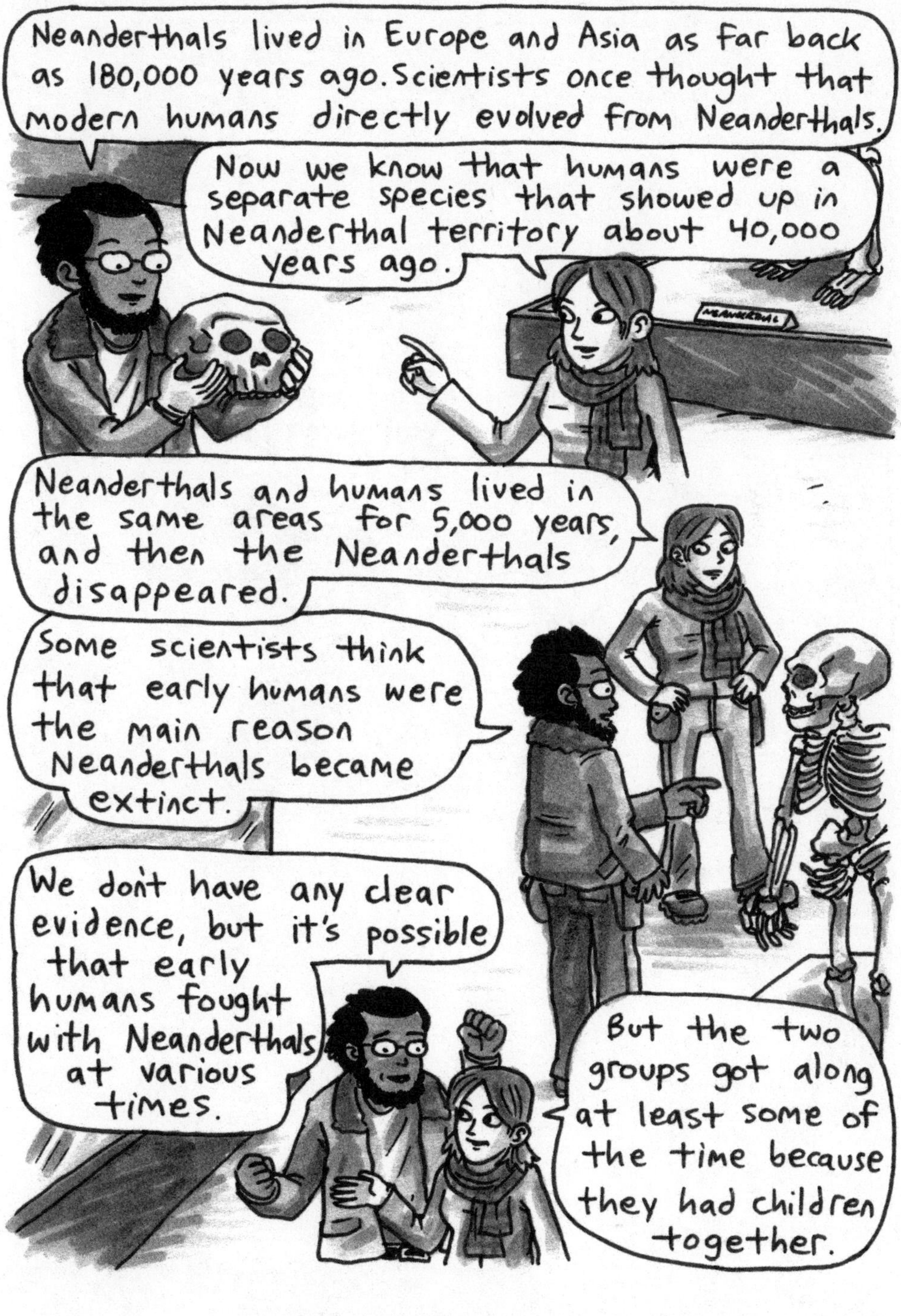

Neanderthals lived in Europe and Asia as far back as 180,000 years ago. Scientists once thought that modern humans directly evolved from Neanderthals.
Now we know that humans were a separate species that showed up in Neanderthal territory about 40,000 years ago.
Neanderthals and humans lived in the same areas for 5,000 years, and then the Neanderthals disappeared.
Some scientists think that early humans were the main reason Neanderthals became extinct.
We don't have any clear evidence, but it's possible that early humans fought with Neanderthals at various times.
But the two groups got along at least some of the time because they had children together.

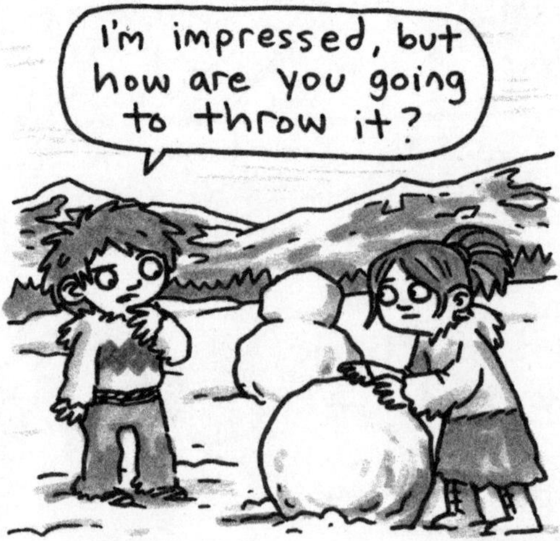
I'm impressed, but how are you going to throw it?

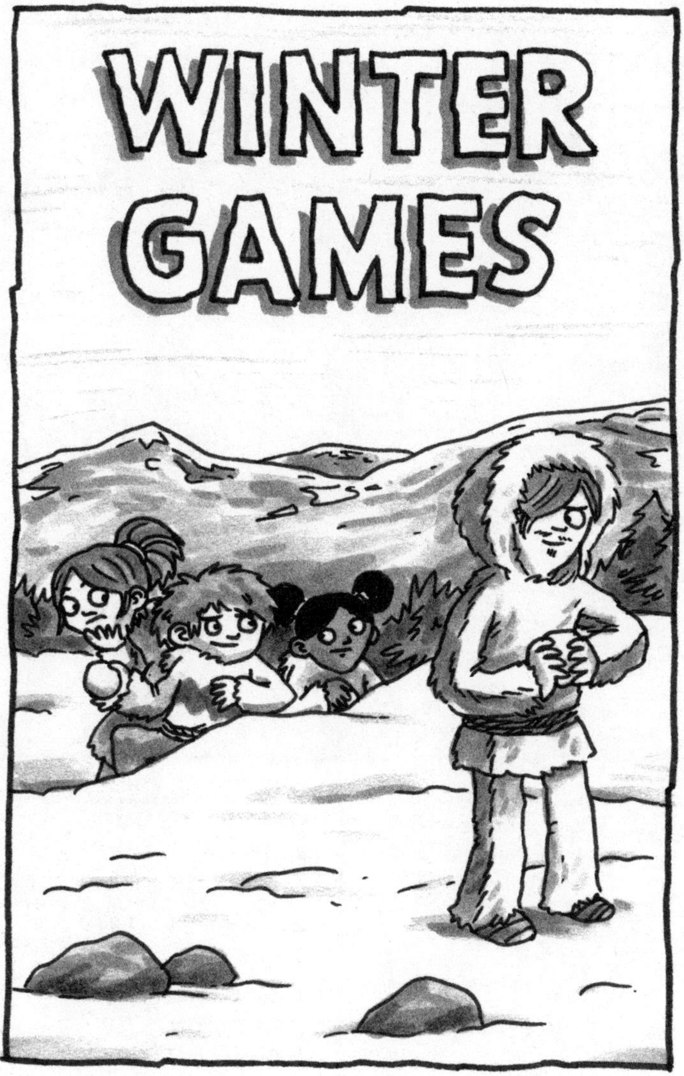
WINTER
GAMES

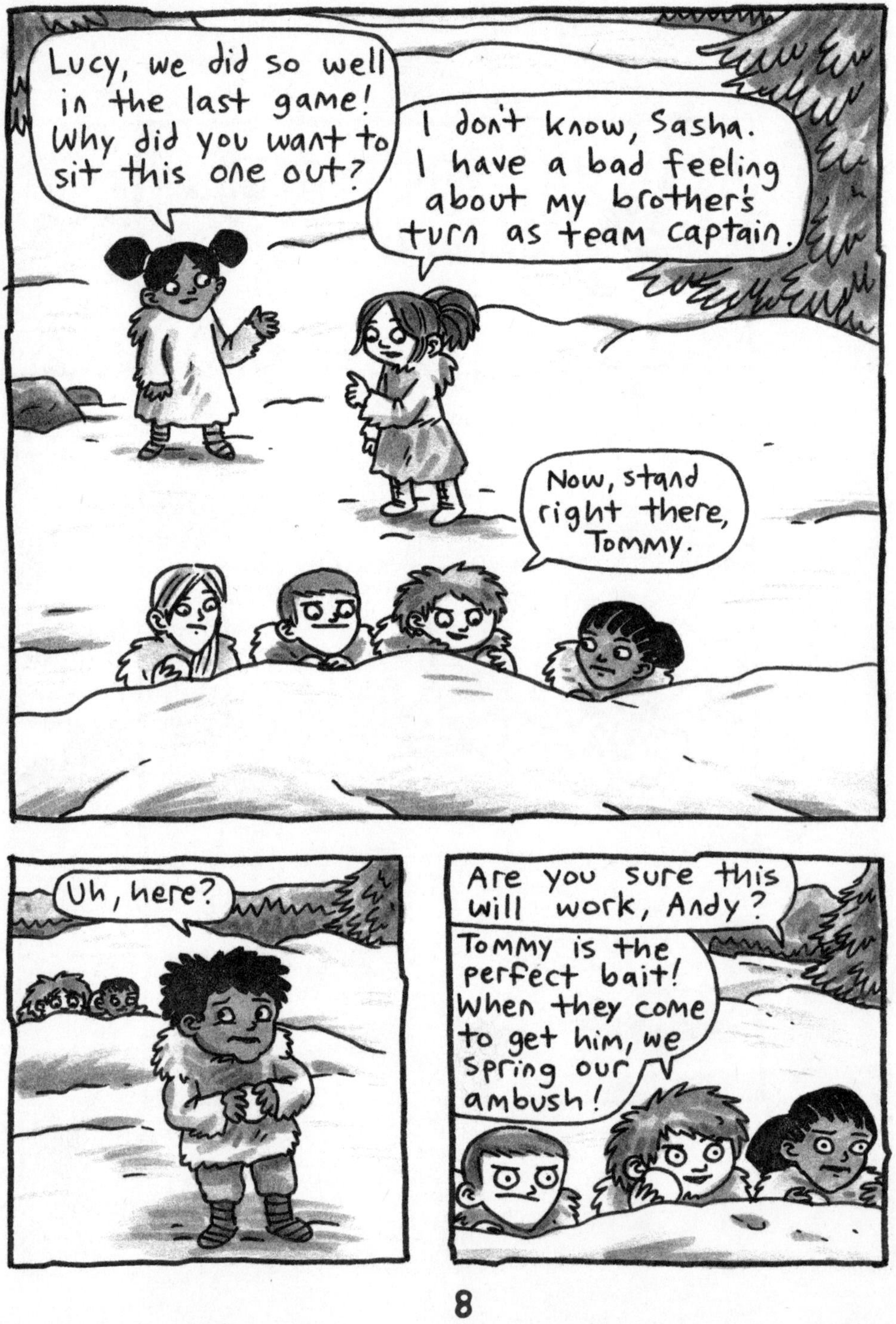
Lucy, we did so well in the last game! Why did you want to sit this one out?
I don't know, Sasha. I have a bad feeling about my brother's turn as team captain.
Now, stand right there, Tommy.
Uh, here?
Are you sure this will work, Andy?
Tommy is the perfect bait! When they come to get him, we spring our ambush!

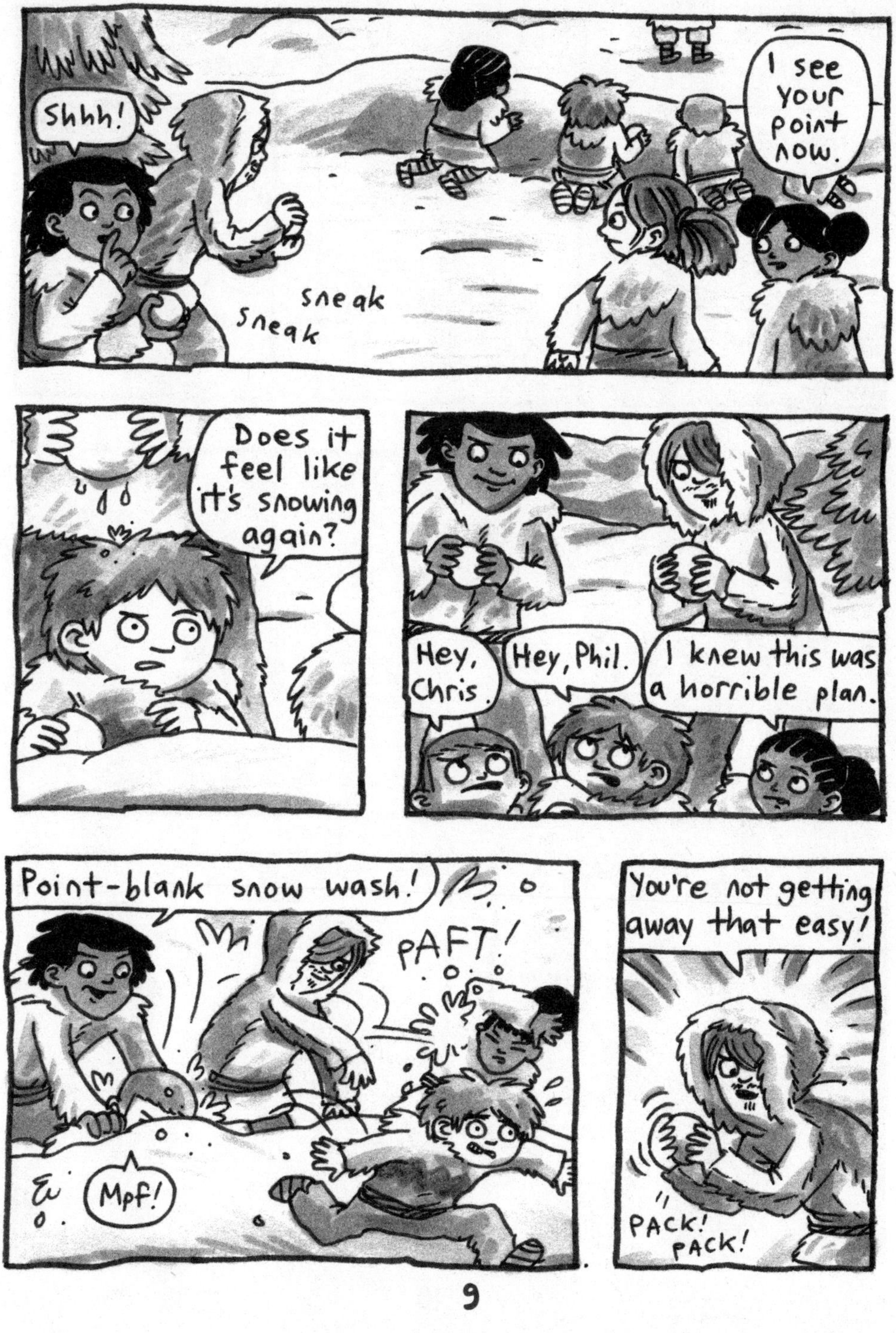
Shhh!
I see your point now.
sneak
sneak
Does it feel like it's snowing again?
Hey, Chris.
Hey, Phil.
I knew this was a horrible plan.
Point-blank snow wash!
PAFT!
Mpf!
You're not getting away that easy!
PACK!
PACK!

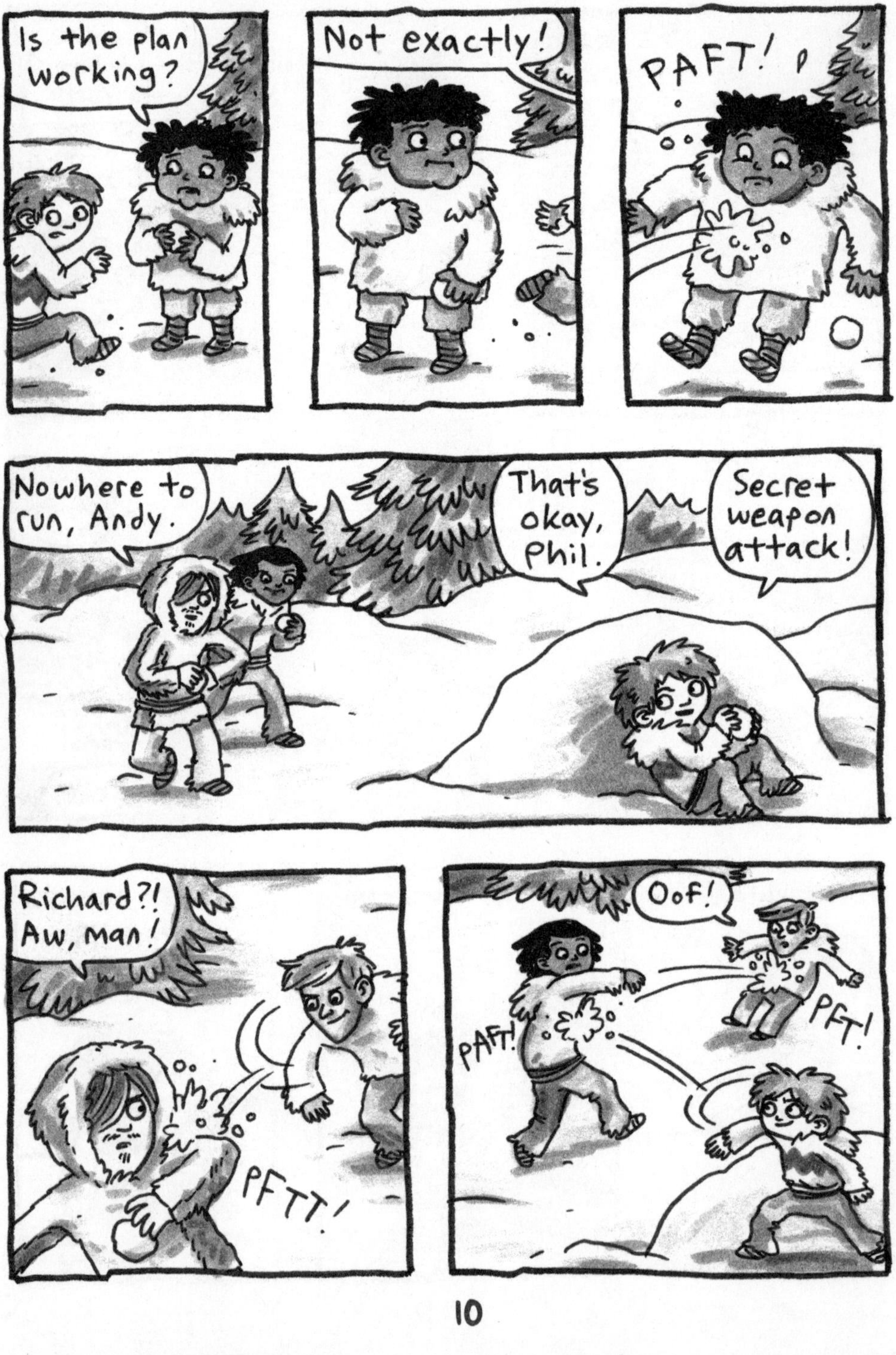
Is the plan working?
Not exactly!
PAFT!
Nowhere to run, Andy.
That's okay, Phil.
Secret weapon attack!
Richard?! Aw, man!
PFTT!
Oof!
PAFT!
PFT!

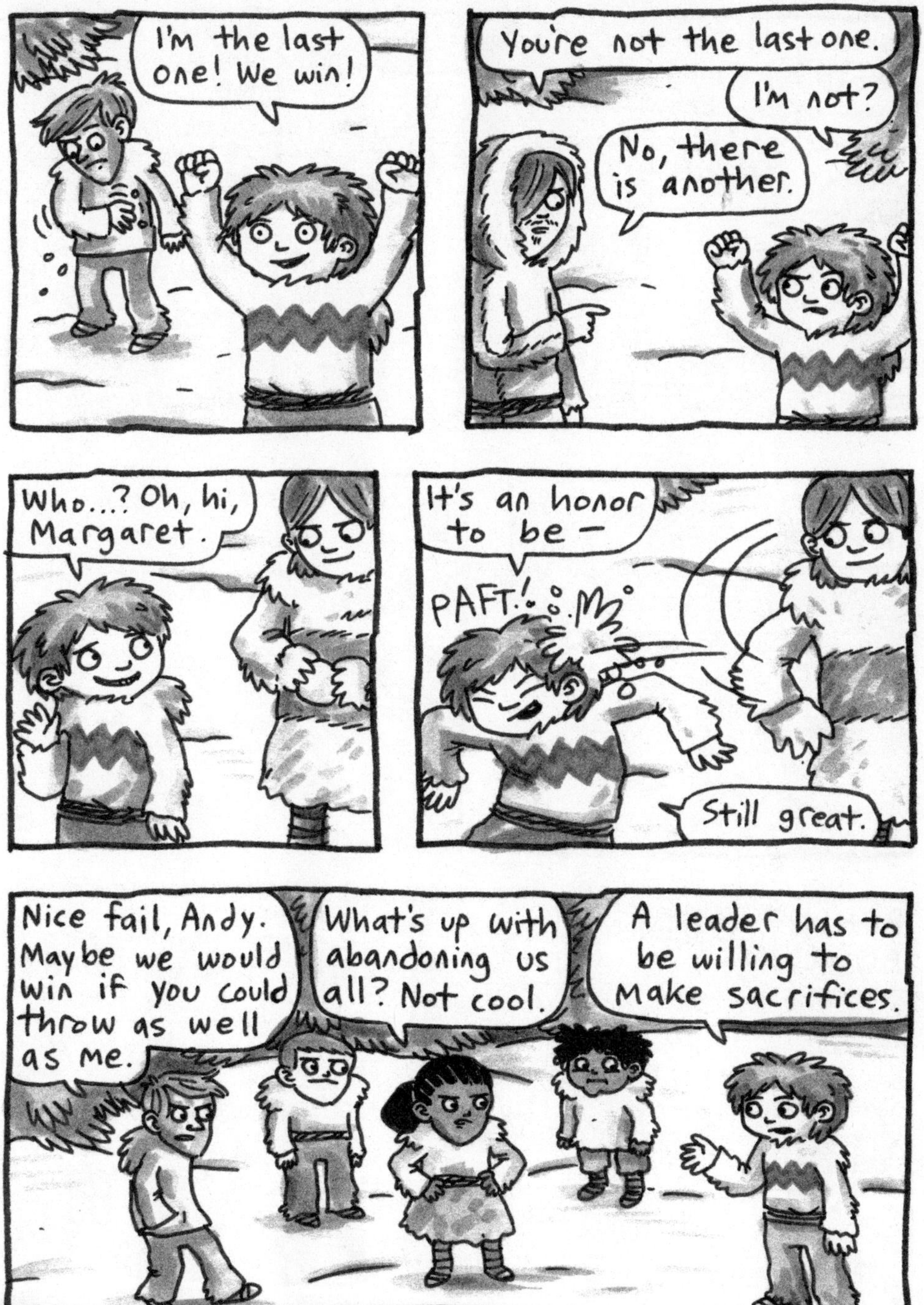

I'm the last one! We win!
You're not the last one.
I'm not?
No, there is another.
Who...? Oh, hi, Margaret.
It's an honor to be -
PAFT!
Still great.
Nice fail, Andy. Maybe we would win if you could throw as well as me.
What's up with abandoning us all? Not cool.
A leader has to be willing to make sacrifices.

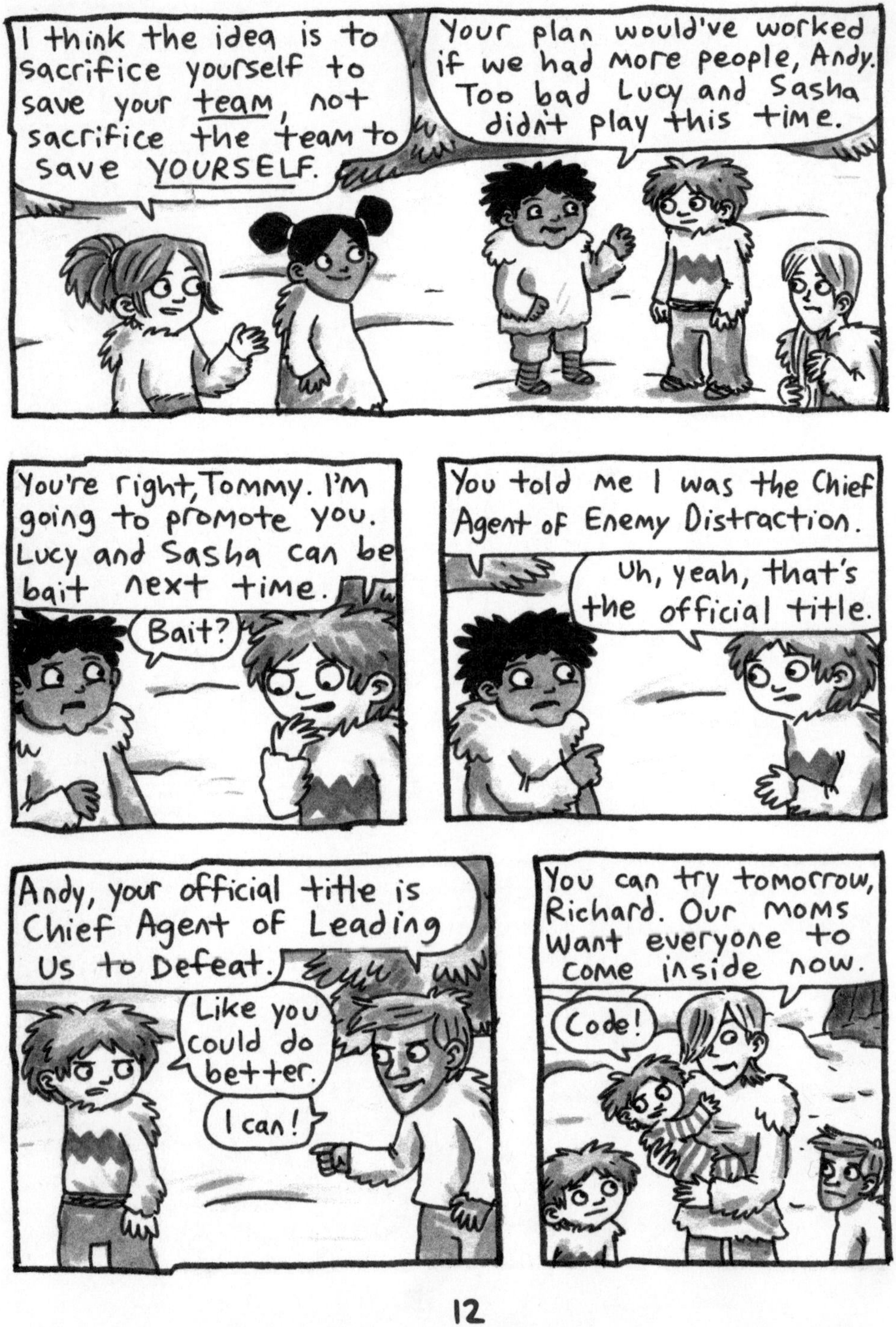
I think the idea is to sacrifice yourself to save your team, not sacrifice the team to save YOURSELF.
Your plan would've worked if we had more people, Andy. Too bad Lucy and Sasha didn't play this time.
You're right, Tommy. I'm going to promote you. Lucy and Sasha can be bait next time.
Bait?
You told me I was the Chief Agent of Enemy Distraction.
Uh, yeah, that's the official title.
Andy, your official title is Chief Agent of Leading Us to Defeat.
Like you could do better.
I can!
You can try tomorrow, Richard. Our moms want everyone to come inside now.
Code!

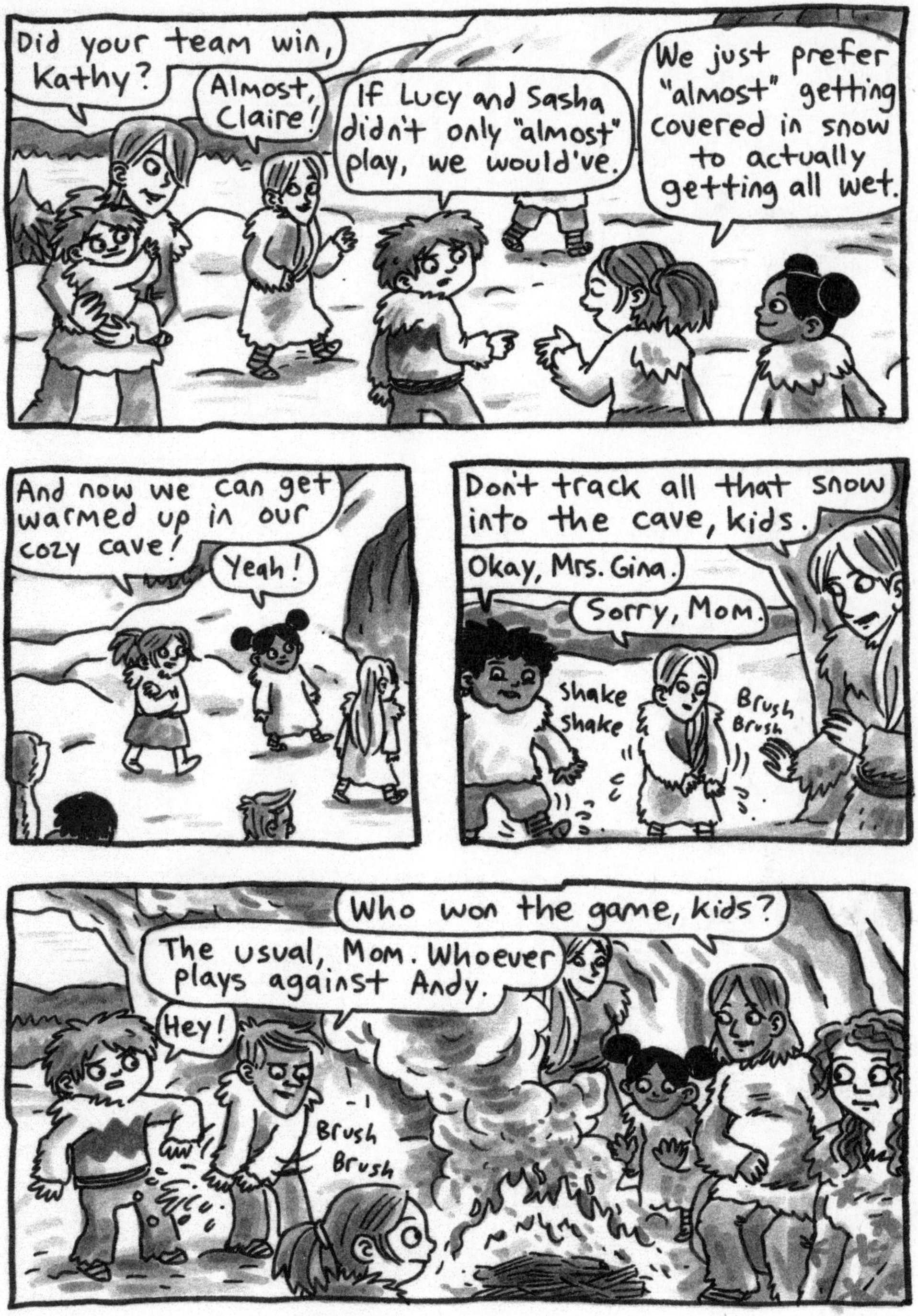
Did your team win, Kathy?
Almost, Claire!
If Lucy and Sasha didn't only "almost" play, we would've.
We just prefer "almost" getting covered in snow to actually getting all wet.
And now we can get warmed up in our cozy cave!
Yeah!
Don't track all that snow into the cave, kids.
Okay, Mrs. Gina.
Sorry, Mom.
Shake Shake
Brush Brush
Who won the game, kids?
The usual, Mom. Whoever plays against Andy.
Hey!
Brush Brush

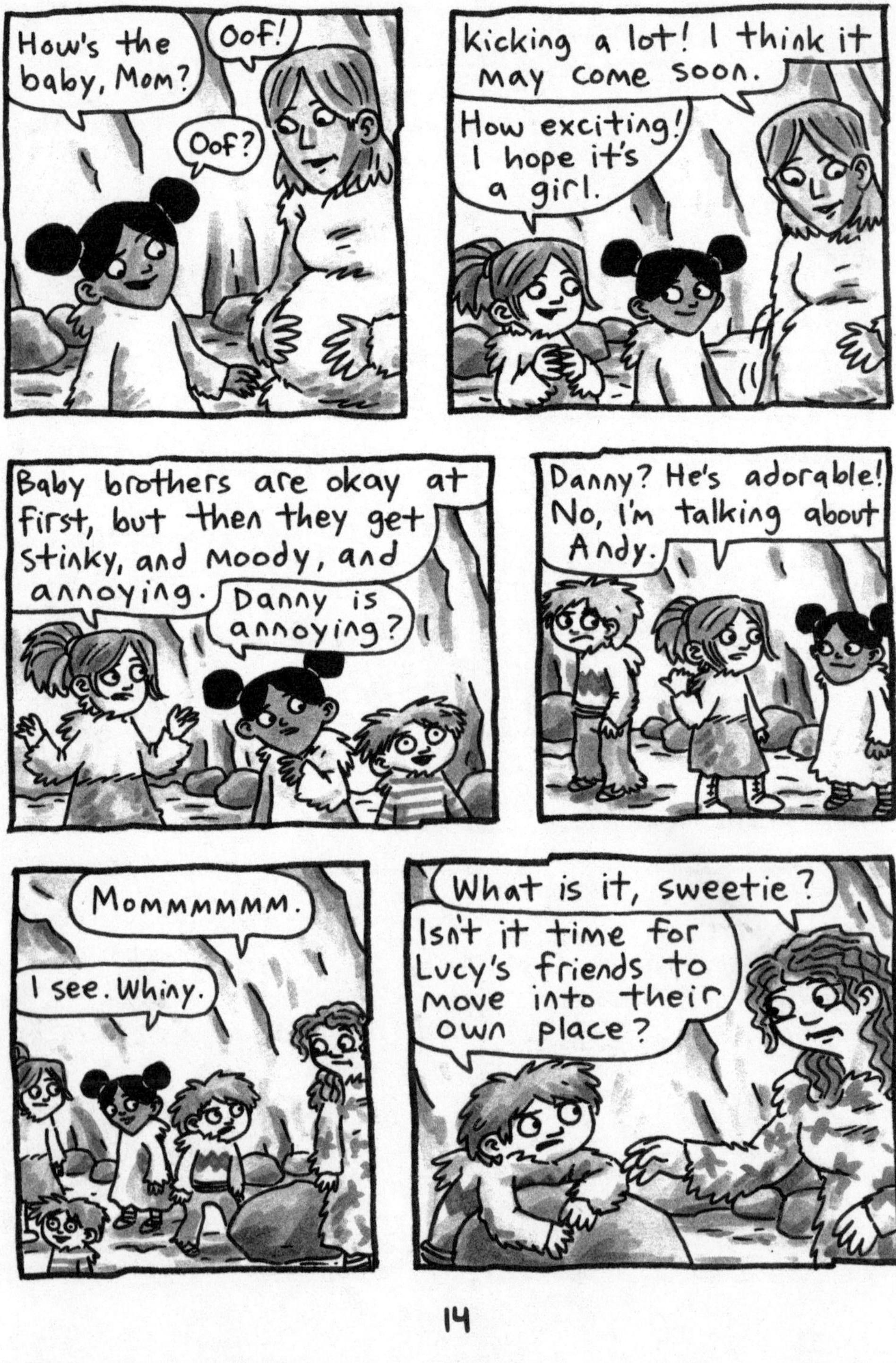
How's the baby, Mom?
Oof!
Oof?
Kicking a lot! I think it may come soon.
How exciting! I hope it's a girl.
Baby brothers are okay at first, but then they get stinky, and moody, and annoying.
Danny is annoying?
Danny? He's adorable! No, I'm talking about Andy.
Mommmmmm.
I see. Whiny.
What is it, sweetie?
Isn't it time for Lucy's friends to move into their own place?

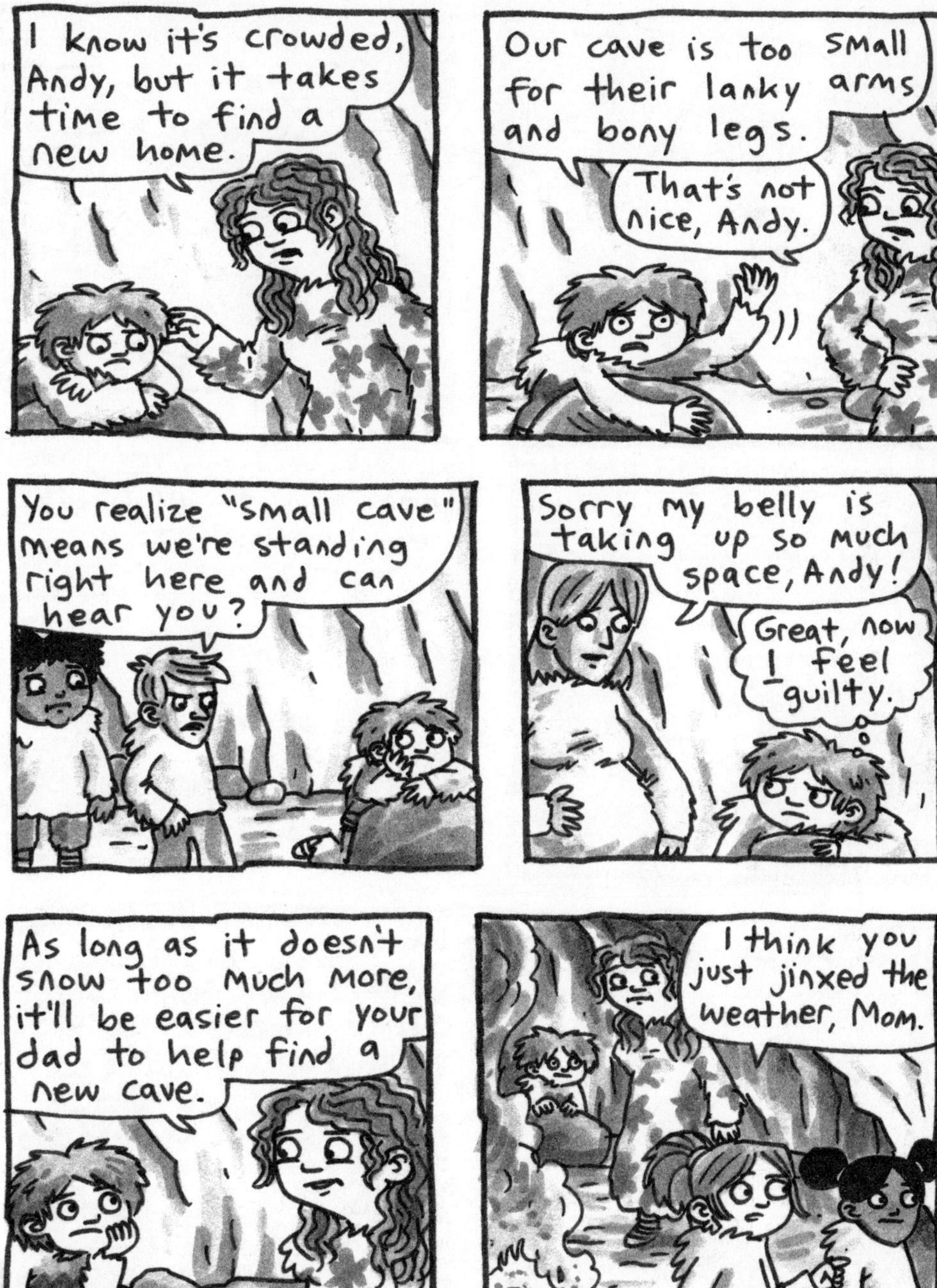
I know it's crowded, Andy, but it takes time to find a new home.
Our cave is too small for their lanky arms and bony legs.
That's not nice, Andy.
You realize "small cave" means we're standing right here and can hear you?
Sorry my belly is taking up so much space, Andy!
Great, now I feel guilty.
As long as it doesn't snow too much more, it'll be easier for your dad to help find a new cave.
I think you just jinxed the weather, Mom.

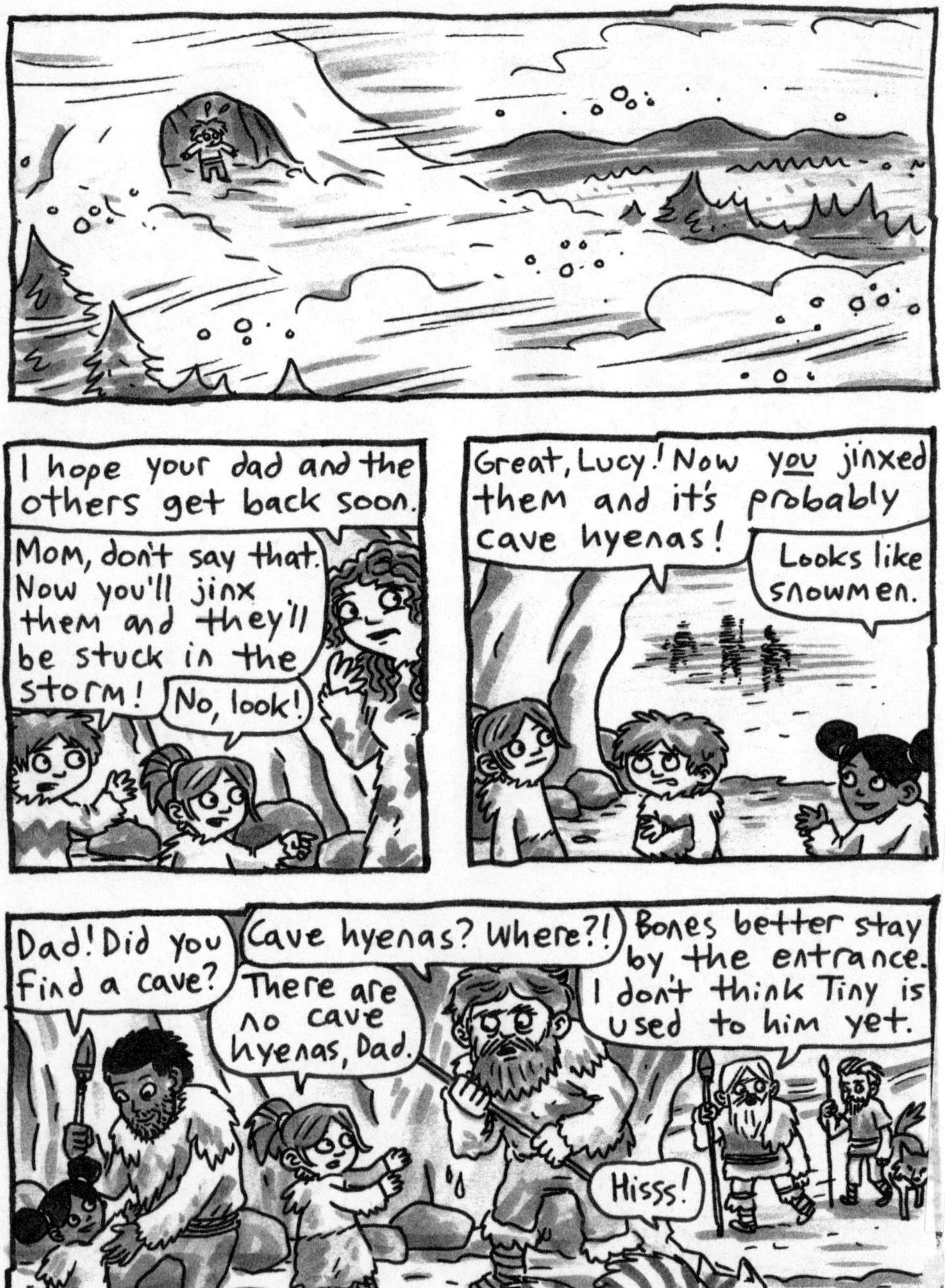
I hope your dad and the others get back soon.
Mom, don't say that. Now you'll jinx them and they'll be stuck in the storm!
No, look!
Great, Lucy! Now you jinxed them and it's probably cave hyenas!
Looks like snowmen.
Dad! Did you find a cave?
Cave hyenas? Where?!
There are no cave hyenas, Dad.
Bones better stay by the entrance. I don't think Tiny is used to him yet.
Hisss!

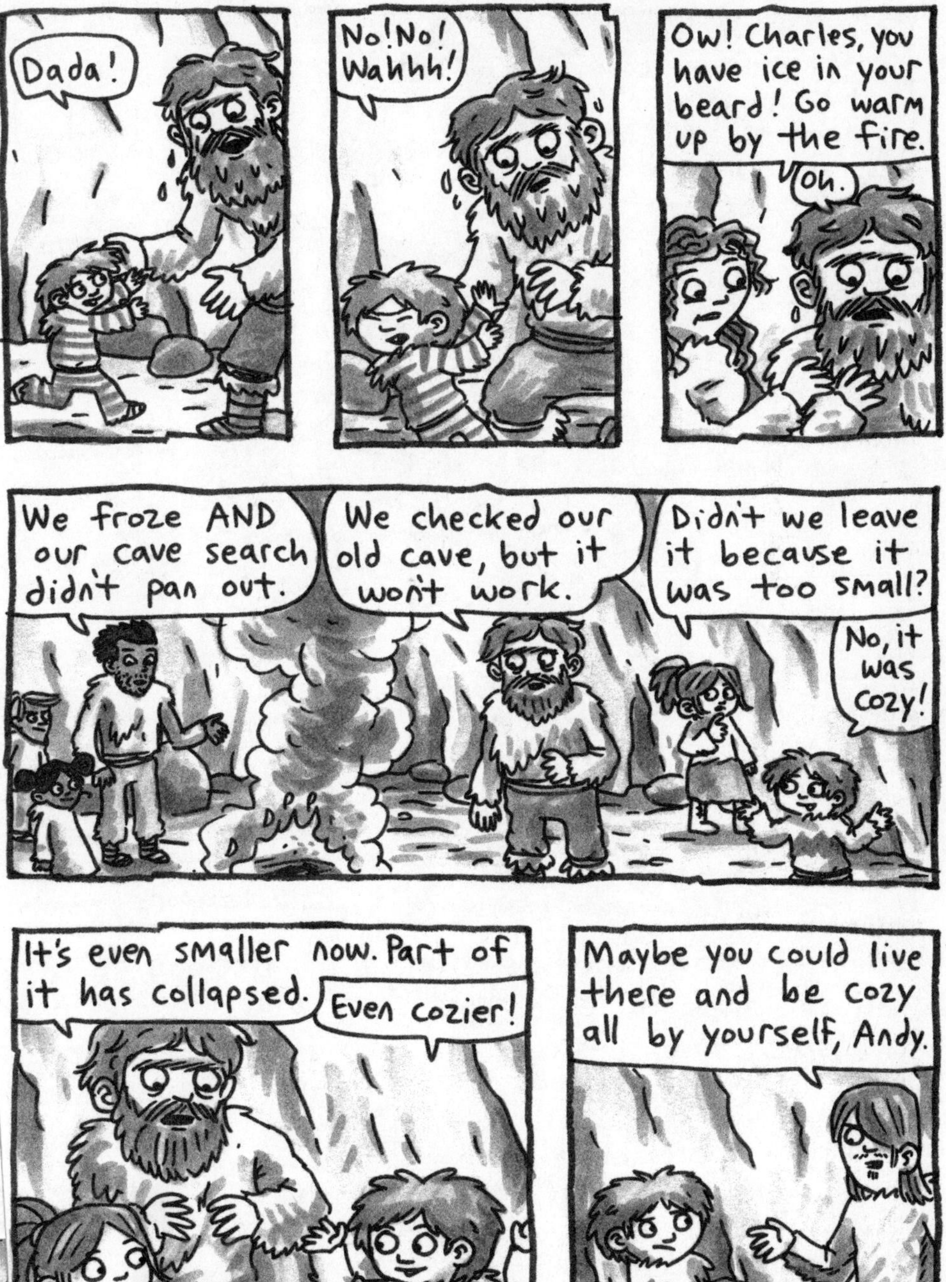
Dada!
No! No! Wahhh!
Ow! Charles, you have ice in your beard! Go warm up by the fire.
Oh.
We froze AND our cave search didn't pan out.
We checked our old cave, but it won't work.
Didn't we leave it because it was too small?
No, it was cozy!
It's even smaller now. Part of it has collapsed.
Even cozier!
Maybe you could live there and be cozy all by yourself, Andy.

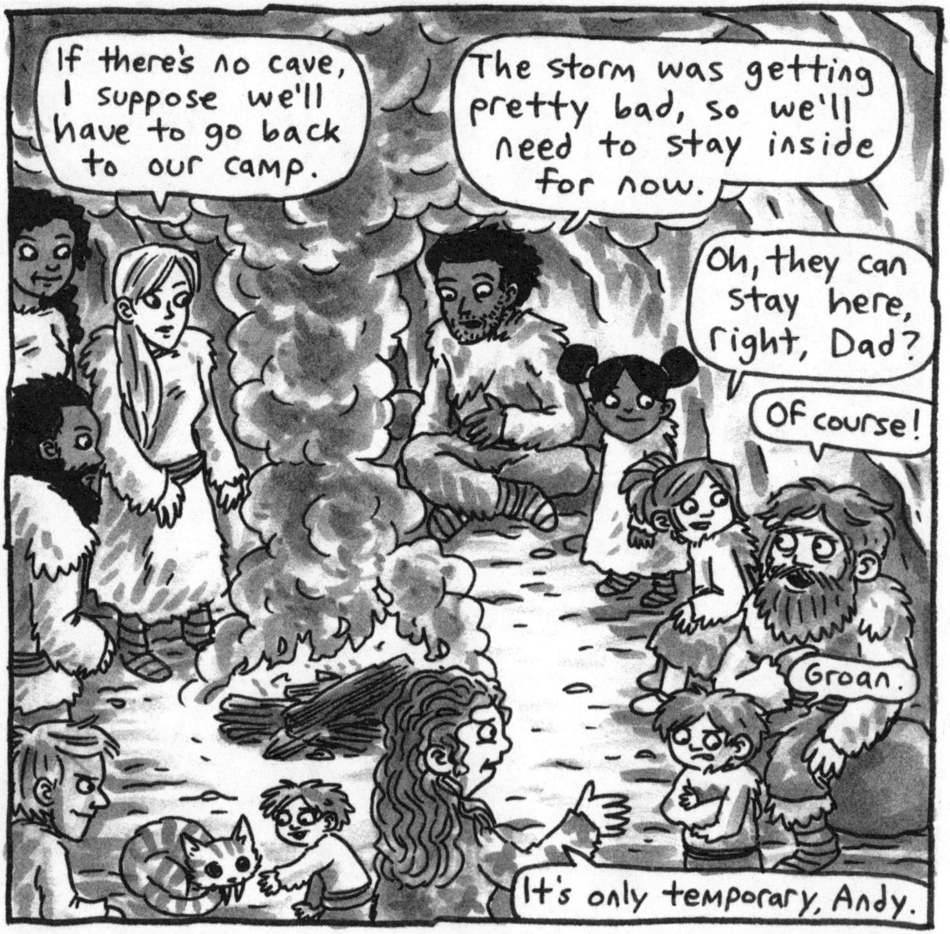
If there's no cave, I suppose we'll have to go back to our camp.
The storm was getting pretty bad, so we'll need to stay inside for now.
Oh, they can stay here, right, Dad?
Of course!
Groan.
It's only temporary, Andy.

Scientists have studied the soil of caves to learn that the smoke and residue from Neanderthal fires was the first man-made pollution!

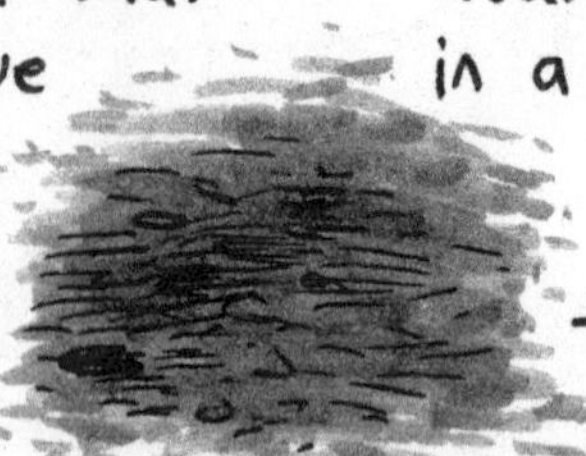

Needing to stay warm while living in a small, enclosed space made exposure to this pollution inevitable.

No warnings about the danger of secondhand smoke have been found in Neanderthal caves.

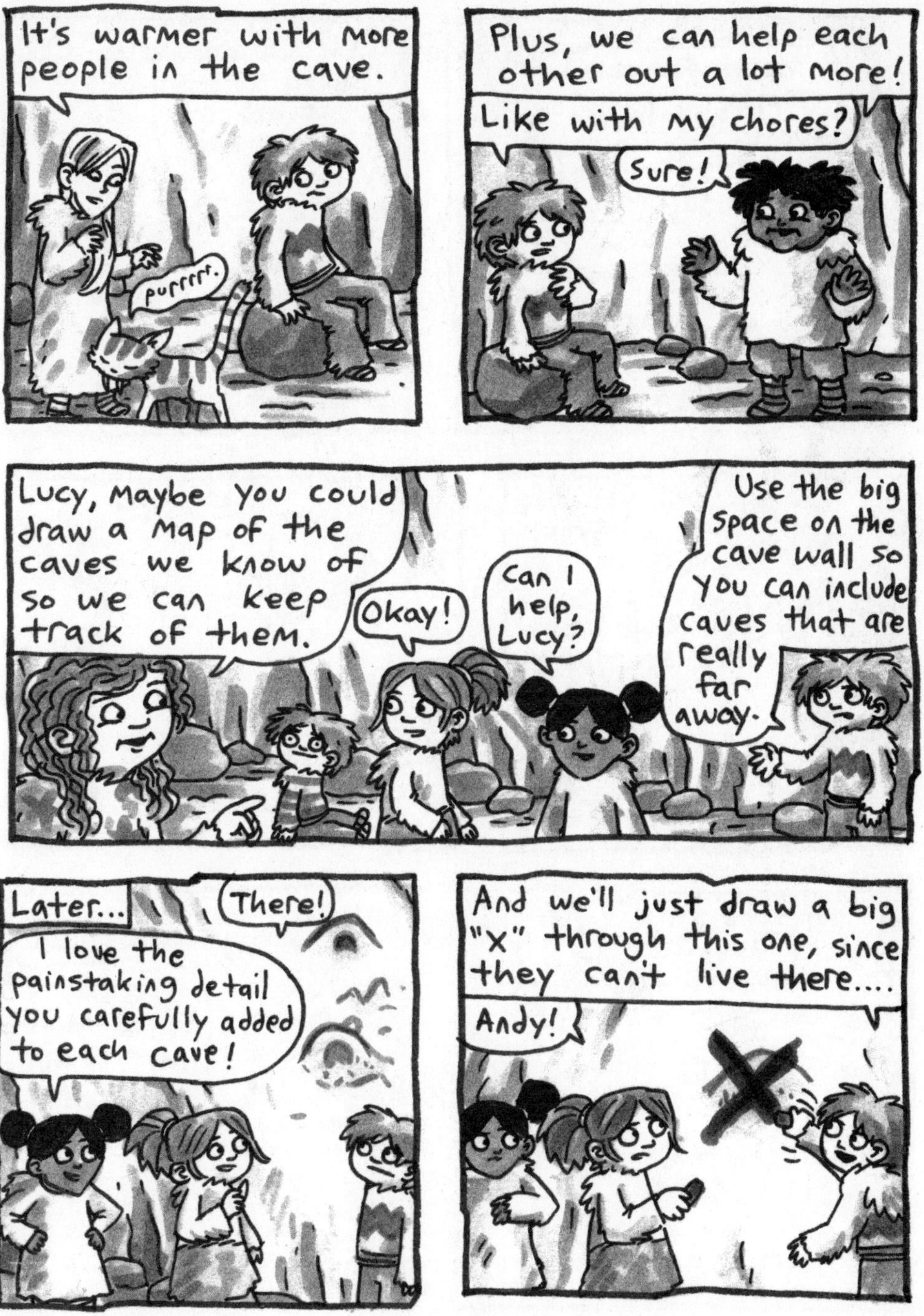
It's warmer with more people in the cave.
purrrrr.
Plus, we can help each other out a lot more!
Like with my chores?
Sure!
Lucy, maybe you could draw a map of the caves we know of so we can keep track of them.
Okay!
Can I help, Lucy?
Use the big space on the cave wall so you can include caves that are really far away.
Later...
There!
I love the painstaking detail you carefully added to each cave!
And we'll just draw a big "X" through this one, since they can't live there....
Andy!

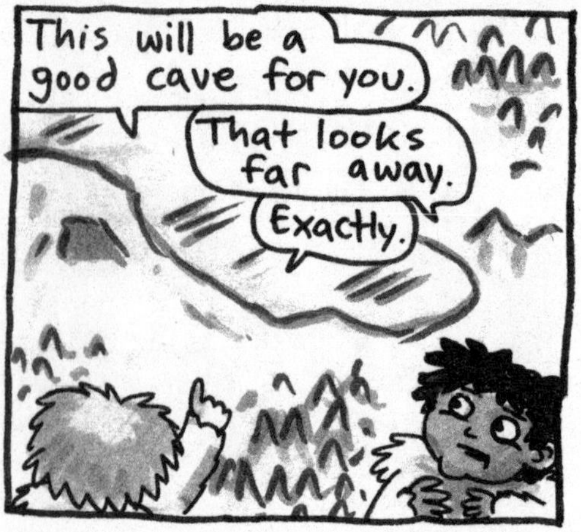
This will be a good cave for you.
That looks far away.
Exactly.
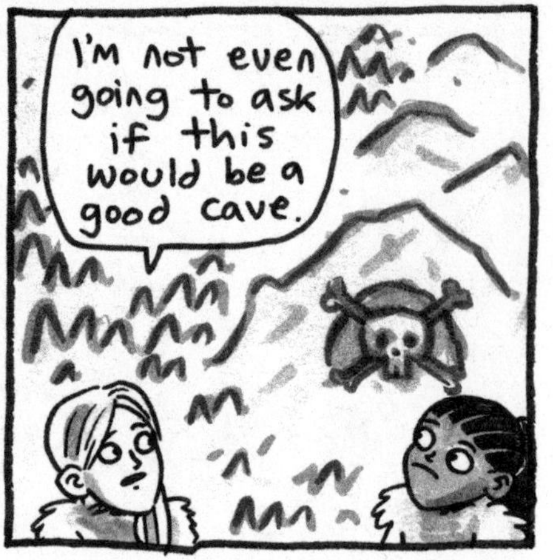
I'm not even going to ask if this would be a good cave.
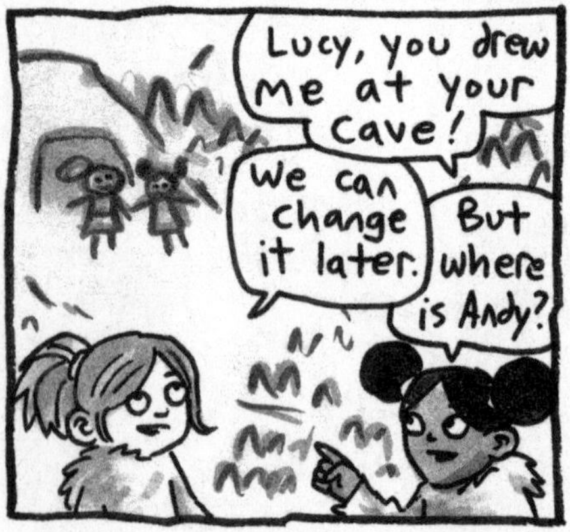
Lucy, you drew me at your cave!
We can change it later.
But where is Andy?
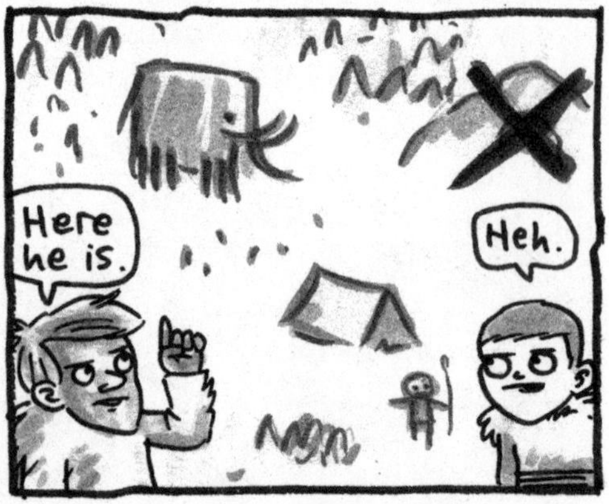
Here he is.
Heh.
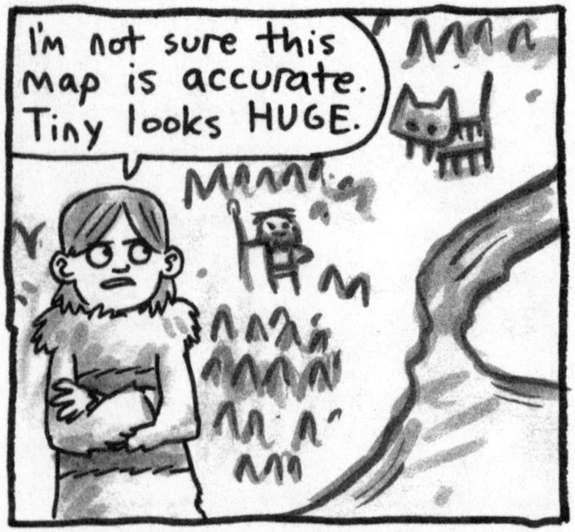
I'm not sure this map is accurate. Tiny looks HUGE.
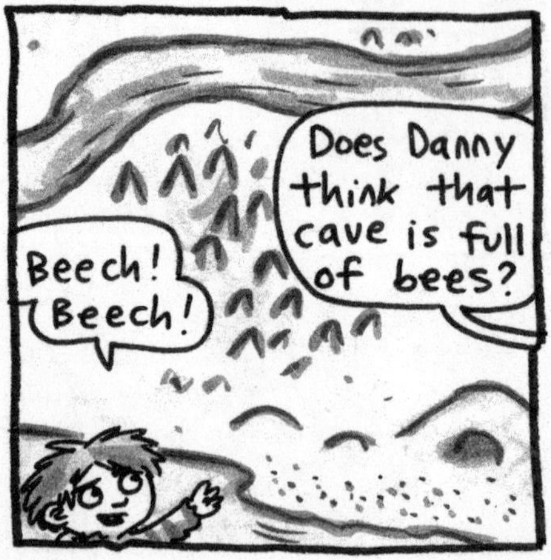
Does Danny think that cave is full of bees?
Beech! Beech!

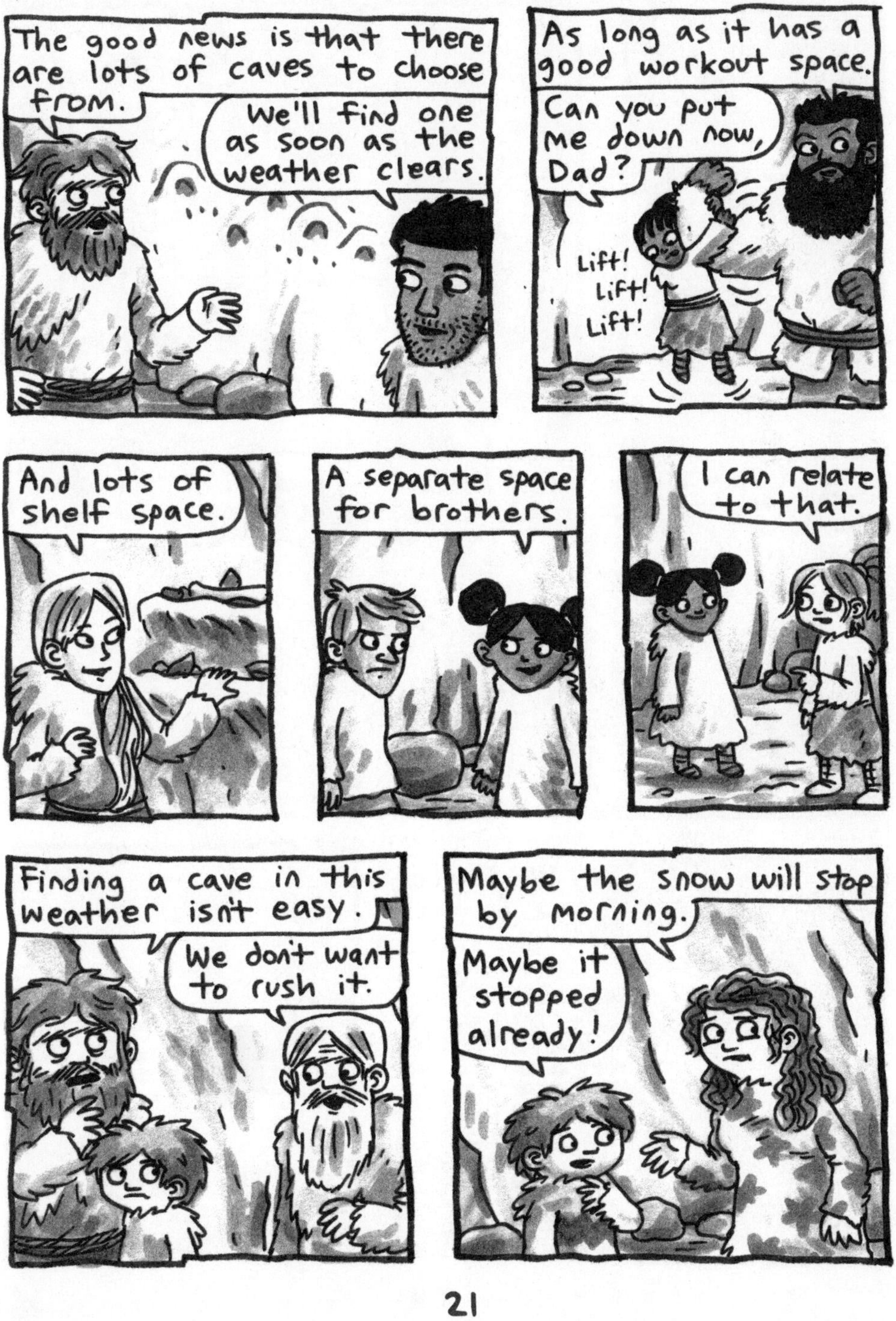
The good news is that there are lots of caves to choose from.
We'll find one as soon as the weather clears.
As long as it has a good workout space.
Can you put me down now, Dad?
Lift! Lift! Lift!
And lots of shelf space.
A separate space for brothers.
I can relate to that.
Finding a cave in this weather isn't easy.
We don't want to rush it.
Maybe the snow will stop by morning.
Maybe it stopped already!

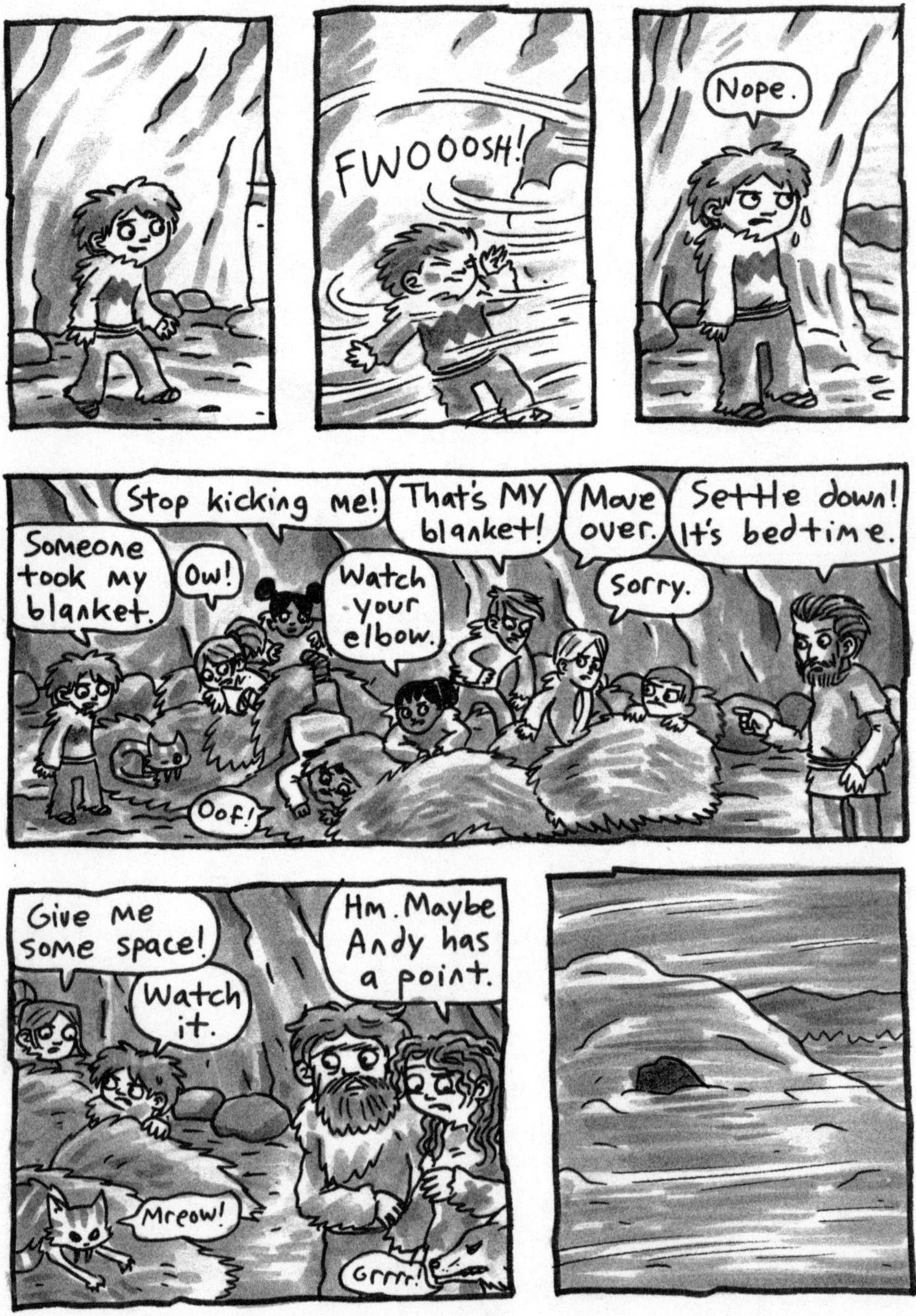
FWOOOSH!
Nope.
Someone took my blanket.
Stop kicking me!
Ow!
Watch your elbow.
That's MY blanket!
Move over.
Sorry.
Settle down! It's bedtime.
Oof!
Give me some space!
Watch it.
Hm. Maybe Andy has a point.
Mreow!
Grrrr!

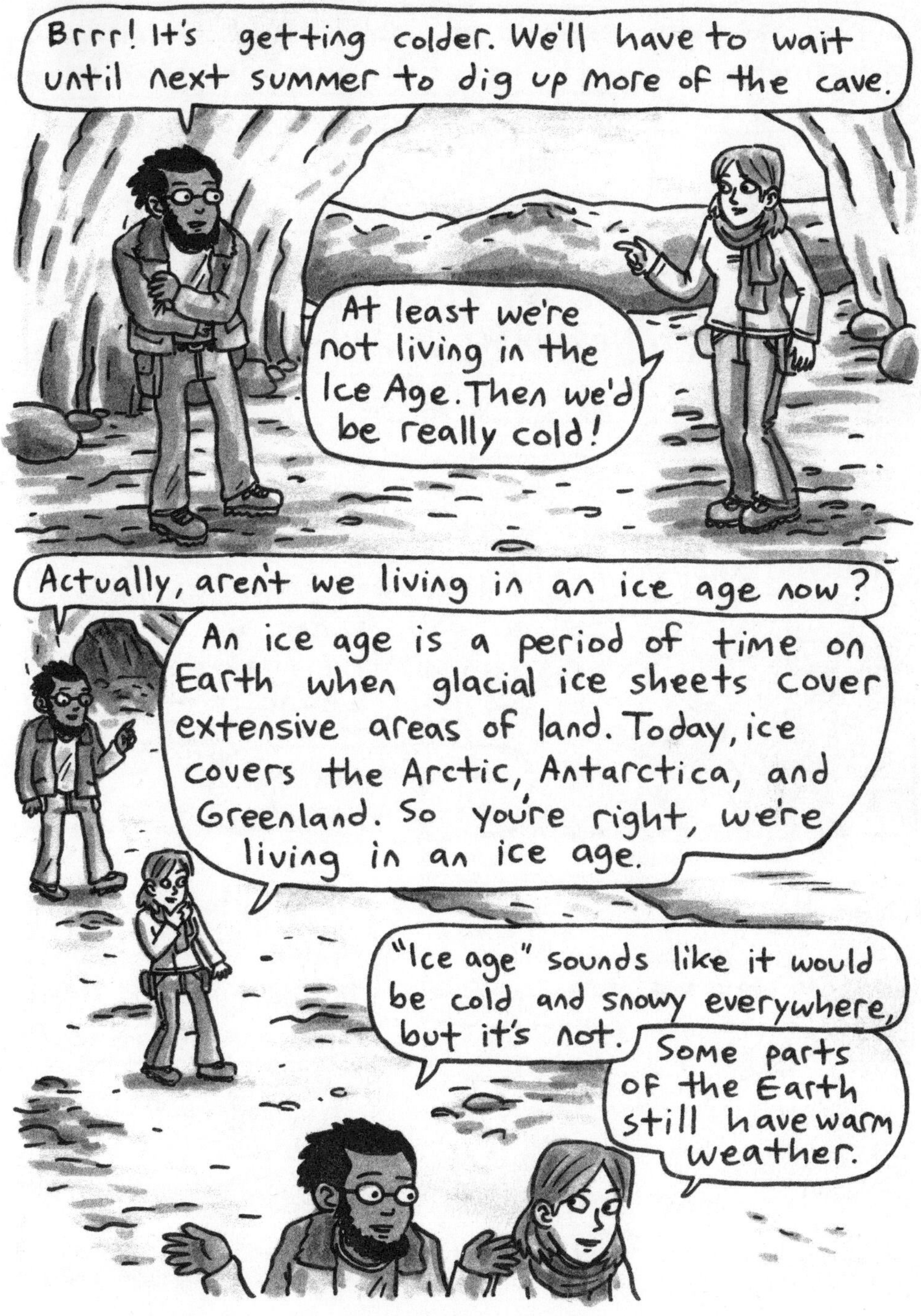

Brrr! It's getting colder. We'll have to wait until next summer to dig up more of the cave.
At least we're not living in the Ice Age. Then we'd be really cold!
Actually, aren't we living in an ice age now?
An ice age is a period of time on Earth when glacial ice sheets cover extensive areas of land. Today, ice covers the Arctic, Antarctica, and Greenland. So you're right, we're living in an ice age.
"Ice age" sounds like it would be cold and snowy everywhere, but it's not.
Some parts of the Earth still have warm weather.

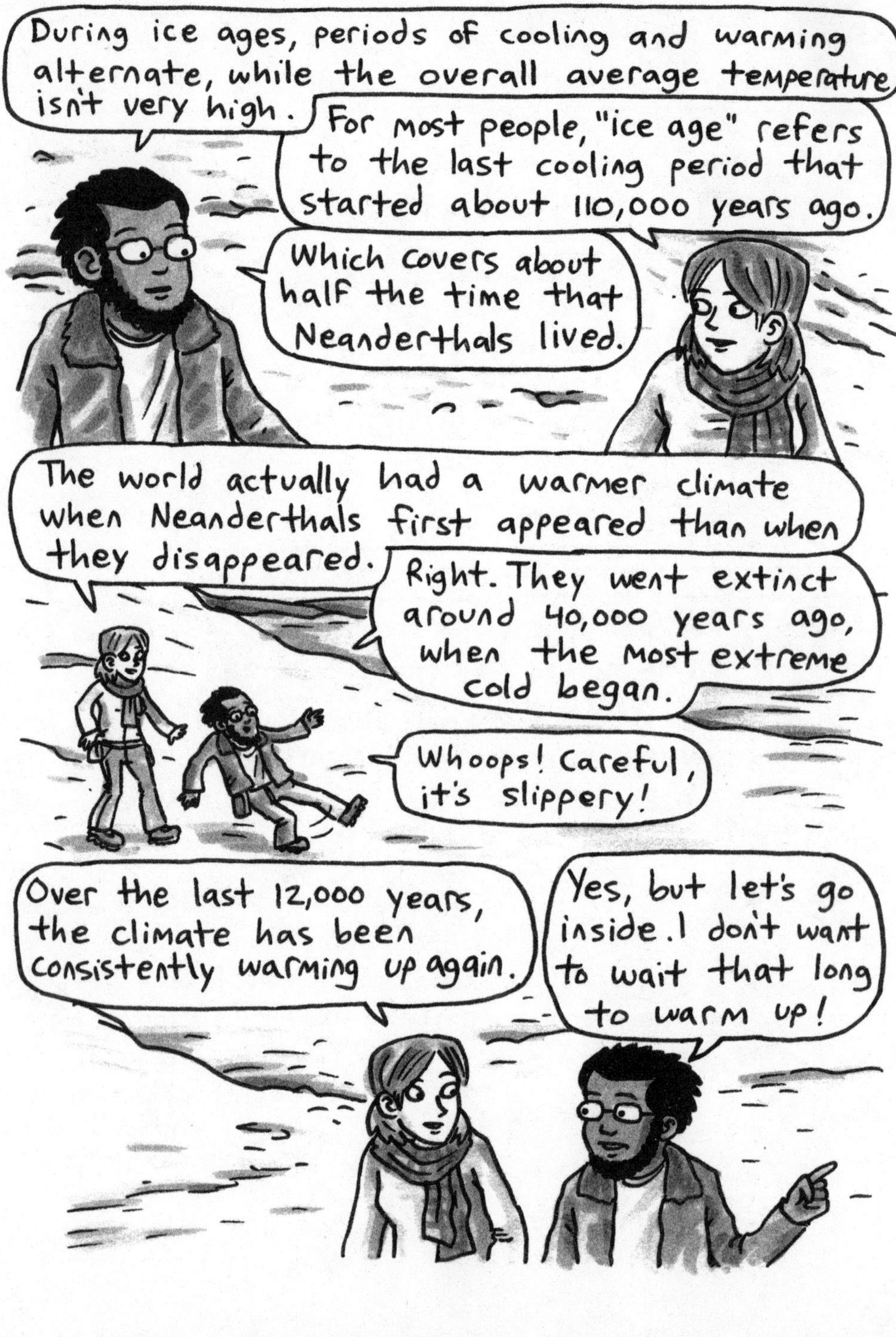
During ice ages, periods of cooling and warming alternate, while the overall average temperature isn't very high.
For most people, "ice age" refers to the last cooling period that started about 110,000 years ago.
Which covers about half the time that Neanderthals lived.
The world actually had a warmer climate when Neanderthals first appeared than when they disappeared.
Right. They went extinct around 40,000 years ago, when the most extreme cold began.
Whoops! Careful, it's slippery!
Over the last 12,000 years, the climate has been consistently warming up again.
Yes, but let's go inside. I don't want to wait that long to warm up!

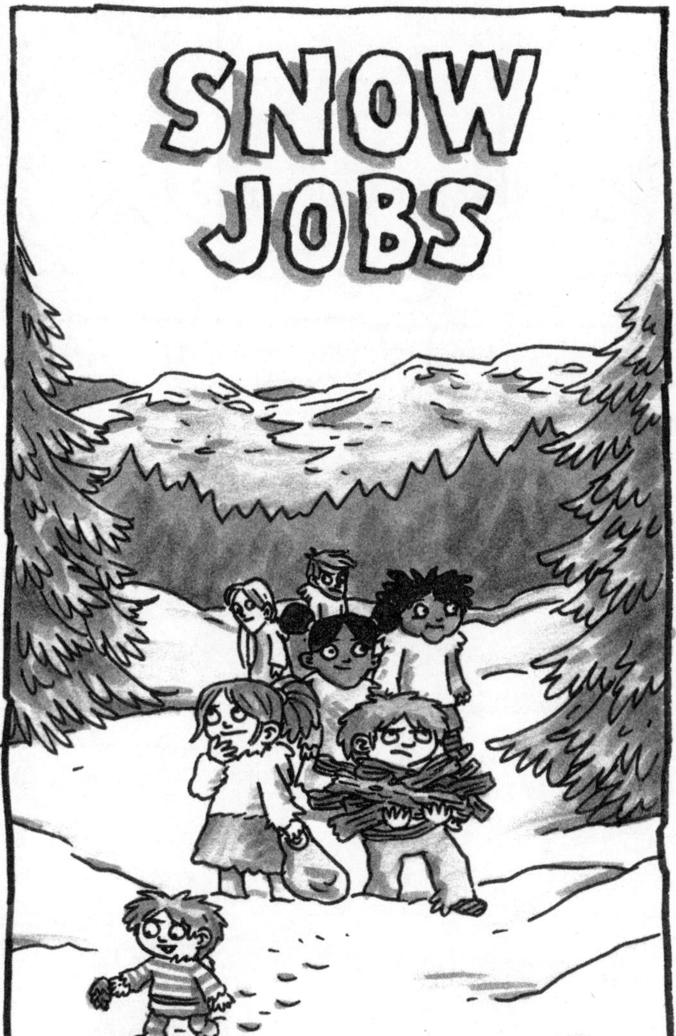
SNOW
JOBS

This is ridiculous.

Maybe a little.

I can't feel my legs.

Hm?

Drool!

YAWN.

It's funny. Usually Richard is a pretty restless sleeper, but he didn't wake me up at all last night.

Tiny didn't like it when I moved.

Look outside. The storm is over!

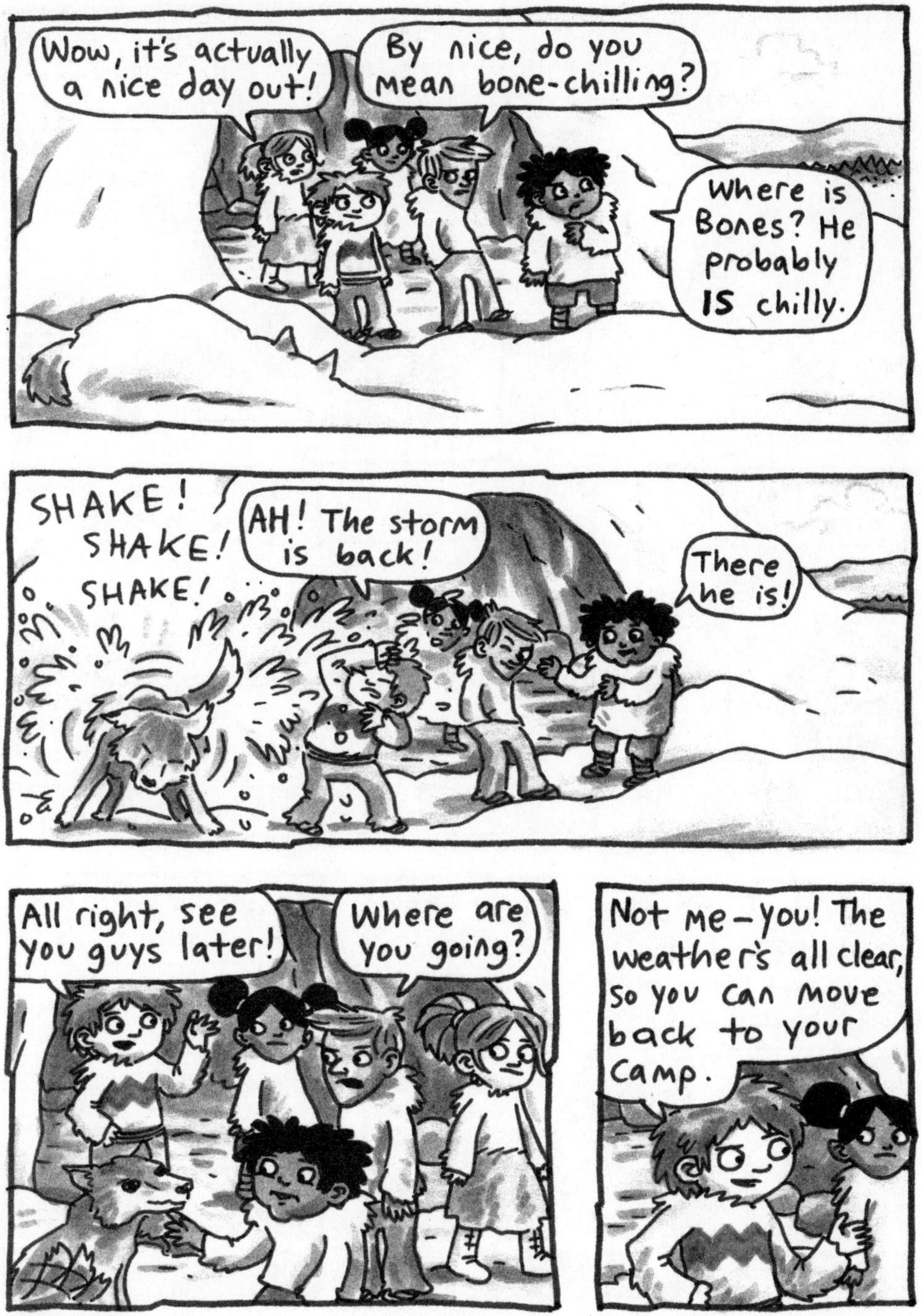
Wow, it's actually a nice day out!
By nice, do you mean bone-chilling?
Where is Bones? He probably IS chilly.
SHAKE! SHAKE! SHAKE!
AH! The storm is back!
There he is!
All right, see you guys later!
Where are you going?
Not me—you! The weather's all clear, so you can move back to your camp.

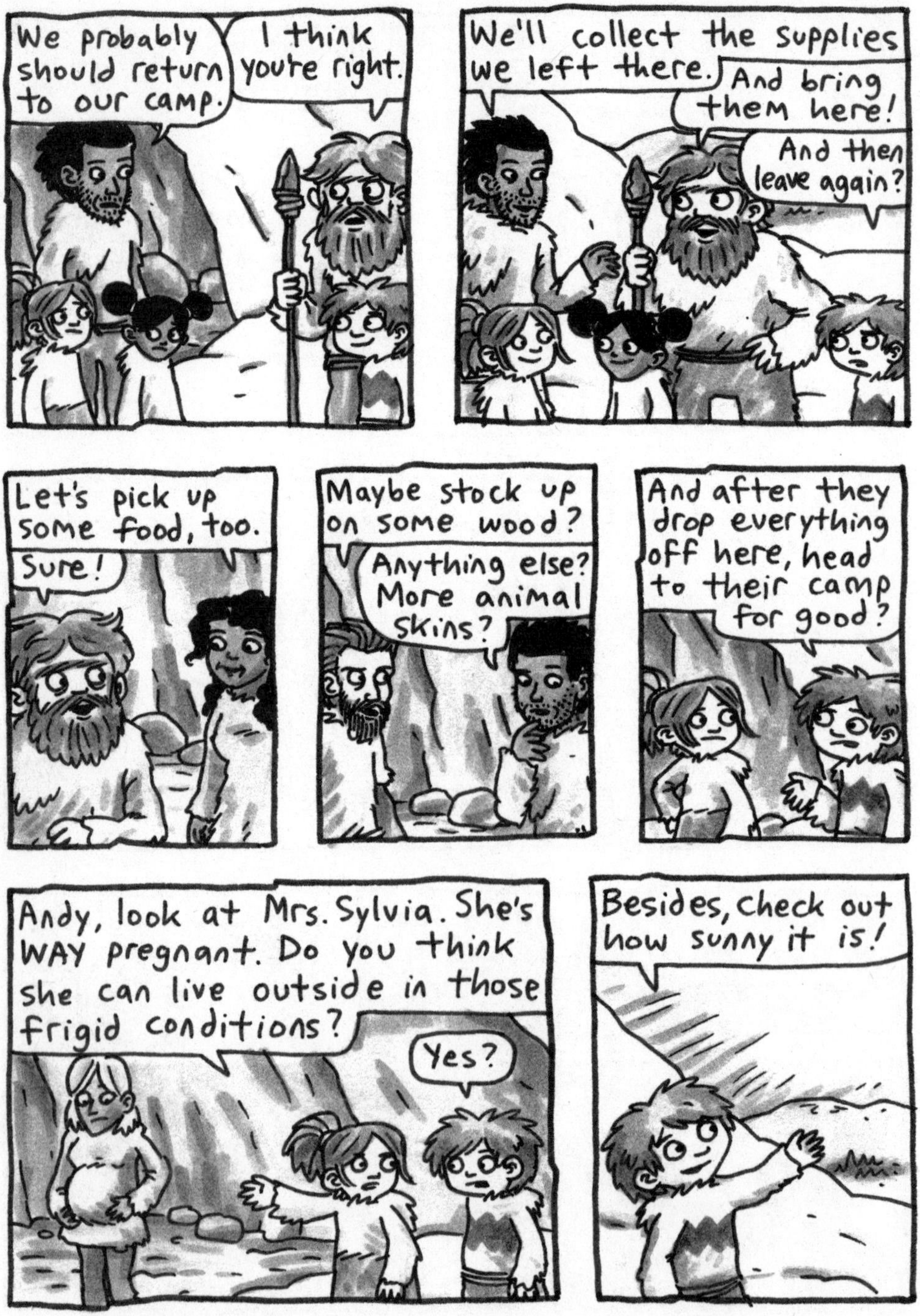
We probably should return to our camp.
I think you're right.
We'll collect the supplies we left there.
And bring them here!
And then leave again?
Let's pick up some food, too.
Sure!
Maybe stock up on some wood?
Anything else? More animal skins?
And after they drop everything off here, head to their camp for good?
Andy, look at Mrs. Sylvia. She's WAY pregnant. Do you think she can live outside in those frigid conditions?
Yes?
Besides, check out how sunny it is!

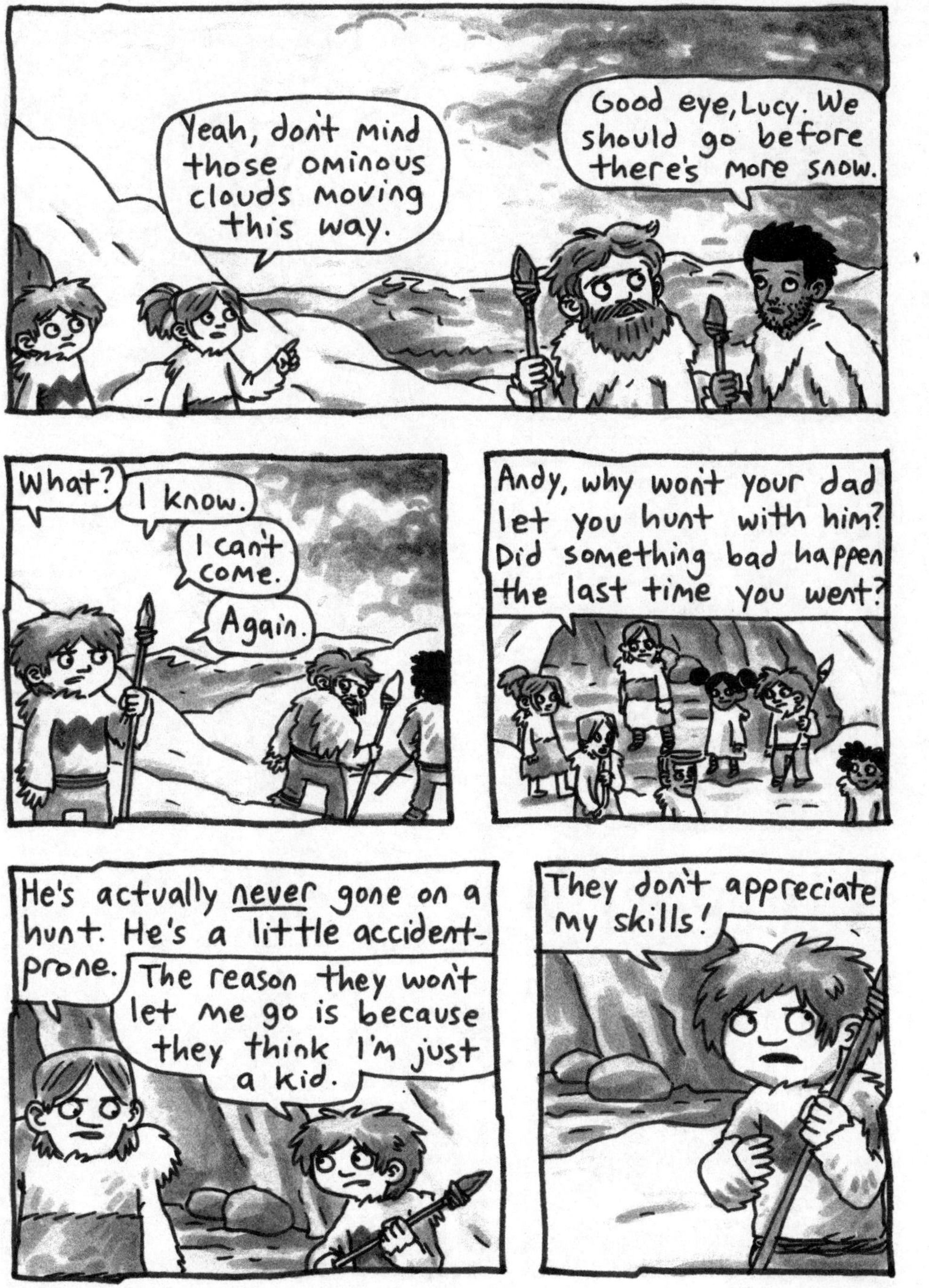
Yeah, don't mind those ominous clouds moving this way.
Good eye, Lucy. We should go before there's more snow.
What?
I know.
I can't come.
Again.
Andy, why won't your dad let you hunt with him? Did something bad happen the last time you went?
He's actually never gone on a hunt. He's a little accident-prone.
The reason they won't let me go is because they think I'm just a kid.
They don't appreciate my skills!

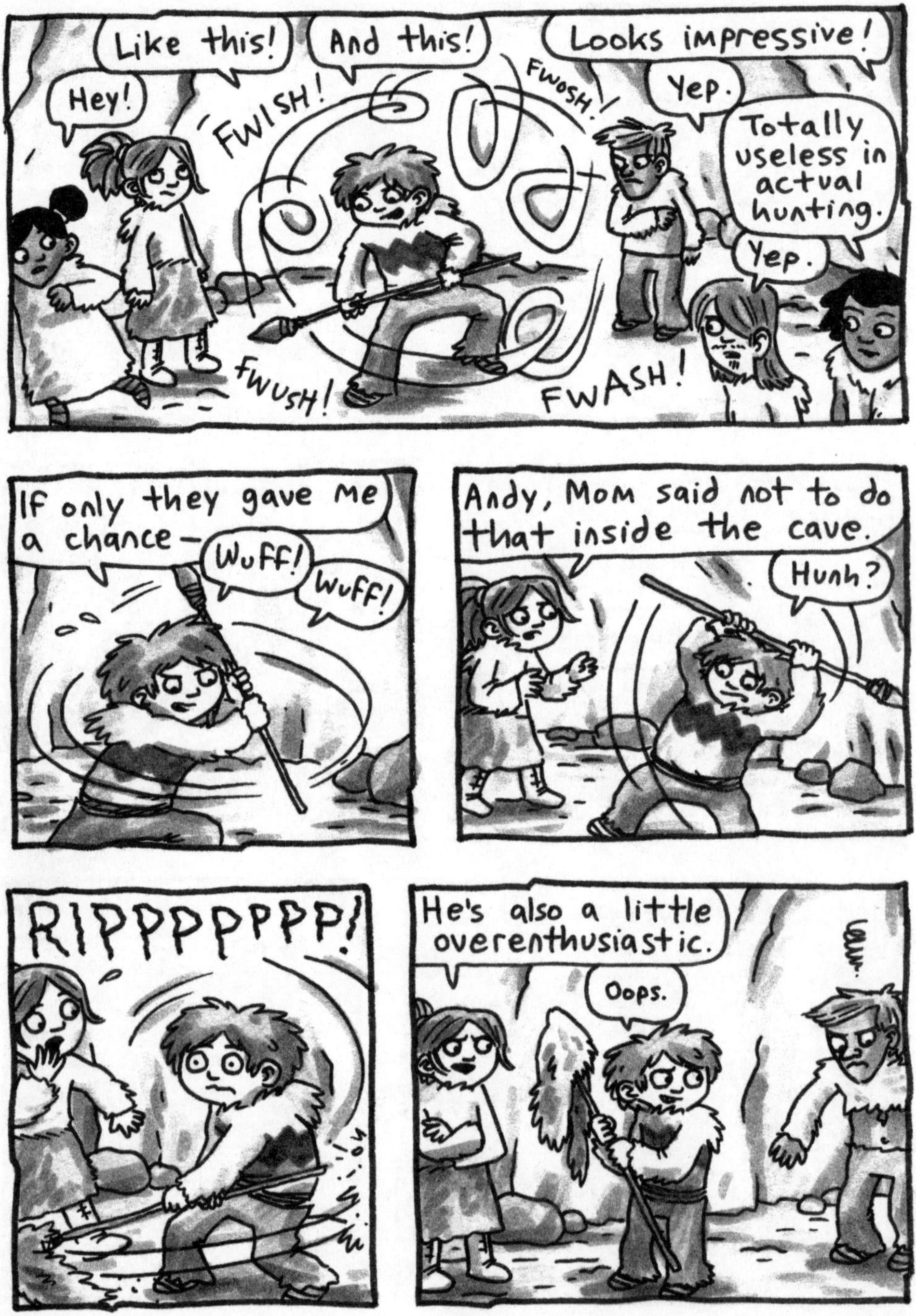
Hey!
Like this!
And this!
FWISH!
FWOSH!
Looks impressive!
Yep.
Totally useless in actual hunting.
Yep.
FWUSH!
FWASH!
If only they gave me a chance—
Wuff!
Wuff!
Andy, Mom said not to do that inside the cave.
Hunh?
RIPPPPPPP!
He's also a little overenthusiastic.
Oops.

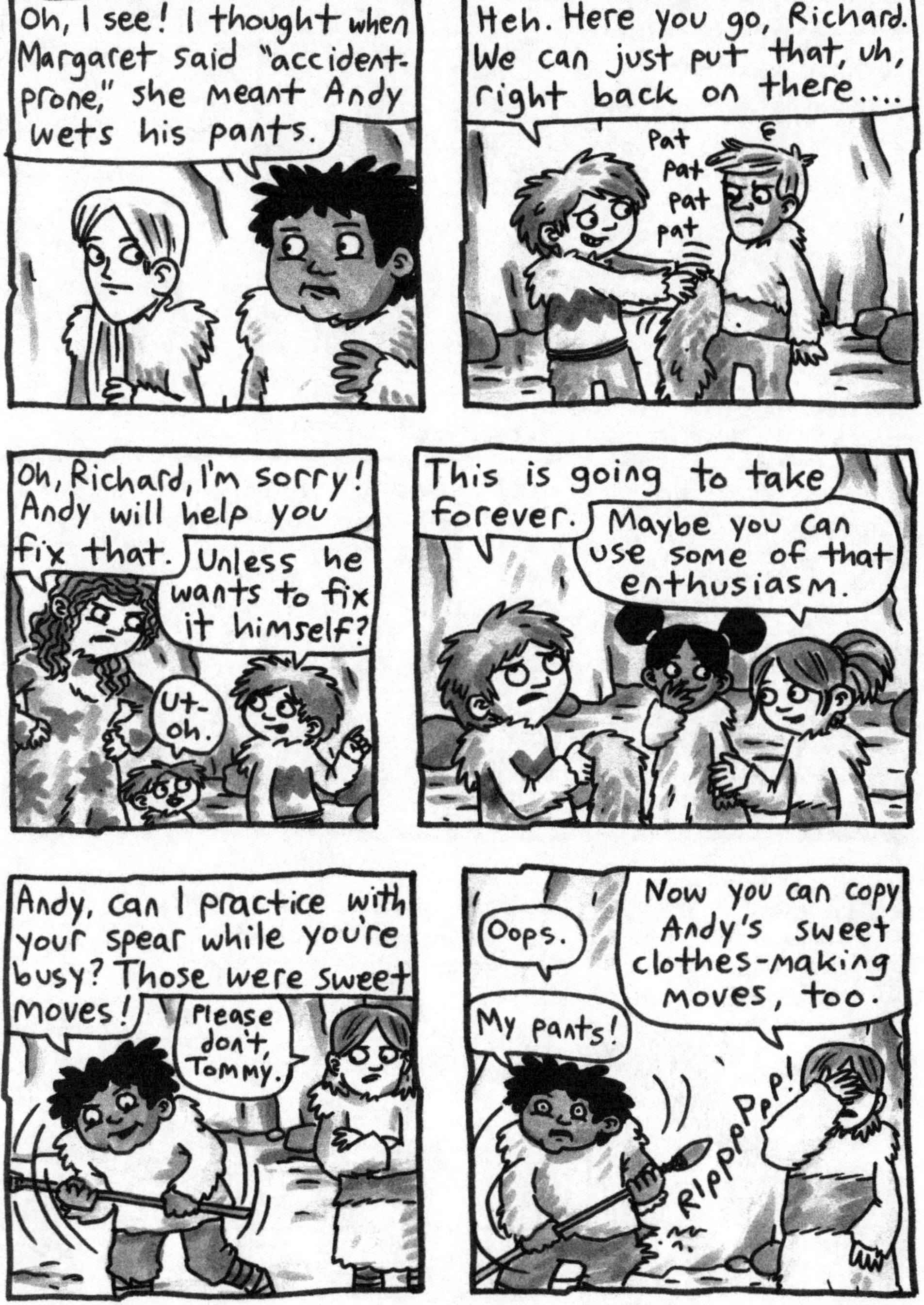

Oh, I see! I thought when Margaret said "accident-prone," she meant Andy wets his pants.
Heh. Here you go, Richard. We can just put that, uh, right back on there....
Pat
pat
pat
pat
Oh, Richard, I'm sorry! Andy will help you fix that.
Unless he wants to fix it himself?
Ut-oh.
This is going to take forever.
Maybe you can use some of that enthusiasm.
Andy, can I practice with your spear while you're busy? Those were sweet moves!
Please don't, Tommy.
Oops.
Now you can copy Andy's sweet clothes-making moves, too.
My pants!
RIPPPPPP!

Neanderthals needed a new outfit every year.

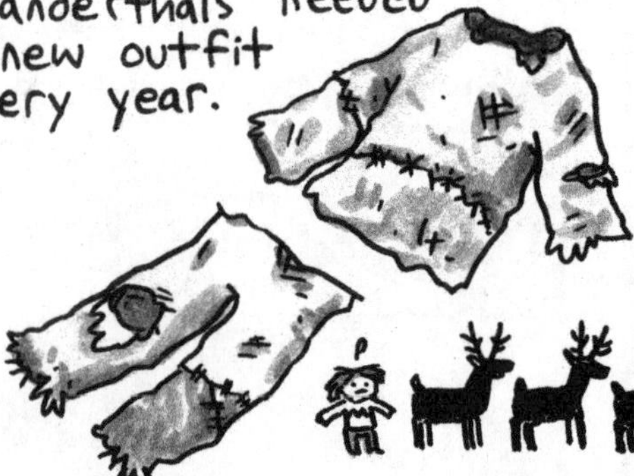

It took the skins of 6 to 8 large deer to make a new outfit, and each skin needed at least 8 hours of scraping.

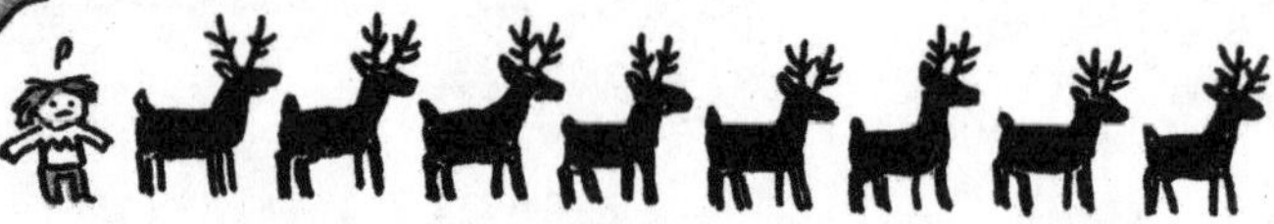

Scientists don't know if Neanderthal kids wore their clothes out faster.

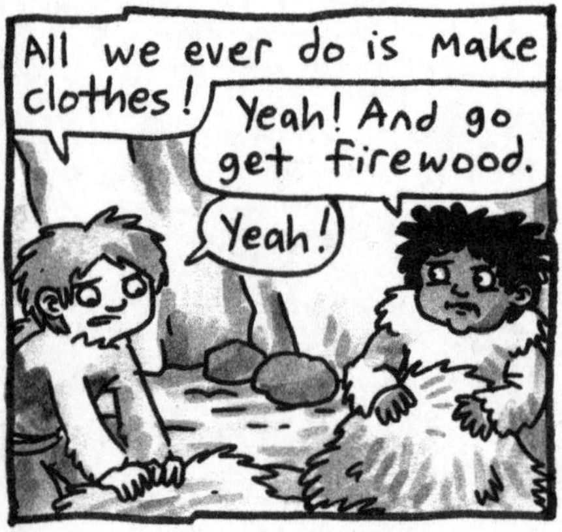
All we ever do is make clothes!
Yeah! And go get firewood.
Yeah!

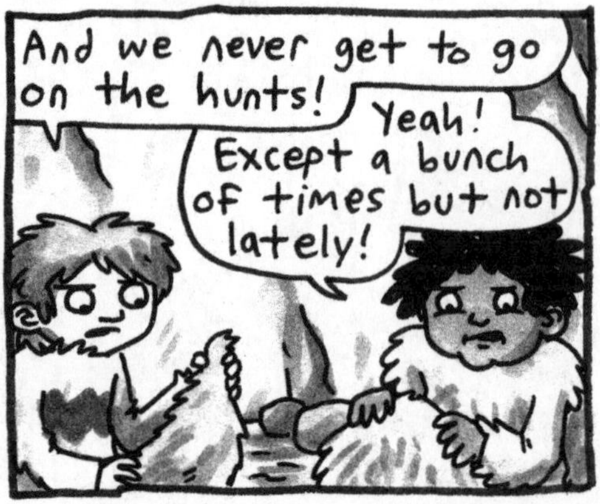
And we never get to go on the hunts!
Yeah! Except a bunch of times but not lately!

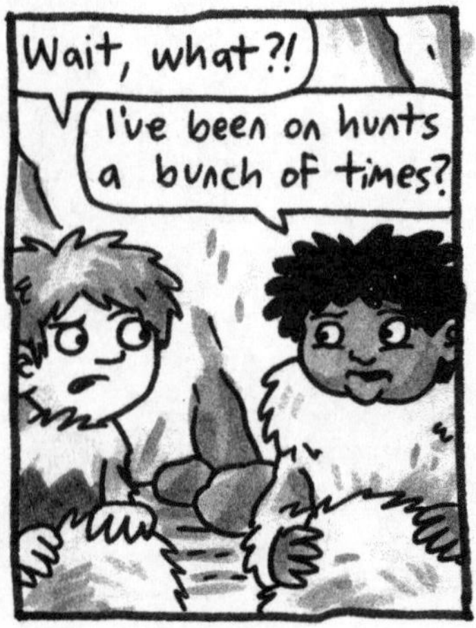
Wait, what?!
I've been on hunts a bunch of times?

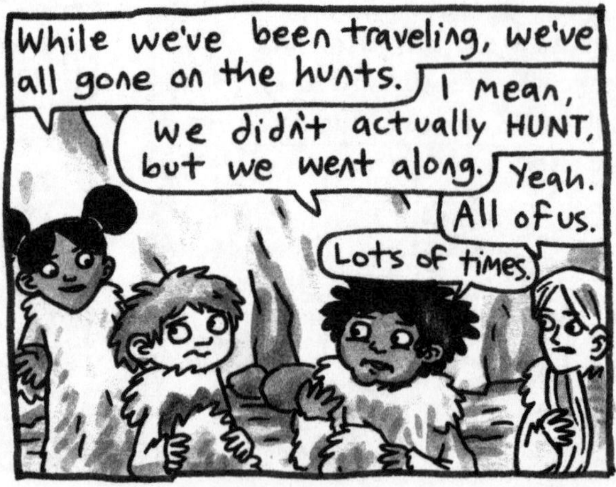
While we've been traveling, we've all gone on the hunts.
I mean, we didn't actually HUNT, but we went along.
Yeah. All of us.
Lots of times.

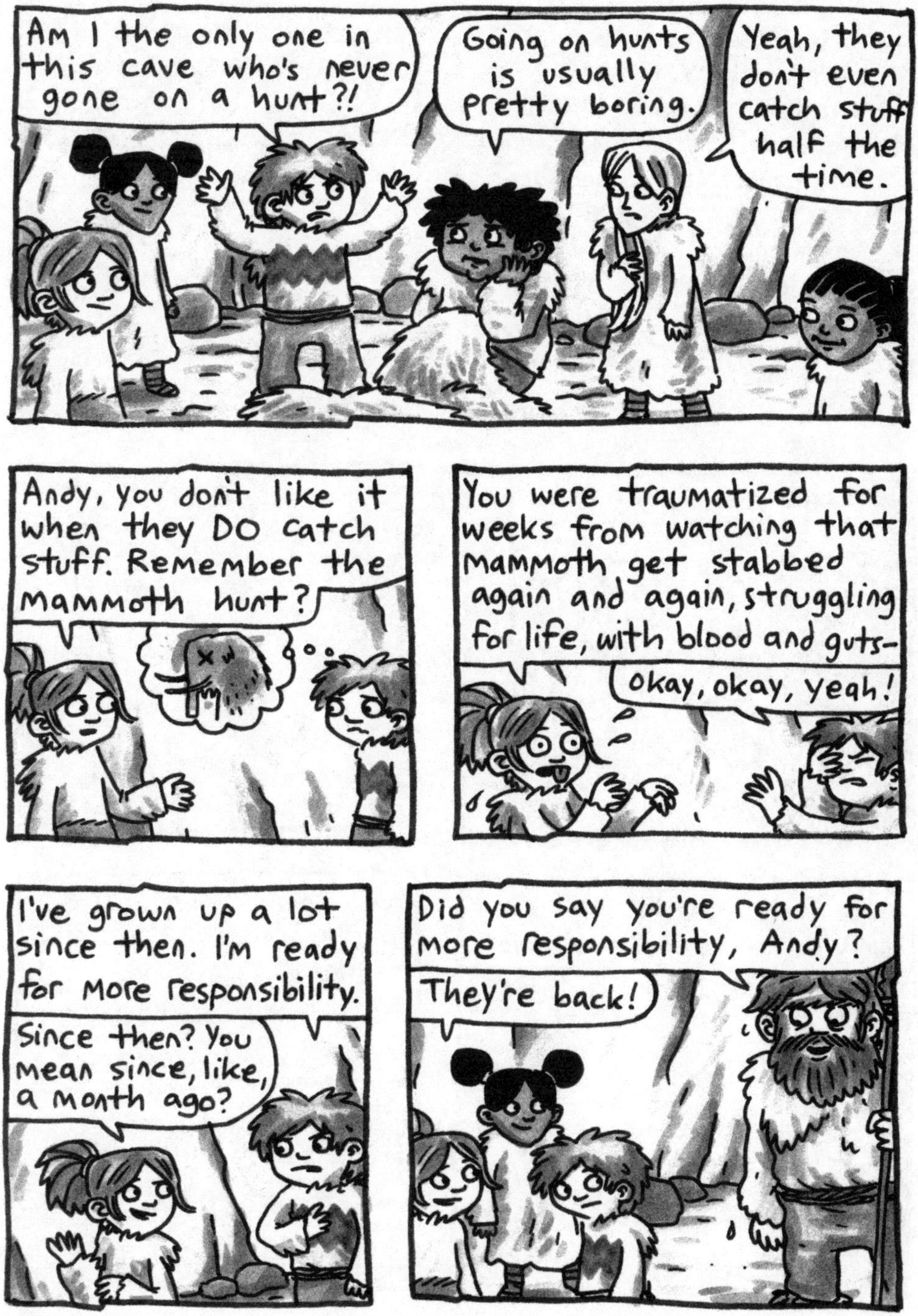
Am I the only one in this cave who's never gone on a hunt?!
Going on hunts is usually pretty boring.
Yeah, they don't even catch stuff half the time.
Andy, you don't like it when they DO catch stuff. Remember the mammoth hunt?
You were traumatized for weeks from watching that mammoth get stabbed again and again, struggling for life, with blood and guts-
okay, okay, yeah!
I've grown up a lot since then. I'm ready for more responsibility.
Since then? You mean since, like, a month ago?
Did you say you're ready for more responsibility, Andy?
They're back!

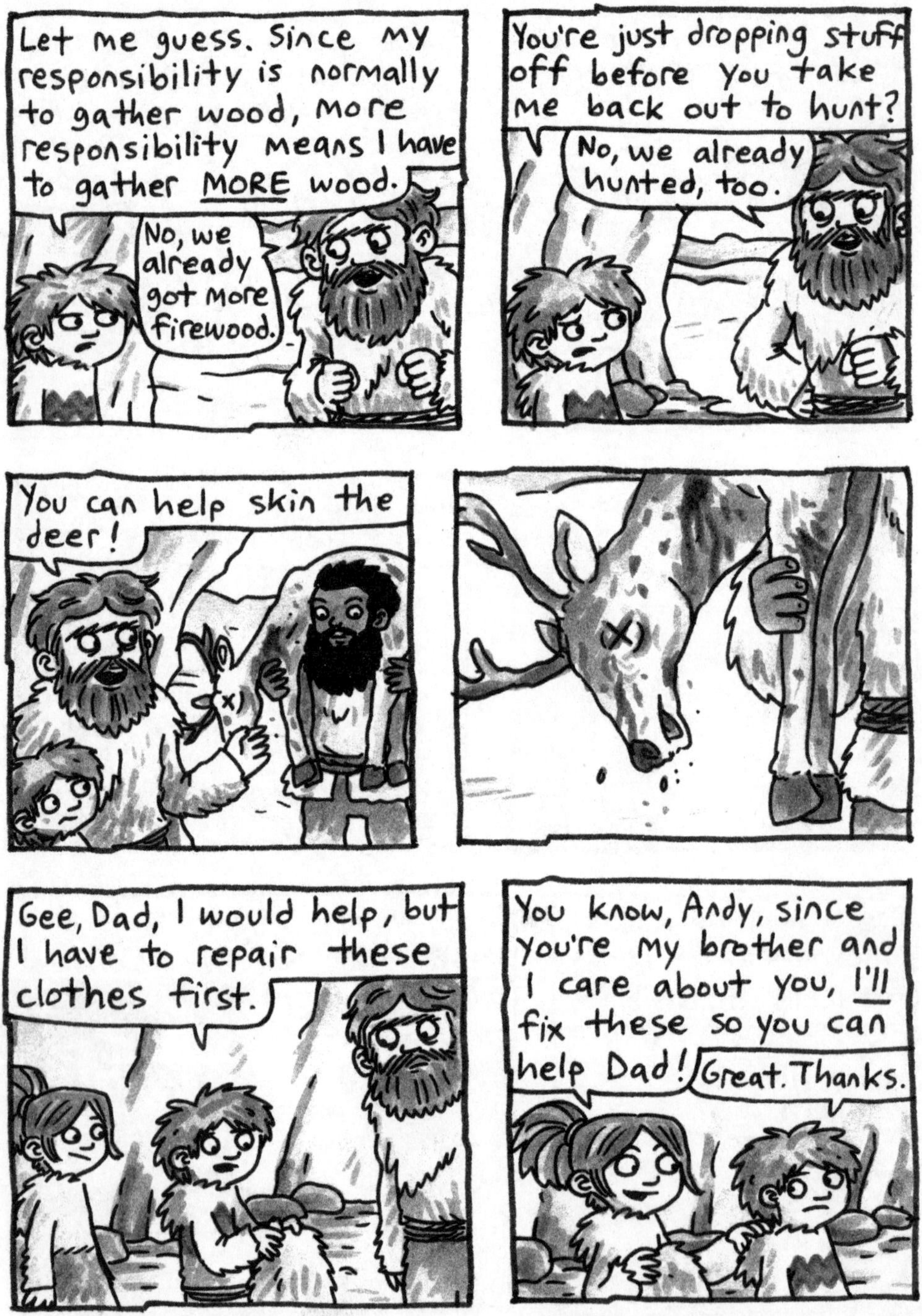
Let me guess. Since my responsibility is normally to gather wood, more responsibility means I have to gather MORE wood.
No, we already got more firewood.
You're just dropping stuff off before you take me back out to hunt?
No, we already hunted, too.
You can help skin the deer!
Gee, Dad, I would help, but I have to repair these clothes first.
You know, Andy, since you're my brother and I care about you, I'll fix these so you can help Dad!
Great. Thanks.

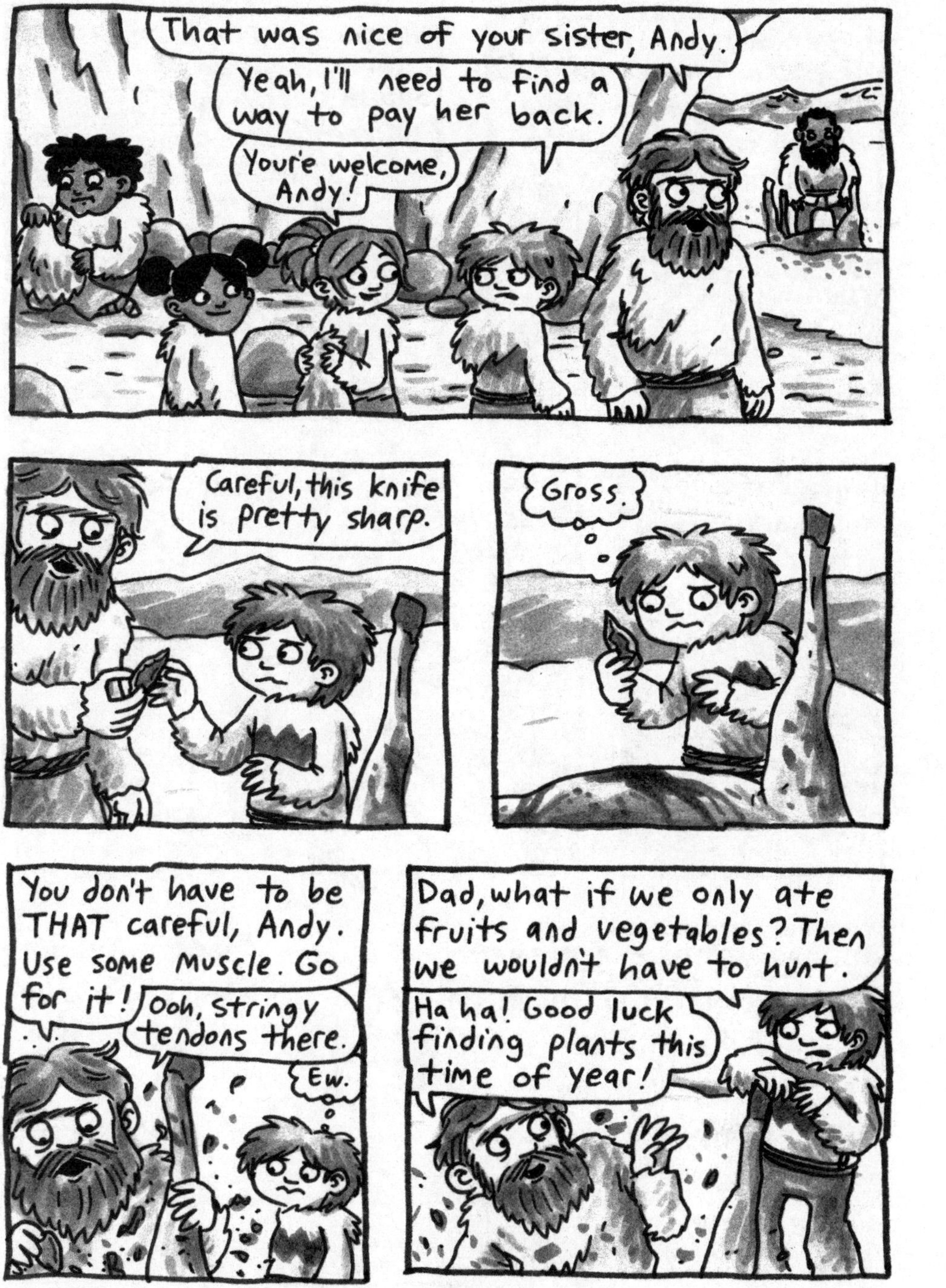
That was nice of your sister, Andy.
Yeah, I'll need to find a way to pay her back.
You're welcome, Andy!
Careful, this knife is pretty sharp.
Gross.
You don't have to be THAT careful, Andy. Use some muscle. Go for it!
Ooh, stringy tendons there.
Ew.
Dad, what if we only ate fruits and vegetables? Then we wouldn't have to hunt.
Ha ha! Good luck finding plants this time of year!

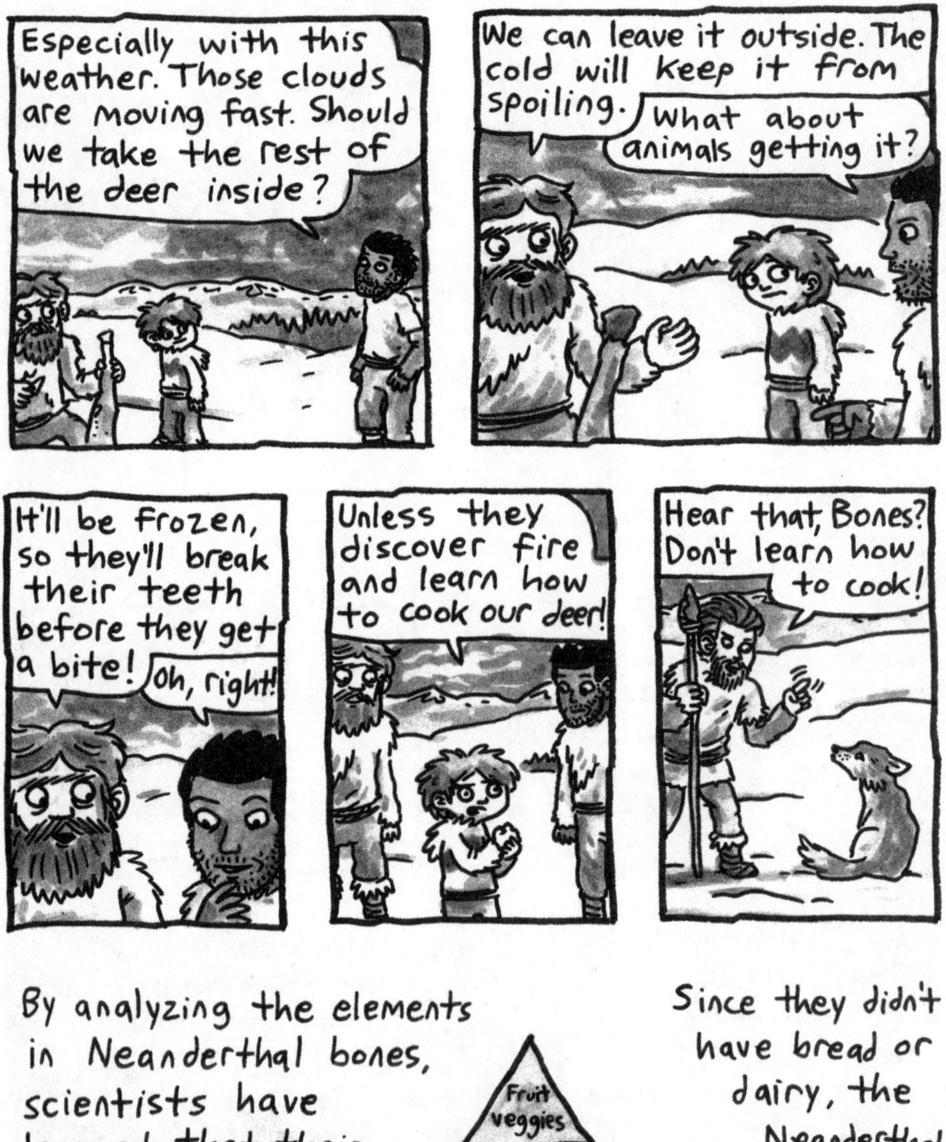
Especially with this weather. Those clouds are moving fast. Should we take the rest of the deer inside?
We can leave it outside. The cold will keep it from spoiling.
What about animals getting it?
It'll be frozen, so they'll break their teeth before they get a bite!
Oh, right!
Unless they discover fire and learn how to cook our deer!
Hear that, Bones? Don't learn how to cook!

By analyzing the elements in Neanderthal bones, scientists have learned that their diet was about 80% meat and 20% vegetables and fruit.

Since they didn't have bread or dairy, the Neanderthal food pyramid looked like this!

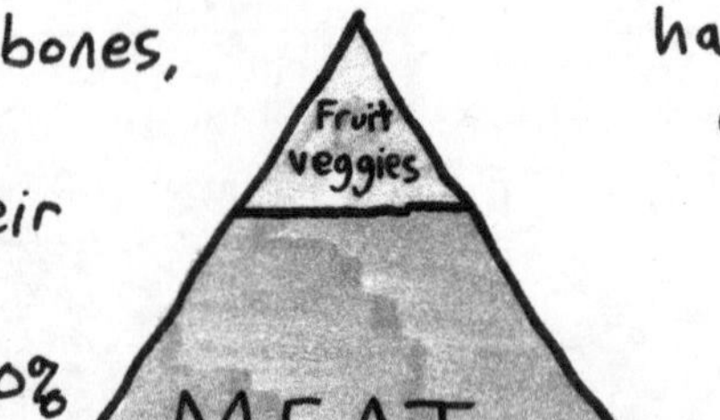
Fruit
veggies
MEAT

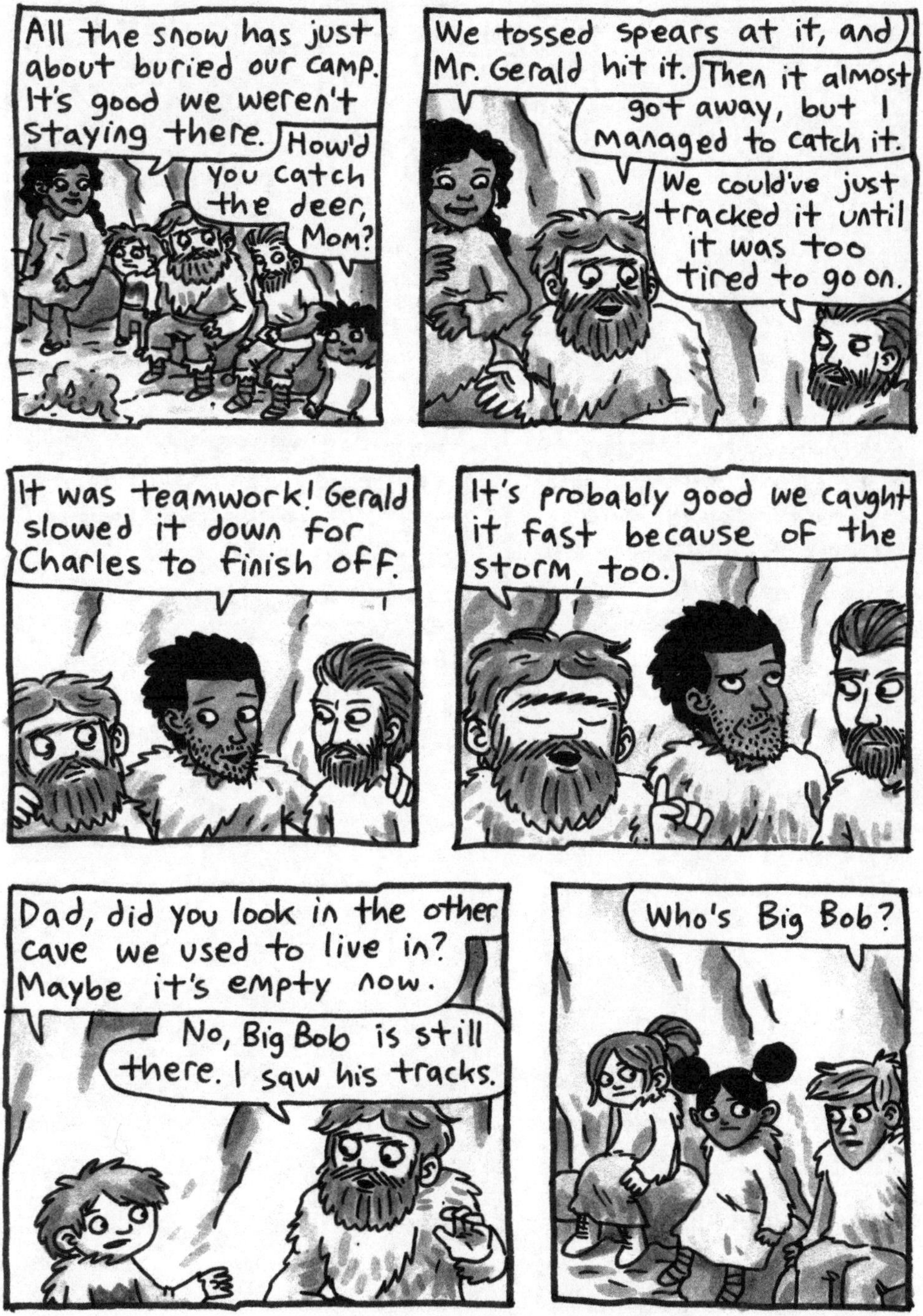
All the snow has just about buried our camp. It's good we weren't staying there.
How'd you catch the deer, Mom?
We tossed spears at it, and Mr. Gerald hit it.
Then it almost got away, but I managed to catch it.
We could've just tracked it until it was too tired to go on.
It was teamwork! Gerald slowed it down for Charles to finish off.
It's probably good we caught it fast because of the storm, too.
Dad, did you look in the other cave we used to live in? Maybe it's empty now.
No, Big Bob is still there. I saw his tracks.
Who's Big Bob?

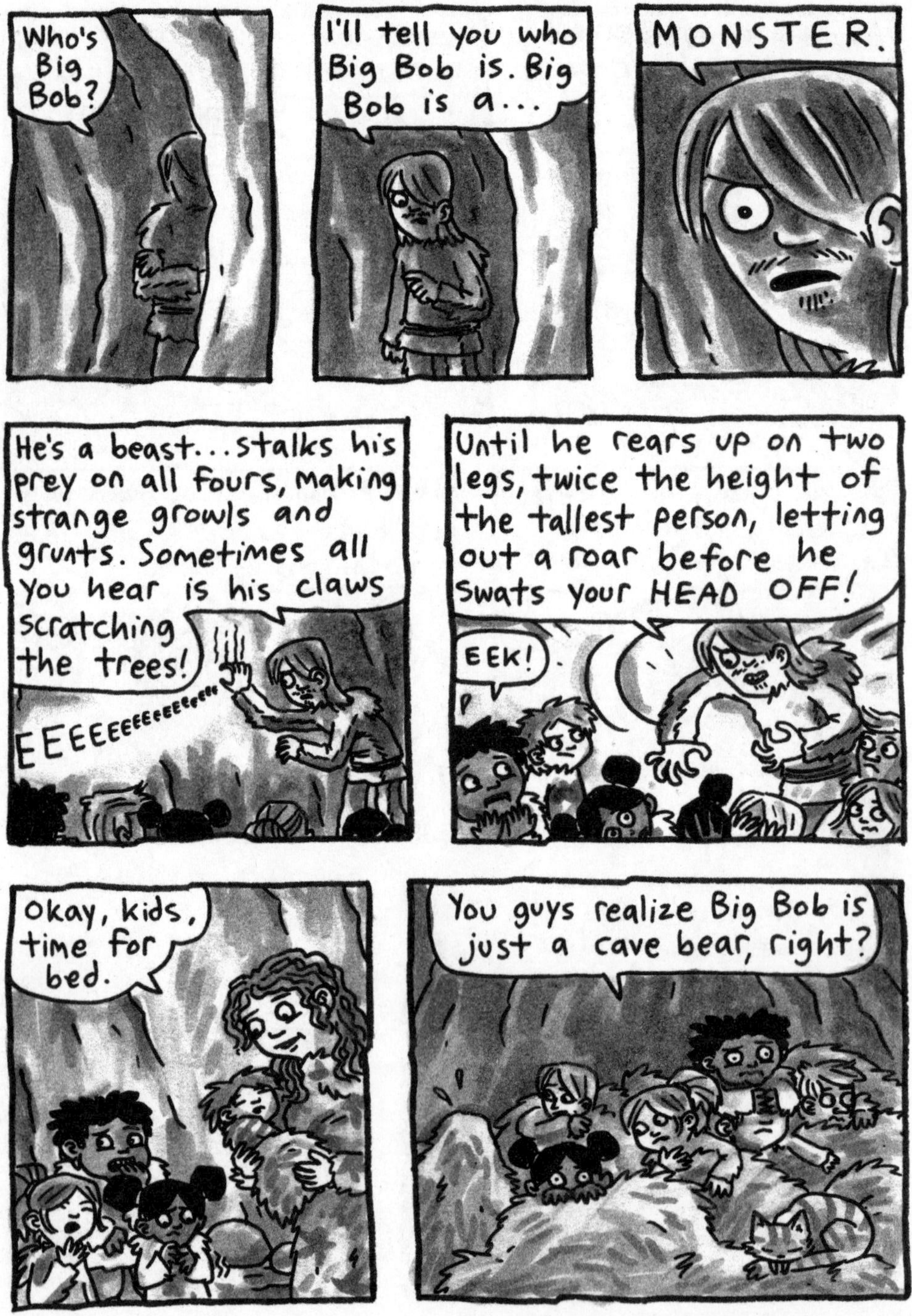
Who's Big Bob?
I'll tell you who Big Bob is. Big Bob is a...
MONSTER.
He's a beast...stalks his prey on all fours, making strange growls and grunts. Sometimes all you hear is his claws scratching the trees!
EEEEeeeeeeeeeee
Until he rears up on two legs, twice the height of the tallest person, letting out a roar before he swats your HEAD OFF!
EEK!
Okay, kids, time for bed.
You guys realize Big Bob is just a cave bear, right?

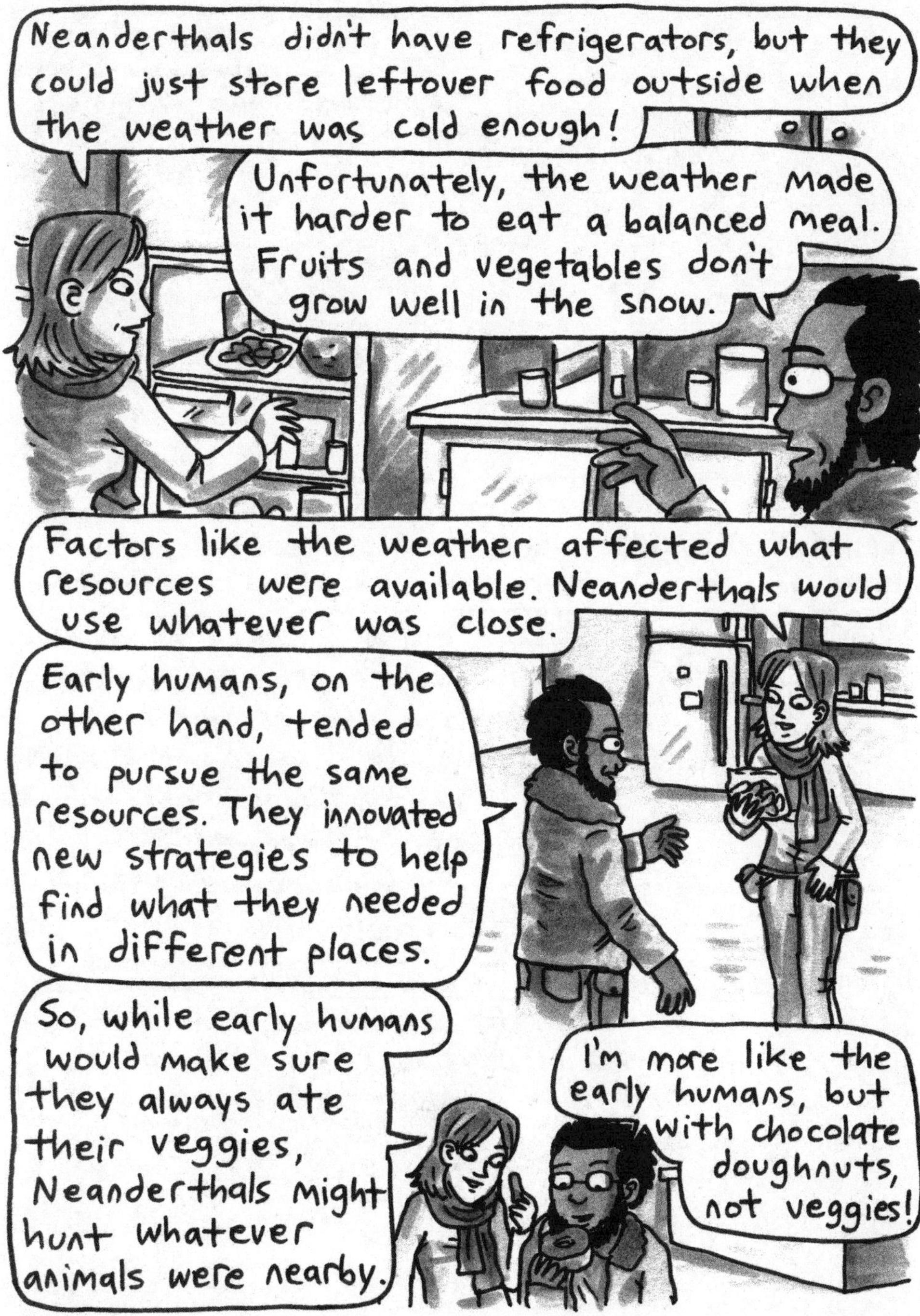
Neanderthals didn't have refrigerators, but they could just store leftover food outside when the weather was cold enough!
Unfortunately, the weather made it harder to eat a balanced meal. Fruits and vegetables don't grow well in the snow.
Factors like the weather affected what resources were available. Neanderthals would use whatever was close.
Early humans, on the other hand, tended to pursue the same resources. They innovated new strategies to help find what they needed in different places.
So, while early humans would make sure they always ate their veggies, Neanderthals might hunt whatever animals were nearby.
I'm more like the early humans, but with chocolate doughnuts, not veggies!

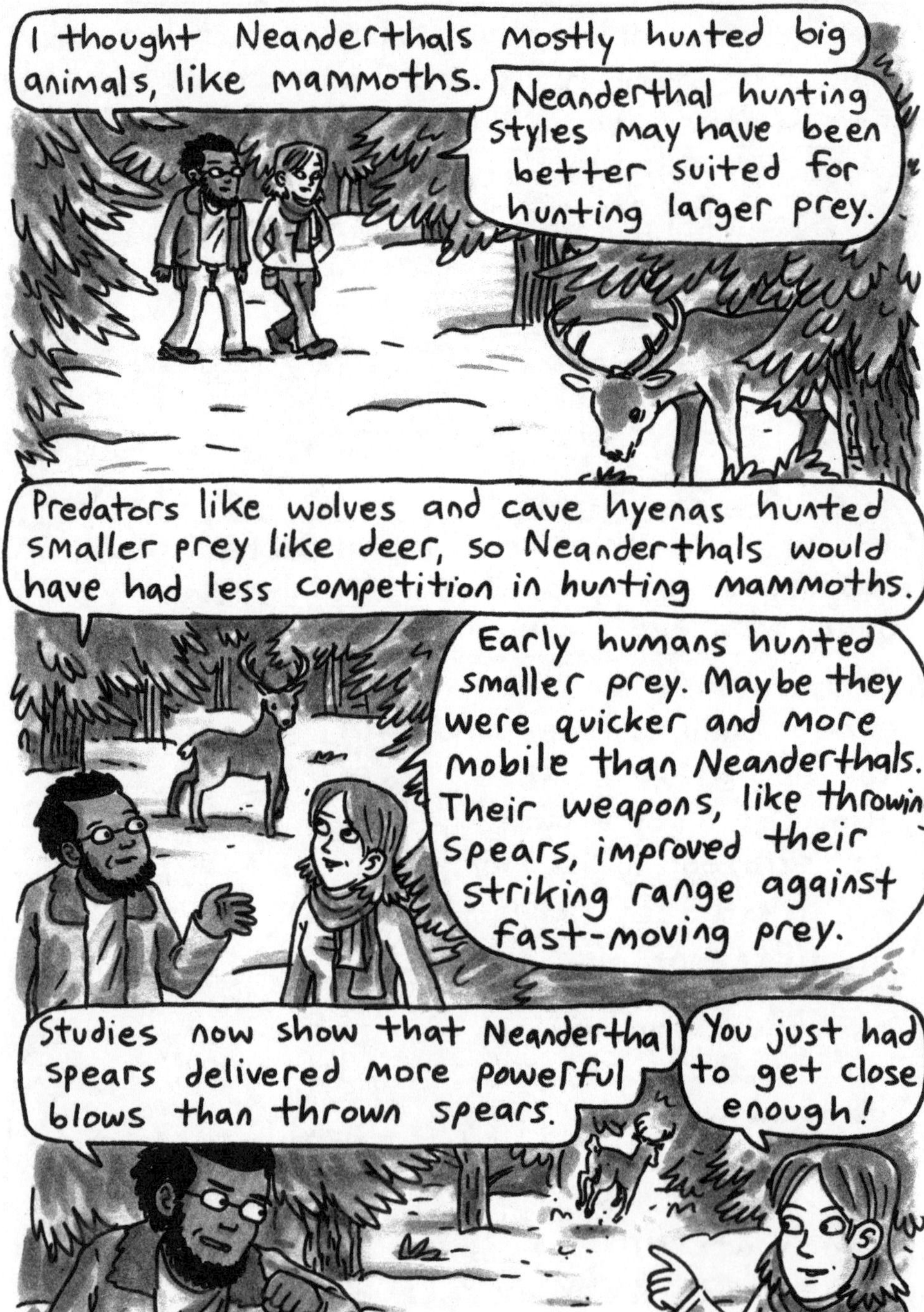
I thought Neanderthals mostly hunted big animals, like mammoths.
Neanderthal hunting styles may have been better suited for hunting larger prey.
Predators like wolves and cave hyenas hunted smaller prey like deer, so Neanderthals would have had less competition in hunting mammoths.
Early humans hunted smaller prey. Maybe they were quicker and more mobile than Neanderthals. Their weapons, like throwing spears, improved their striking range against fast-moving prey.
Studies now show that Neanderthal spears delivered more powerful blows than thrown spears.
You just had to get close enough!

CAVE
BEARS
101

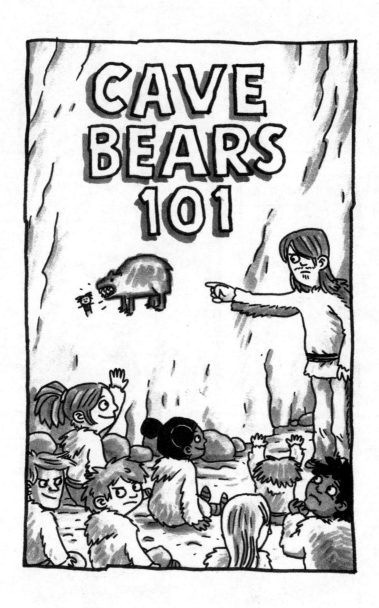

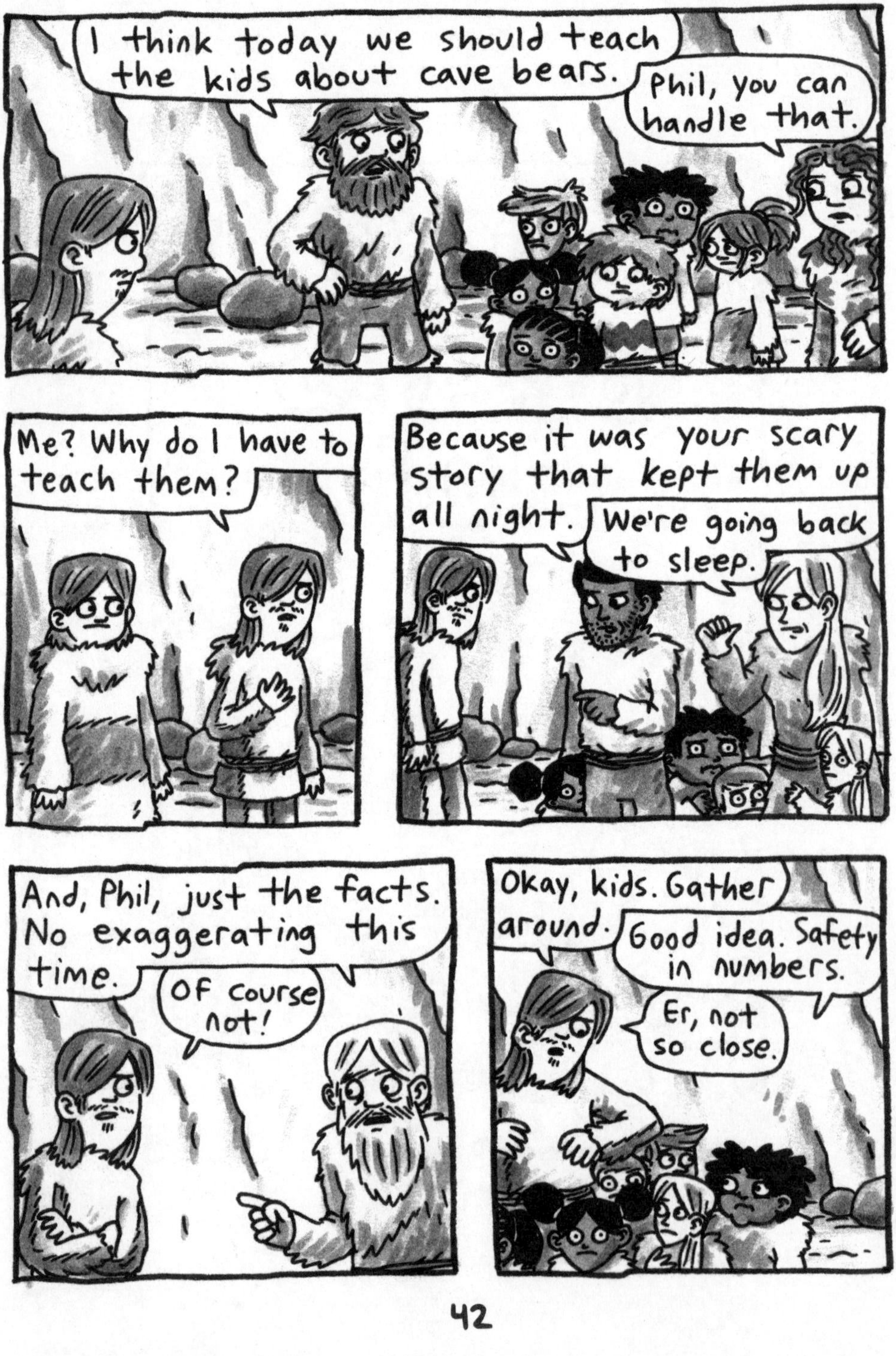
I think today we should teach the kids about cave bears.
Phil, you can handle that.
Me? Why do I have to teach them?
Because it was your scary story that kept them up all night.
We're going back to sleep.
And, Phil, just the facts. No exaggerating this time.
Of course not!
Okay, kids. Gather around.
Good idea. Safety in numbers.
Er, not so close.

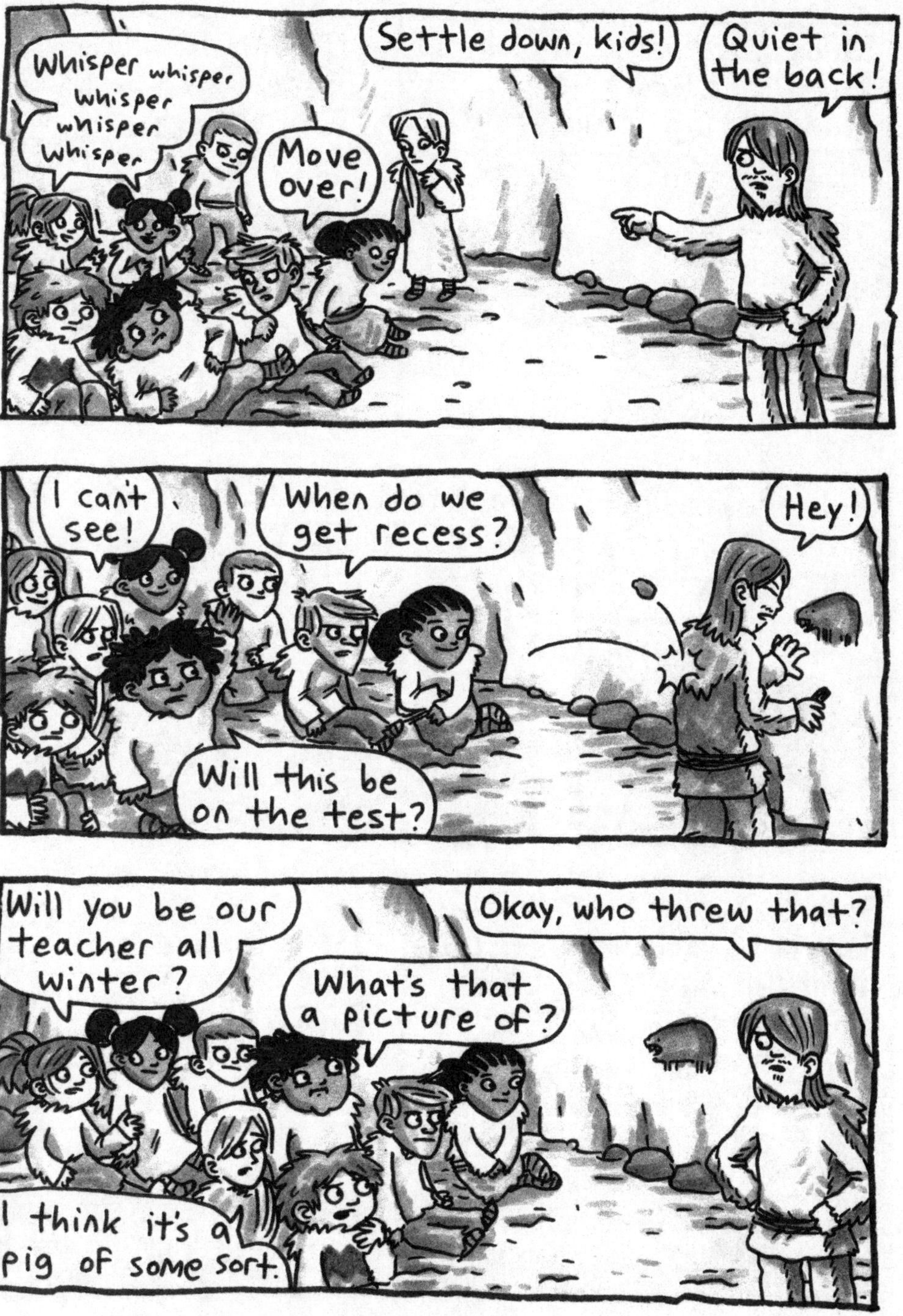
Whisper whisper whisper whisper whisper
Move over!
Settle down, kids!
Quiet in the back!
I can't see!
When do we get recess?
Will this be on the test?
Hey!
Will you be our teacher all winter?
What's that a picture of?
I think it's a pig of some sort.
Okay, who threw that?

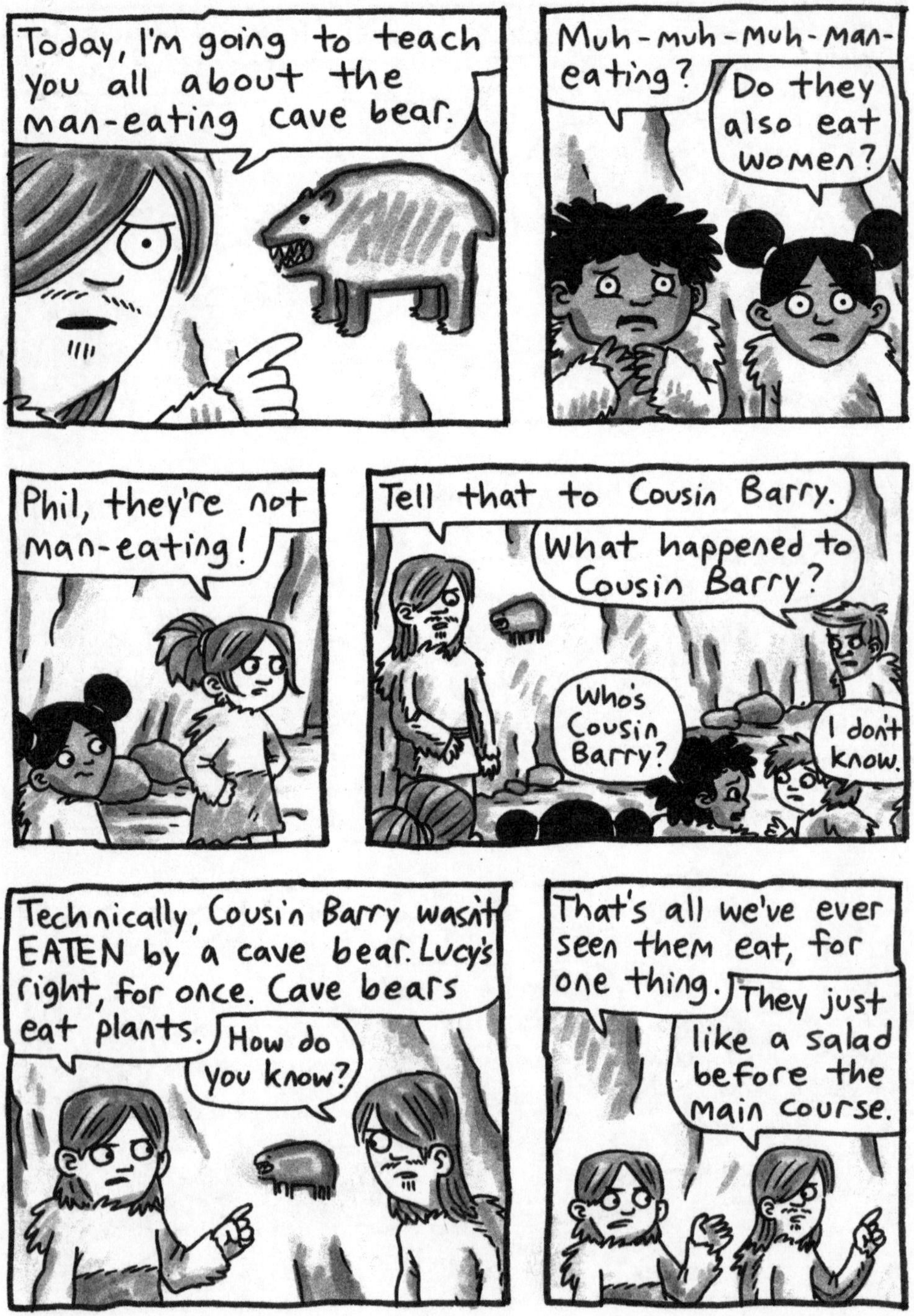
Today, I'm going to teach you all about the man-eating cave bear.
Muh-muh-muh-man-eating?
Do they also eat women?
Phil, they're not man-eating!
Tell that to Cousin Barry.
What happened to Cousin Barry?
Who's Cousin Barry?
I don't know.
Technically, Cousin Barry wasn't EATEN by a cave bear. Lucy's right, for once. Cave bears eat plants.
How do you know?
That's all we've ever seen them eat, for one thing.
They just like a salad before the main course.

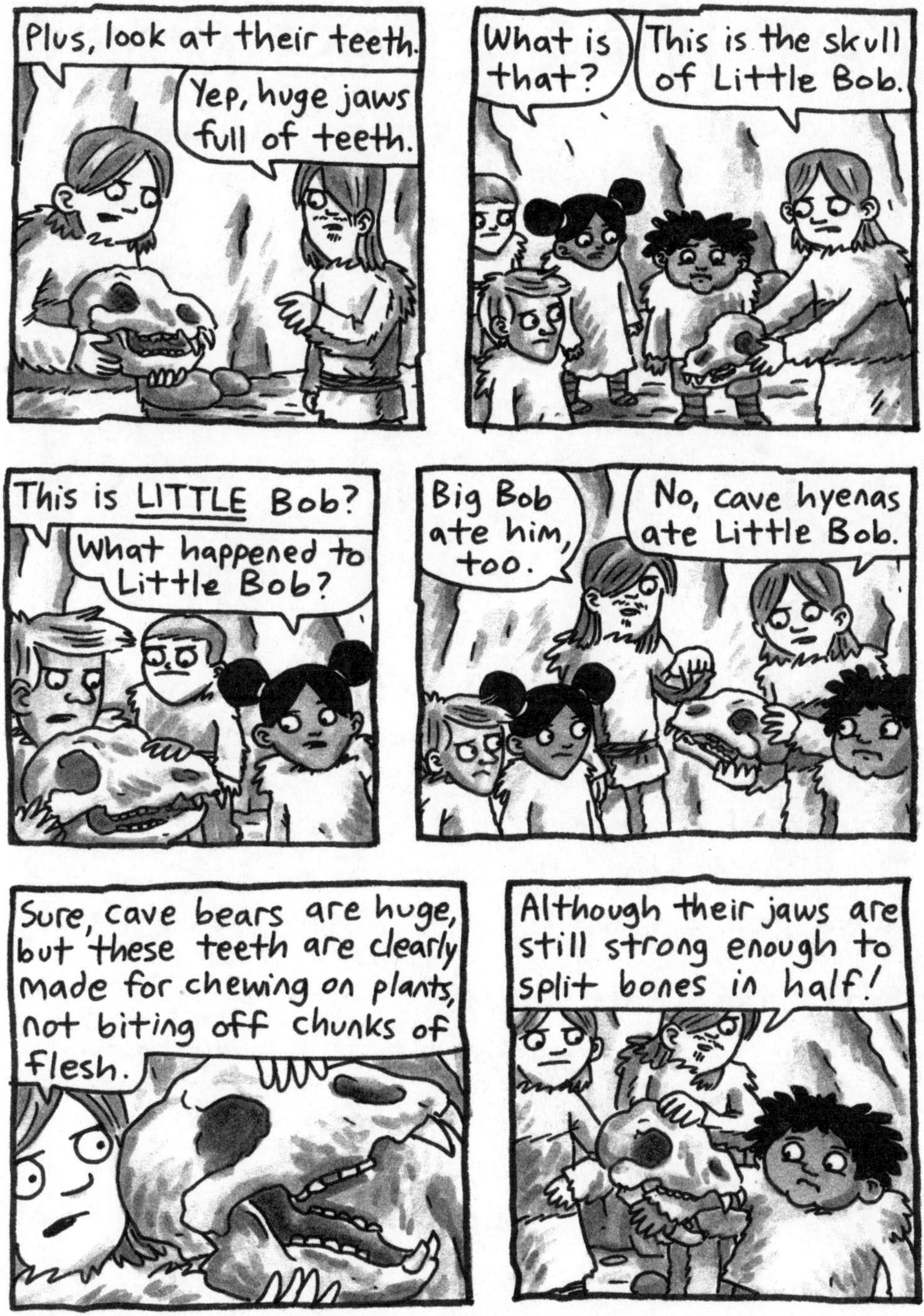
Plus, look at their teeth.
Yep, huge jaws full of teeth.
What is that?
This is the skull of Little Bob.
This is LITTLE Bob?
What happened to Little Bob?
Big Bob ate him, too.
No, cave hyenas ate Little Bob.
Sure, cave bears are huge, but these teeth are clearly made for chewing on plants, not biting off chunks of flesh.
Although their jaws are still strong enough to split bones in half!

CAVE BEAR CLASS NOTES!

The cave bear lived in Europe and western Asia from about 300,000 years ago until around 28,000 years ago.

shoulder was about 4 feet tall

Stood about 10 feet tall on hind legs!

Male: 800-1,000 lbs
Female: 500-550 lbs

Were polar bears the dominant bear during the Ice Age? No! During the time of the Neanderthals, cave bears and the smaller brown bear were the most common bears found in Europe and Asia. The biggest bear, the short-faced bear, occupied North America until about 12,000 years ago.

6 feet tall at the shoulder

12 feet tall on hind legs!

Up to 2,000 lbs

Please stay on that side of the ocean.

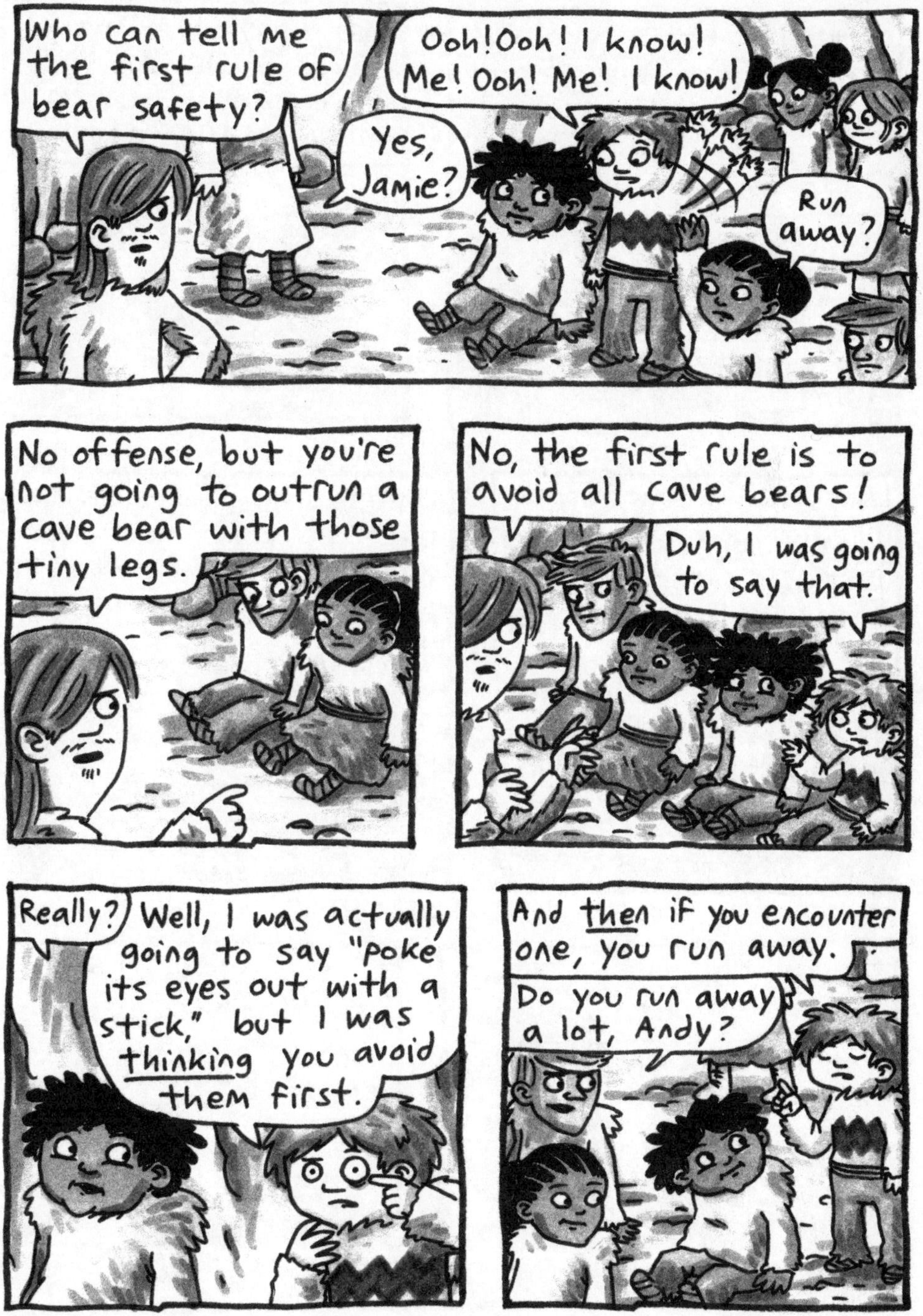
Who can tell me the first rule of bear safety?
Ooh! Ooh! I know! Me! Ooh! Me! I know!
Yes, Jamie?
Run away?
No offense, but you're not going to outrun a cave bear with those tiny legs.
No, the first rule is to avoid all cave bears!
Duh, I was going to say that.
Really?
Well, I was actually going to say "poke its eyes out with a stick," but I was thinking you avoid them first.
And then if you encounter one, you run away.
Do you run away a lot, Andy?

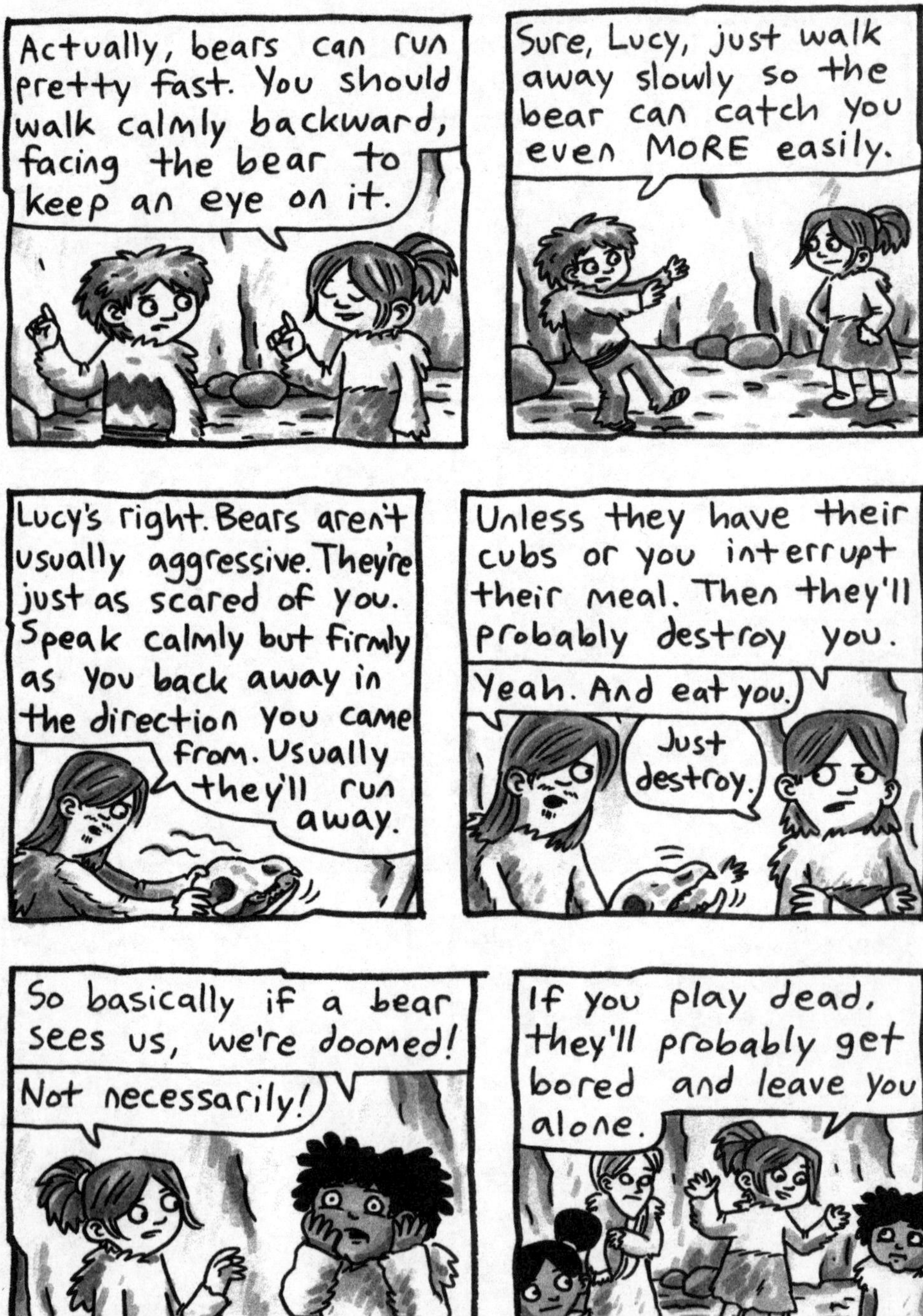

Actually, bears can run pretty fast. You should walk calmly backward, facing the bear to keep an eye on it.
Sure, Lucy, just walk away slowly so the bear can catch you even MORE easily.
Lucy's right. Bears aren't usually aggressive. They're just as scared of you. Speak calmly but firmly as you back away in the direction you came from. Usually they'll run away.
Unless they have their cubs or you interrupt their meal. Then they'll probably destroy you.
Yeah. And eat you.
Just destroy.
So basically if a bear sees us, we're doomed!
Not necessarily!
If you play dead, they'll probably get bored and leave you alone.

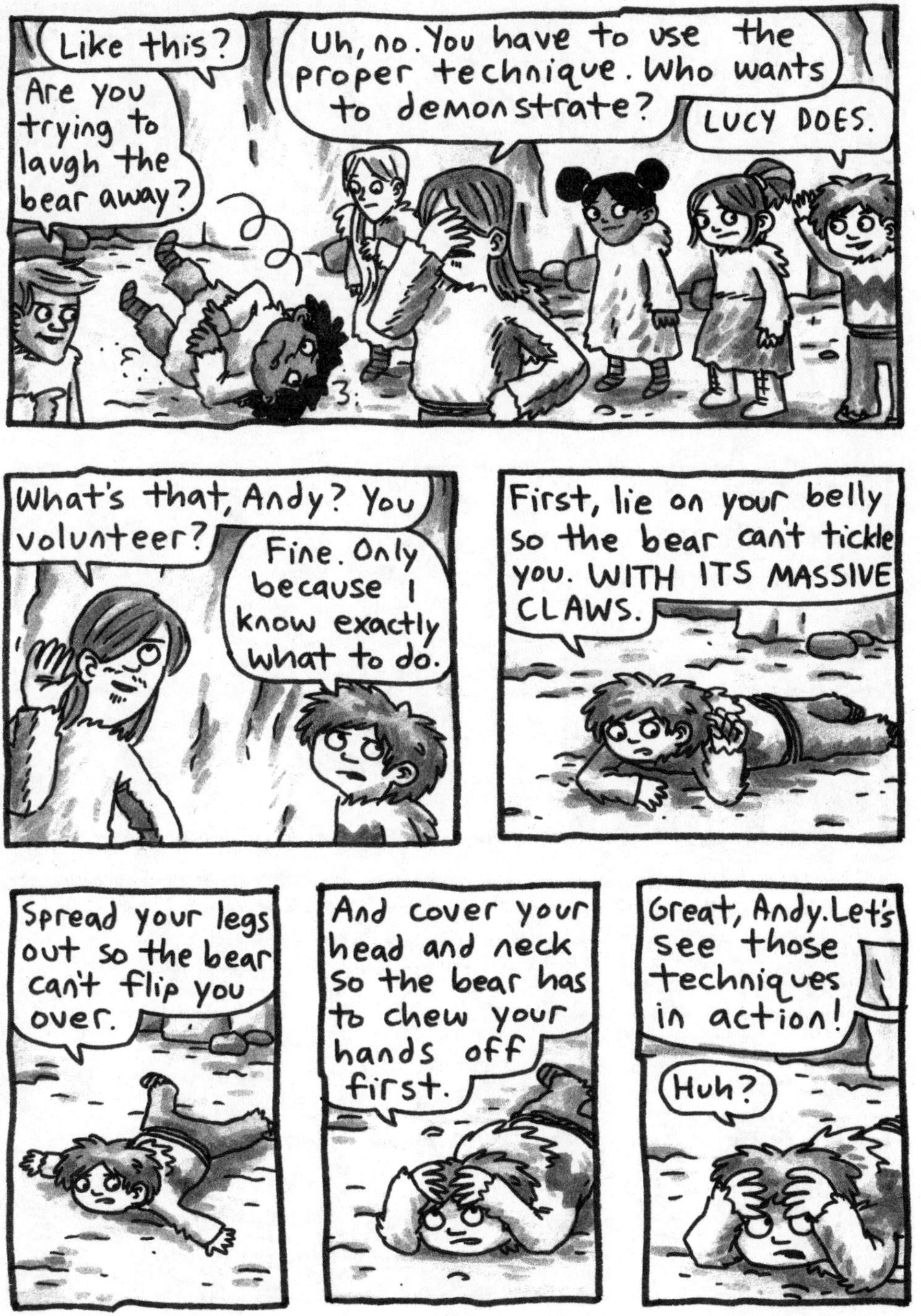
Like this?
Are you trying to laugh the bear away?
Uh, no. You have to use the proper technique. Who wants to demonstrate?
LUCY DOES.
What's that, Andy? You volunteer?
Fine. Only because I know exactly what to do.
First, lie on your belly so the bear can't tickle you. WITH ITS MASSIVE CLAWS.
Spread your legs out so the bear can't flip you over.
And cover your head and neck so the bear has to chew your hands off first.
Great, Andy. Let's see those techniques in action!
Huh?

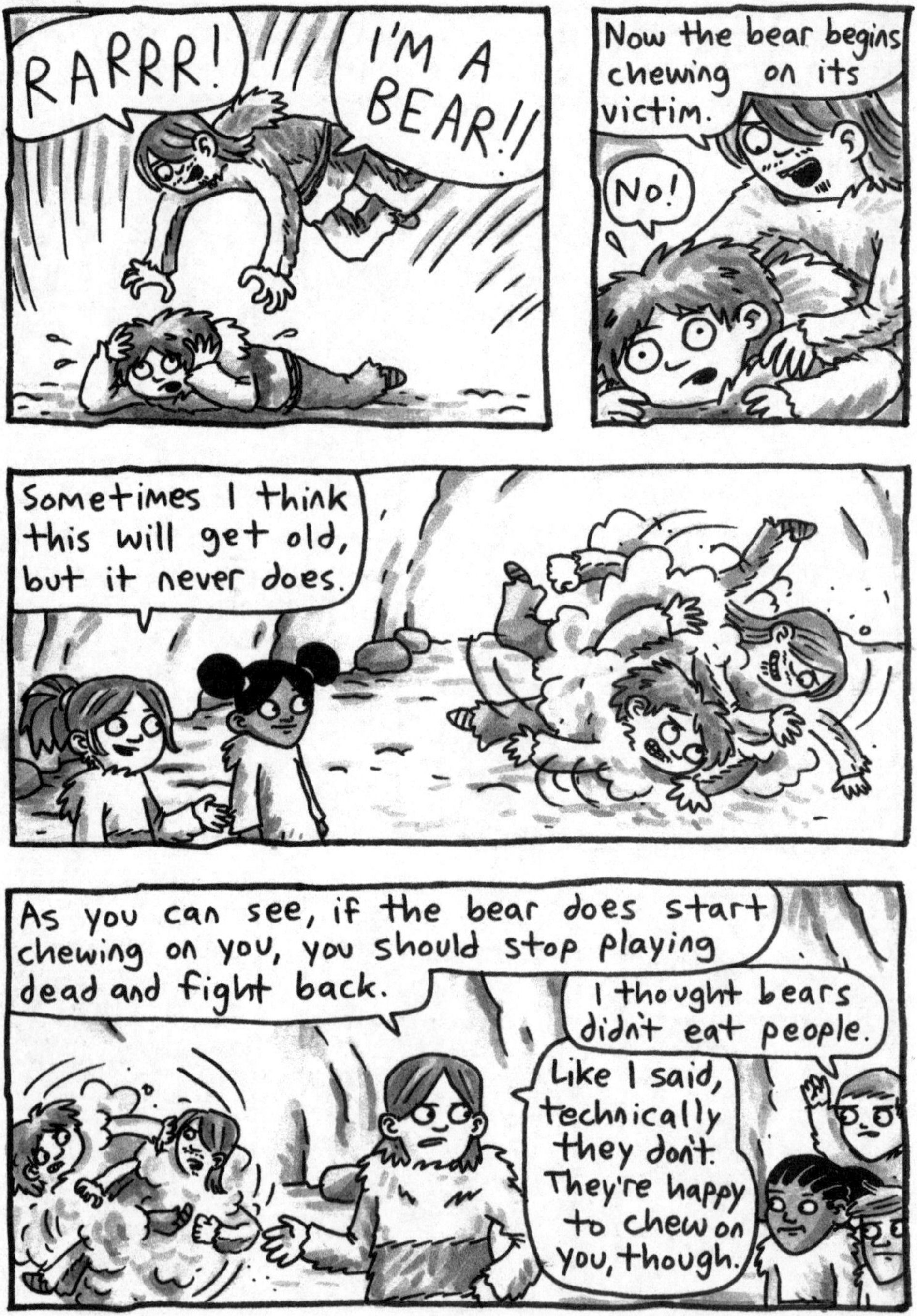
RARRR!
I'M A BEAR!!
Now the bear begins chewing on its victim.
No!
Sometimes I think this will get old, but it never does.
As you can see, if the bear does start chewing on you, you should stop playing dead and fight back.
I thought bears didn't eat people.
Like I said, technically they don't. They're happy to chew on you, though.

If the bear stops chewing on you, play dead again until it leaves...
I'm not leaving any time soon.
...or until you can surprise it!
OOF!
RRRRRRR.
And then run!
That was rad, Andy! Have you ever done that with a real bear?
I've never gotten that close.
No, I meant the running. I want to be that fast!

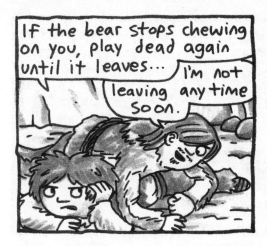

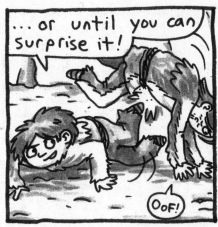

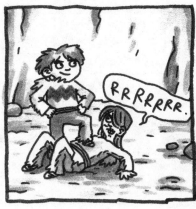

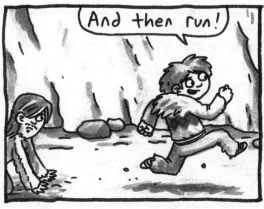

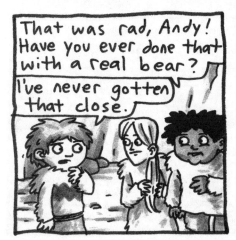

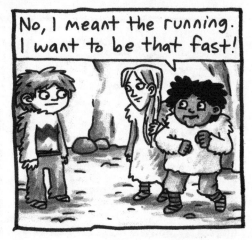

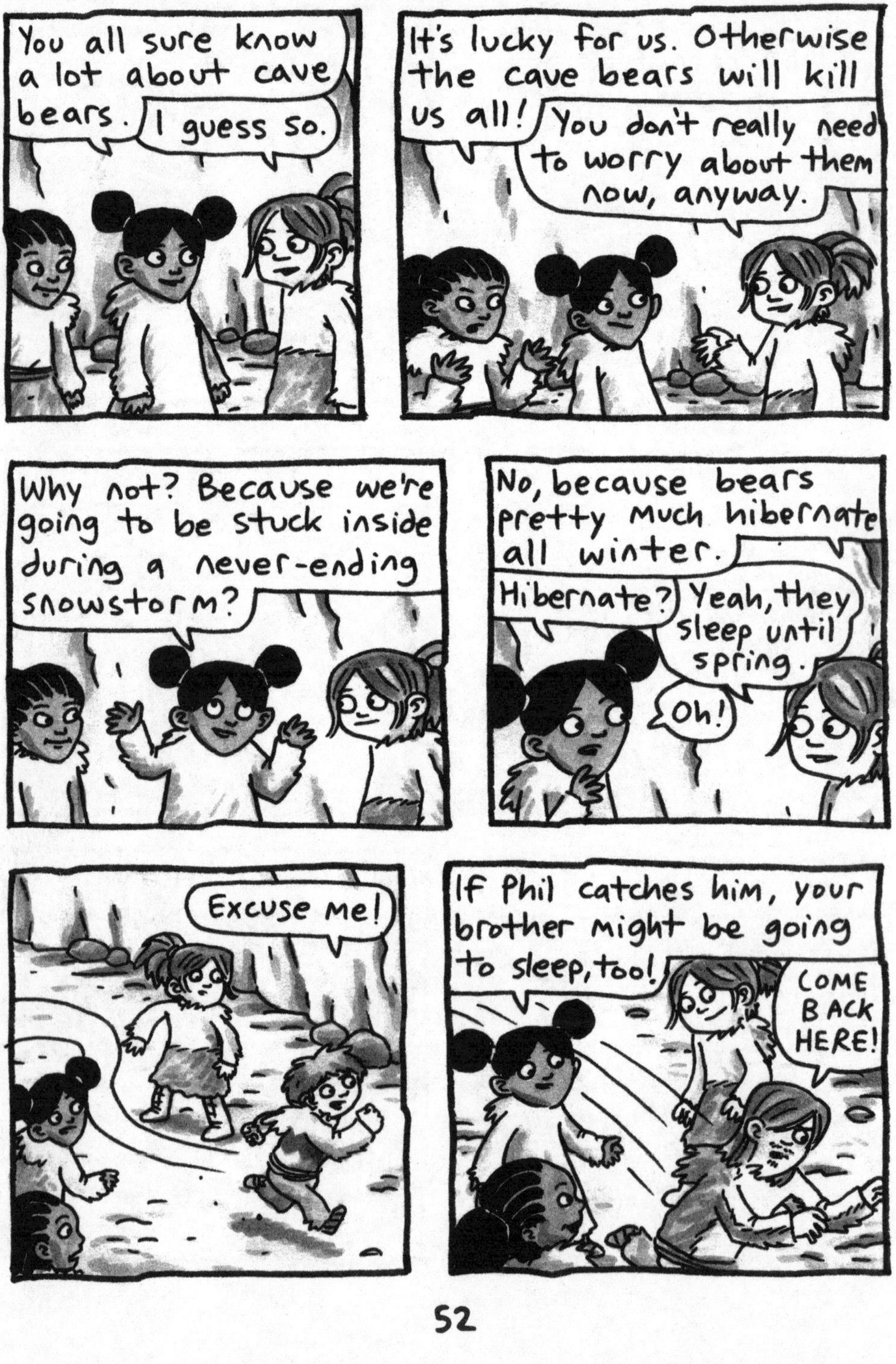
You all sure know a lot about cave bears.
I guess so.
It's lucky for us. Otherwise the cave bears will kill us all!
You don't really need to worry about them now, anyway.
Why not? Because we're going to be stuck inside during a never-ending snowstorm?
No, because bears pretty much hibernate all winter.
Hibernate?
Yeah, they sleep until spring.
Oh!
Excuse me!
If Phil catches him, your brother might be going to sleep, too!
COME BACK HERE!

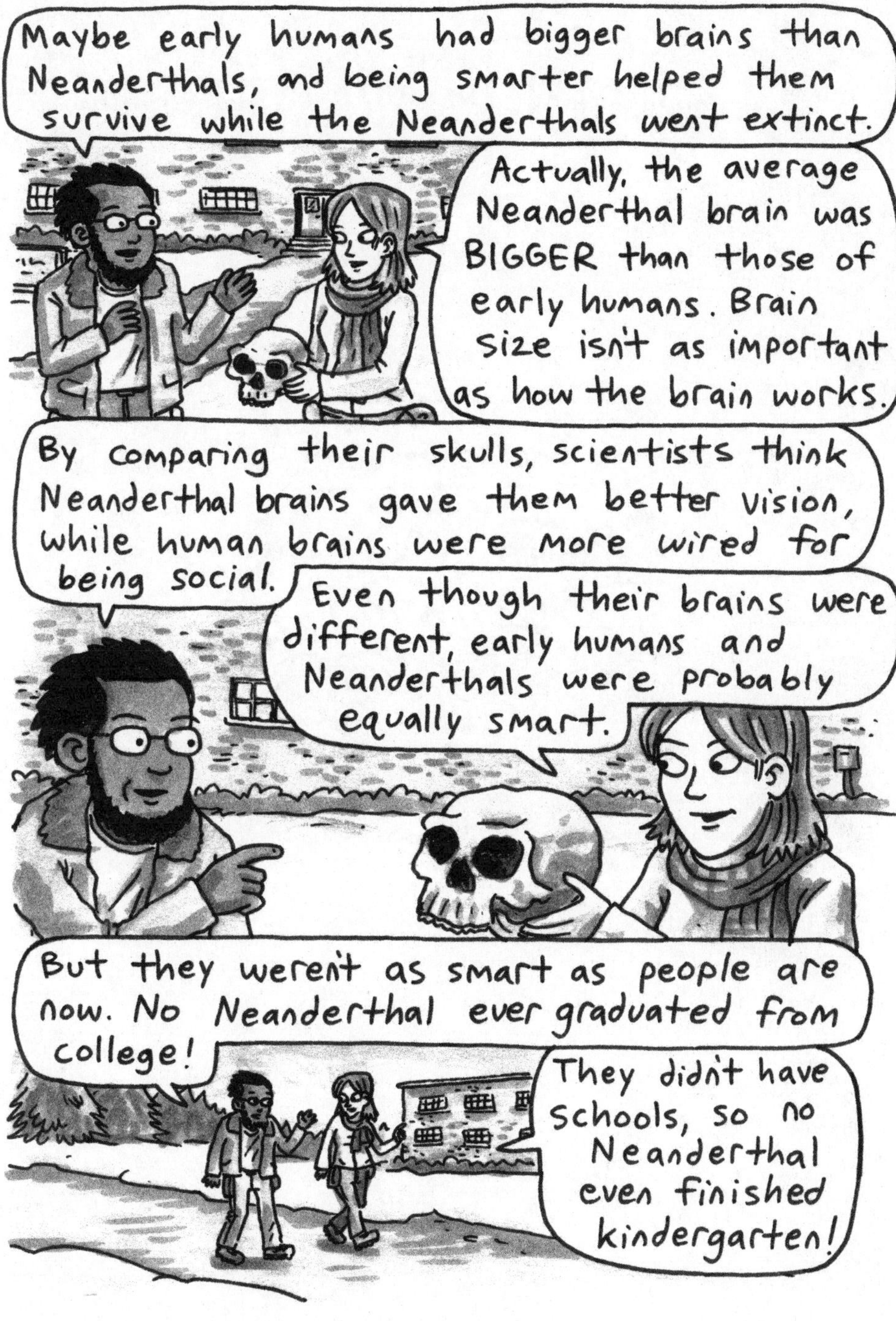
Maybe early humans had bigger brains than Neanderthals, and being smarter helped them survive while the Neanderthals went extinct.
Actually, the average Neanderthal brain was BIGGER than those of early humans. Brain size isn't as important as how the brain works.
By comparing their skulls, scientists think Neanderthal brains gave them better vision, while human brains were more wired for being social.
Even though their brains were different, early humans and Neanderthals were probably equally smart.
But they weren't as smart as people are now. No Neanderthal ever graduated from college!
They didn't have schools, so no Neanderthal even finished kindergarten!

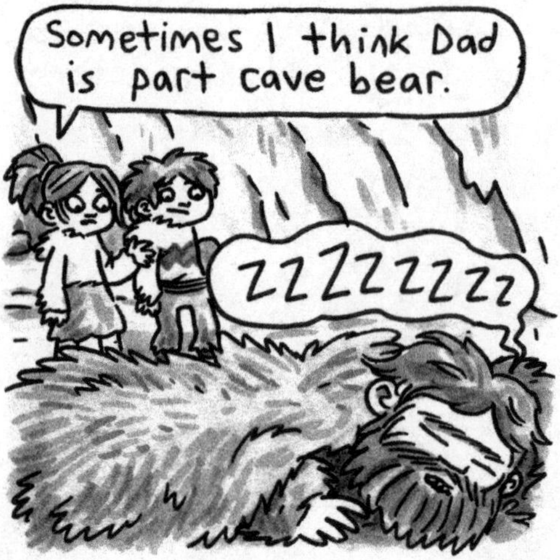
Sometimes I think Dad is part cave bear.
ZZZZZZZZZ

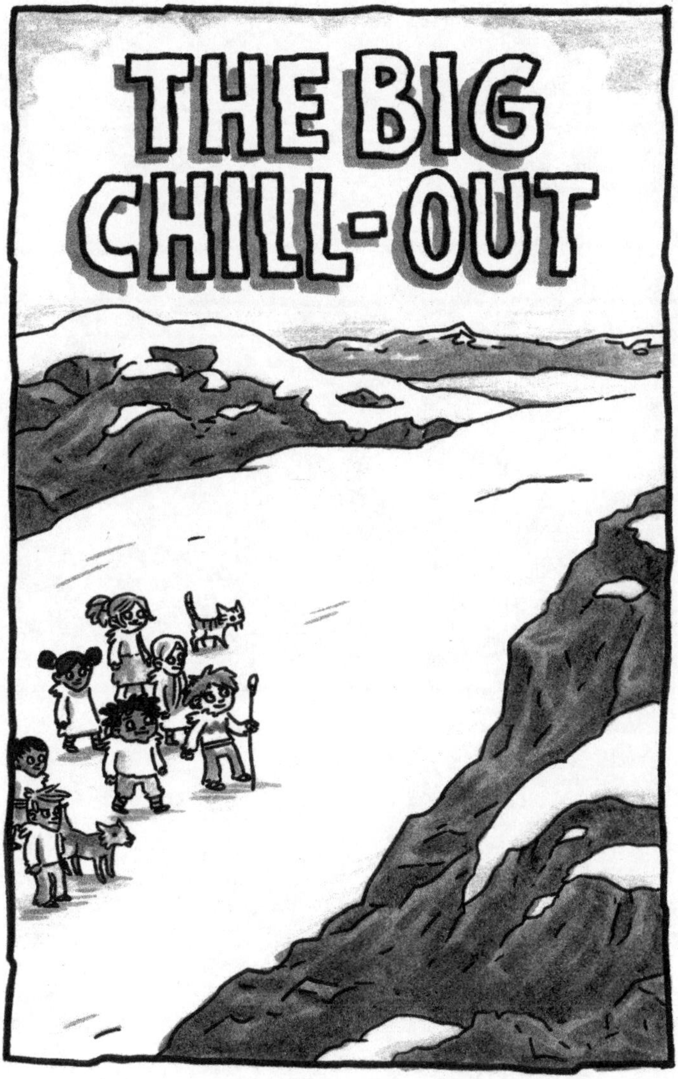
THE BIG
CHILL-OUT

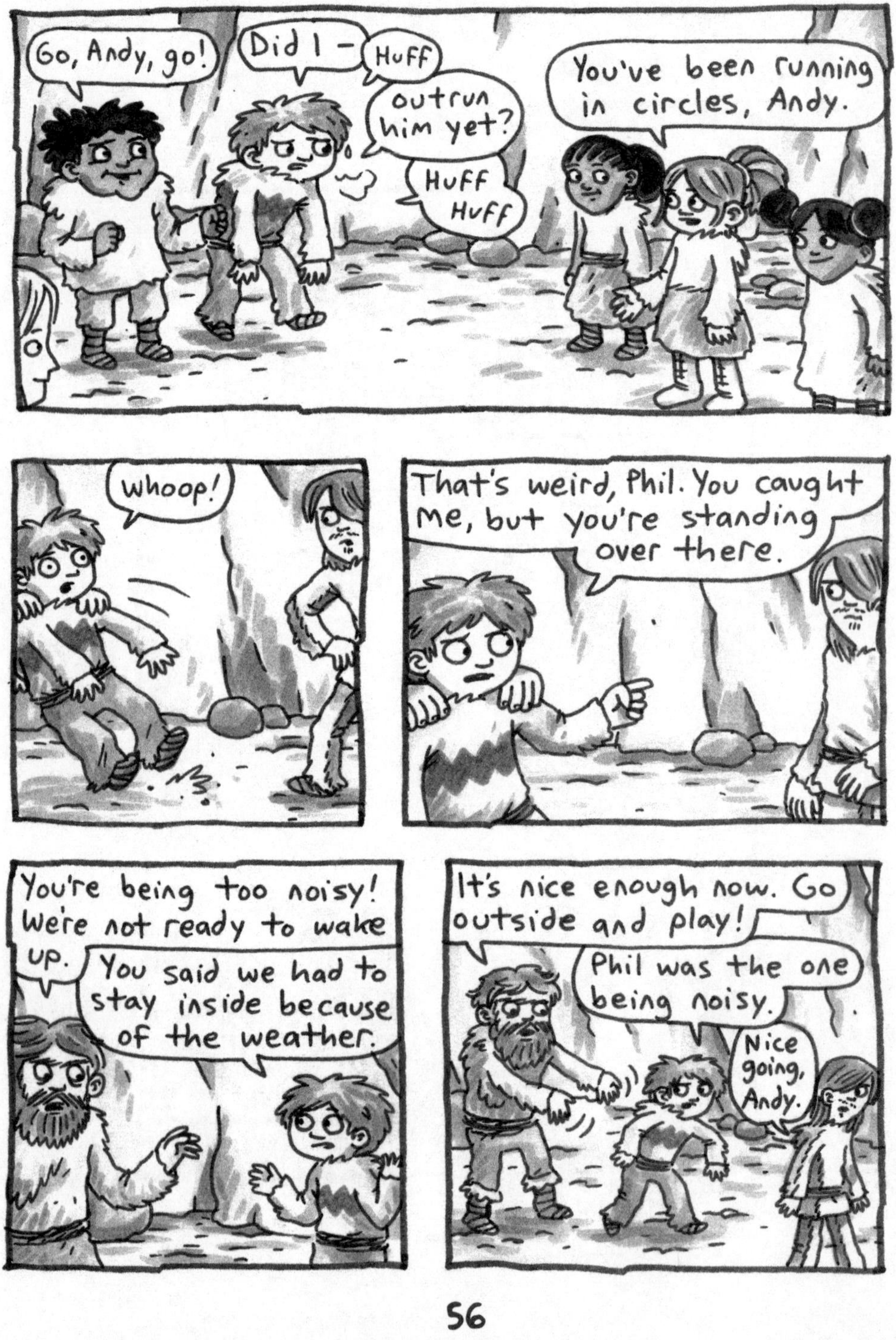
Go, Andy, go!
Did I -
Huff
outrun him yet?
Huff Huff
You've been running in circles, Andy.
whoop!
That's weird, Phil. You caught me, but you're standing over there.
You're being too noisy! We're not ready to wake up.
You said we had to stay inside because of the weather.
It's nice enough now. Go outside and play!
Phil was the one being noisy.
Nice going, Andy.

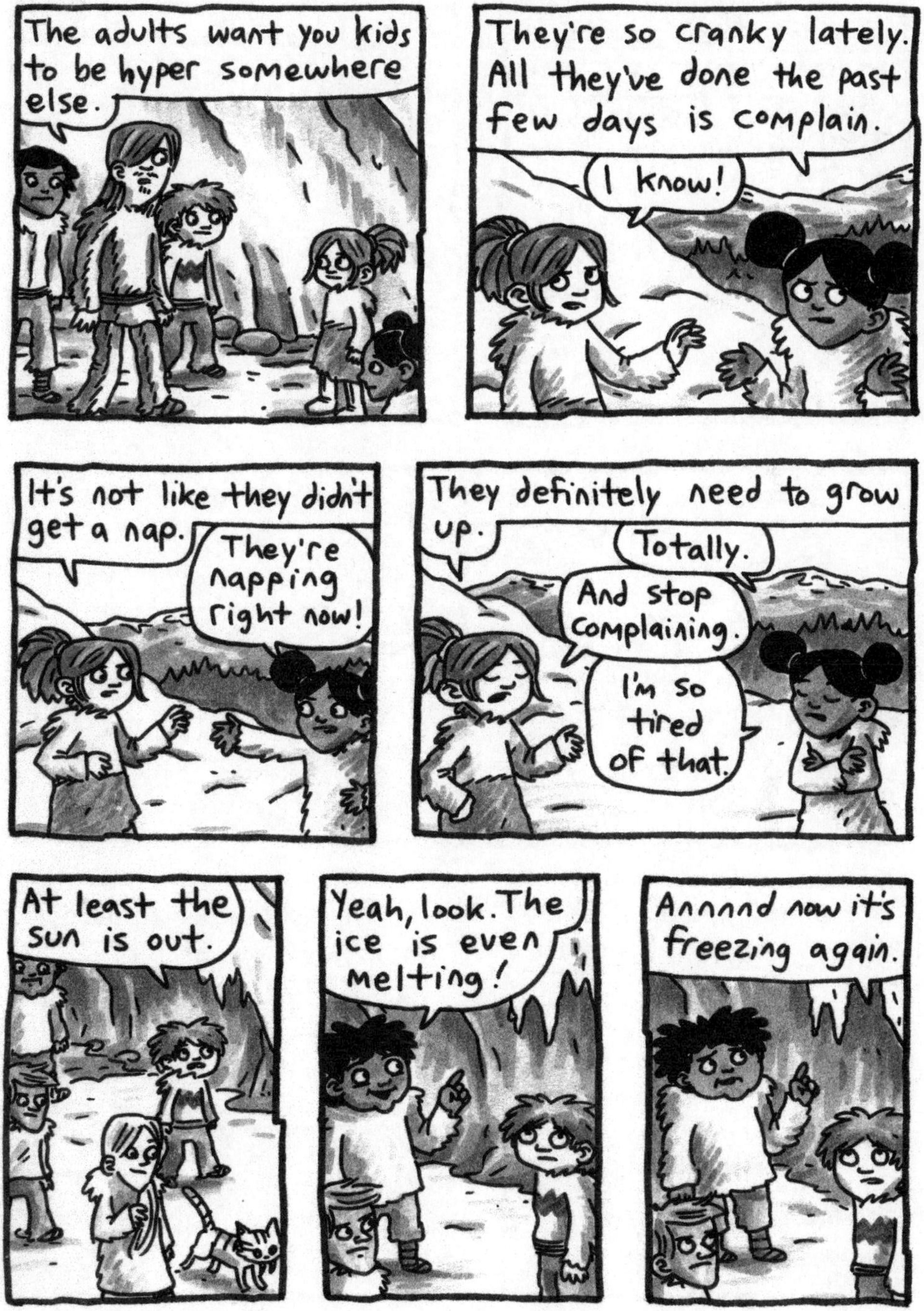

The adults want you kids to be hyper somewhere else.
They're so cranky lately. All they've done the past few days is complain.
I know!
It's not like they didn't get a nap.
They're napping right now!
They definitely need to grow up.
Totally.
And stop complaining.
I'm so tired of that.
At least the sun is out.
Yeah, look. The ice is even melting!
Annnnd now it's freezing again.

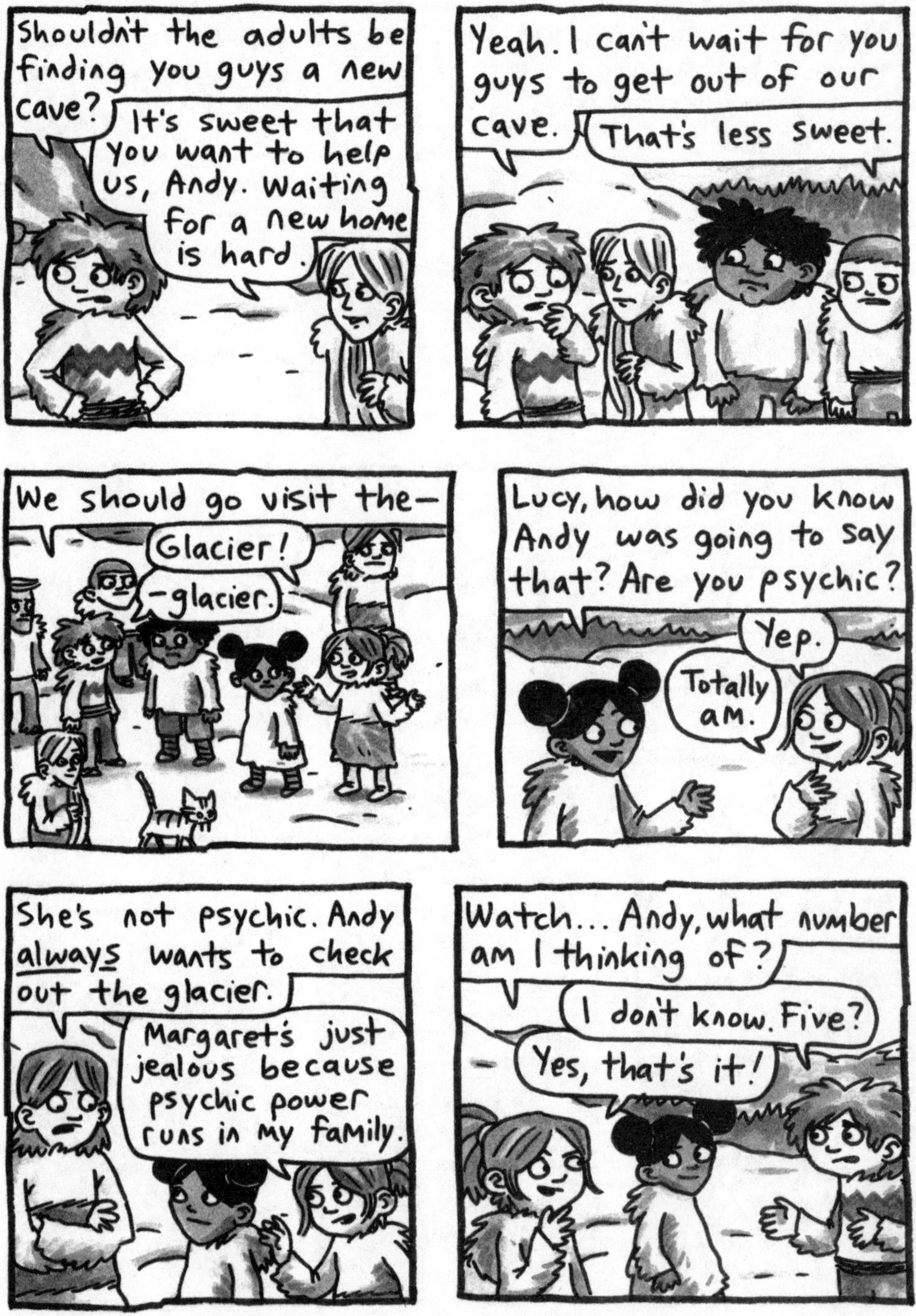
Shouldn't the adults be finding you guys a new cave?
It's sweet that you want to help us, Andy. Waiting for a new home is hard.
Yeah. I can't wait for you guys to get out of our cave.
That's less sweet.
We should go visit the—
Glacier!
—glacier.
Lucy, how did you know Andy was going to say that? Are you psychic?
Yep.
Totally am.
She's not psychic. Andy always wants to check out the glacier.
Margaret's just jealous because psychic power runs in my family.
Watch... Andy, what number am I thinking of?
I don't know. Five?
Yes, that's it!

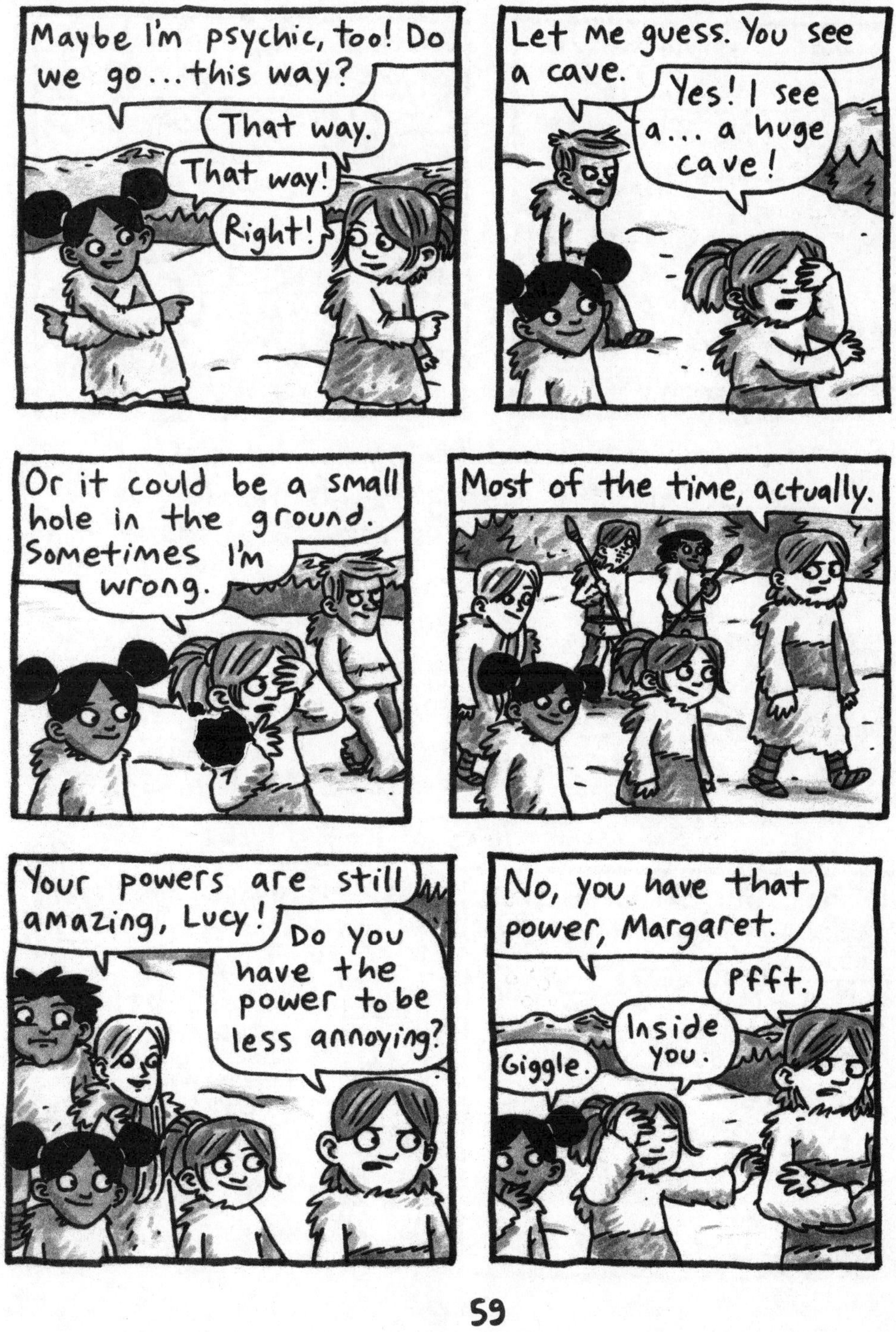
Maybe I'm psychic, too! Do we go...this way?
That way.
That way!
Right!
Let me guess. You see a cave.
Yes! I see a... a huge cave!
Or it could be a small hole in the ground. Sometimes I'm wrong.
Most of the time, actually.
Your powers are still amazing, Lucy!
Do you have the power to be less annoying?
No, you have that power, Margaret.
Pfft.
Inside you.
Giggle.

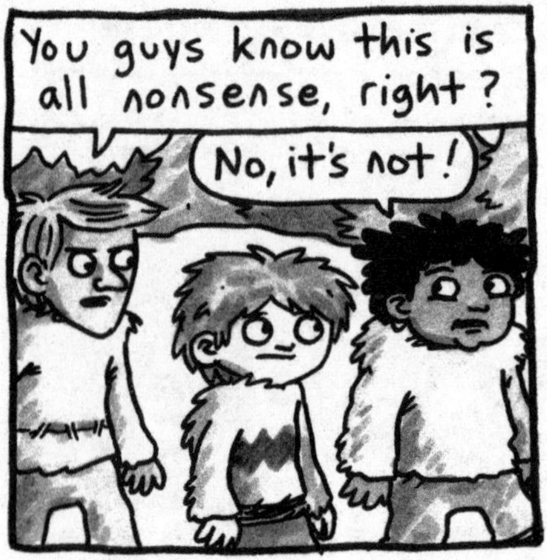
You guys know this is all nonsense, right?
No, it's not!
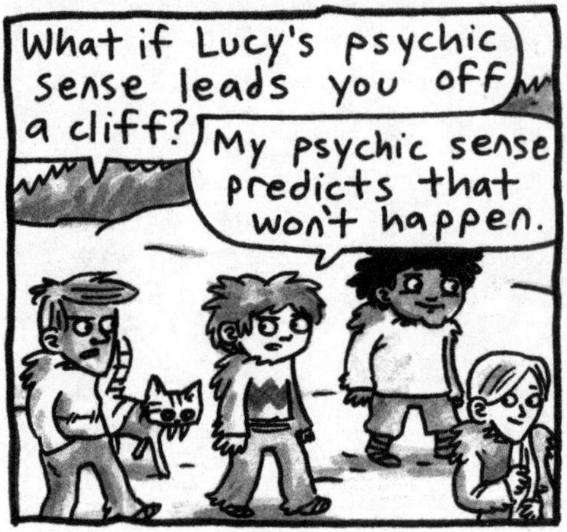
What if Lucy's psychic sense leads you off a cliff?
My psychic sense predicts that won't happen.

If psychic powers were real, paleontologists would have an easier time finding fossils. People who claim to be psychic are correct about as often as random guessing!

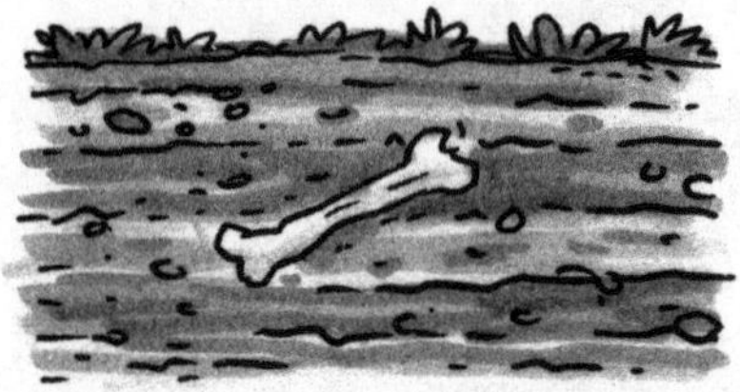

Instead, paleontologists rely on knowing where to look based on previous discoveries, help from locals who know that area, experience, and practice.

And sometimes a little luck!

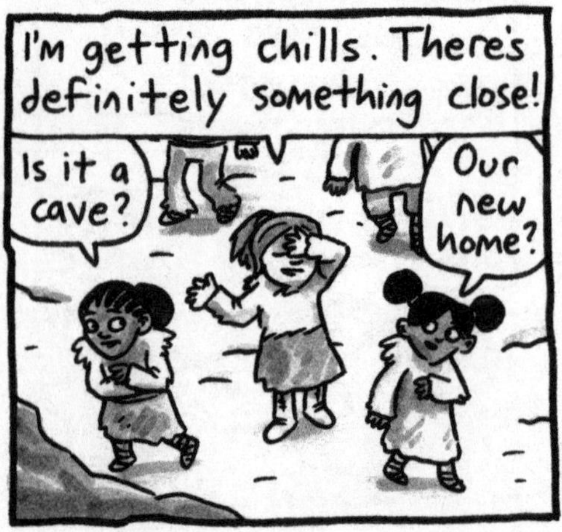
I'm getting chills. There's definitely something close!
Is it a cave?
Our new home?
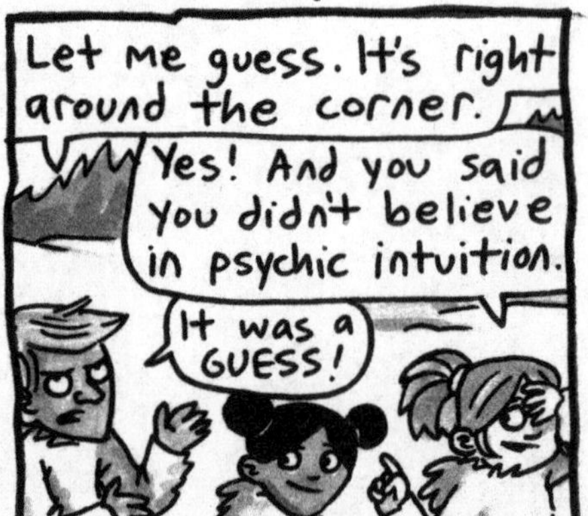
Let me guess. It's right around the corner.
Yes! And you said you didn't believe in psychic intuition.
It was a GUESS!

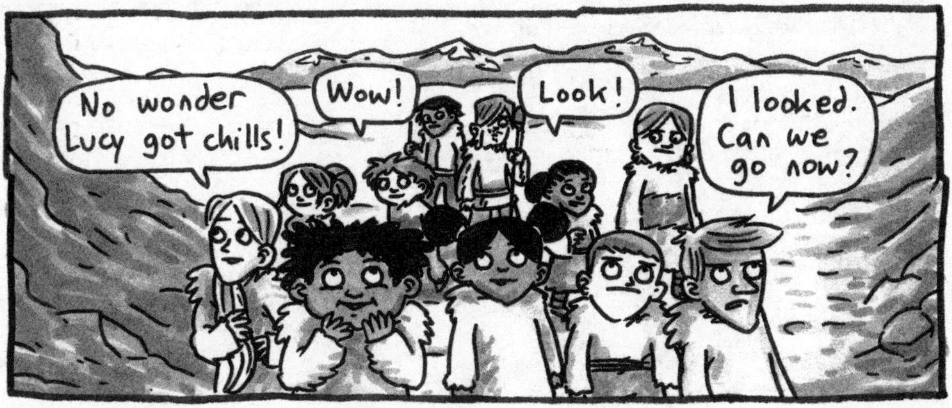
No wonder Lucy got chills!
Wow!
Look!
I looked. Can we go now?

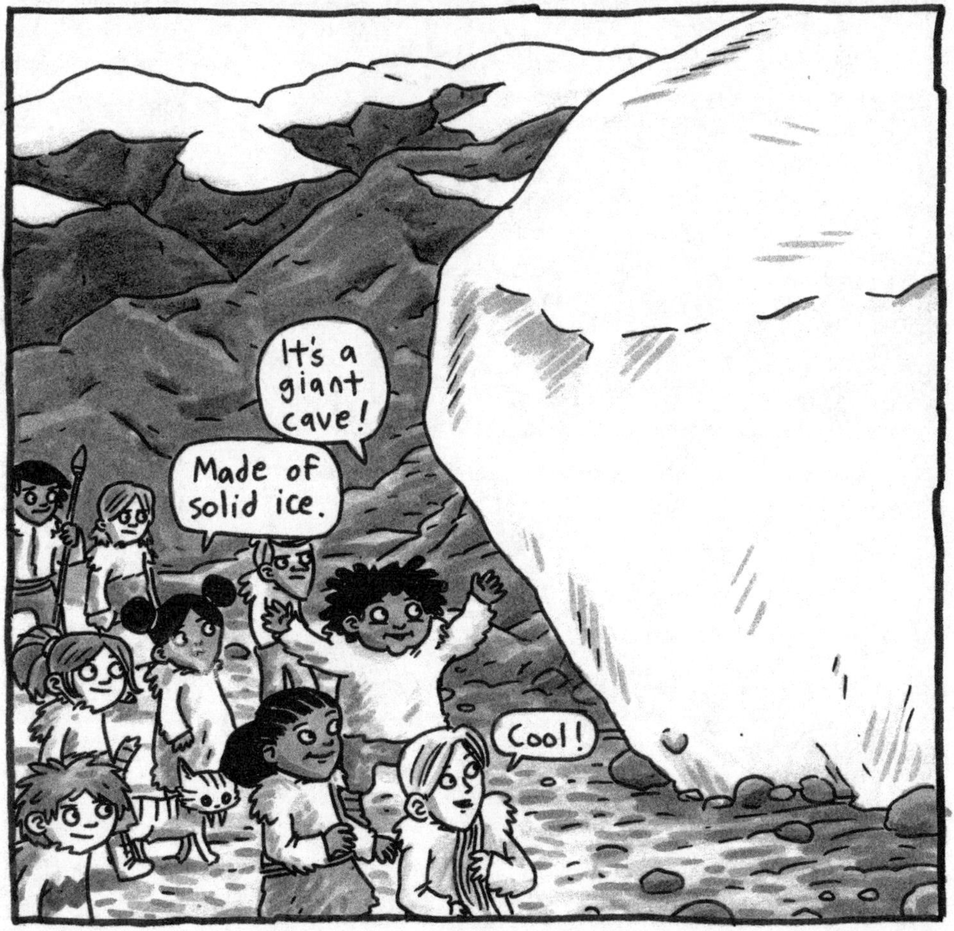
It's a giant cave!
Made of solid ice.
Cool!

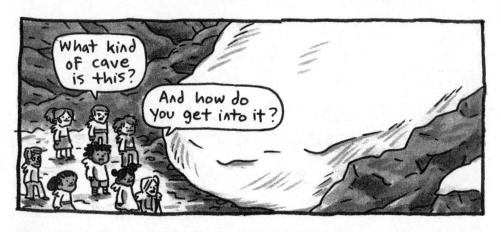

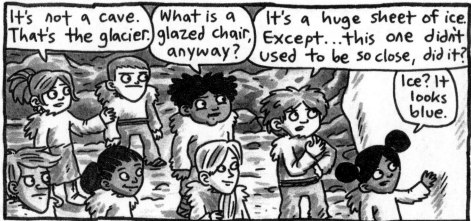

What kind of cave is this?
And how do you get into it?
It's not a cave. That's the glacier.
What is a glazed chair, anyway?
It's a huge sheet of ice. Except...this one didn't used to be so close, did it?
Ice? It looks blue.
A glacier forms when enough snow and ice gather creating an ice sheet—almost like a river of ice!
The thickest glaciers can be almost a mile thick—taller than a skyscraper!
The weight of the ice causes a glacier to move downhill—usually slowly, but sometimes 100 feet a day!

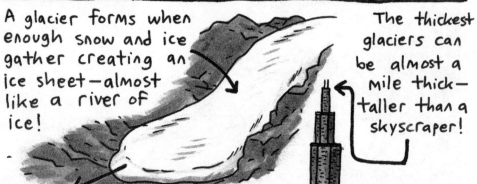

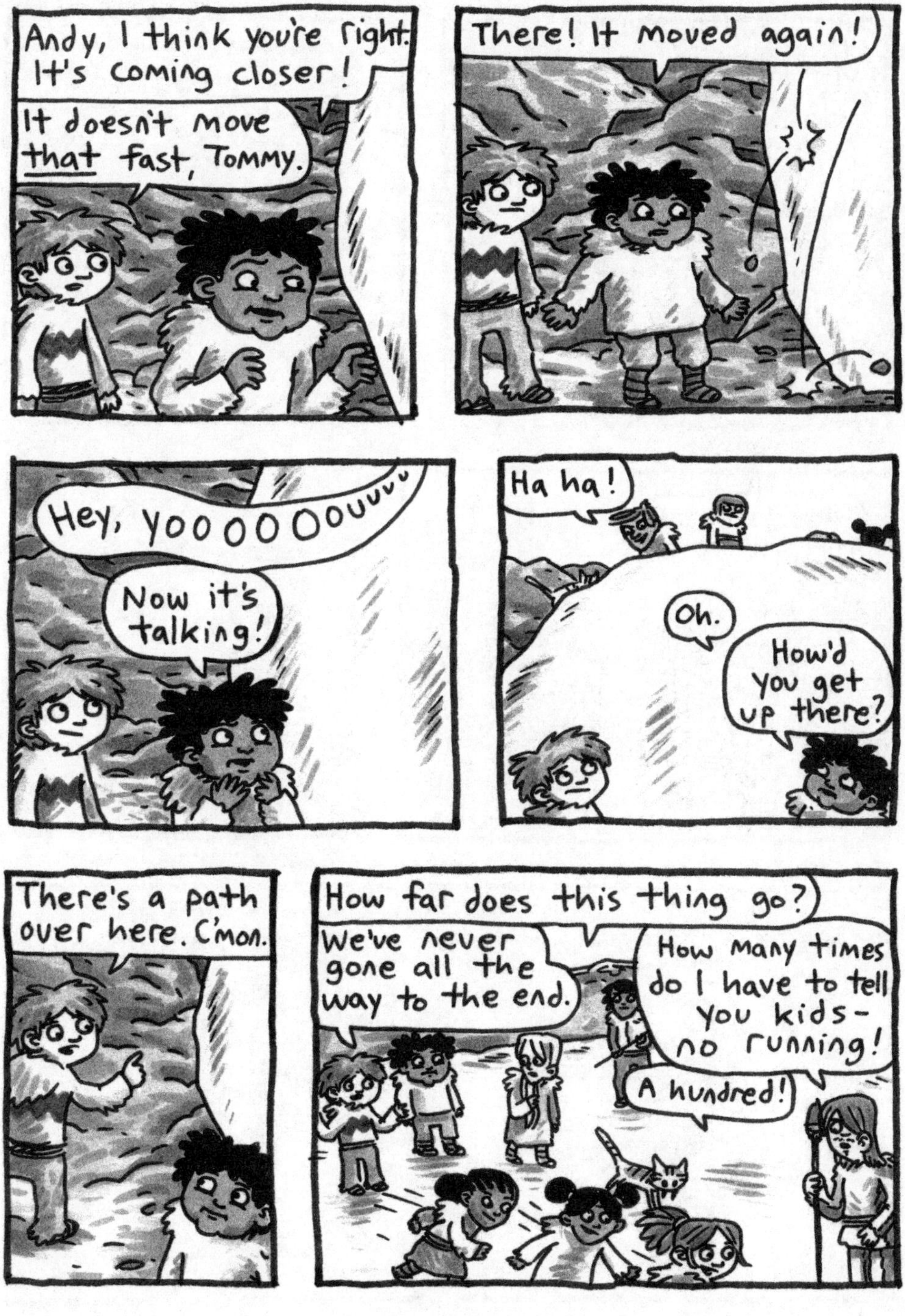
Andy, I think you're right. It's coming closer!
It doesn't move that fast, Tommy.
There! It moved again!
Hey, yooOOOOuuvvv
Now it's talking!
Ha ha!
Oh.
How'd you get up there?
There's a path over here. C'mon.
How far does this thing go?
We've never gone all the way to the end.
How many times do I have to tell you kids- no running!
A hundred!

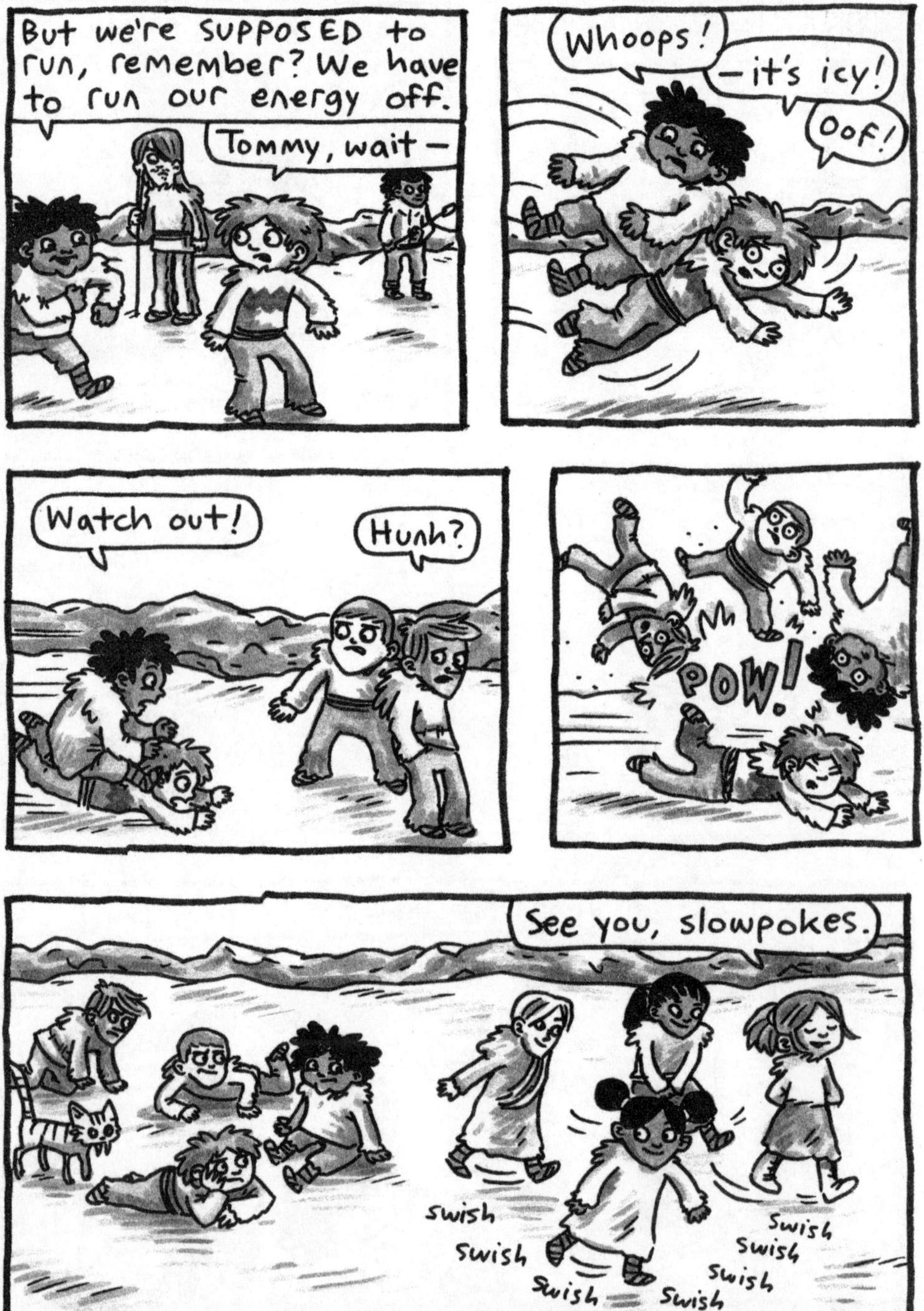
But we're SUPPOSED to run, remember? We have to run our energy off.
Tommy, wait—
Whoops!
—it's icy!
Oof!
Watch out!
Hunh?
POW!
See you, slowpokes.
swish
swish
swish
swish
swish
swish
swish

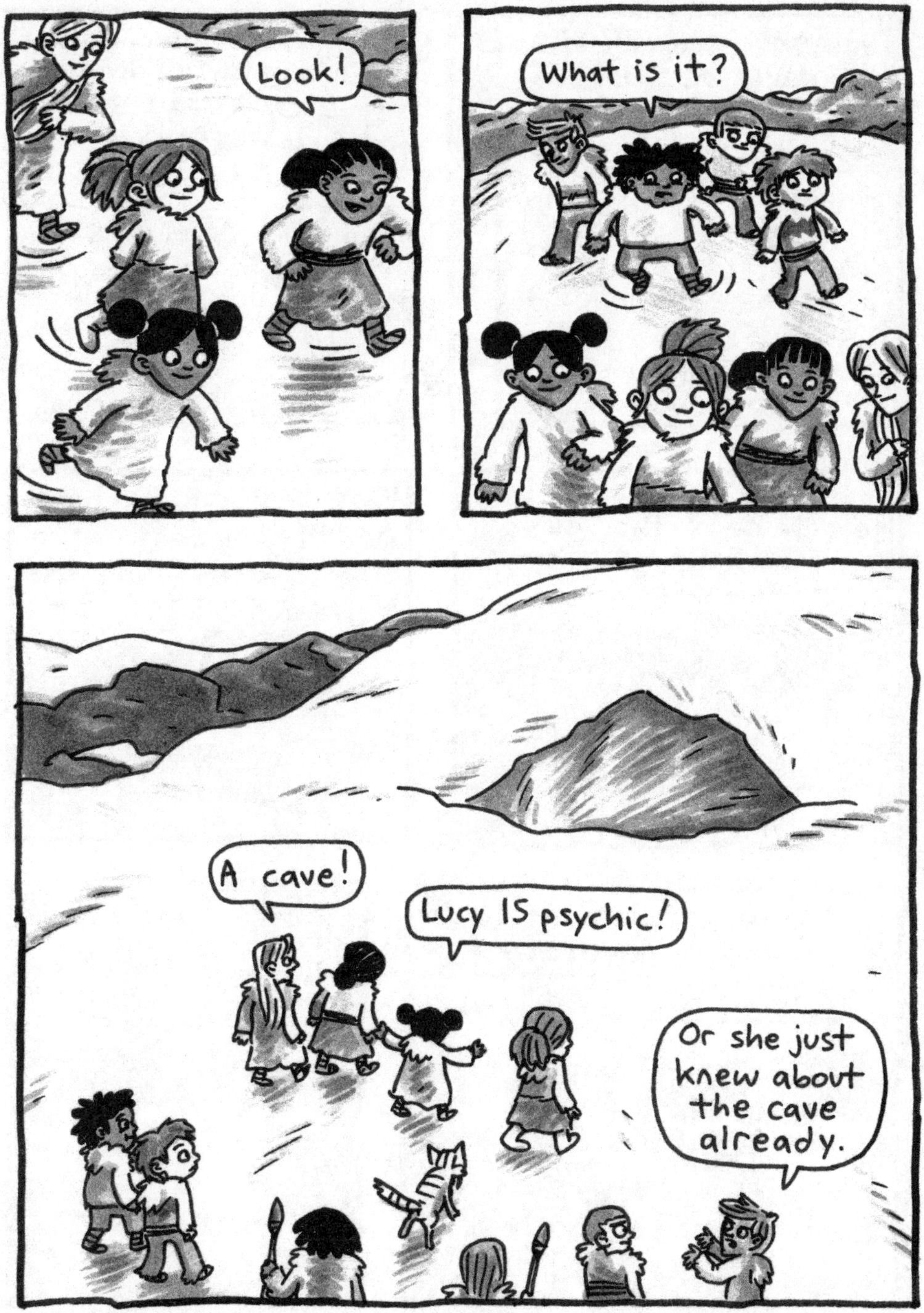
Look!
What is it?
A cave!
Lucy IS psychic!
Or she just knew about the cave already.

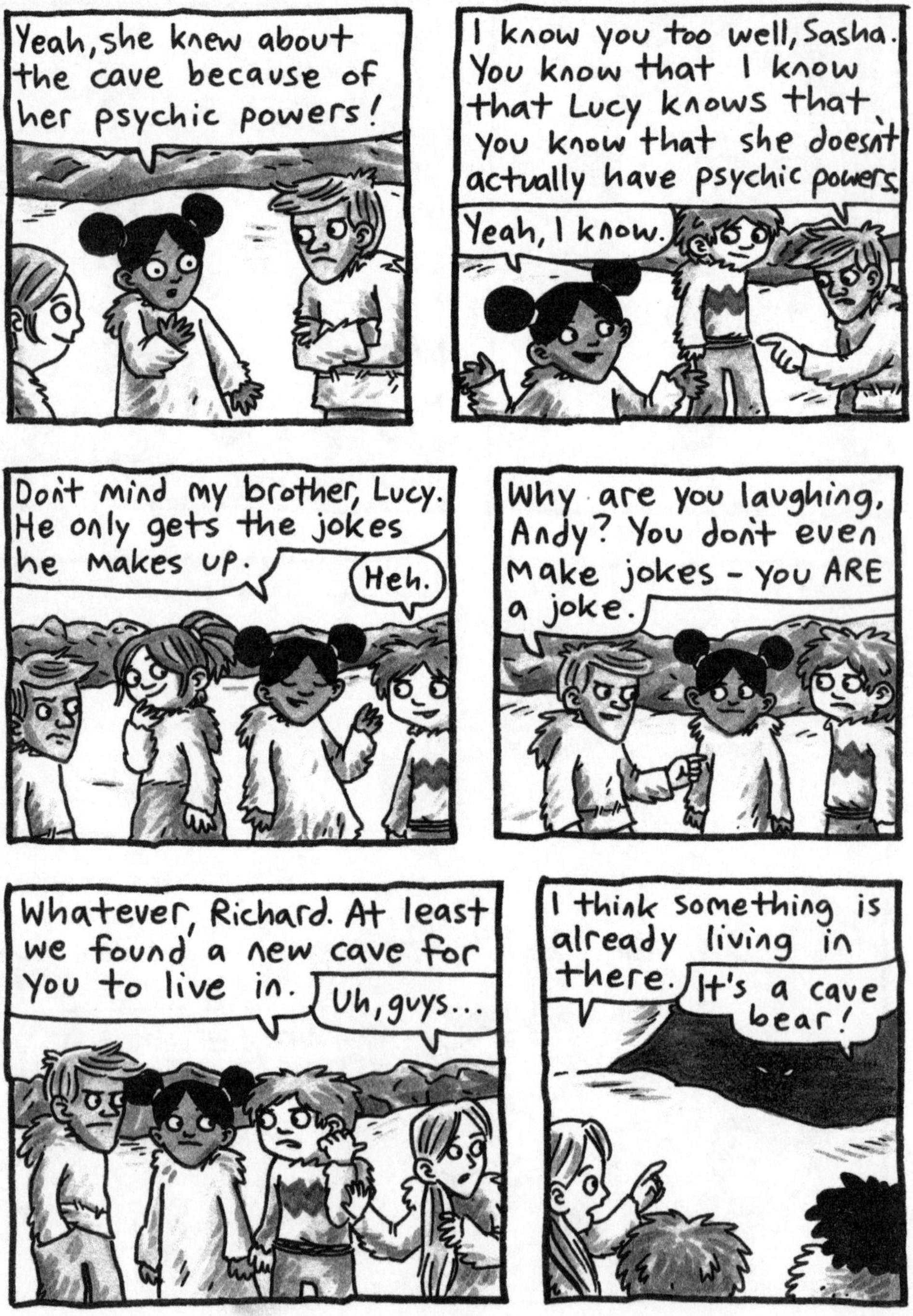
Yeah, she knew about the cave because of her psychic powers!
I know you too well, Sasha. You know that I know that Lucy knows that you know that she doesn't actually have psychic powers.
Yeah, I know.
Don't mind my brother, Lucy. He only gets the jokes he makes up.
Heh.
Why are you laughing, Andy? You don't even make jokes - you ARE a joke.
Whatever, Richard. At least we found a new cave for you to live in.
Uh, guys...
I think something is already living in there.
It's a cave bear!

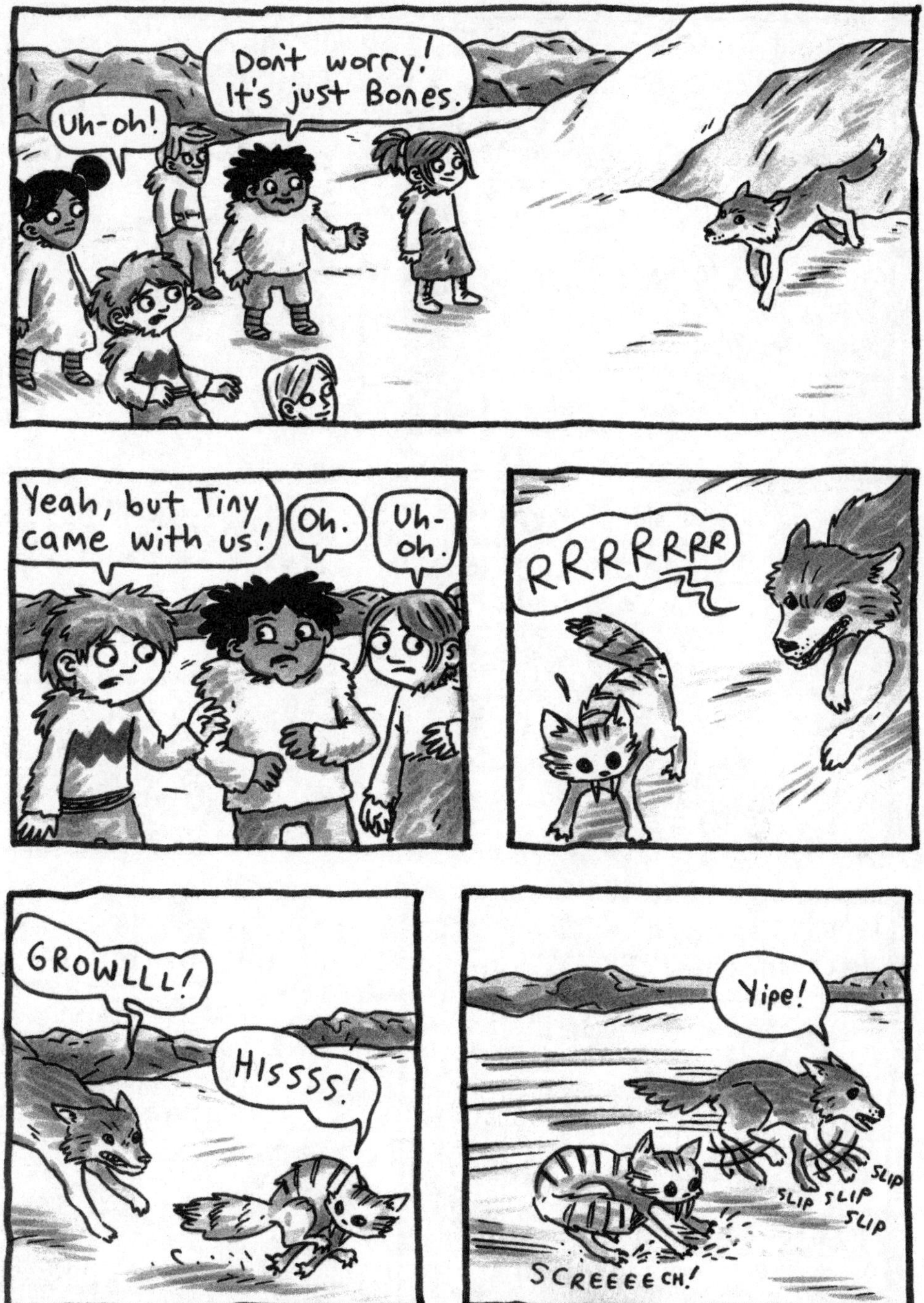
Uh-oh!
Don't worry! It's just Bones.
Yeah, but Tiny came with us!
Oh.
Uh-oh.
RRRRRRR
GROWLLL!
HISSSS!
Yipe!
SLIP
SLIP SLIP
SLIP
SCREEEEECH!

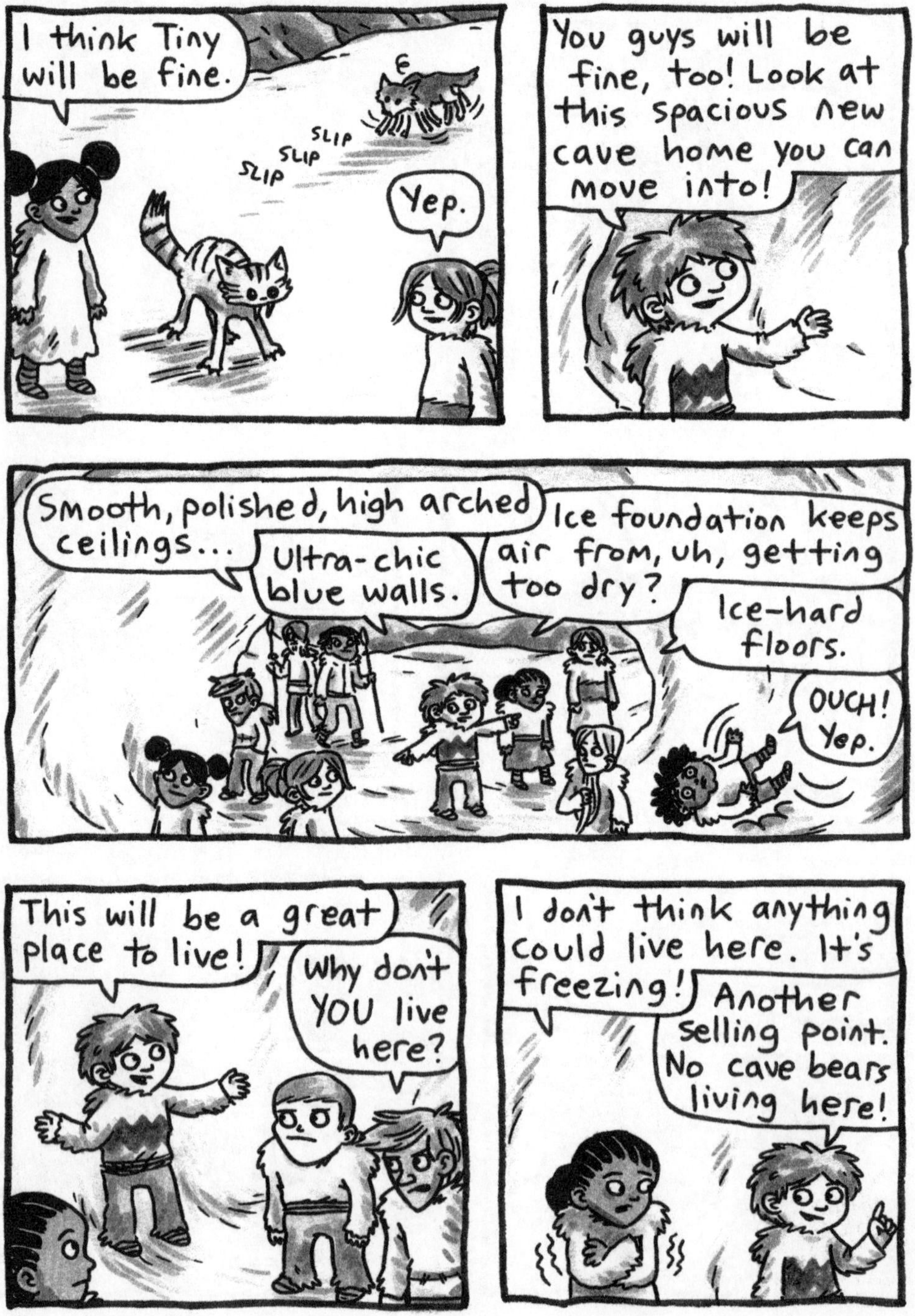
I think Tiny will be fine.
SLIP
SLIP
SLIP
Yep.
You guys will be fine, too! Look at this spacious new cave home you can move into!
Smooth, polished, high arched ceilings...
Ultra-chic blue walls.
Ice foundation keeps air from, uh, getting too dry?
Ice-hard floors.
OUCH! Yep.
This will be a great place to live!
Why don't YOU live here?
I don't think anything could live here. It's freezing!
Another selling point. No cave bears living here!

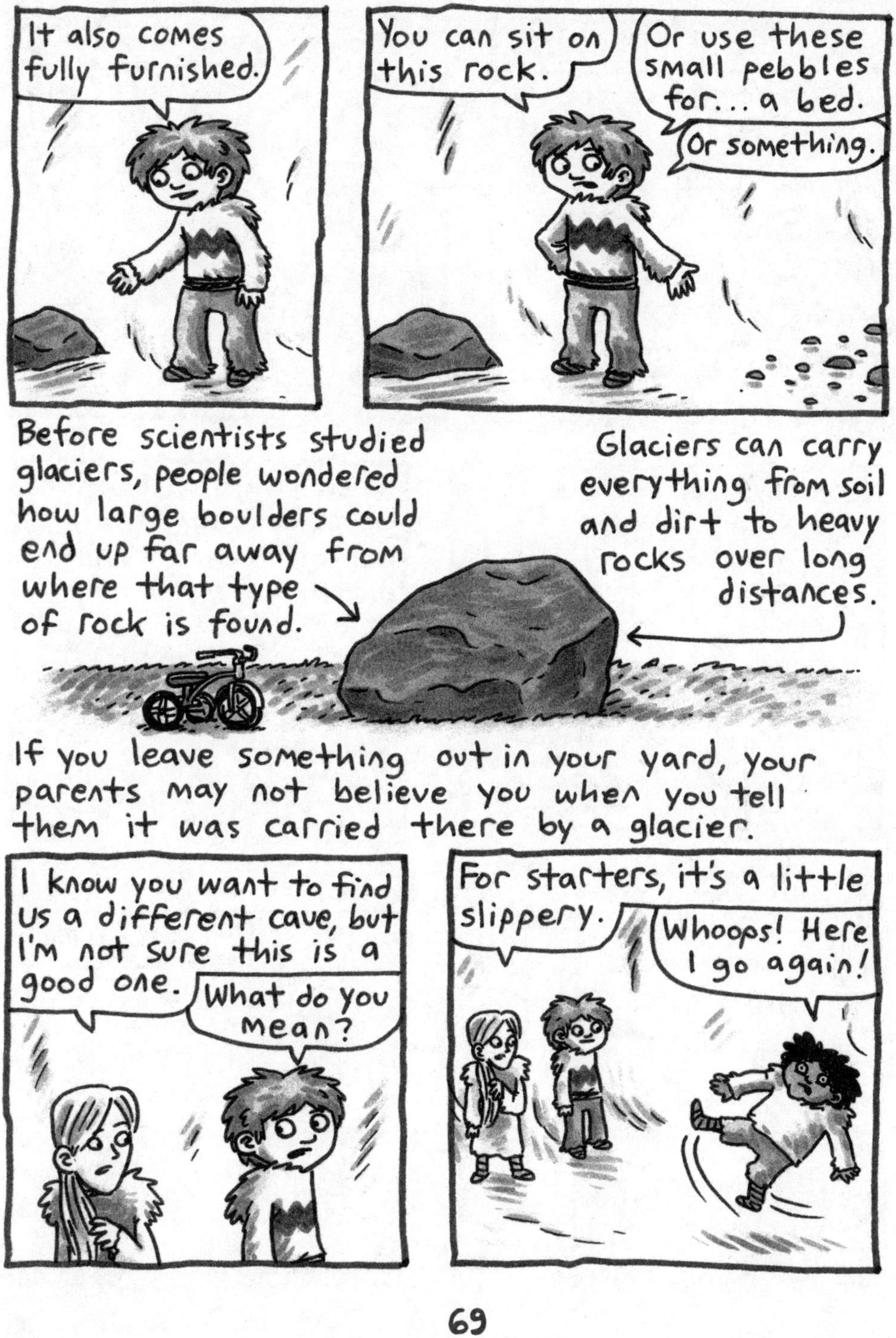
It also comes fully furnished.
You can sit on this rock.
Or use these small pebbles for... a bed.
Or something.
Before scientists studied glaciers, people wondered how large boulders could end up far away from where that type of rock is found.
Glaciers can carry everything from soil and dirt to heavy rocks over long distances.
If you leave something out in your yard, your parents may not believe you when you tell them it was carried there by a glacier.
I know you want to find us a different cave, but I'm not sure this is a good one.
What do you mean?
For starters, it's a little slippery.
Whoops! Here I go again!

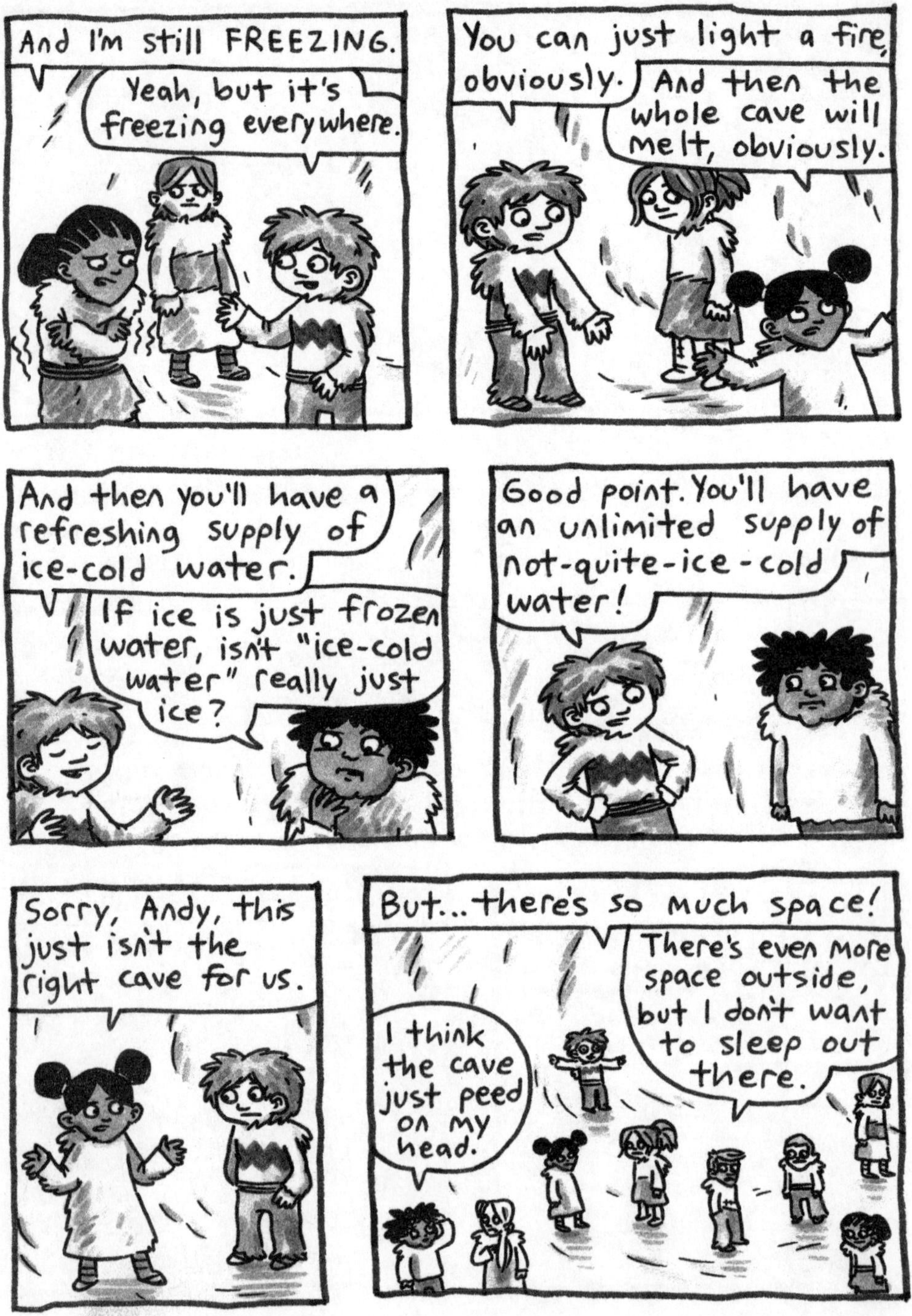
And I'm still FREEZING.
Yeah, but it's freezing everywhere.
You can just light a fire, obviously.
And then the whole cave will melt, obviously.
And then you'll have a refreshing supply of ice-cold water.
If ice is just frozen water, isn't "ice-cold water" really just ice?
Good point. You'll have an unlimited supply of not-quite-ice-cold water!
Sorry, Andy, this just isn't the right cave for us.
But... there's so much space!
There's even more space outside, but I don't want to sleep out there.
I think the cave just peed on my head.

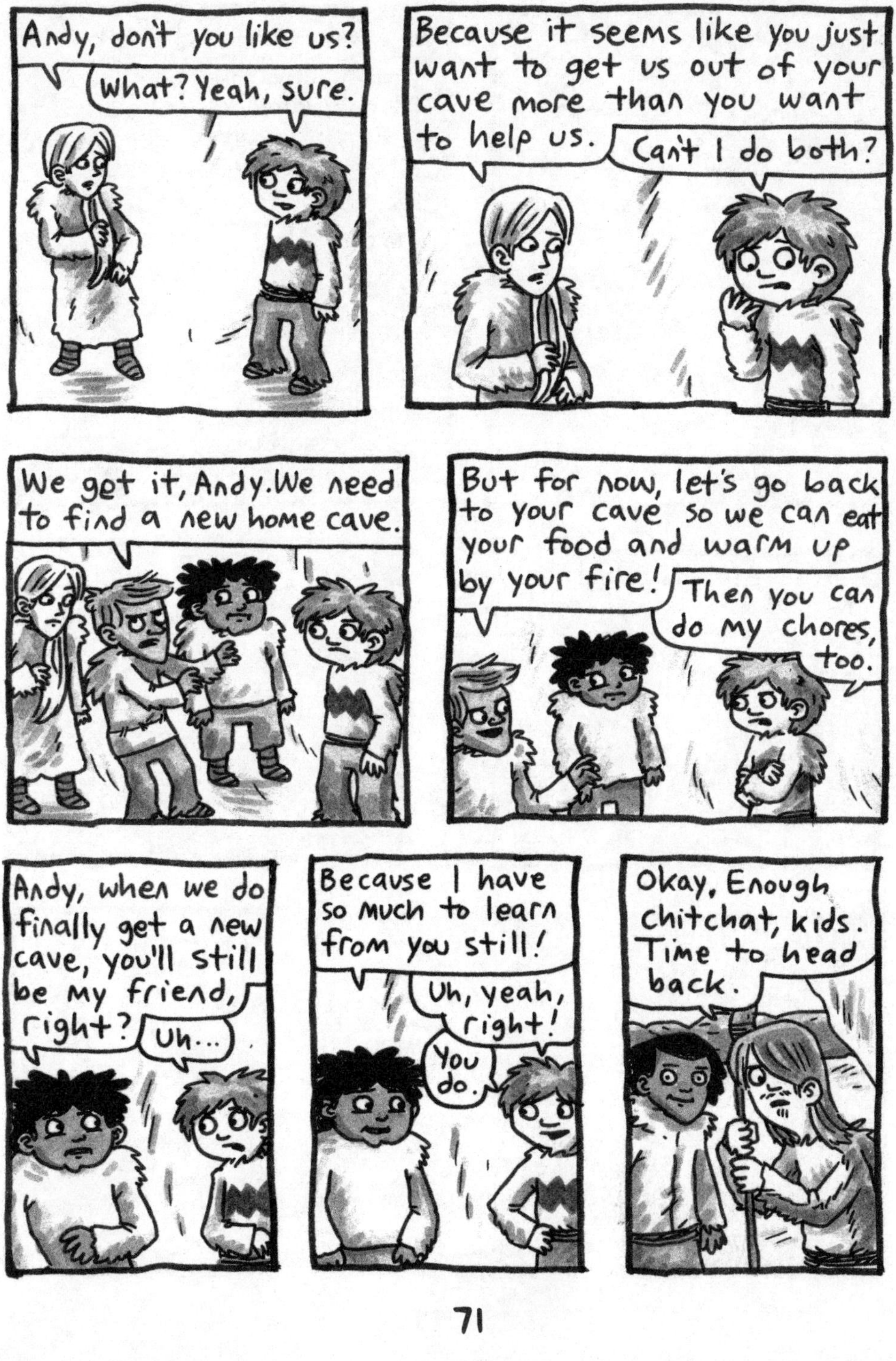
Andy, don't you like us?
What? Yeah, sure.
Because it seems like you just want to get us out of your cave more than you want to help us.
Can't I do both?
We get it, Andy. We need to find a new home cave.
But for now, let's go back to your cave so we can eat your food and warm up by your fire!
Then you can do my chores, too.
Andy, when we do finally get a new cave, you'll still be my friend, right?
Uh...
Because I have so much to learn from you still!
Uh, yeah, right!
You do.
Okay, Enough chitchat, kids. Time to head back.

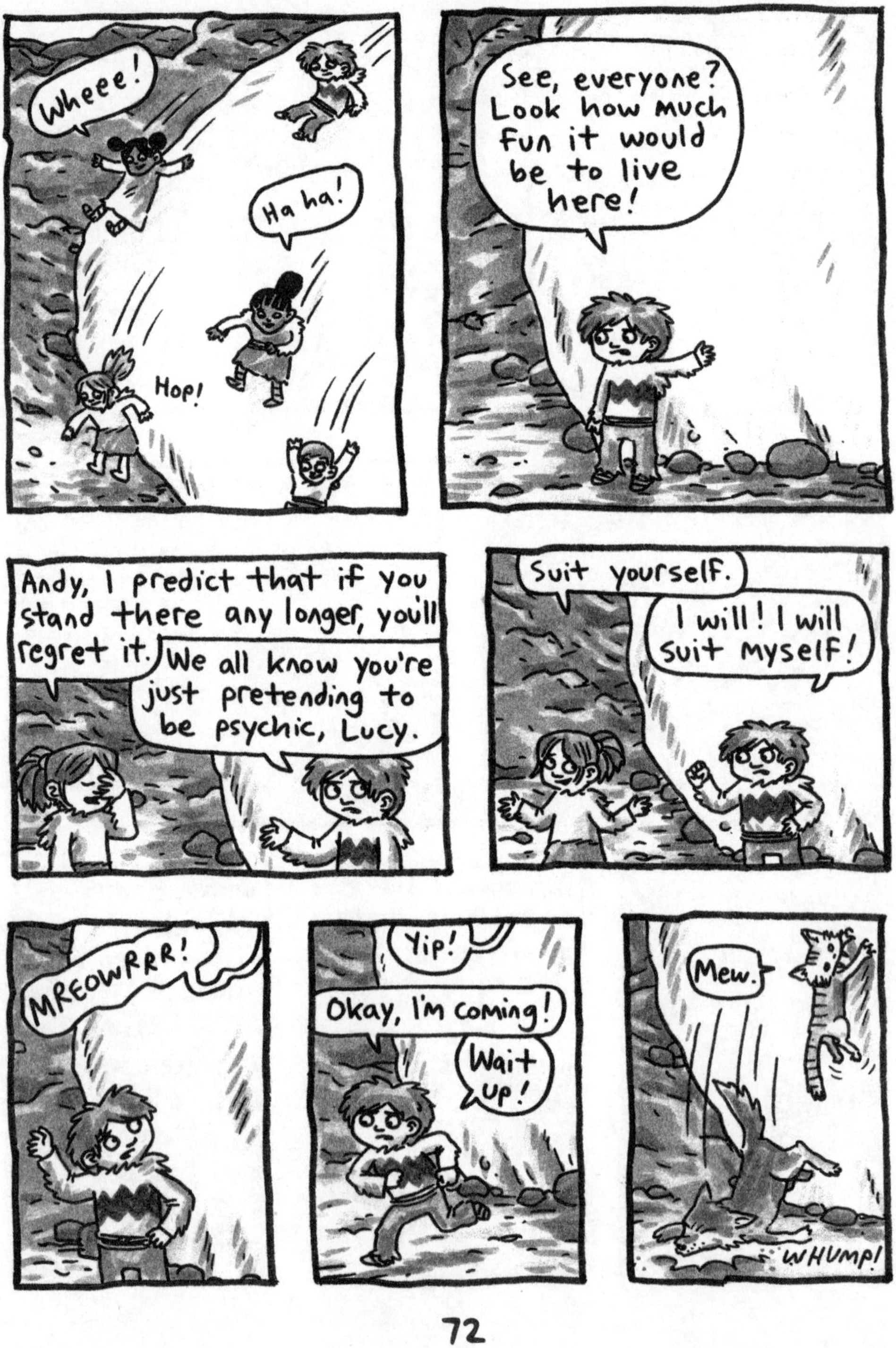
Wheee!
Ha ha!
Hop!
See, everyone? Look how much fun it would be to live here!
Andy, I predict that if you stand there any longer, you'll regret it.
We all know you're just pretending to be psychic, Lucy.
Suit yourself.
I will! I will suit myself!
MREOWRRR!
Yip!
Okay, I'm coming!
Wait up!
Mew.
WHUMP!

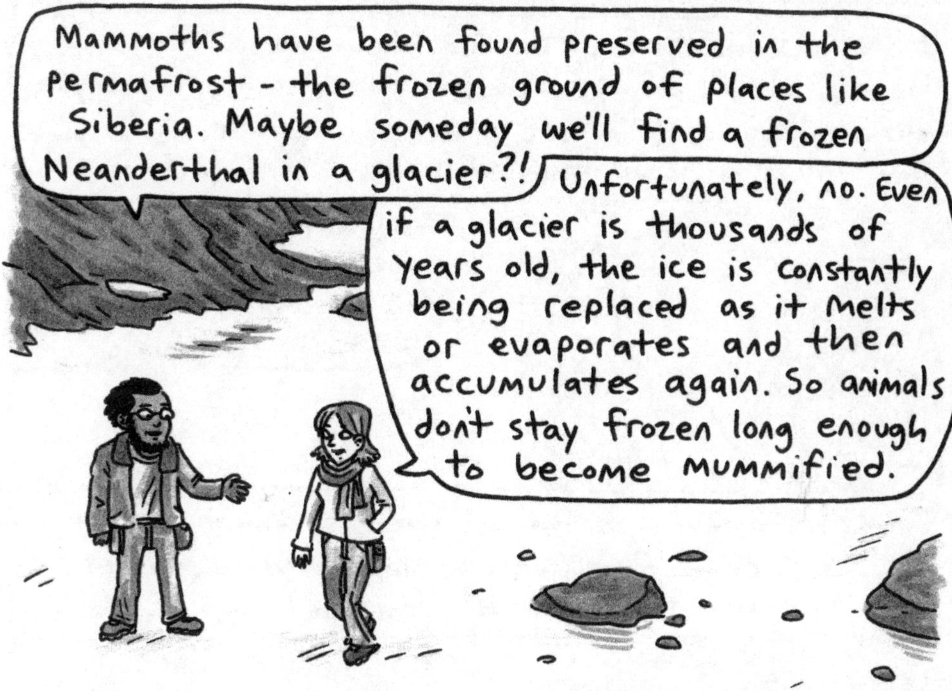
Mammoths have been found preserved in the permafrost - the frozen ground of places like Siberia. Maybe someday we'll find a frozen Neanderthal in a glacier?!
Unfortunately, no. Even if a glacier is thousands of years old, the ice is constantly being replaced as it melts or evaporates and then accumulates again. So animals don't stay frozen long enough to become mummified.
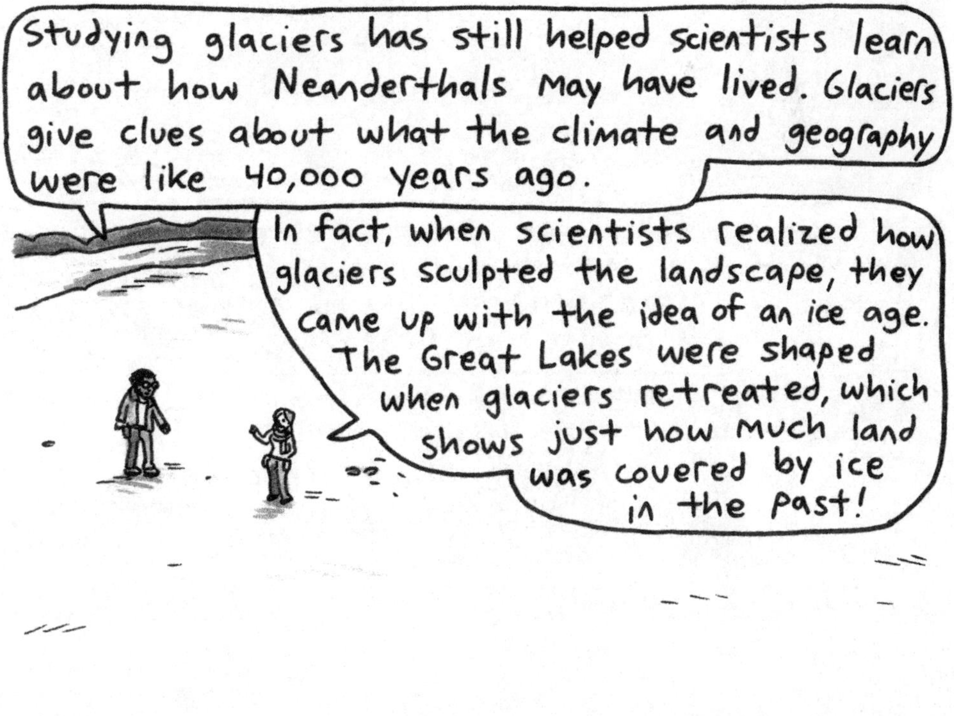
Studying glaciers has still helped scientists learn about how Neanderthals may have lived. Glaciers give clues about what the climate and geography were like 40,000 years ago.
In fact, when scientists realized how glaciers sculpted the landscape, they came up with the idea of an ice age. The Great Lakes were shaped when glaciers retreated, which shows just how much land was covered by ice in the past!

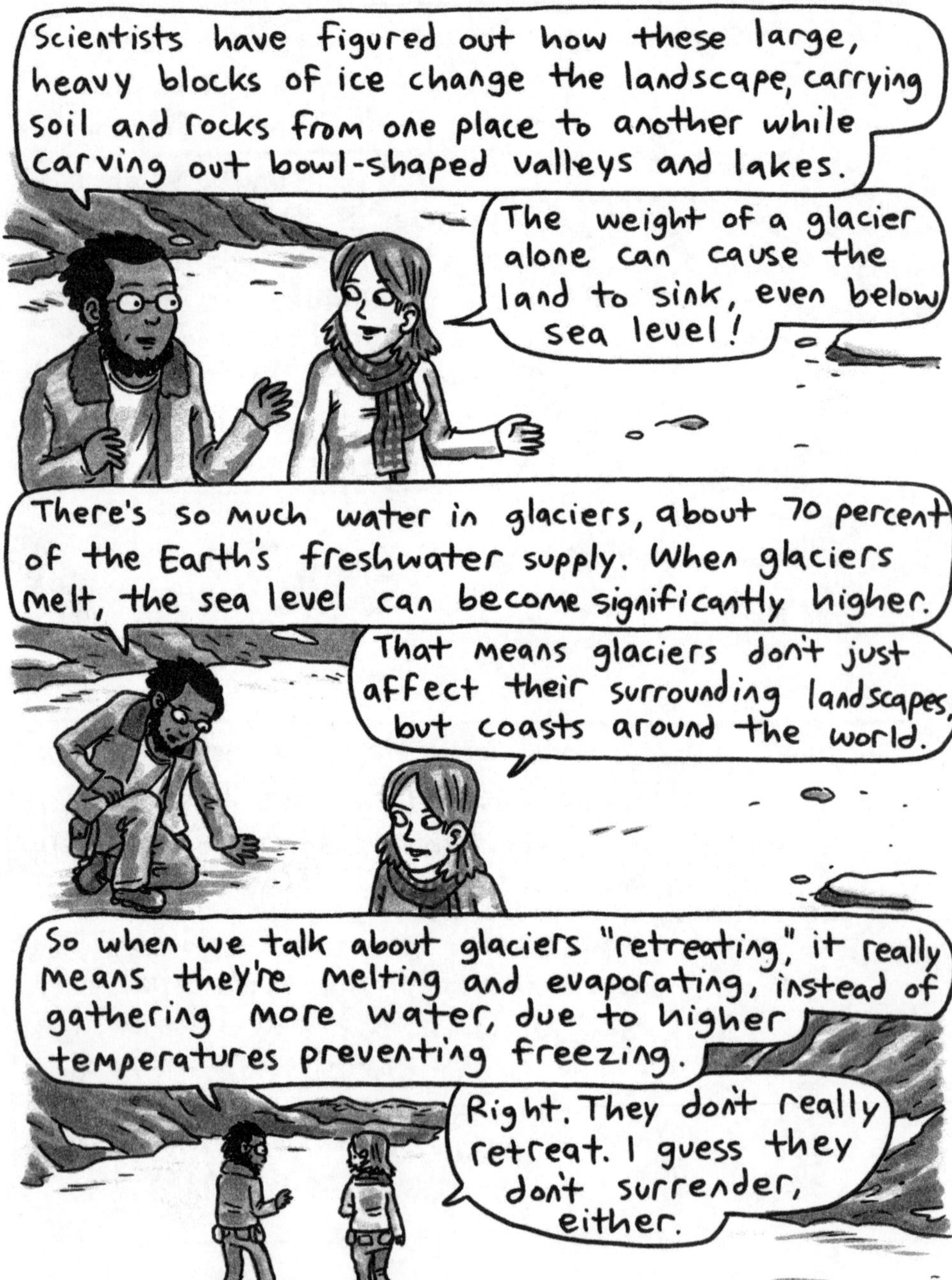
Scientists have figured out how these large, heavy blocks of ice change the landscape, carrying soil and rocks from one place to another while carving out bowl-shaped valleys and lakes.
The weight of a glacier alone can cause the land to sink, even below sea level!
There's so much water in glaciers, about 70 percent of the Earth's freshwater supply. When glaciers melt, the sea level can become significantly higher.
That means glaciers don't just affect their surrounding landscapes, but coasts around the world.
So when we talk about glaciers "retreating," it really means they're melting and evaporating, instead of gathering more water, due to higher temperatures preventing freezing.
Right. They don't really retreat. I guess they don't surrender, either.

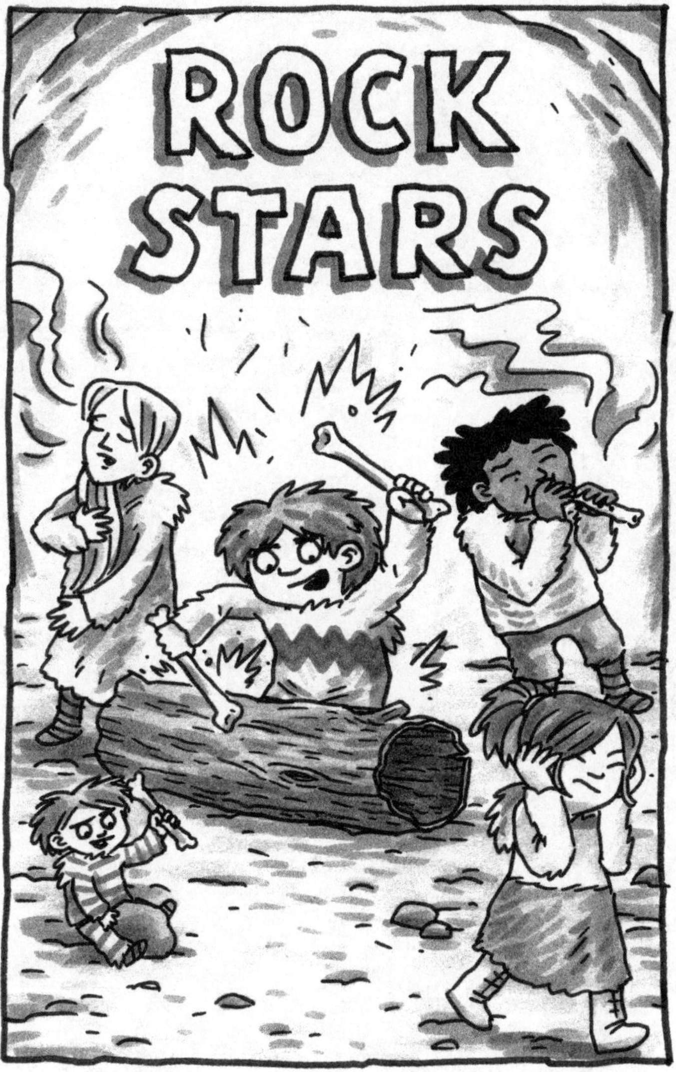
ROCK
STARS

On the way back, let's stop by our camp.
Sure, we can take the other path.
But...what about the cave bears?
They'll be hibernating.
But what if they wake up?
We have Bones with us.
Ha!
One wolf won't scare a bear. But we'll be in a big group, and bears are usually alone.

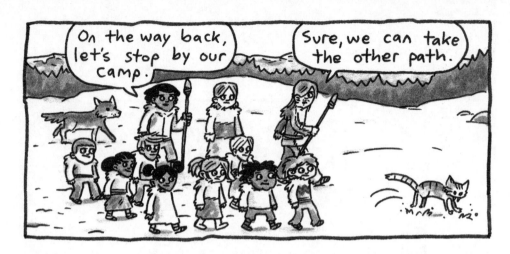

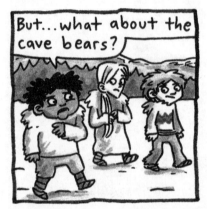

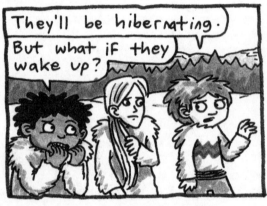

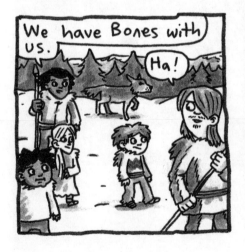

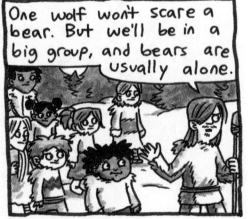

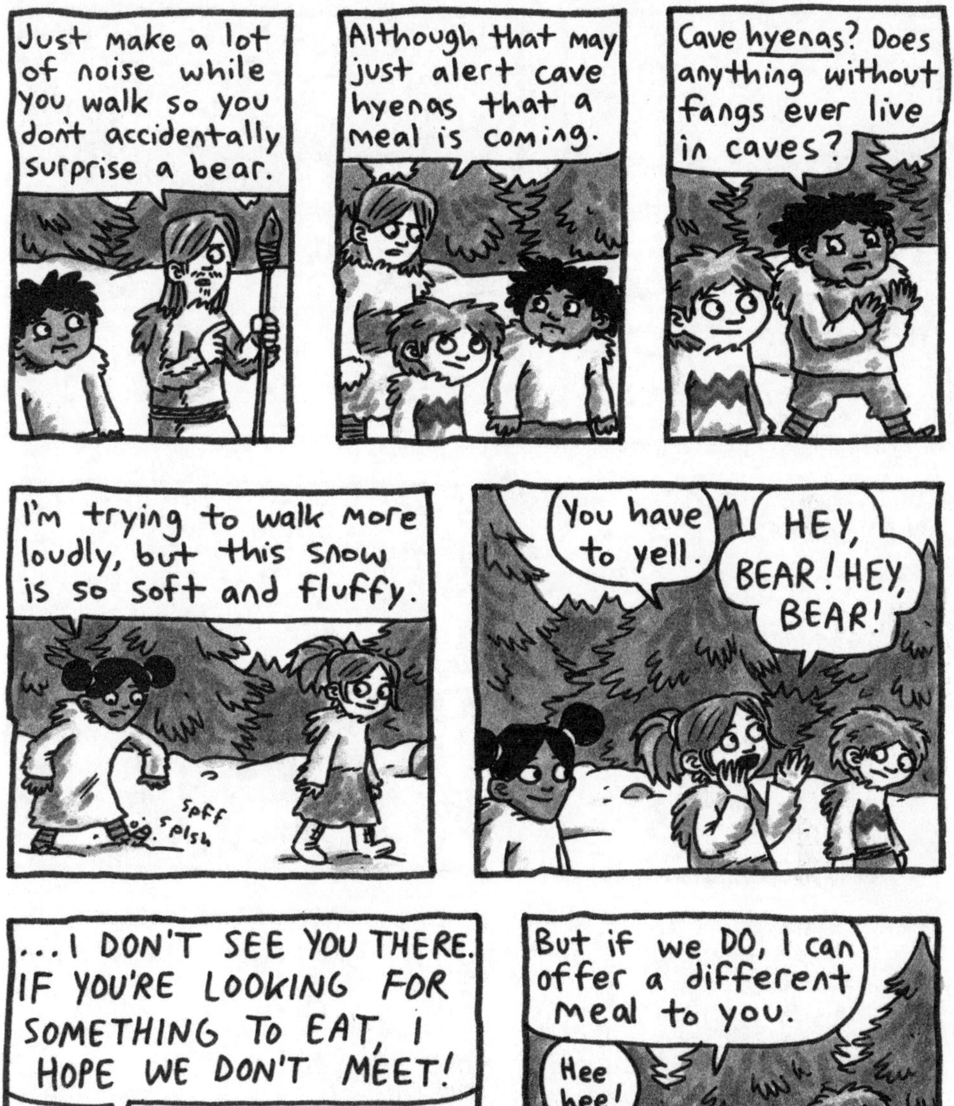
Just make a lot of noise while you walk so you don't accidentally surprise a bear.
Although that may just alert cave hyenas that a meal is coming.
Cave hyenas? Does anything without fangs ever live in caves?
I'm trying to walk more loudly, but this snow is so soft and fluffy.
spff
splsh
You have to yell.
HEY, BEAR! HEY, BEAR!
...I DON'T SEE YOU THERE. IF YOU'RE LOOKING FOR SOMETHING TO EAT, I HOPE WE DON'T MEET!
But if we DO, I can offer a different meal to you.
Hee hee!

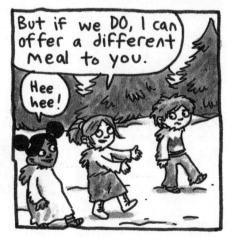

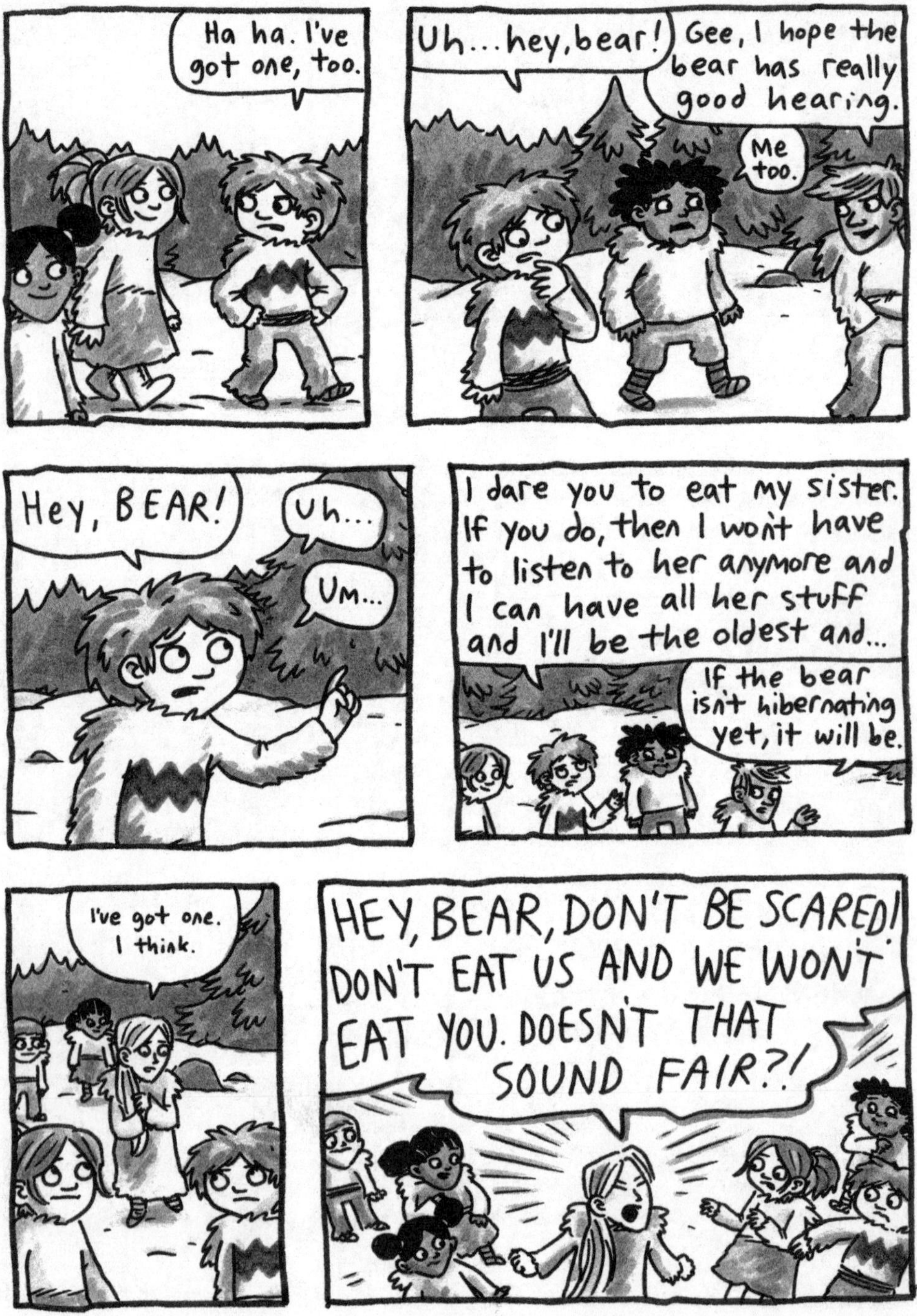
Ha ha. I've got one, too.
Uh... hey, bear!
Gee, I hope the bear has really good hearing.
Me too.
Hey, BEAR!
Uh...
Um...
I dare you to eat my sister. If you do, then I won't have to listen to her anymore and I can have all her stuff and I'll be the oldest and...
If the bear isn't hibernating yet, it will be.
I've got one. I think.
HEY, BEAR, DON'T BE SCARED! DON'T EAT US AND WE WON'T EAT YOU. DOESN'T THAT SOUND FAIR?!

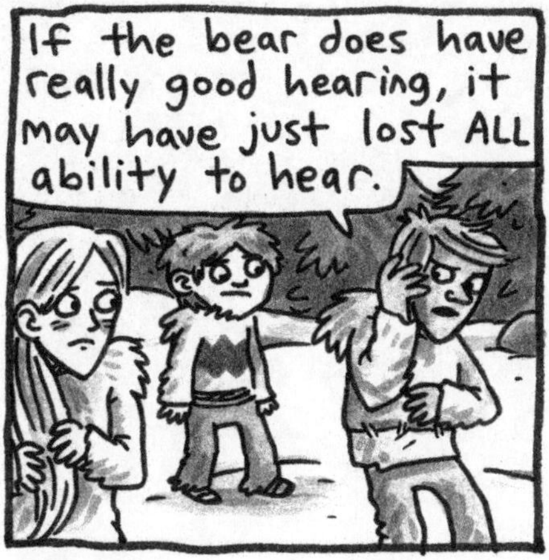
If the bear does have really good hearing, it may have just lost ALL ability to hear.

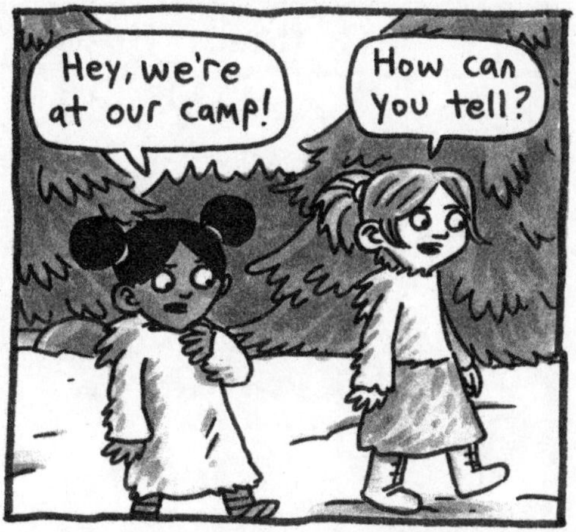
Hey, we're at our camp!
How can you tell?

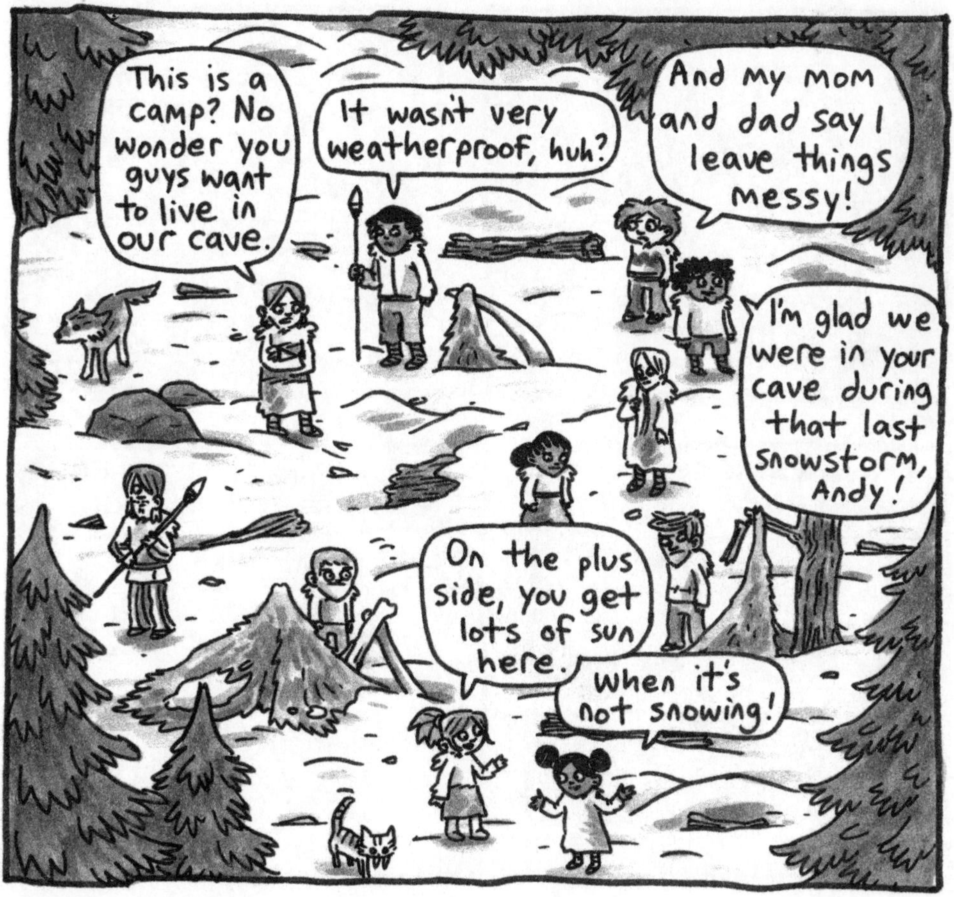
This is a camp? No wonder you guys want to live in our cave.
It wasn't very weatherproof, huh?
And my mom and dad say I leave things messy!
I'm glad we were in your cave during that last snowstorm, Andy!
On the plus side, you get lots of sun here.
When it's not snowing!

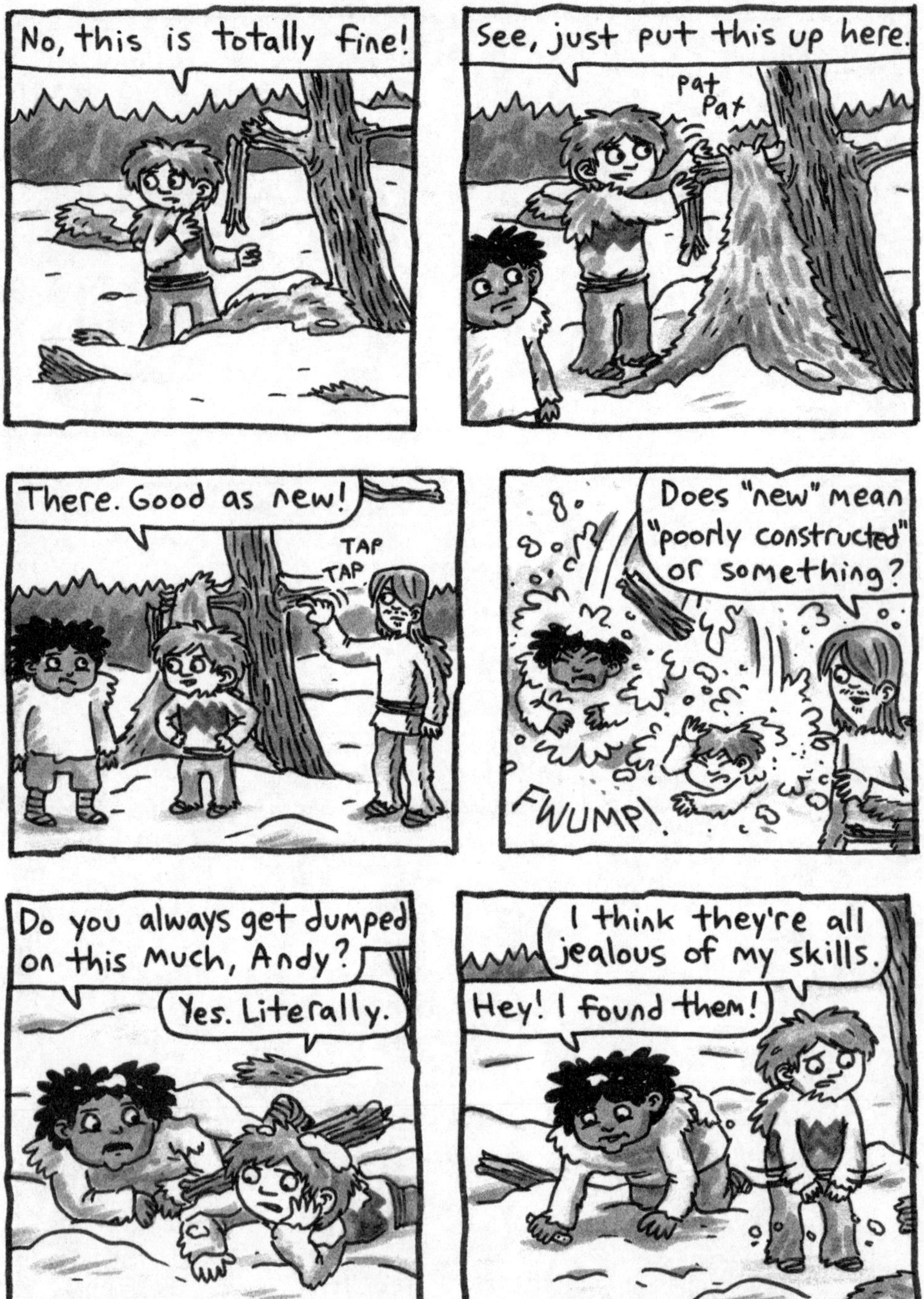
No, this is totally fine!
See, just put this up here.
pat
pat
There. Good as new!
TAP
TAP
Does "new" mean "poorly constructed" or something?
FWUMP!
Do you always get dumped on this much, Andy?
Yes. Literally.
I think they're all jealous of my skills.
Hey! I found them!

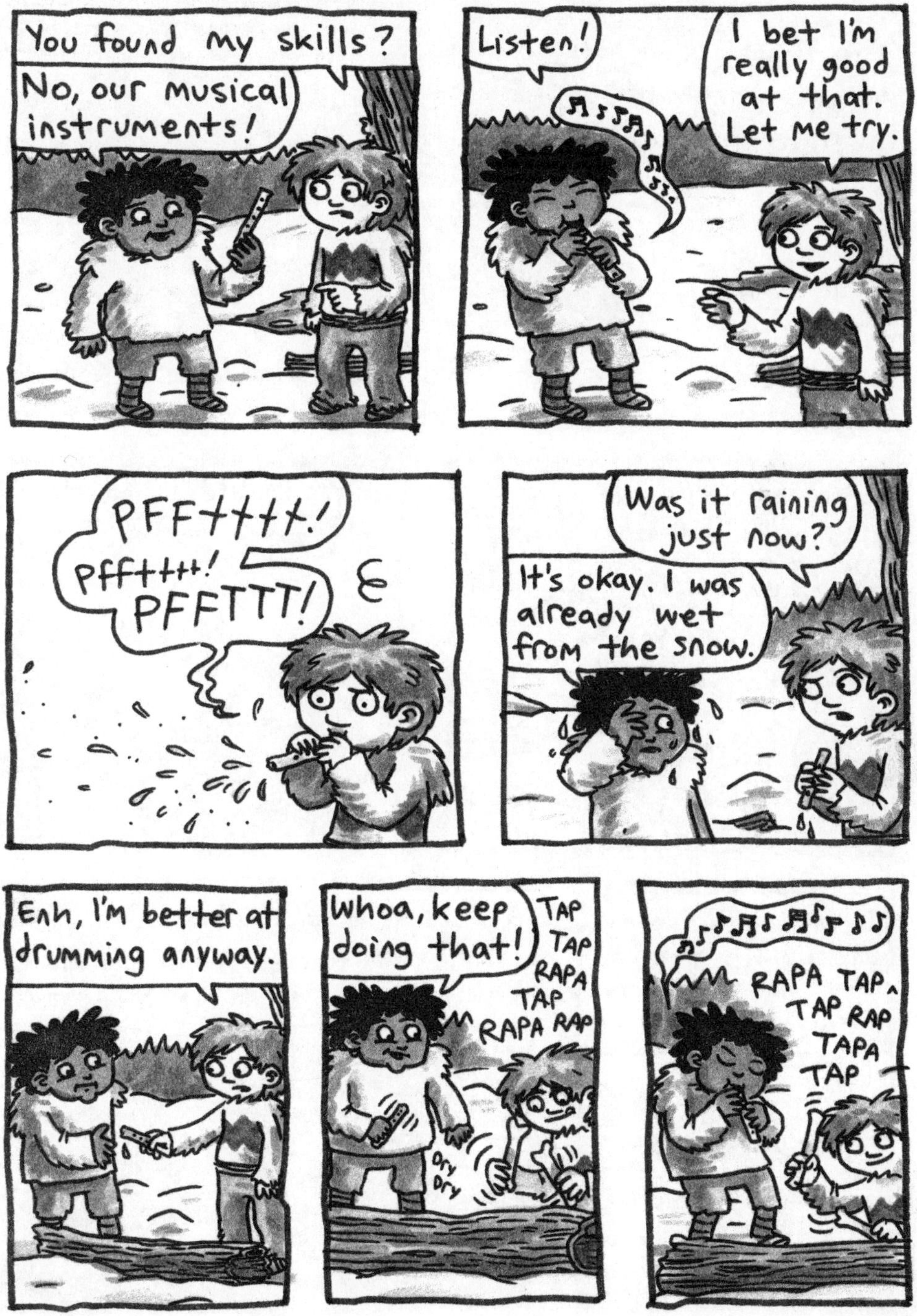
You found my skills?
No, our musical instruments!
Listen!
I bet I'm really good at that. Let me try.
PFFtttt!
pfftttt!
PFFTTT!
Was it raining just now?
It's okay. I was already wet from the snow.
Enh, I'm better at drumming anyway.
Whoa, keep doing that!
TAP TAP RAPA TAP RAPA RAP
Dry Dry
RAPA TAP TAP RAP TAPA TAP

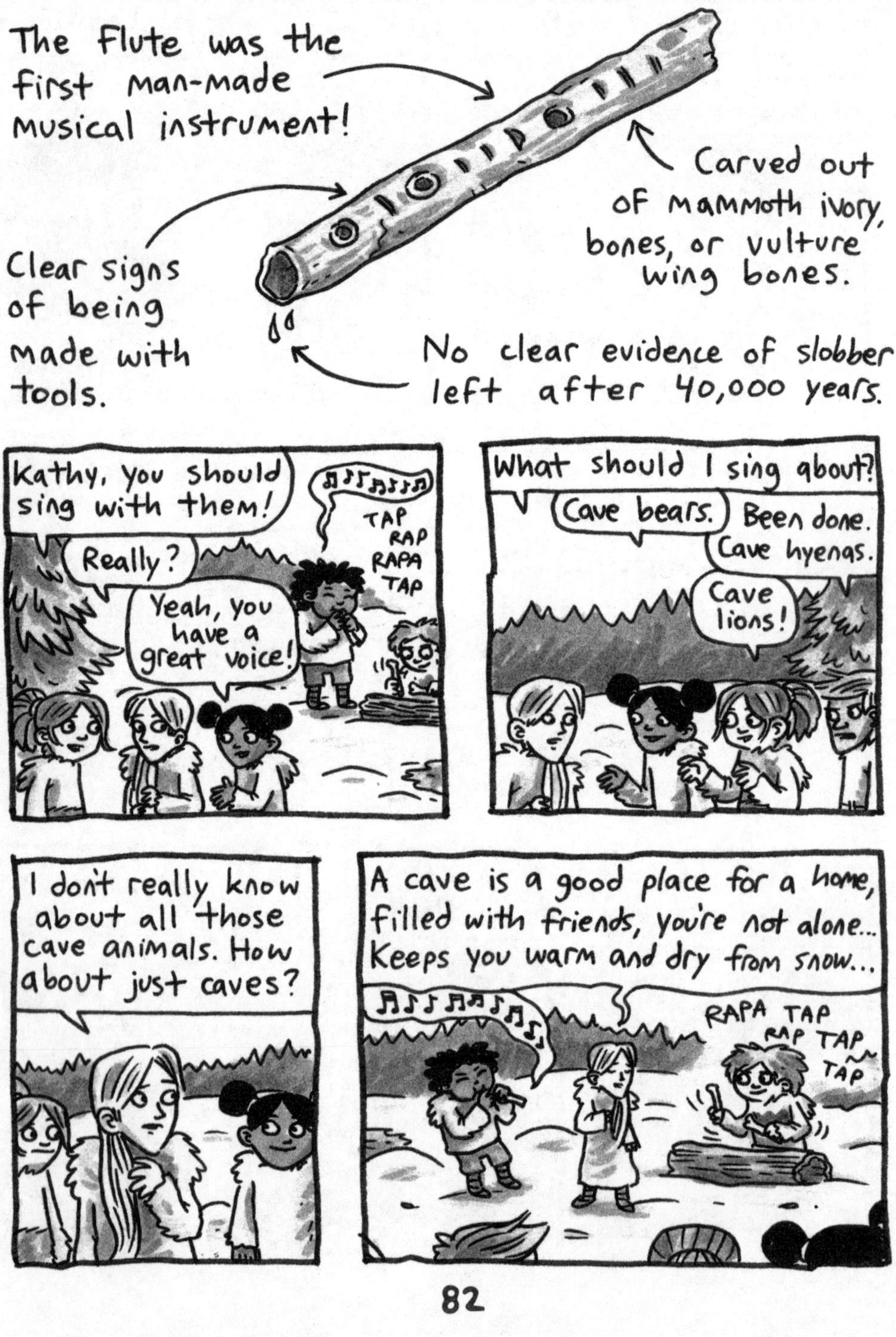
The Flute was the first man-made musical instrument!
Carved out of mammoth ivory, bones, or vulture wing bones.
Clear signs of being made with tools.
No clear evidence of slobber left after 40,000 years.
Kathy, you should sing with them!
TAP RAP RAPA TAP
Really?
Yeah, you have a great voice!
What should I sing about?
Cave bears.
Been done. Cave hyenas.
Cave lions!
I don't really know about all those cave animals. How about just caves?
A cave is a good place for a home, filled with friends, you're not alone... Keeps you warm and dry from snow...
RAPA TAP
RAP TAP
TAP

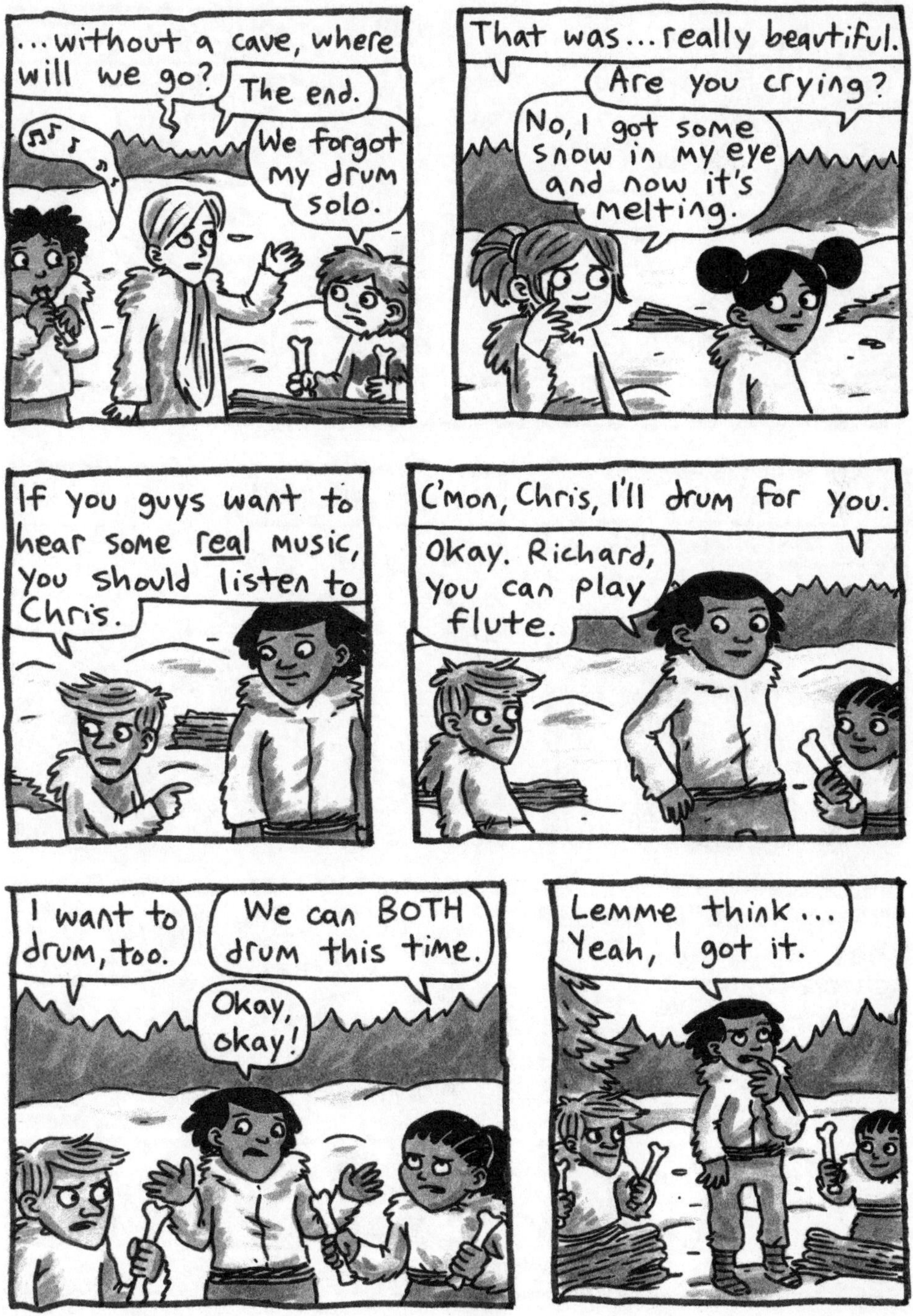
...without a cave, where will we go?
The end.
We forgot my drum solo.
That was...really beautiful.
Are you crying?
No, I got some snow in my eye and now it's melting.
If you guys want to hear some real music, you should listen to Chris.
C'mon, Chris, I'll drum for you.
Okay. Richard, you can play flute.
I want to drum, too.
We can BOTH drum this time.
Okay, okay!
Lemme think... Yeah, I got it.

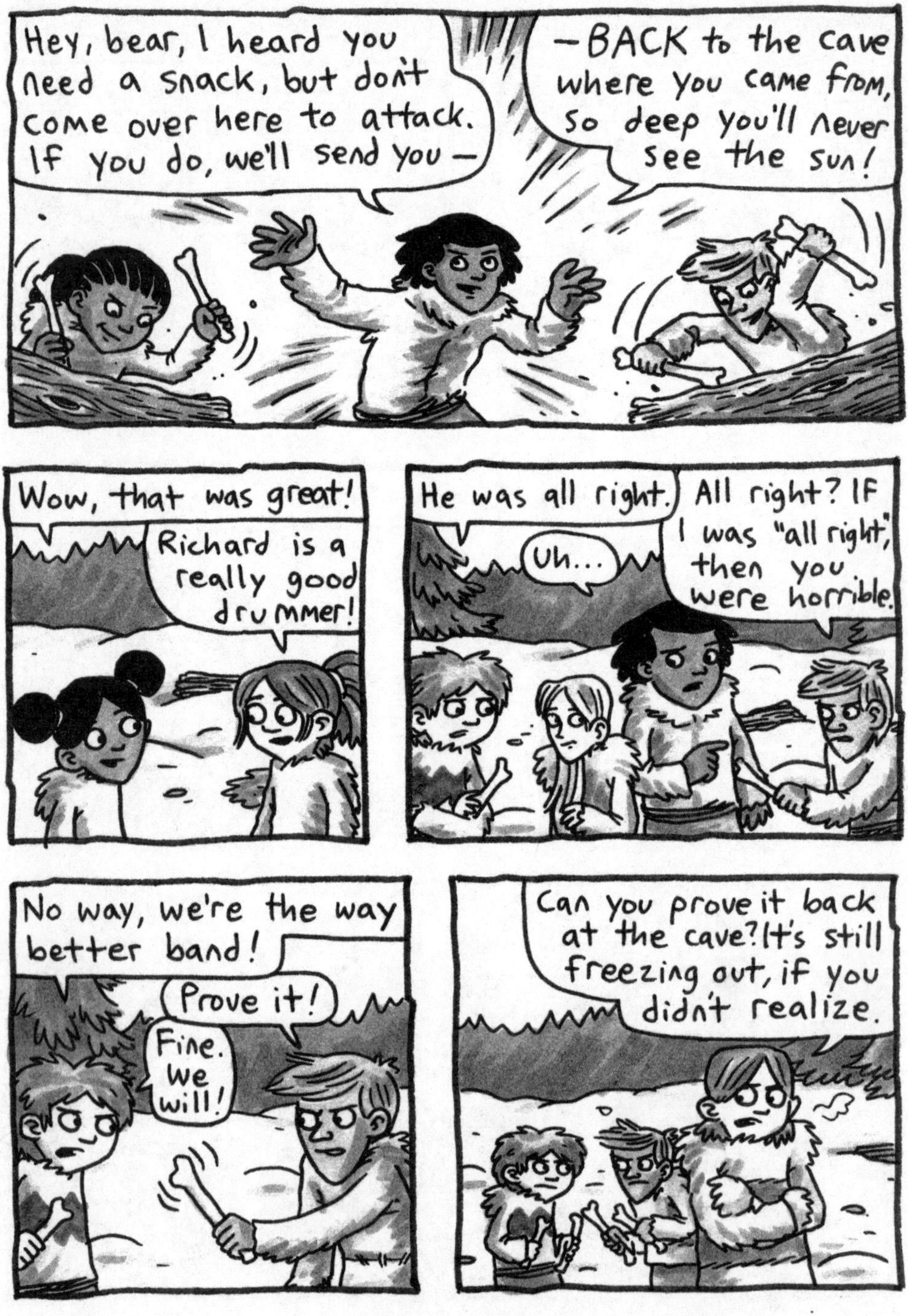

Hey, bear, I heard you need a snack, but don't come over here to attack. If you do, we'll send you —
—BACK to the cave where you came from, so deep you'll never see the sun!
Wow, that was great!
Richard is a really good drummer!
He was all right.
Uh...
All right? If I was "all right," then you were horrible.
No way, we're the way better band!
Prove it!
Fine. We will!
Can you prove it back at the cave? It's still freezing out, if you didn't realize.

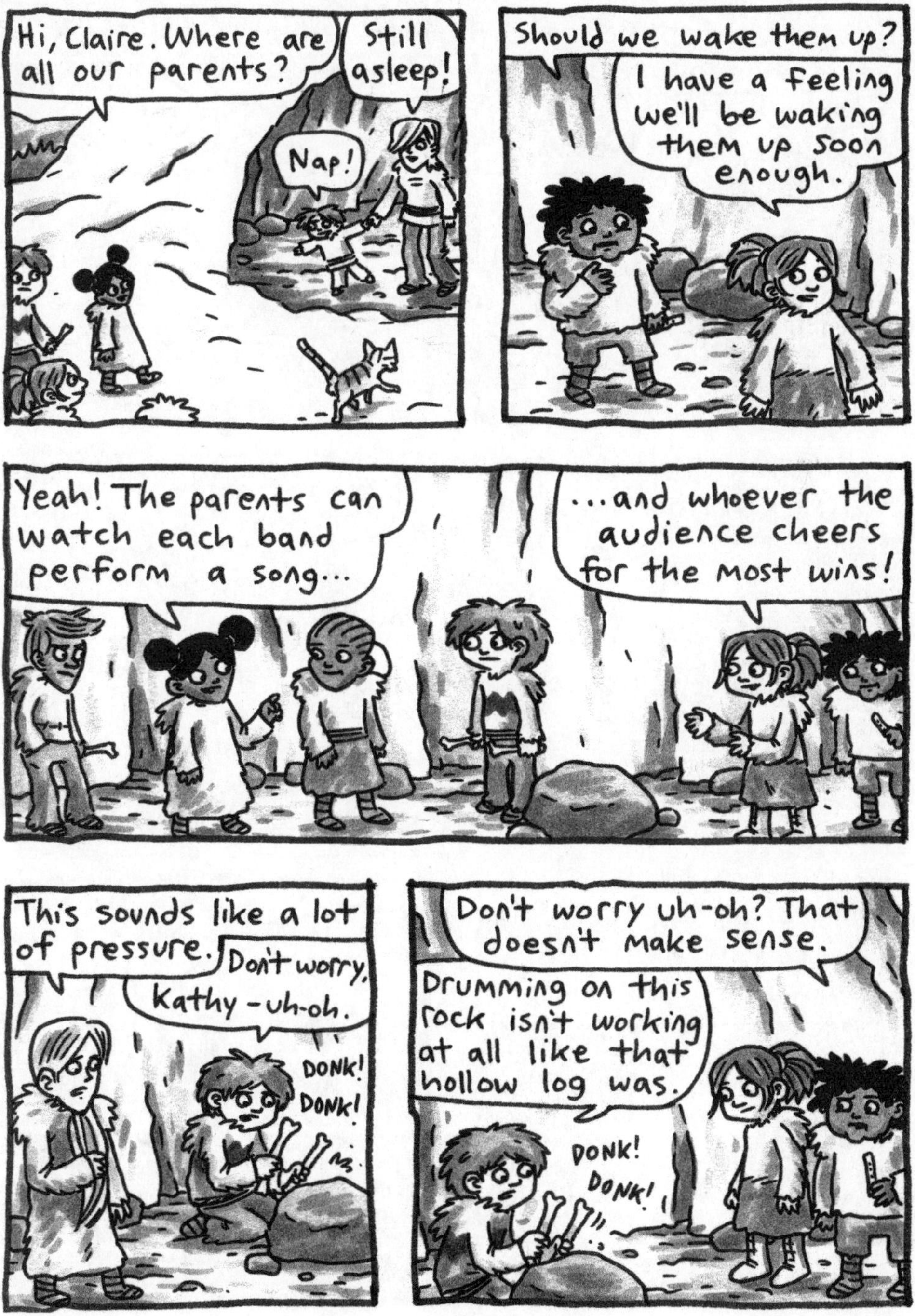
Hi, Claire. Where are all our parents?
Still asleep!
Nap!
Should we wake them up?
I have a feeling we'll be waking them up soon enough.
Yeah! The parents can watch each band perform a song...
...and whoever the audience cheers for the most wins!
This sounds like a lot of pressure.
Don't worry, Kathy-uh-oh.
DONK!
DONK!
Don't worry uh-oh? That doesn't make sense.
Drumming on this rock isn't working at all like that hollow log was.
DONK!
DONK!

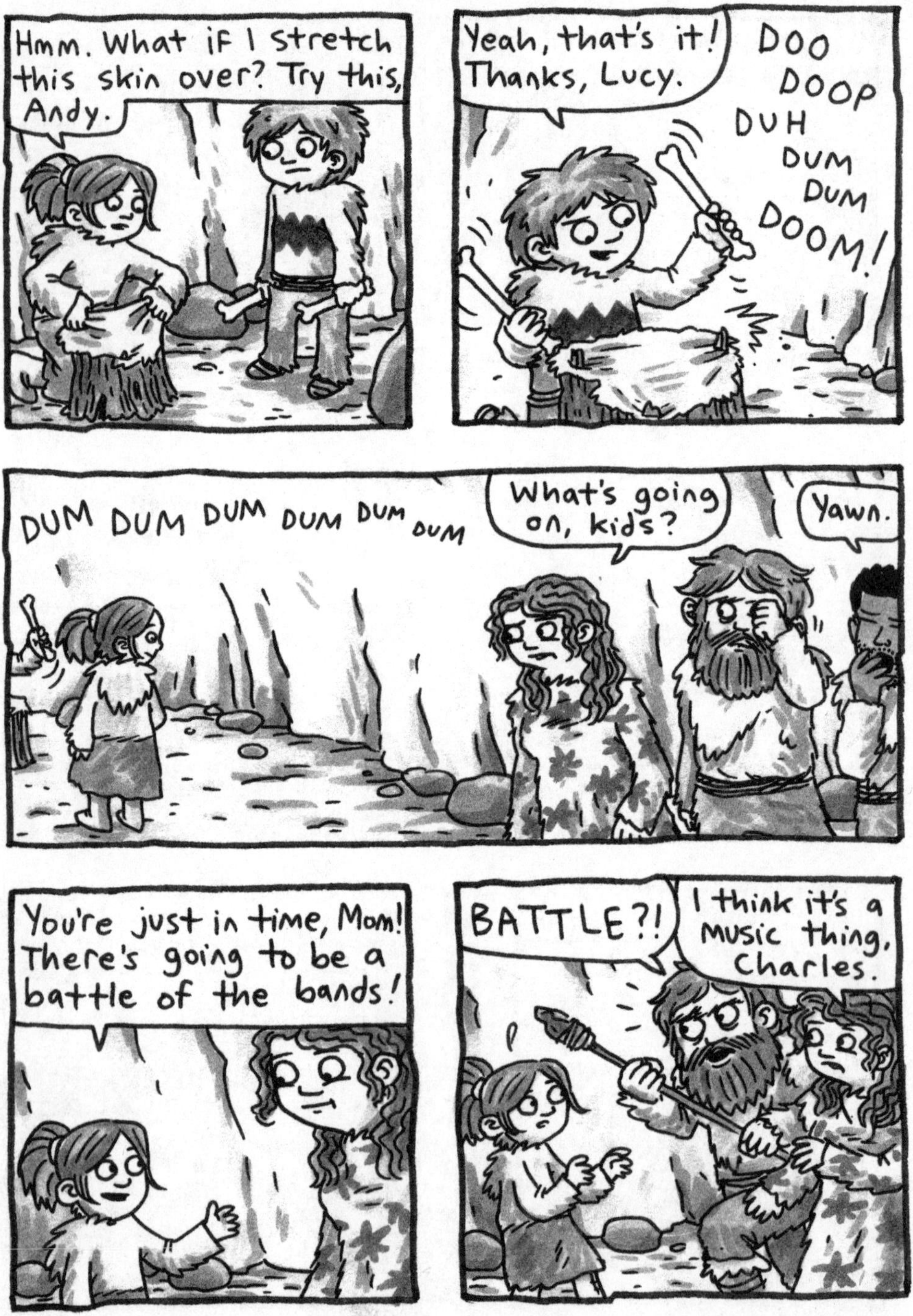
Hmm. What if I stretch this skin over? Try this, Andy.
Yeah, that's it! Thanks, Lucy.
DOO DOOP DUH DUM DUM DOOM!
DUM DUM DUM DUM DUM DUM
What's going on, kids?
Yawn.
You're just in time, Mom! There's going to be a battle of the bands!
BATTLE?!
I think it's a music thing, Charles.

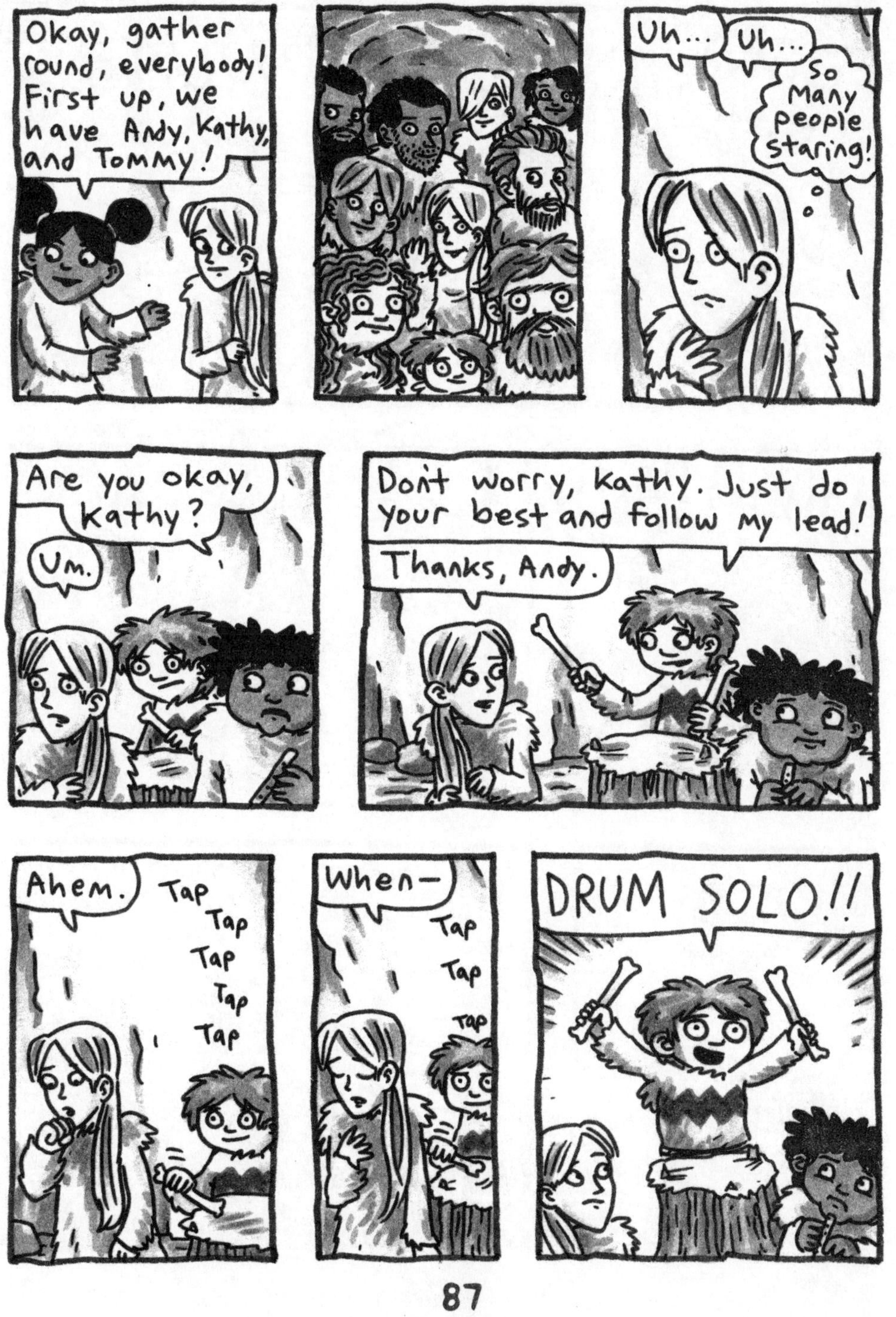
Okay, gather round, everybody! First up, we have Andy, Kathy, and Tommy!
Uh...
Uh...
So Many people staring!
Are you okay, Kathy?
Um.
Don't worry, Kathy. Just do your best and follow my lead!
Thanks, Andy.
Ahem.
Tap
Tap
Tap
Tap
Tap
When—
Tap
Tap
Tap
DRUM SOLO!!

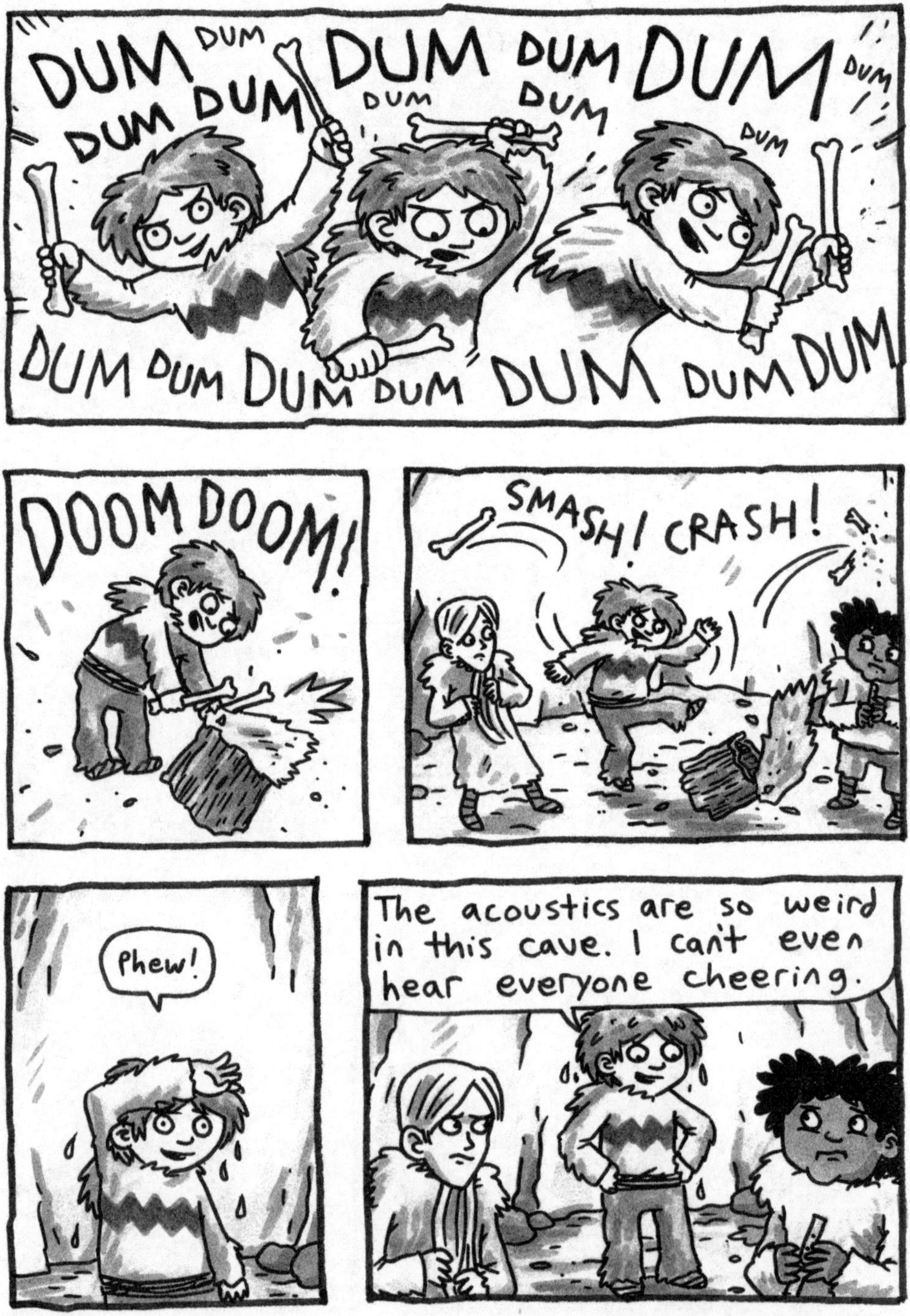
DUM DUM
DUM DUM
DUM DUM DUM DUM DUM DUM DUM DUM
DUM DUM DUM DUM DUM DUM DUM
DOOM DOOM!
SMASH! CRASH!
Phew!
The acoustics are so weird in this cave. I can't even hear everyone cheering.

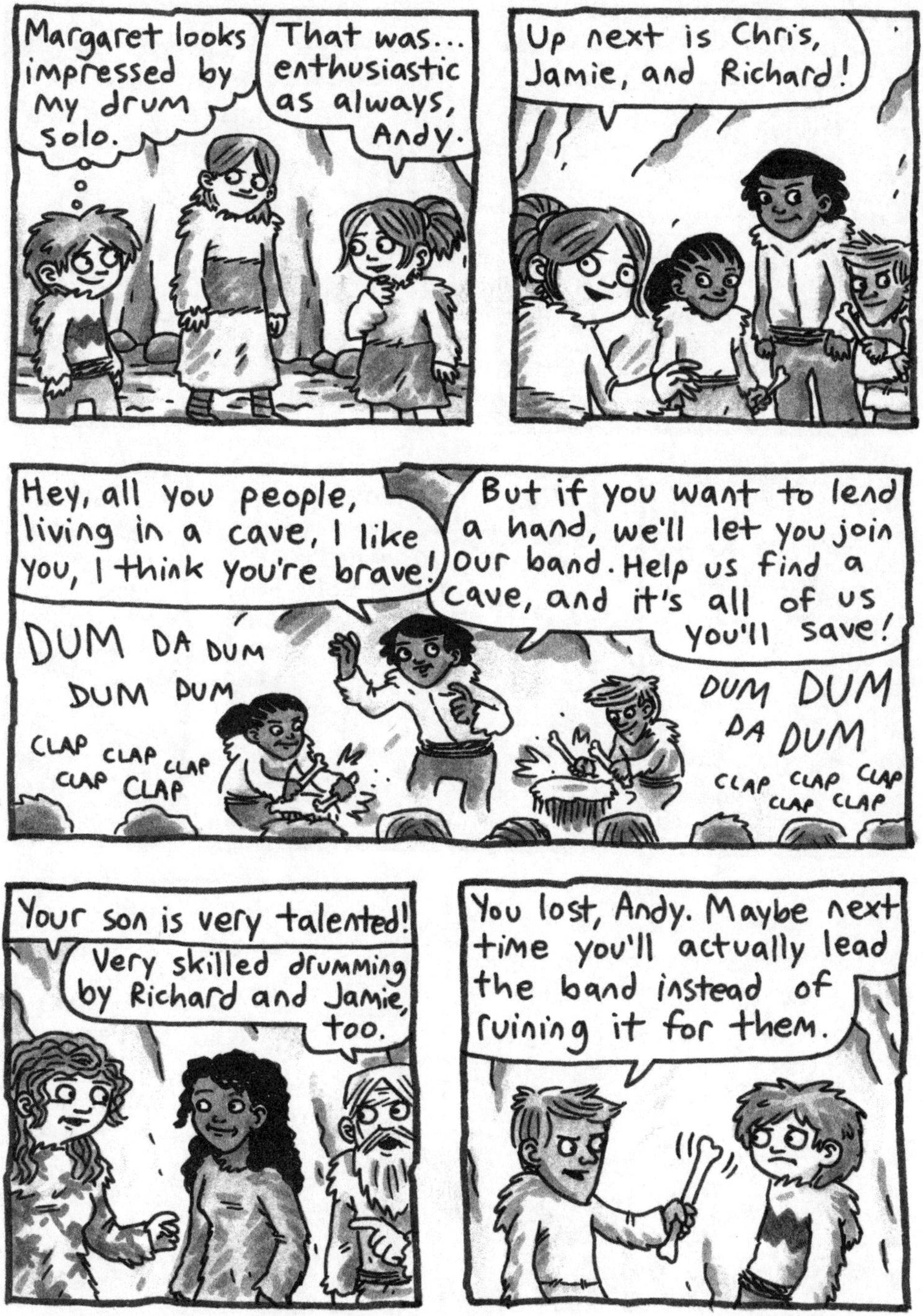
Margaret looks impressed by my drum solo.
That was... enthusiastic as always, Andy.
Up next is Chris, Jamie, and Richard!
Hey, all you people, living in a cave, I like you, I think you're brave!
But if you want to lend a hand, we'll let you join our band. Help us find a cave, and it's all of us you'll save!
DUM DA DUM
DUM DUM
CLAP CLAP CLAP CLAP CLAP
DUM DUM DA DUM
CLAP CLAP CLAP CLAP CLAP
Your son is very talented!
Very skilled drumming by Richard and Jamie, too.
You lost, Andy. Maybe next time you'll actually lead the band instead of ruining it for them.

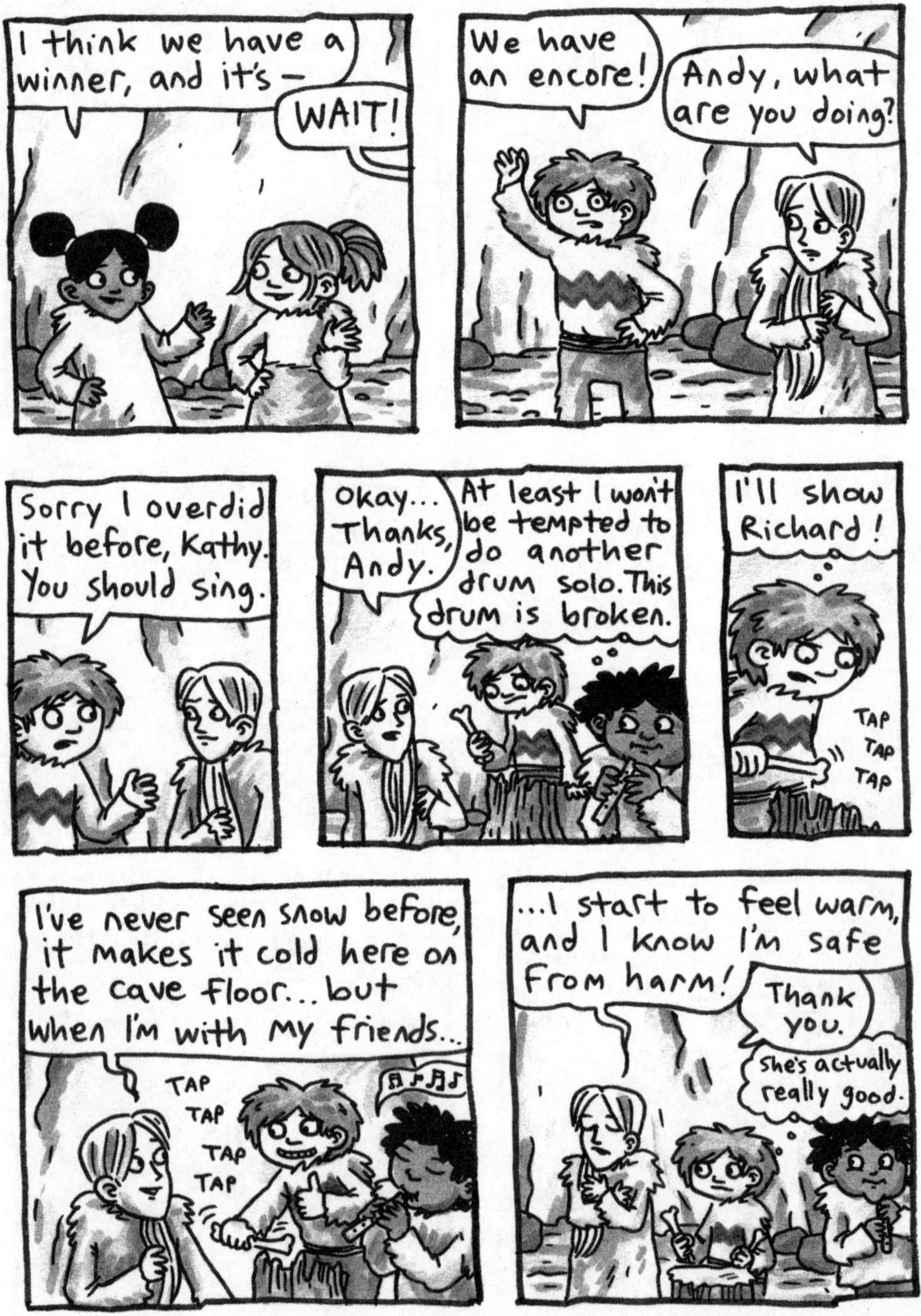
I think we have a winner, and it's—
WAIT!
We have an encore!
Andy, what are you doing?
Sorry I overdid it before, Kathy. You should sing.
Okay... Thanks, Andy.
At least I won't be tempted to do another drum solo. This drum is broken.
I'll show Richard!
TAP
TAP
TAP
I've never seen snow before, it makes it cold here on the cave floor... but when I'm with my friends...
TAP
TAP
TAP
TAP
...I start to feel warm, and I know I'm safe from harm!
Thank you.
She's actually really good.

CLAP CLAP CLAP CLAP CLAP
CLAP CLAP CLAP CLAP CLAP
CLAP
That was beautiful, sweetie. I'm proud of you.
Wow, I think we have a tie!
Yeah!
SUDDEN-DEATH FACE-OFF!
Sudden death?!
Uh, maybe we should just leave it a tie.
Is this another music thing?
Yep. Definitely a tie.

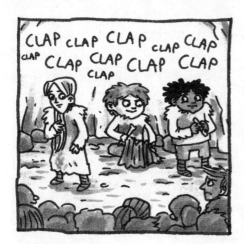

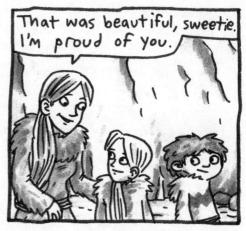

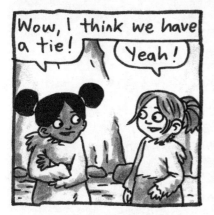

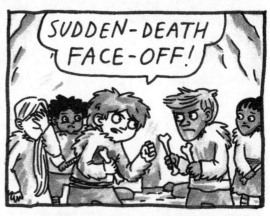

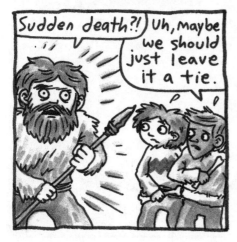

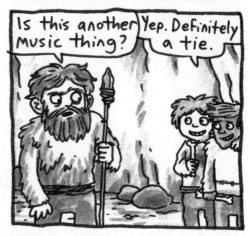

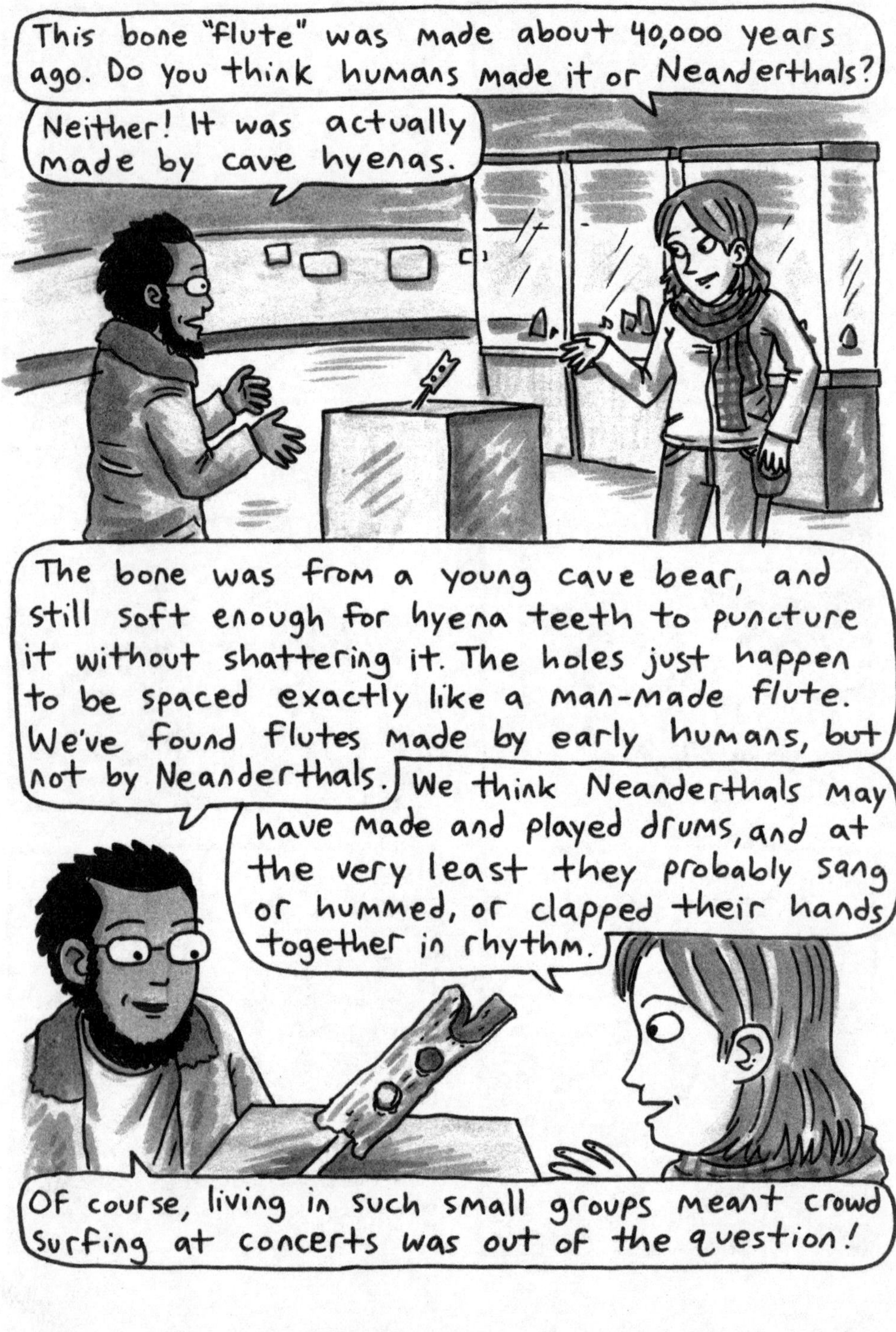

This bone "flute" was made about 40,000 years ago. Do you think humans made it or Neanderthals?
Neither! It was actually made by cave hyenas.
The bone was from a young cave bear, and still soft enough for hyena teeth to puncture it without shattering it. The holes just happen to be spaced exactly like a man-made flute. We've found flutes made by early humans, but not by Neanderthals.
We think Neanderthals may have made and played drums, and at the very least they probably sang or hummed, or clapped their hands together in rhythm.
Of course, living in such small groups meant crowd surfing at concerts was out of the question!

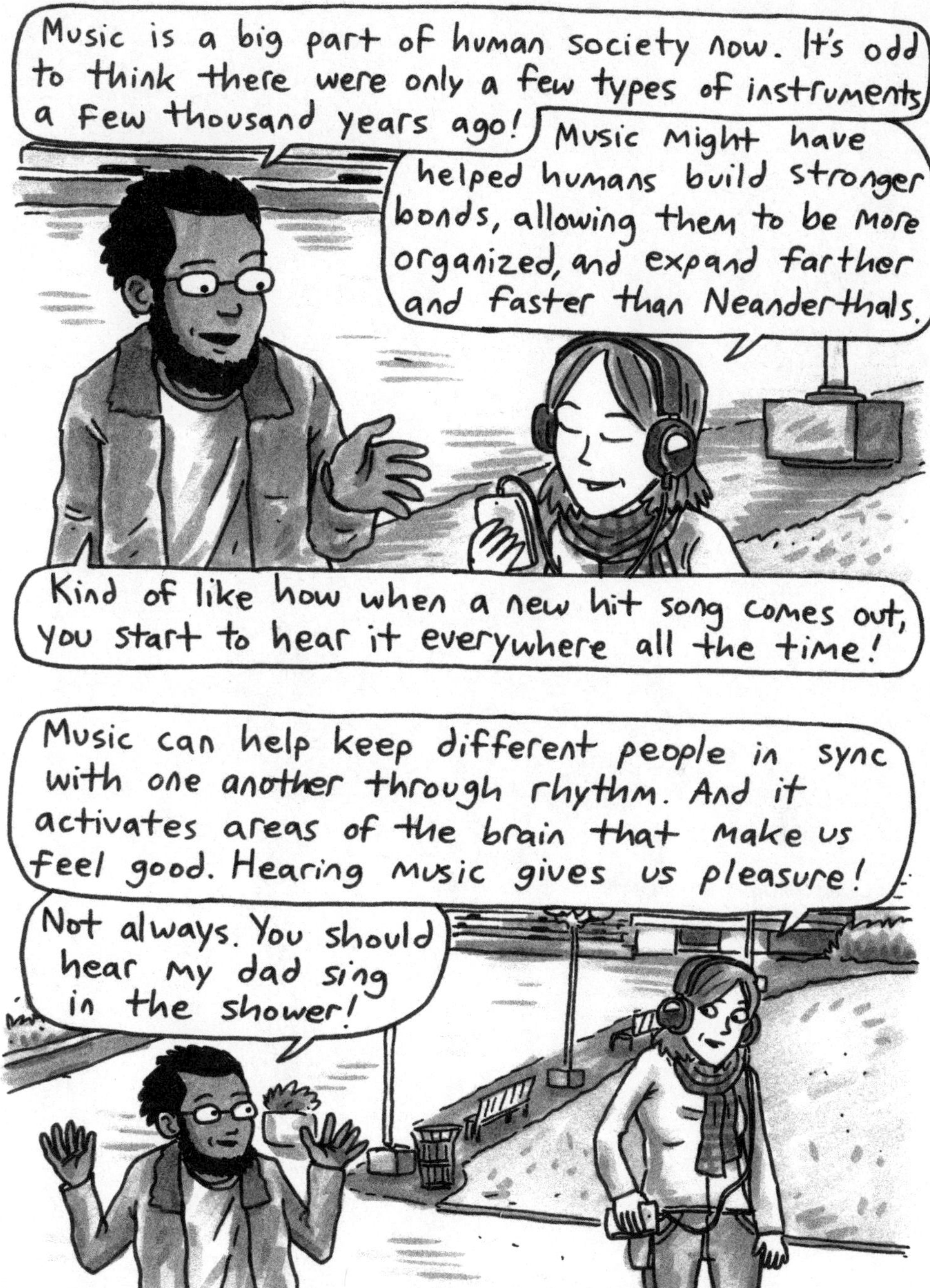
Music is a big part of human society now. It's odd to think there were only a few types of instruments a few thousand years ago!
Music might have helped humans build stronger bonds, allowing them to be more organized, and expand farther and faster than Neanderthals.
Kind of like how when a new hit song comes out, you start to hear it everywhere all the time!
Music can help keep different people in sync with one another through rhythm. And it activates areas of the brain that make us feel good. Hearing music gives us pleasure!
Not always. You should hear my dad sing in the shower!

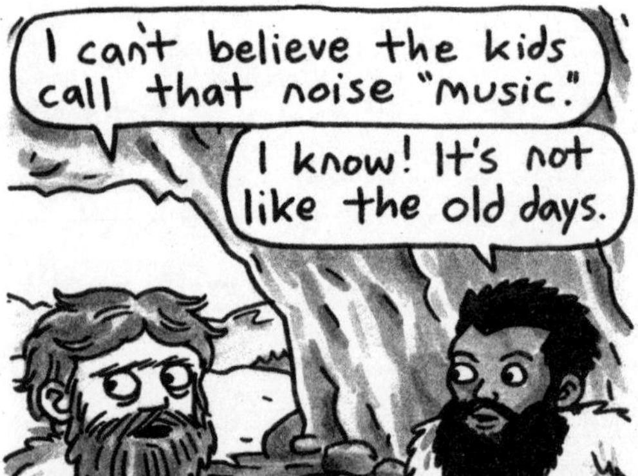
I can't believe the kids call that noise "music."
I know! It's not like the old days.

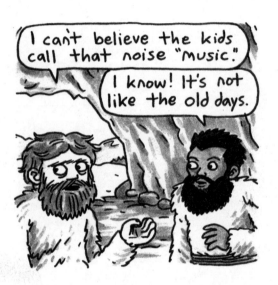

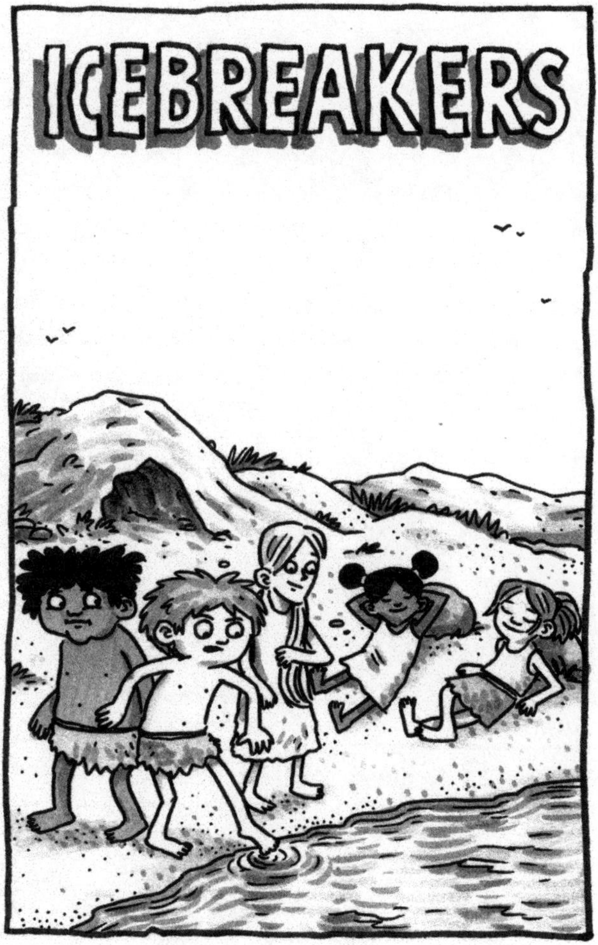
ICEBREAKERS

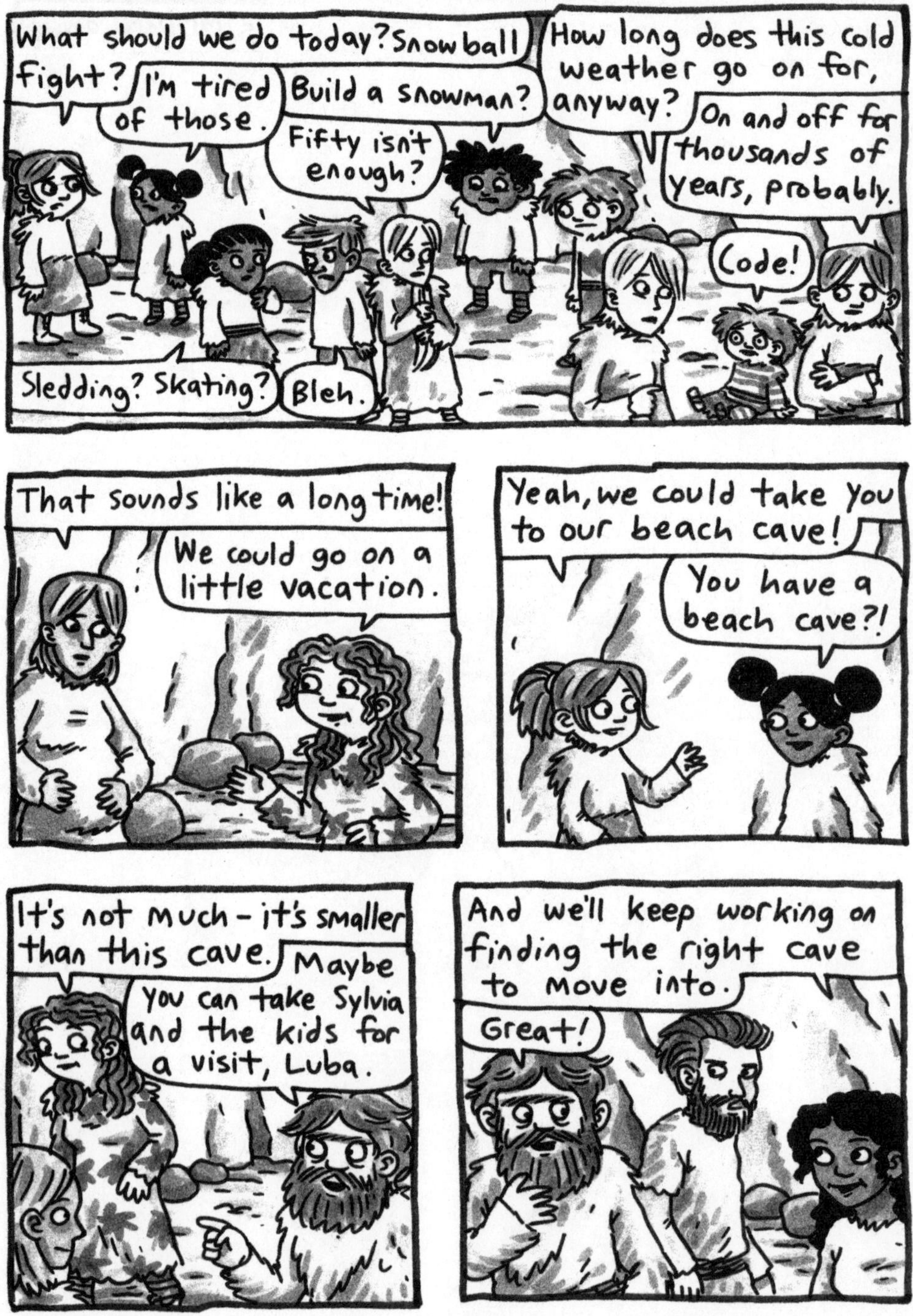

What should we do today? Snowball fight?
I'm tired of those.
Build a snowman?
Fifty isn't enough?
Sledding? Skating?
Bleh.
How long does this cold weather go on for, anyway?
On and off for thousands of years, probably.
Code!
That sounds like a long time!
We could go on a little vacation.
Yeah, we could take you to our beach cave!
You have a beach cave?!
It's not much - it's smaller than this cave.
Maybe you can take Sylvia and the kids for a visit, Luba.
And we'll keep working on finding the right cave to move into.
Great!

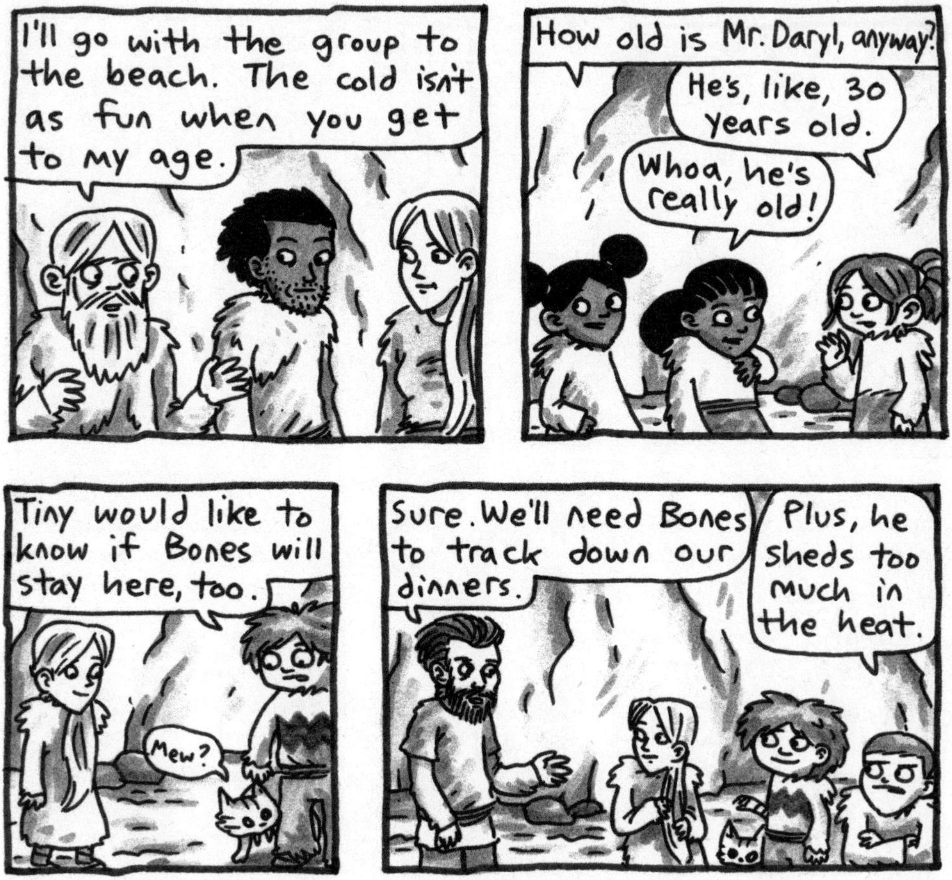
I'll go with the group to the beach. The cold isn't as fun when you get to my age.
How old is Mr. Daryl, anyway?
He's, like, 30 years old.
Whoa, he's really old!
Tiny would like to know if Bones will stay here, too.
Mew?
Sure. We'll need Bones to track down our dinners.
Plus, he sheds too much in the heat.

By studying the bones of the animals Neanderthals hunted, scientists know they had a harder time finding food in the cold climate.

Neanderthals broke open bones to get the nutritious marrow inside. During cold times, the bones were more thoroughly picked over.

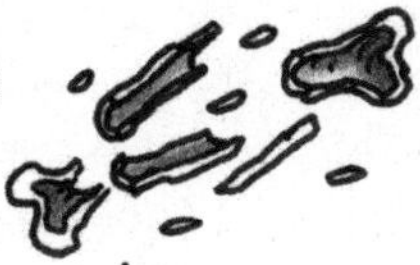

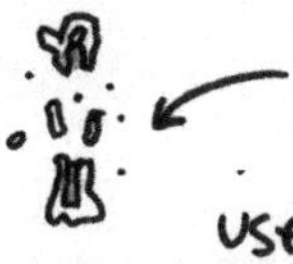

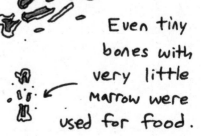

Even tiny bones with very little marrow were used for food.

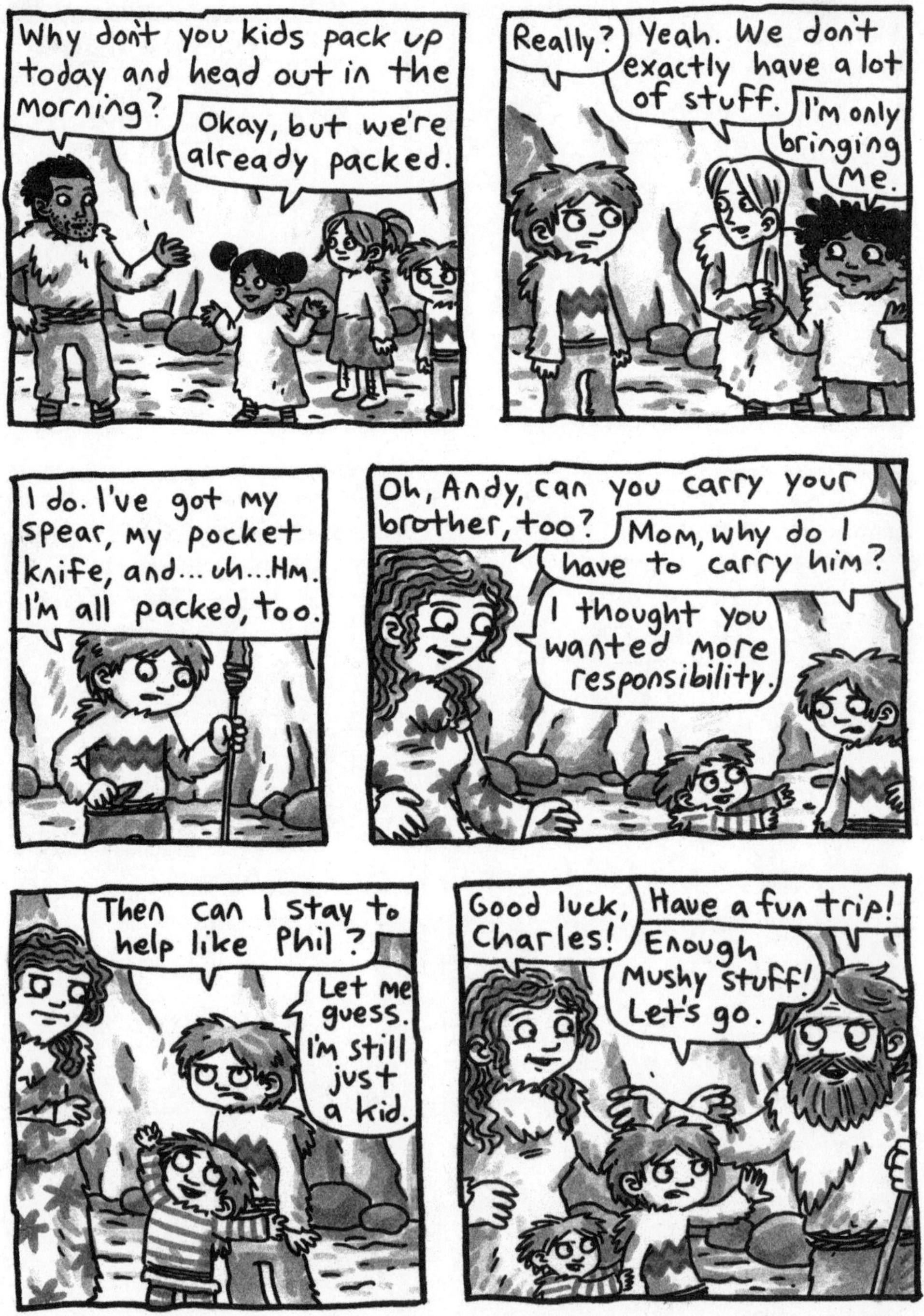
Why don't you kids pack up today and head out in the morning?
Okay, but we're already packed.
Really?
Yeah. We don't exactly have a lot of stuff.
I'm only bringing me.
I do. I've got my spear, my pocket knife, and... uh... Hm. I'm all packed, too.
Oh, Andy, can you carry your brother, too?
Mom, why do I have to carry him?
I thought you wanted more responsibility.
Then can I stay to help like Phil?
Let me guess. I'm still just a kid.
Good luck, Charles!
Have a fun trip!
Enough mushy stuff! Let's go.

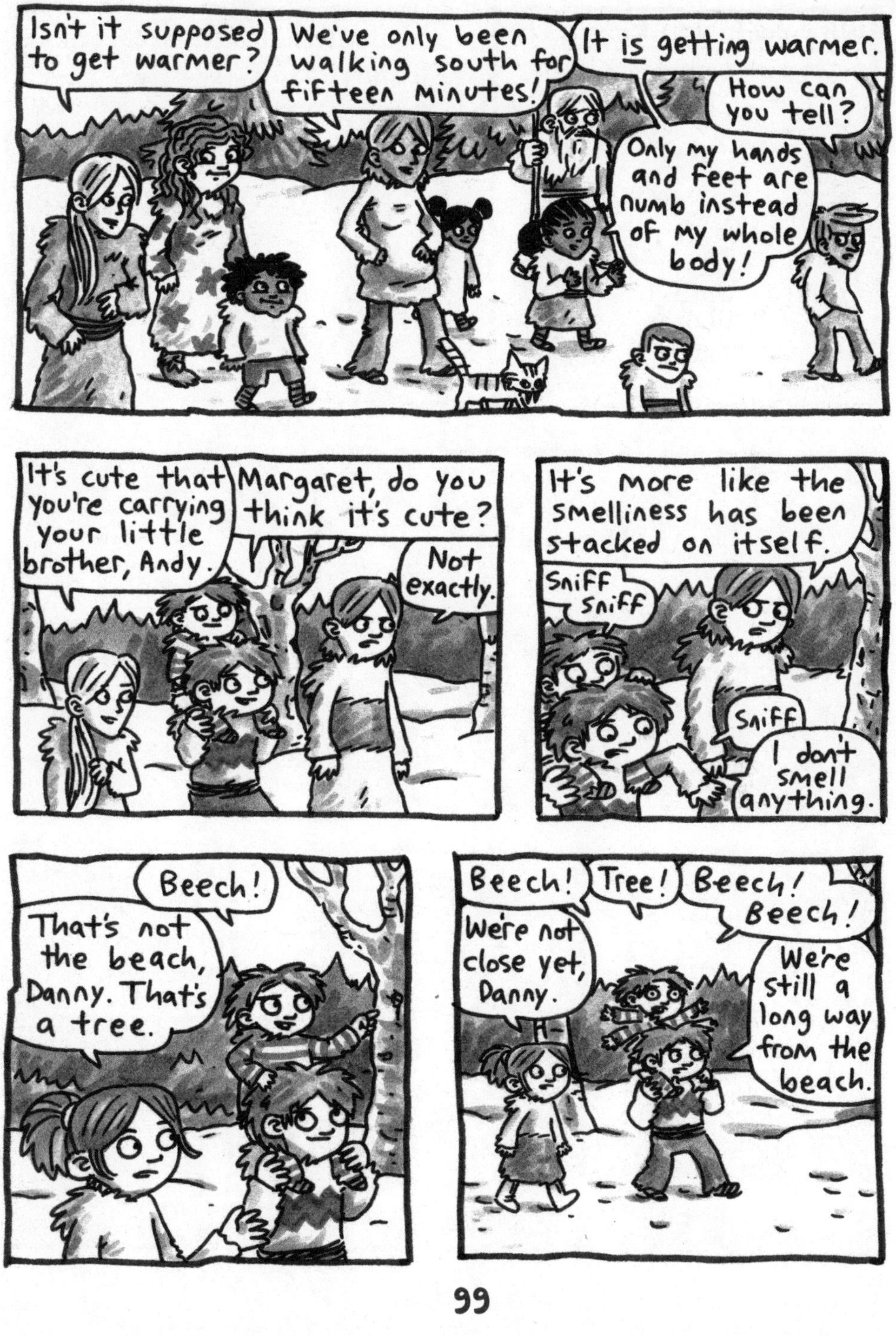
Isn't it supposed to get warmer?
We've only been walking south for fifteen minutes!
It is getting warmer.
How can you tell?
Only my hands and feet are numb instead of my whole body!
It's cute that you're carrying your little brother, Andy.
Margaret, do you think it's cute?
Not exactly.
It's more like the smelliness has been stacked on itself.
Sniff sniff
Sniff
I don't smell anything.
Beech!
That's not the beach, Danny. That's a tree.
Beech!
Tree!
Beech! Beech!
We're not close yet, Danny.
We're still a long way from the beach.

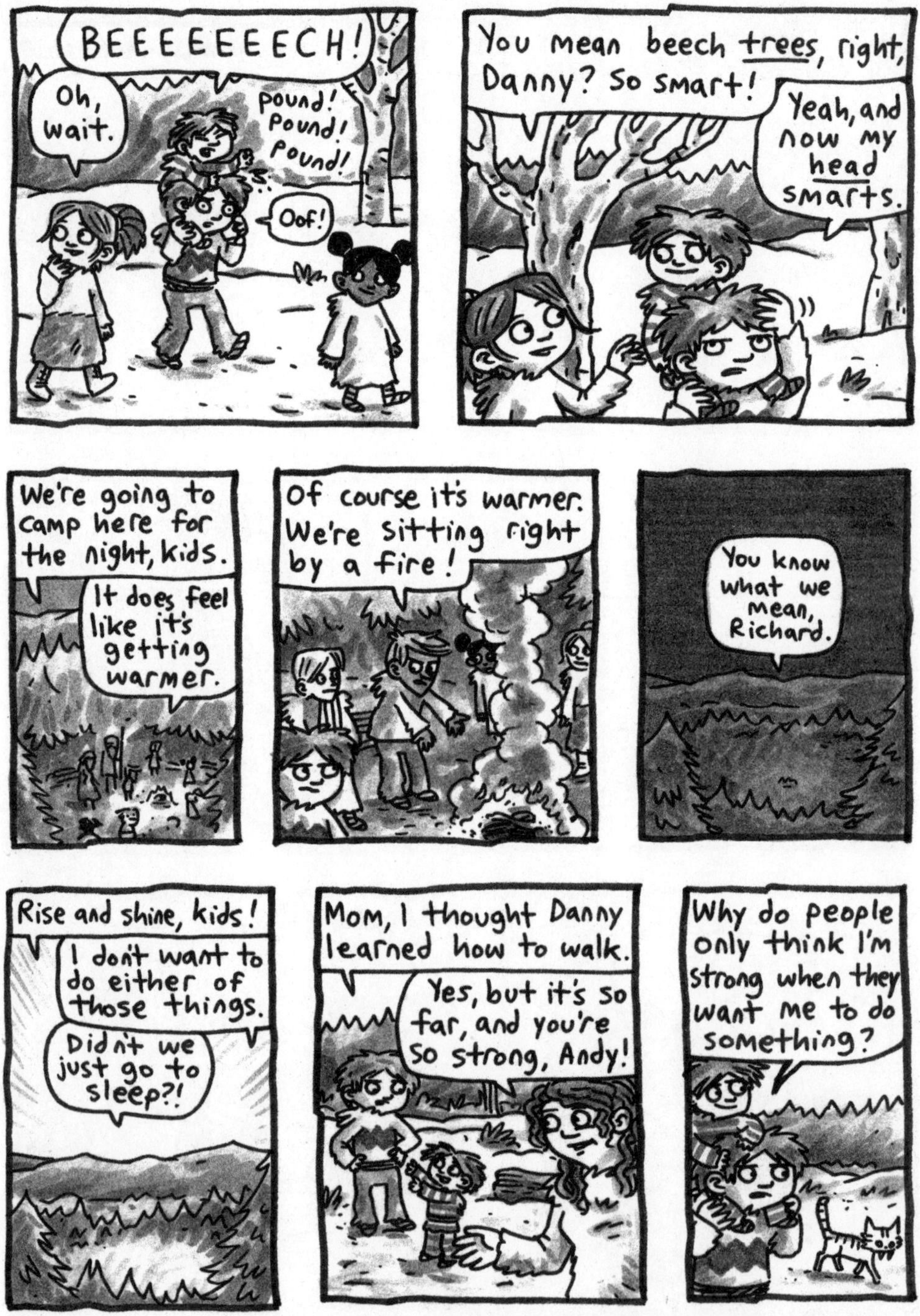
BEEEEEEECH!
Oh, wait.
Pound! Pound! Pound!
Oof!
You mean beech trees, right, Danny? So smart!
Yeah, and now my head smarts.
We're going to camp here for the night, kids.
It does feel like it's getting warmer.
Of course it's warmer. We're sitting right by a fire!
You know what we mean, Richard.
Rise and shine, kids!
I don't want to do either of those things.
Didn't we just go to sleep?!
Mom, I thought Danny learned how to walk.
Yes, but it's so far, and you're so strong, Andy!
Why do people only think I'm strong when they want me to do something?

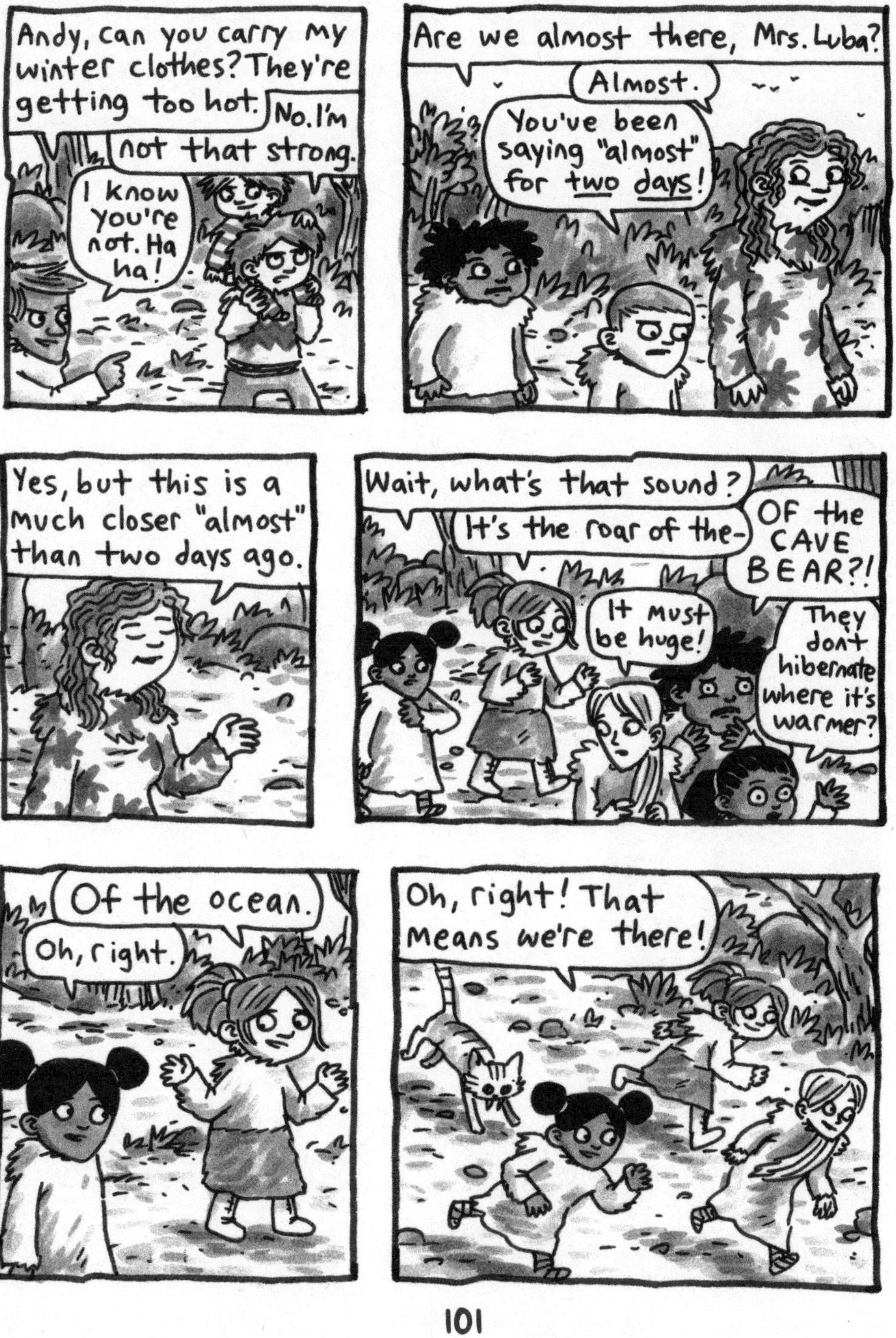
Andy, can you carry my winter clothes? They're getting too hot.
No. I'm not that strong.
I know you're not. Ha ha!
Are we almost there, Mrs. Luba?
Almost.
You've been saying "almost" for two days!
Yes, but this is a much closer "almost" than two days ago.
Wait, what's that sound?
It's the roar of the-
OF the CAVE BEAR?!
It must be huge!
They don't hibernate where it's warmer?
Of the ocean.
Oh, right.
Oh, right! That means we're there!

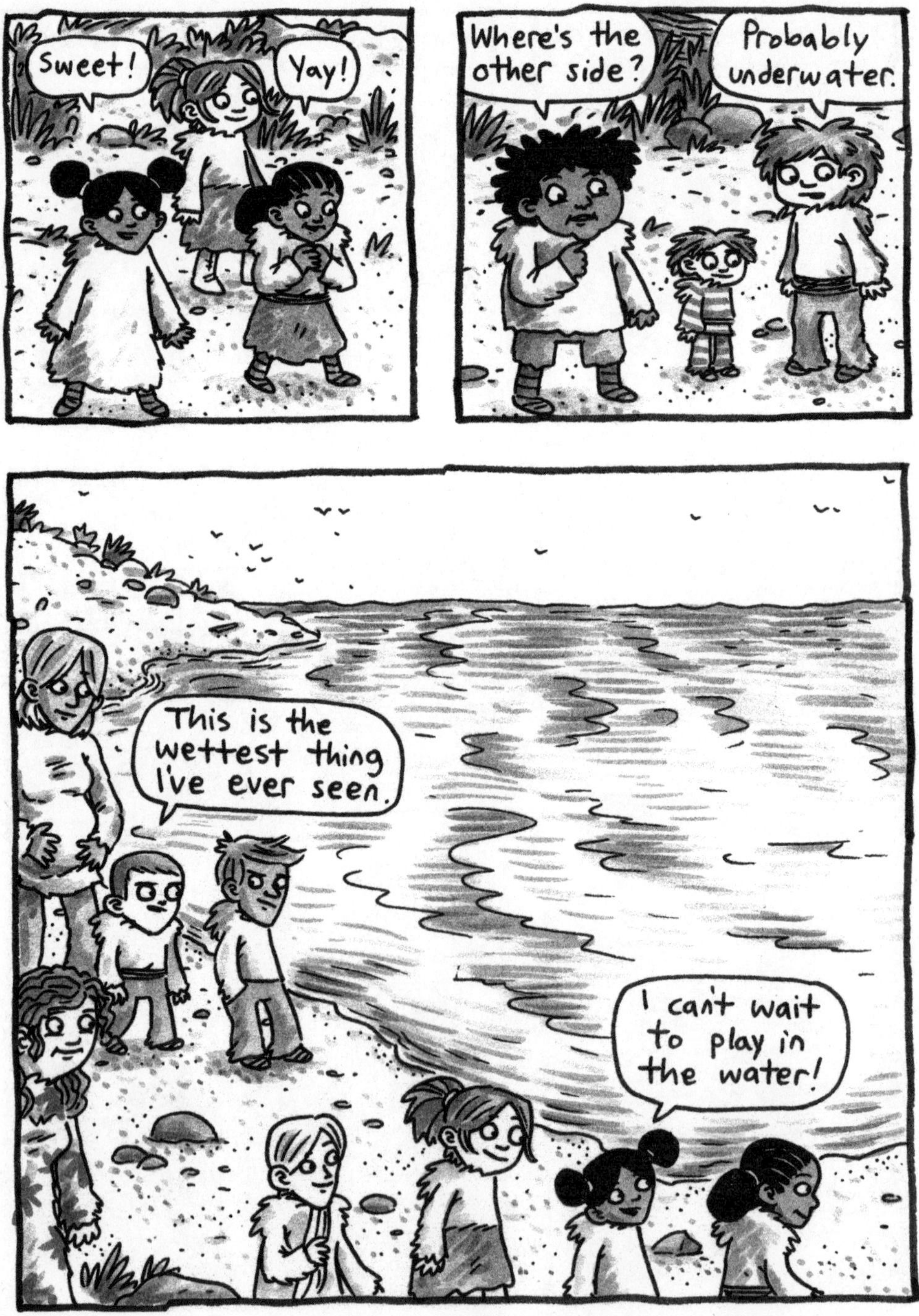
Sweet!
Yay!
Where's the other side?
Probably underwater.
This is the wettest thing I've ever seen.
I can't wait to play in the water!

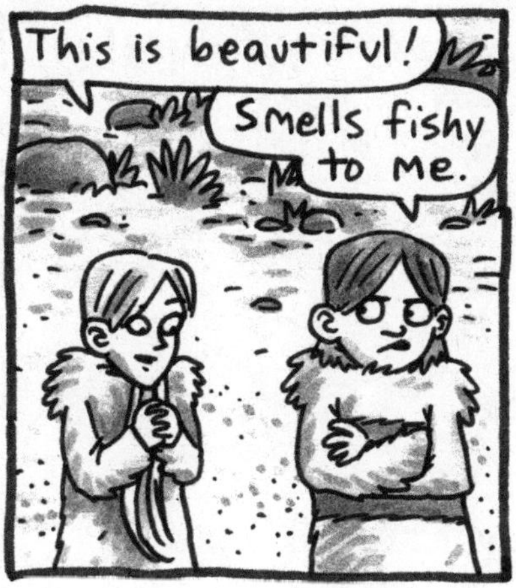
This is beautiful!
Smells fishy to me.
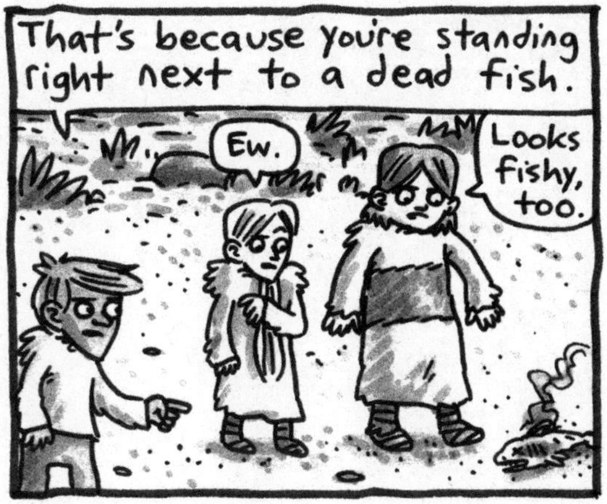
That's because you're standing right next to a dead fish.
Ew.
Looks fishy, too.
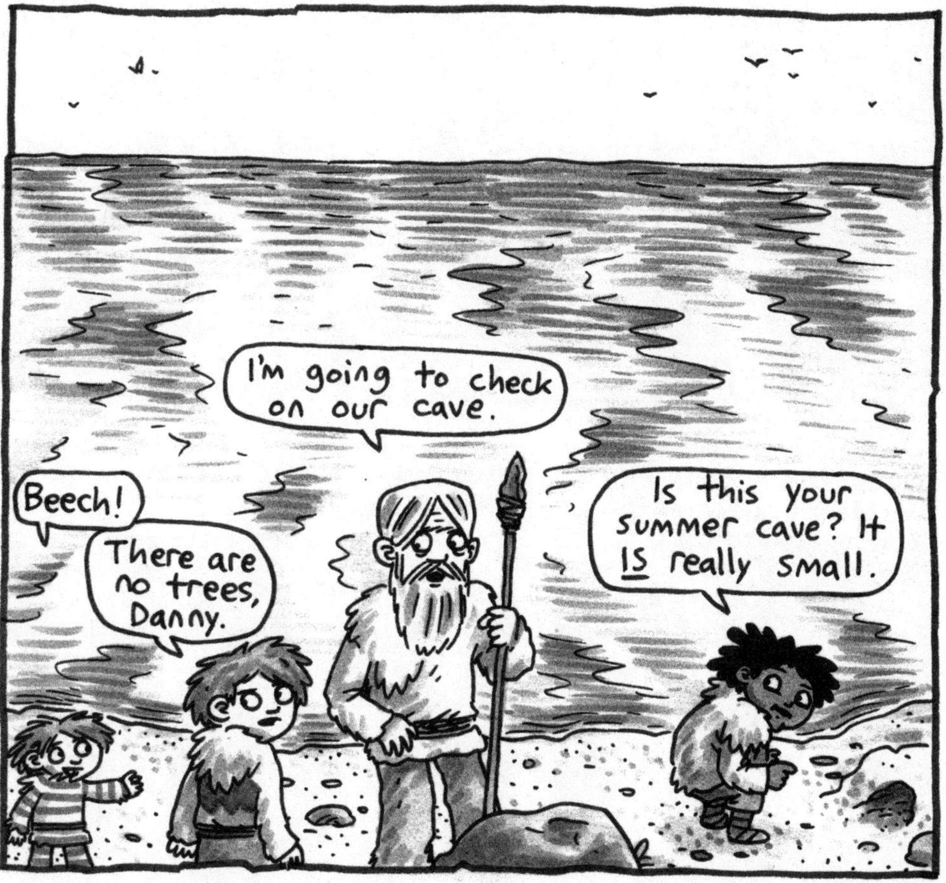
I'm going to check on our cave.
Beech!
There are no trees, Danny.
Is this your summer cave? It IS really small.

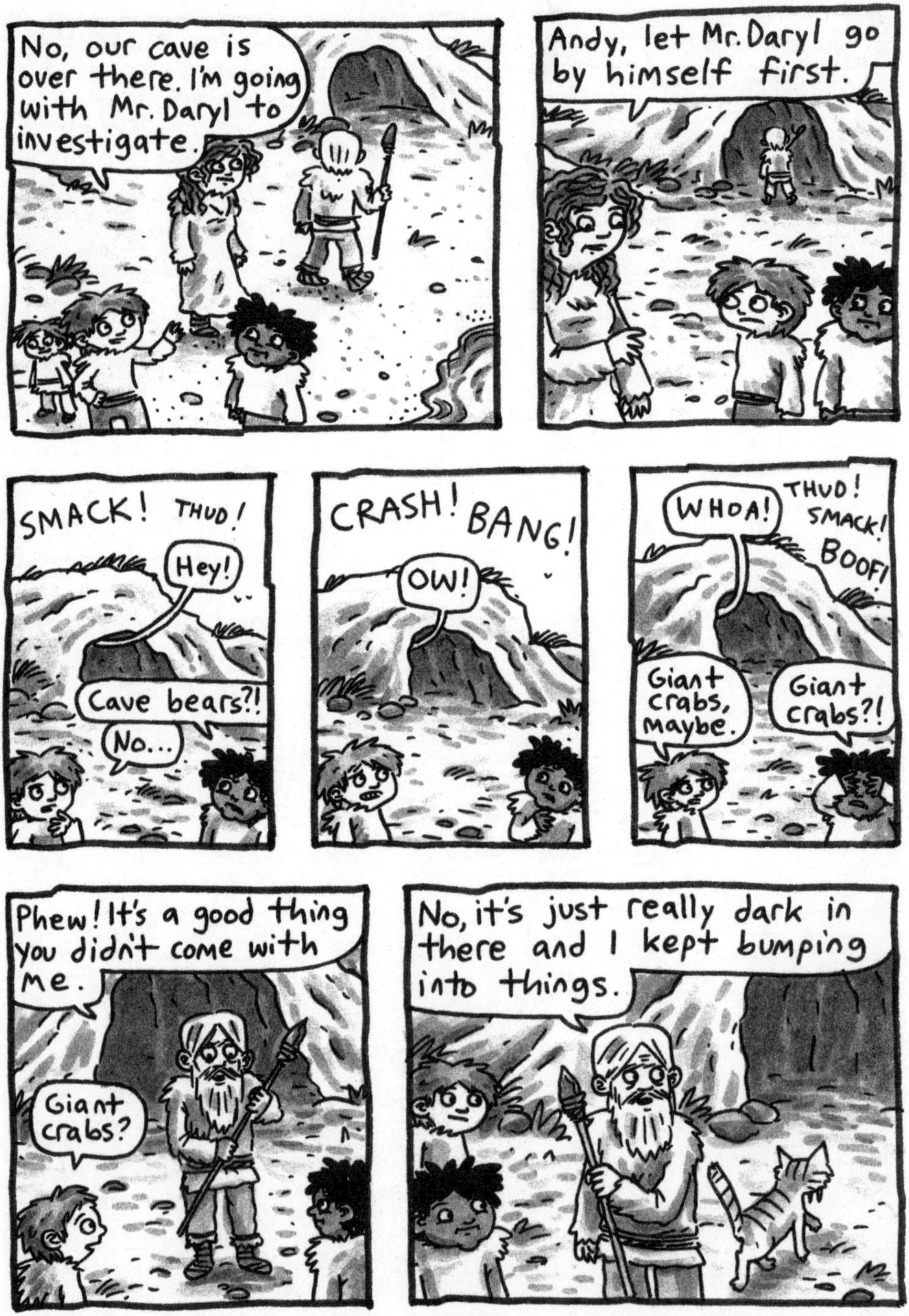

No, our cave is over there. I'm going with Mr. Daryl to investigate.
Andy, let Mr. Daryl go by himself first.
SMACK! THUD!
Hey!
Cave bears?!
No...
CRASH! BANG!
OW!
WHOA!
THUD! SMACK! BOOF!
Giant crabs, maybe.
Giant crabs?!
Phew! It's a good thing you didn't come with me.
Giant crabs?
No, it's just really dark in there and I kept bumping into things.

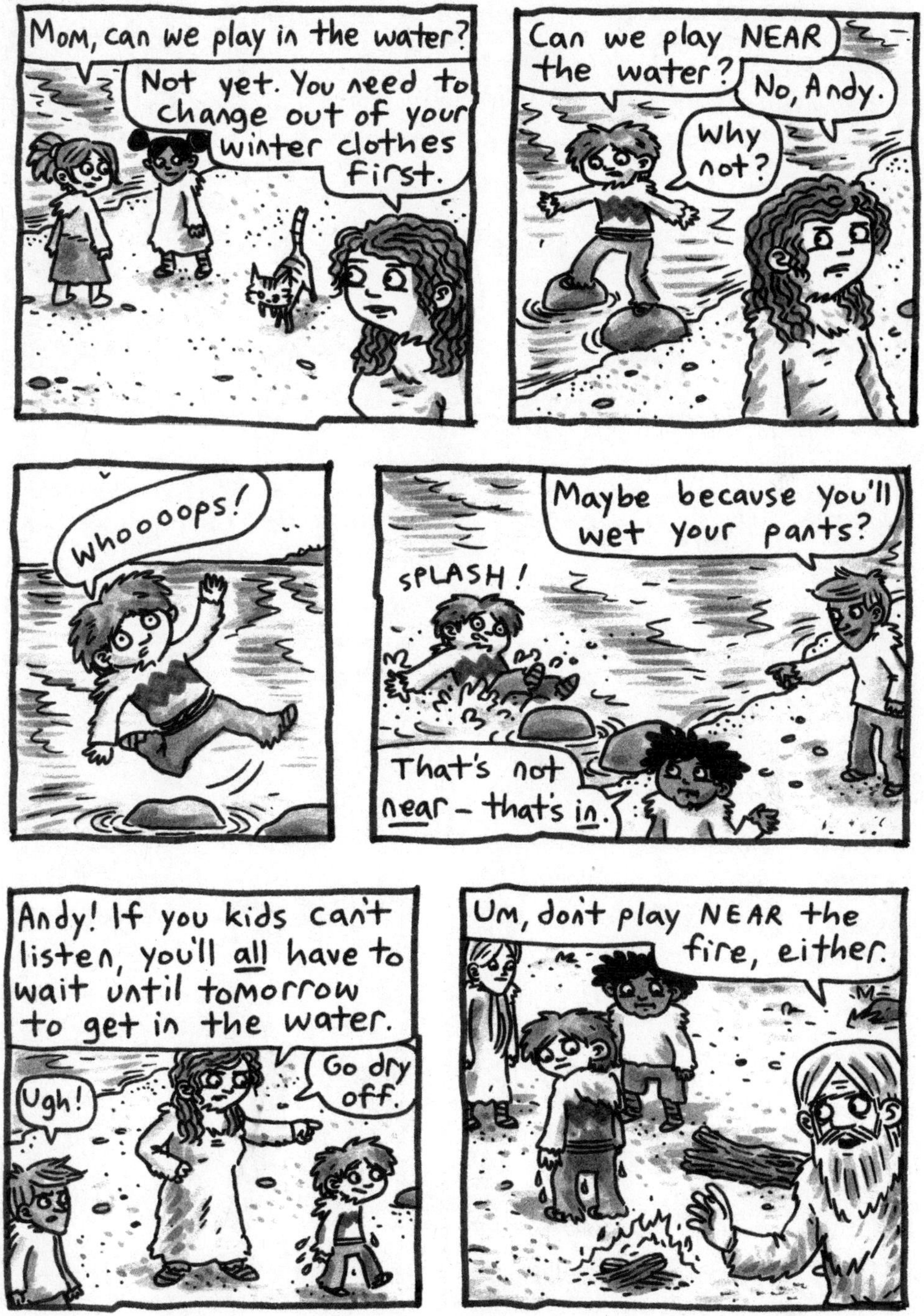
Mom, can we play in the water?
Not yet. You need to change out of your winter clothes first.
Can we play NEAR the water?
No, Andy.
Why not?
Whoooops!
Maybe because you'll wet your pants?
SPLASH!
That's not near – that's in.
Andy! If you kids can't listen, you'll all have to wait until tomorrow to get in the water.
Ugh!
Go dry off.
Um, don't play NEAR the fire, either.

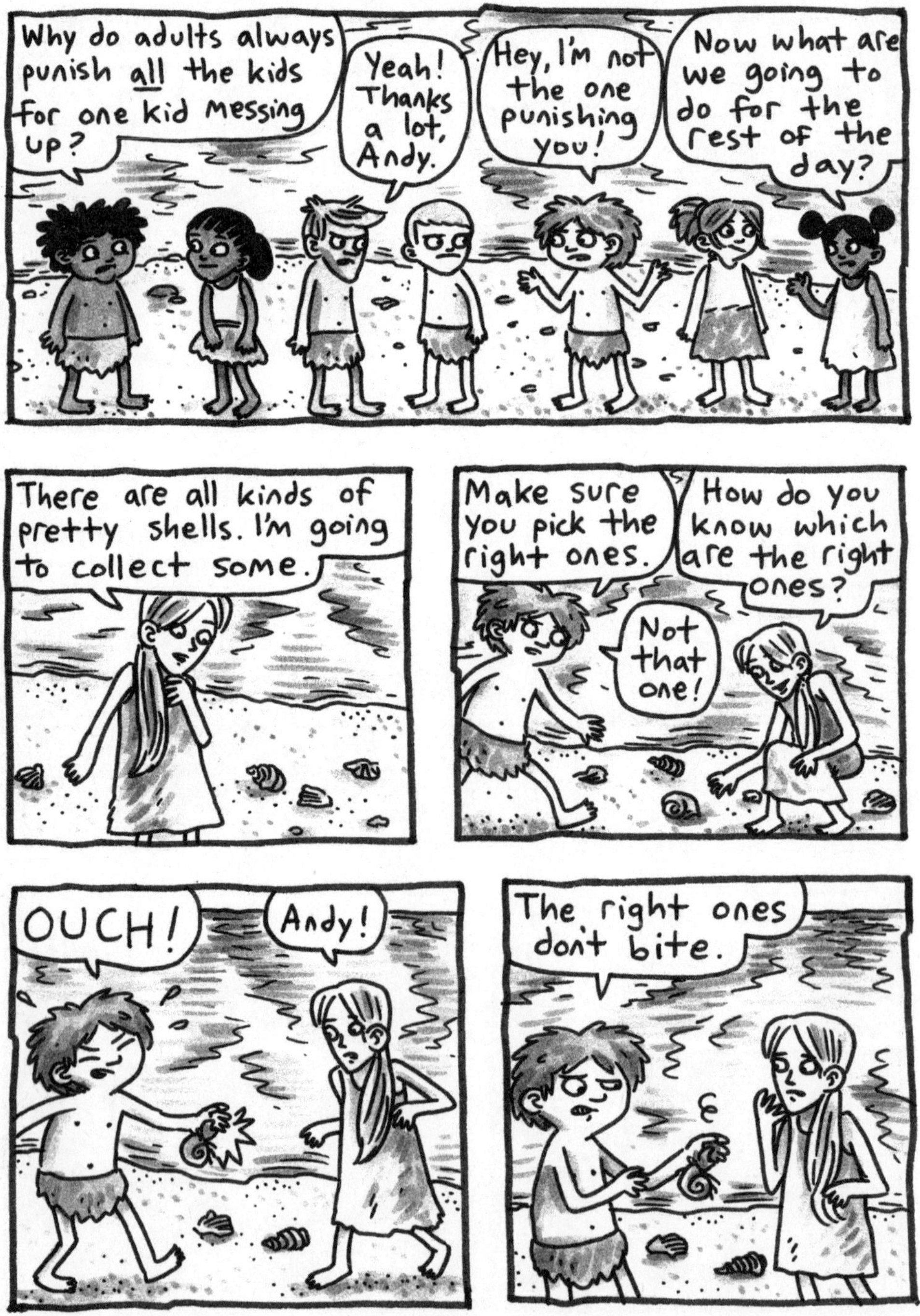
Why do adults always punish all the kids for one kid messing up?
Yeah! Thanks a lot, Andy.
Hey, I'm not the one punishing you!
Now what are we going to do for the rest of the day?
There are all kinds of pretty shells. I'm going to collect some.
Make sure you pick the right ones.
How do you know which are the right ones?
Not that one!
OUCH!
Andy!
The right ones don't bite.

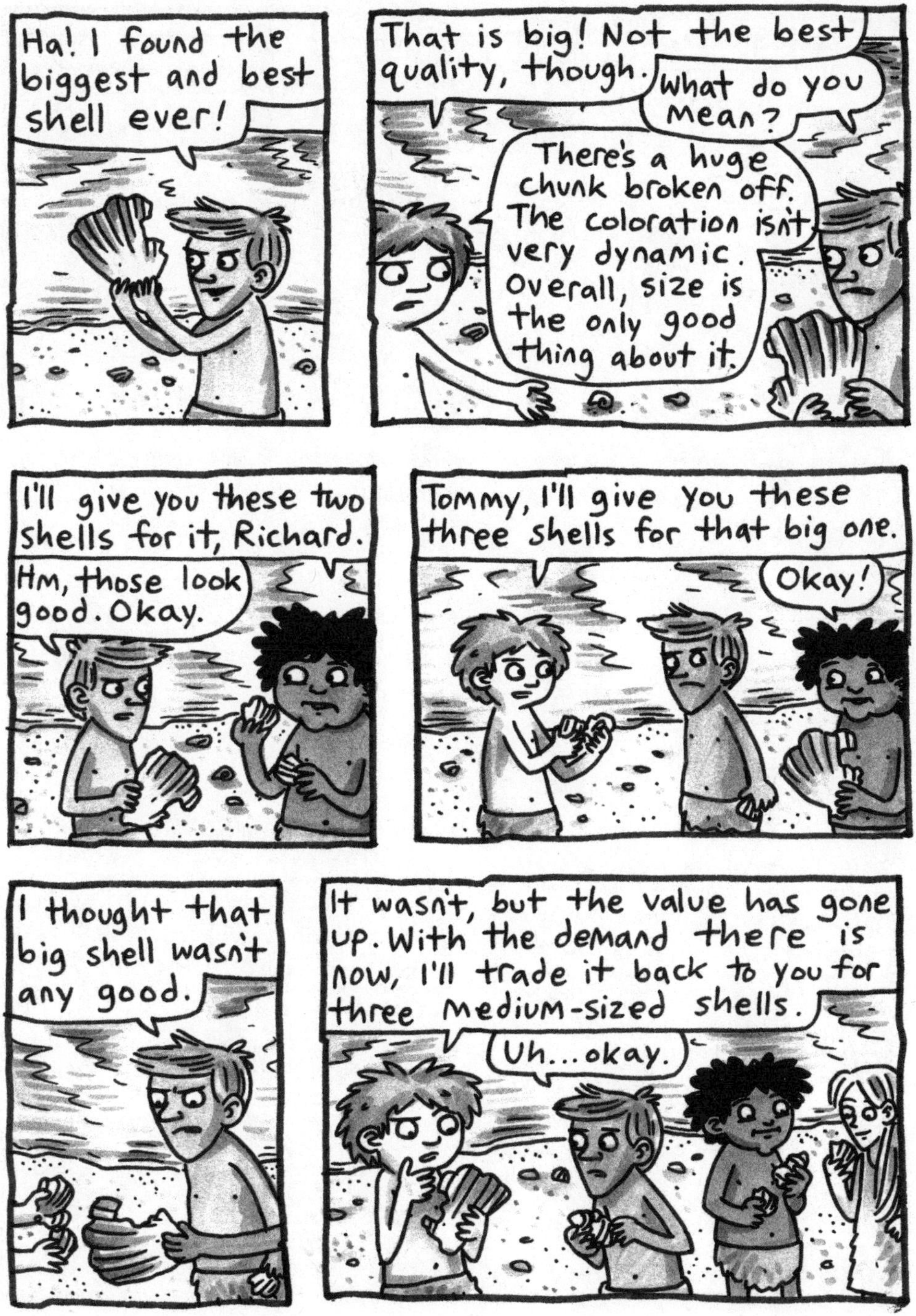
Ha! I found the biggest and best shell ever!
That is big! Not the best quality, though.
What do you mean?
There's a huge chunk broken off. The coloration isn't very dynamic. Overall, size is the only good thing about it.
I'll give you these two shells for it, Richard.
Hm, those look good. Okay.
Tommy, I'll give you these three shells for that big one.
Okay!
I thought that big shell wasn't any good.
It wasn't, but the value has gone up. With the demand there is now, I'll trade it back to you for three medium-sized shells.
Uh...okay.

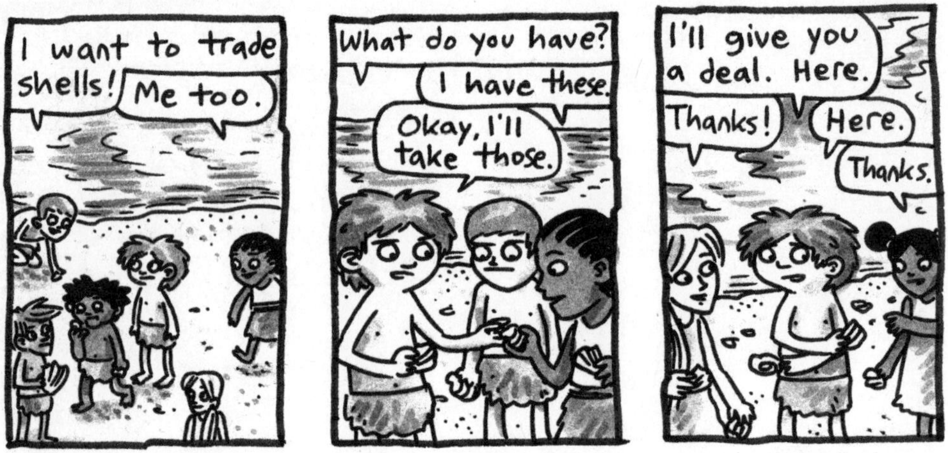
I want to trade shells!
Me too.
What do you have?
I have these.
Okay, I'll take those.
I'll give you a deal. Here.
Thanks!
Here.
Thanks.

Coins weren't invented until about 2,700 years ago, so early humans and Neanderthals would have had to barter — exchange goods or services for other goods or services.

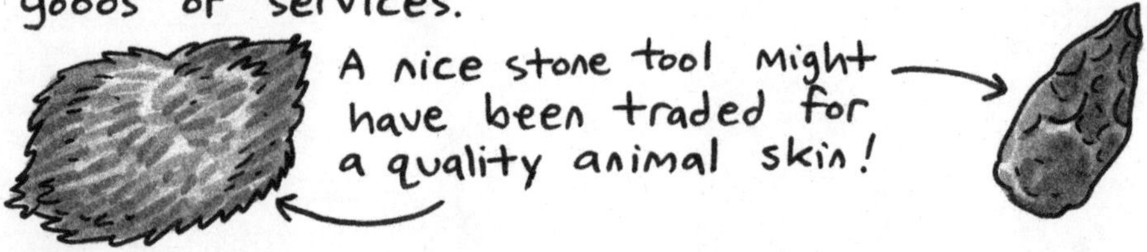
A nice stone tool might have been traded for a quality animal skin!

Trading could benefit both sides and lead to the spread of new ideas!

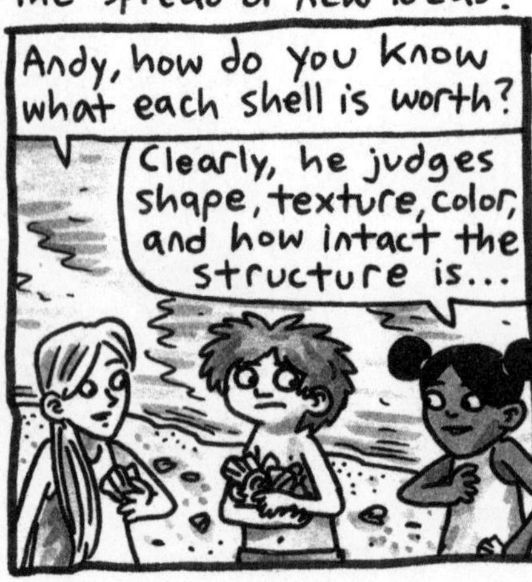
Andy, how do you know what each shell is worth?
Clearly, he judges shape, texture, color, and how intact the structure is...

However, the stock market did NOT originate from a prehistoric rock market.

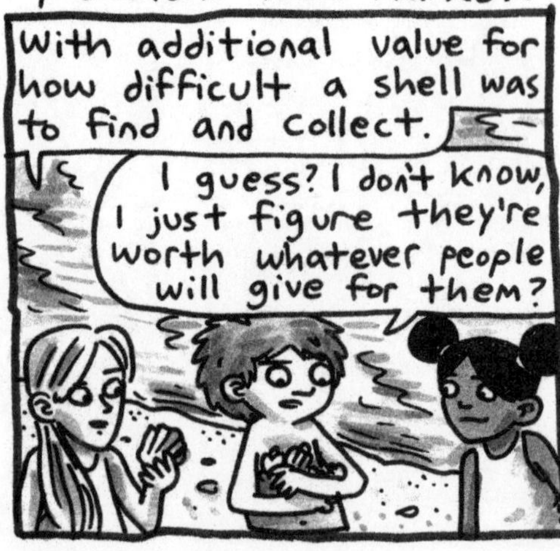
With additional value for how difficult a shell was to find and collect.
I guess? I don't know, I just figure they're worth whatever people will give for them?

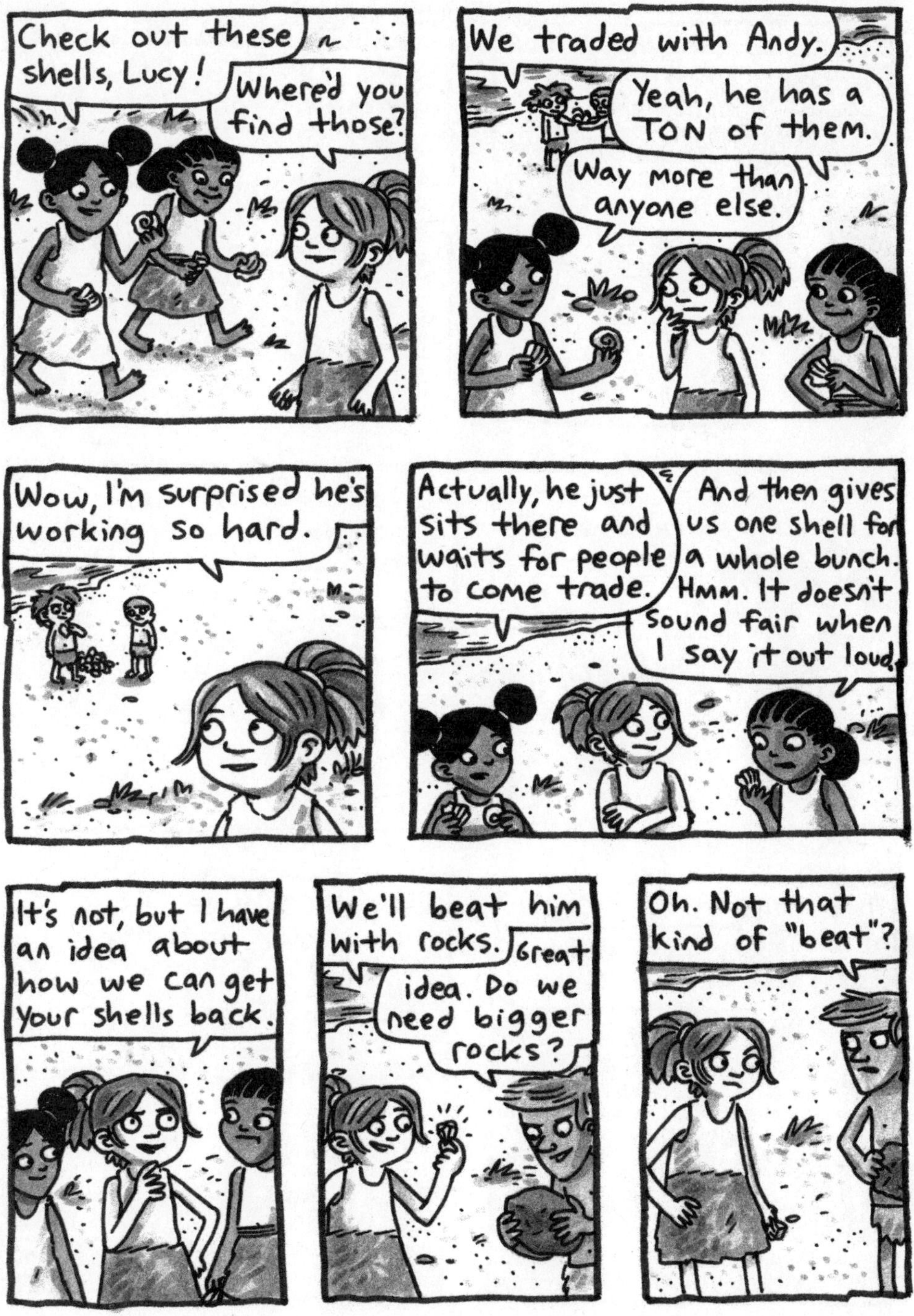
Check out these shells, Lucy!
Where'd you find those?
We traded with Andy.
Yeah, he has a TON of them.
Way more than anyone else.
Wow, I'm surprised he's working so hard.
Actually, he just sits there and waits for people to come trade.
And then gives us one shell for a whole bunch.
Hmm. It doesn't sound fair when I say it out loud.
It's not, but I have an idea about how we can get your shells back.
We'll beat him with rocks.
Great idea. Do we need bigger rocks?
Oh. Not that kind of "beat"?

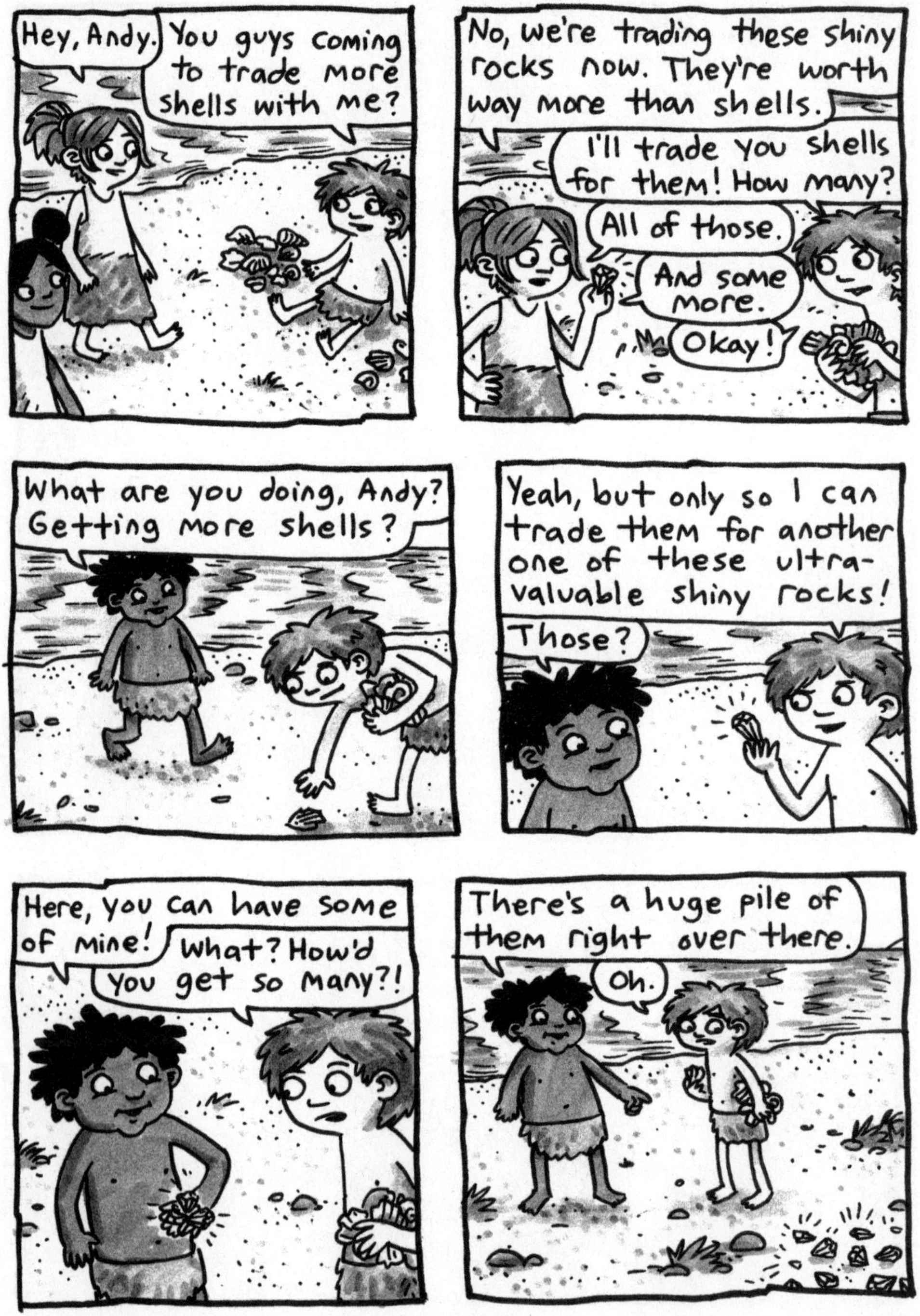
Hey, Andy.
You guys coming to trade more shells with me?
No, we're trading these shiny rocks now. They're worth way more than shells.
I'll trade you shells for them! How many?
All of those.
And some more.
Okay!
What are you doing, Andy? Getting more shells?
Yeah, but only so I can trade them for another one of these ultra-valuable shiny rocks!
Those?
Here, you can have some of mine!
What? How'd you get so many?!
There's a huge pile of them right over there.
Oh.

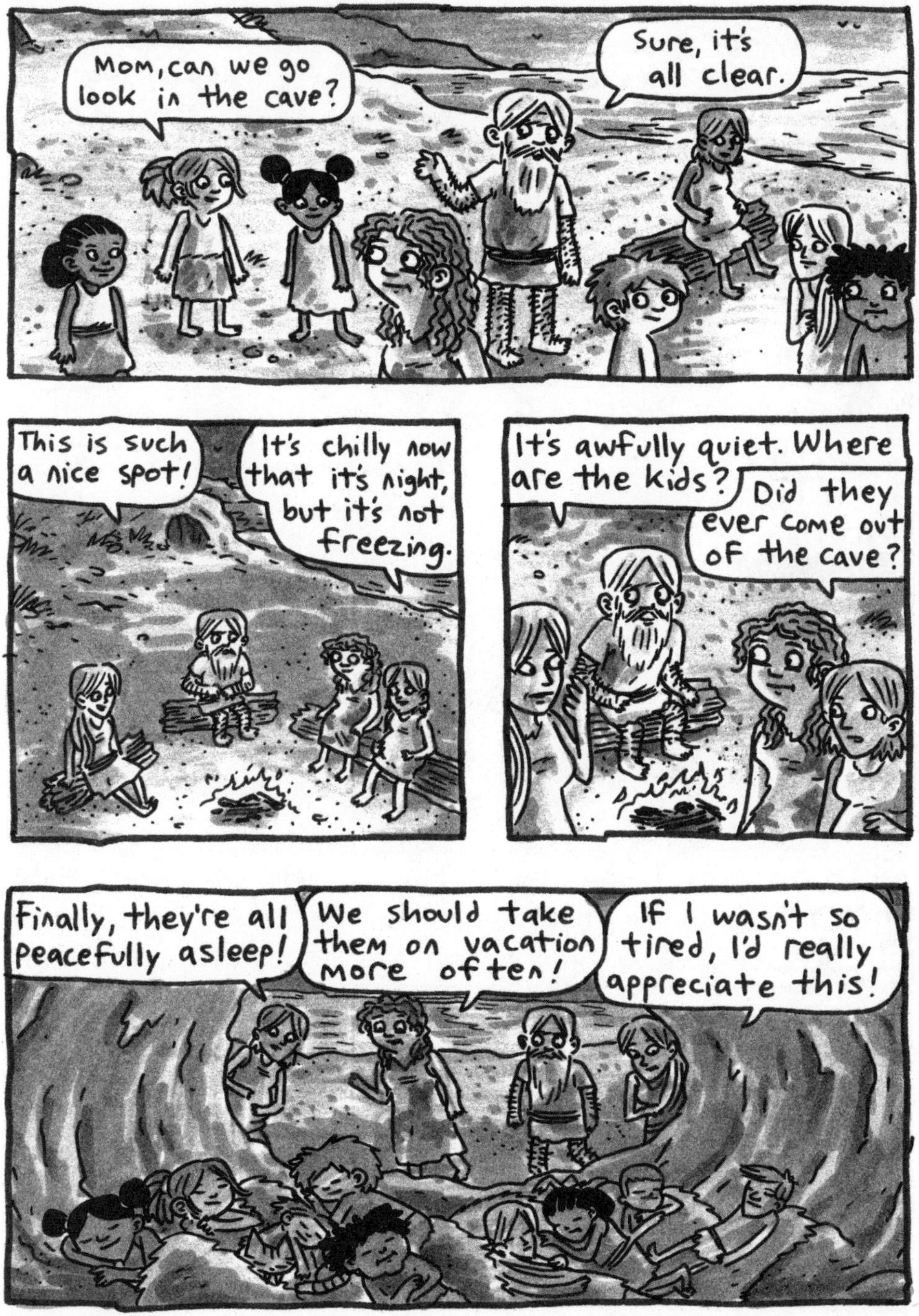
Mom, can we go look in the cave?
Sure, it's all clear.
This is such a nice spot!
It's chilly now that it's night, but it's not freezing.
It's awfully quiet. Where are the kids?
Did they ever come out of the cave?
Finally, they're all peacefully asleep!
We should take them on vacation more often!
If I wasn't so tired, I'd really appreciate this!

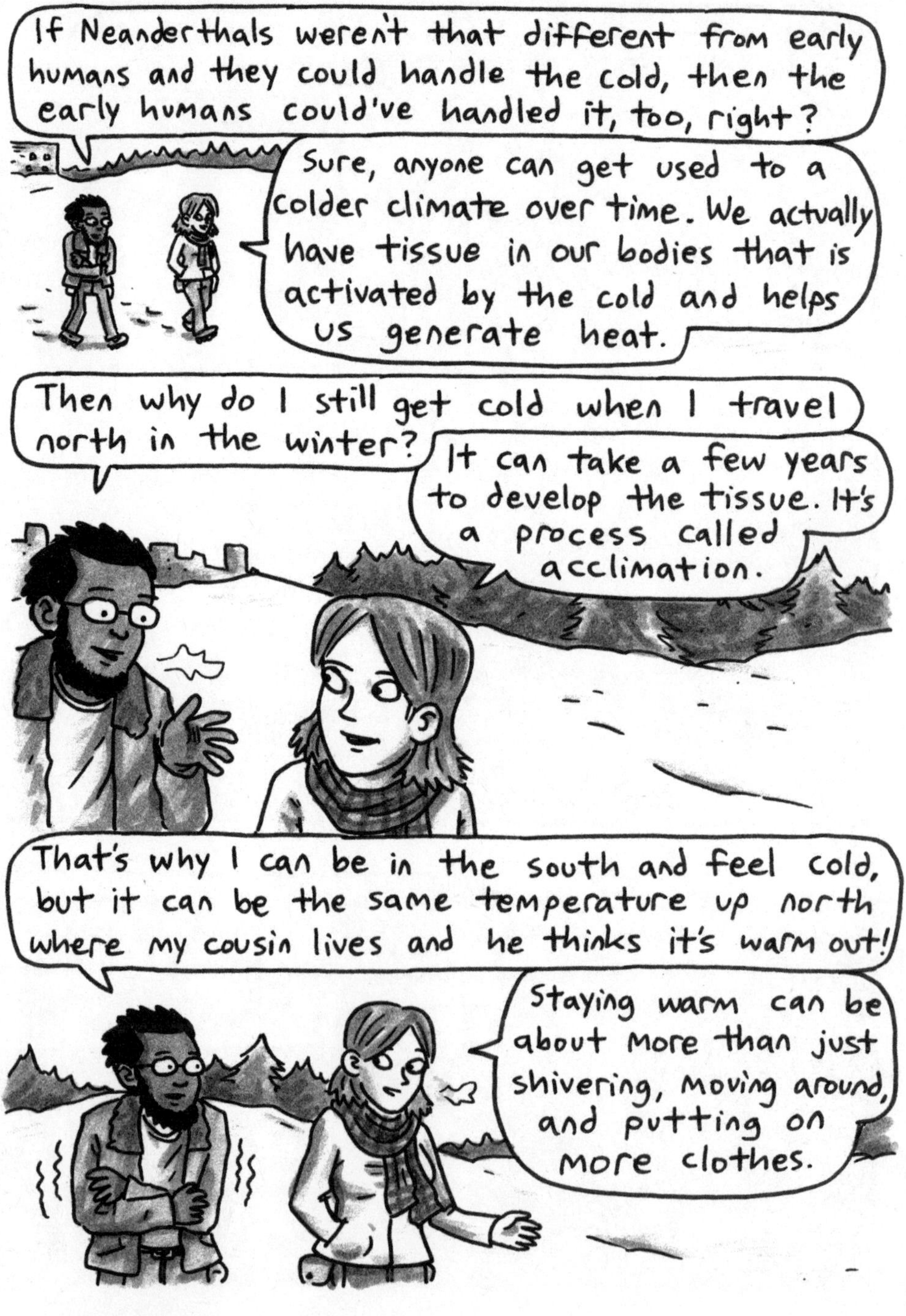
If Neanderthals weren't that different from early humans and they could handle the cold, then the early humans could've handled it, too, right?
Sure, anyone can get used to a colder climate over time. We actually have tissue in our bodies that is activated by the cold and helps us generate heat.
Then why do I still get cold when I travel north in the winter?
It can take a few years to develop the tissue. It's a process called acclimation.
That's why I can be in the south and feel cold, but it can be the same temperature up north where my cousin lives and he thinks it's warm out!
Staying warm can be about more than just shivering, moving around, and putting on more clothes.

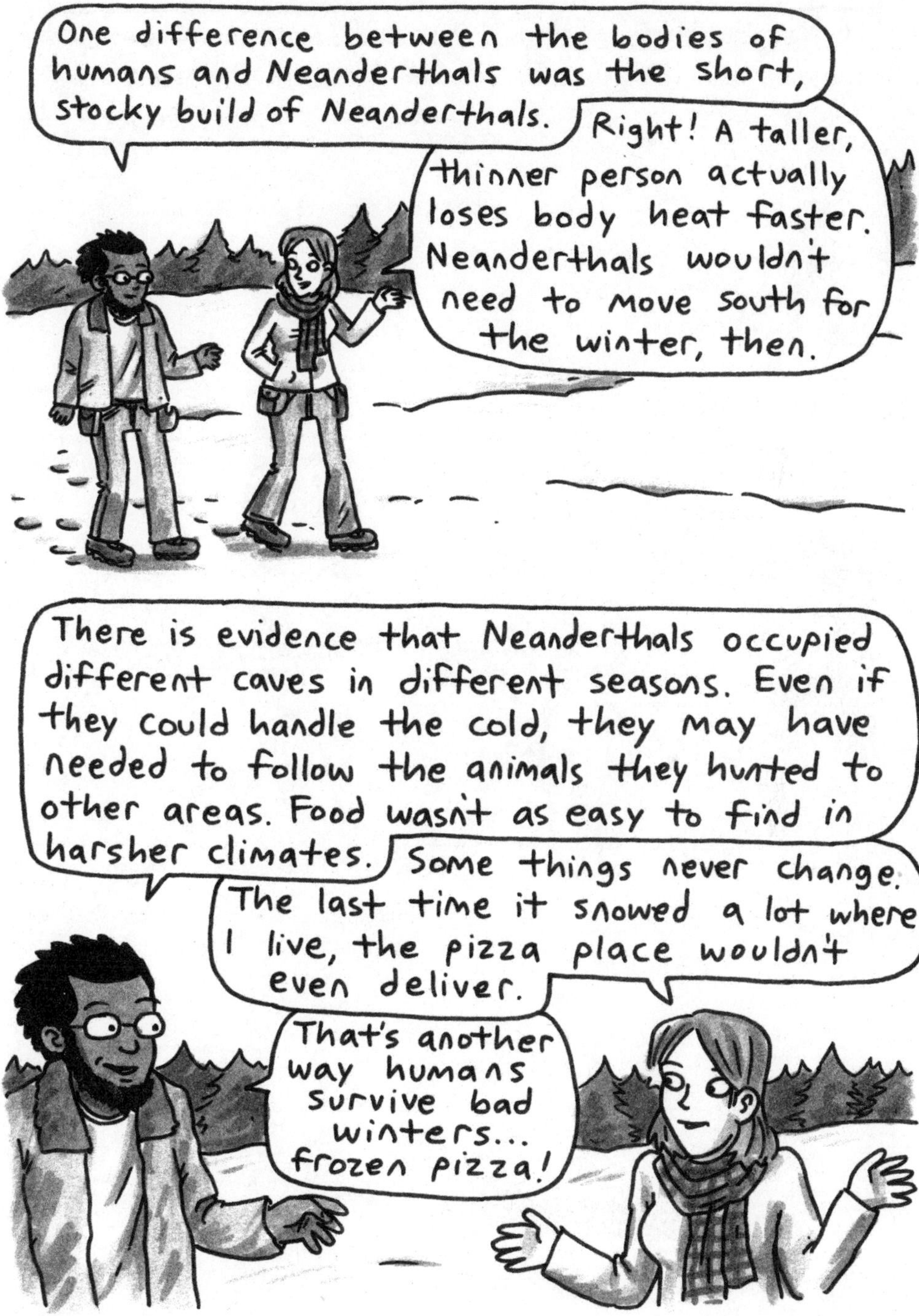
One difference between the bodies of humans and Neanderthals was the short, stocky build of Neanderthals.
Right! A taller, thinner person actually loses body heat faster. Neanderthals wouldn't need to move south for the winter, then.
There is evidence that Neanderthals occupied different caves in different seasons. Even if they could handle the cold, they may have needed to follow the animals they hunted to other areas. Food wasn't as easy to find in harsher climates.
Some things never change. The last time it snowed a lot where I live, the pizza place wouldn't even deliver.
That's another way humans survive bad winters... frozen pizza!

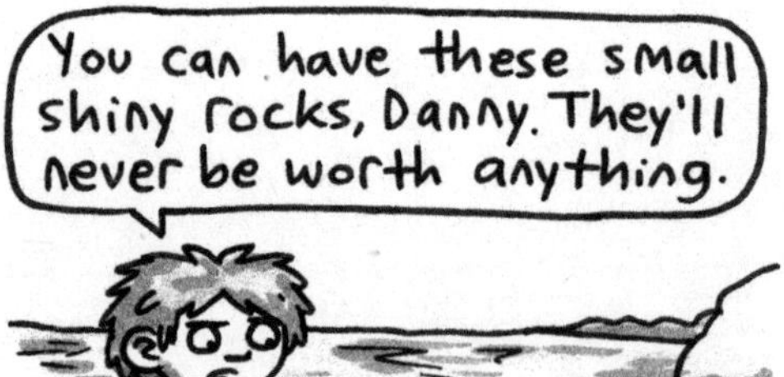
You can have these small shiny rocks, Danny. They'll never be worth anything.

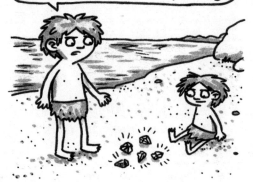

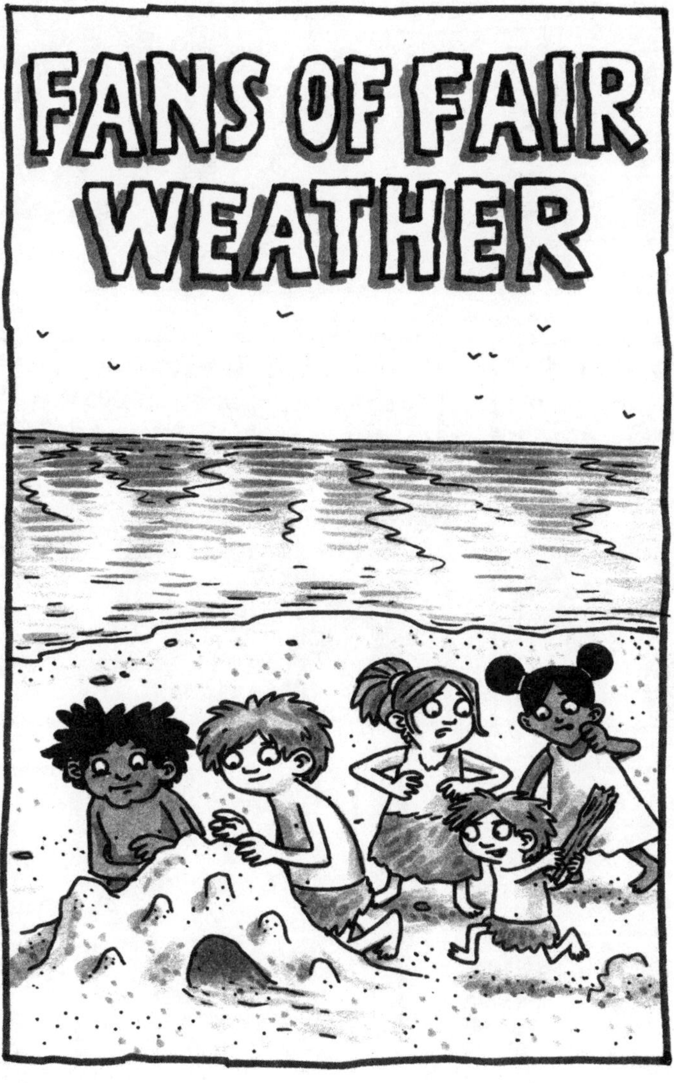
FANS OF FAIR WEATHER

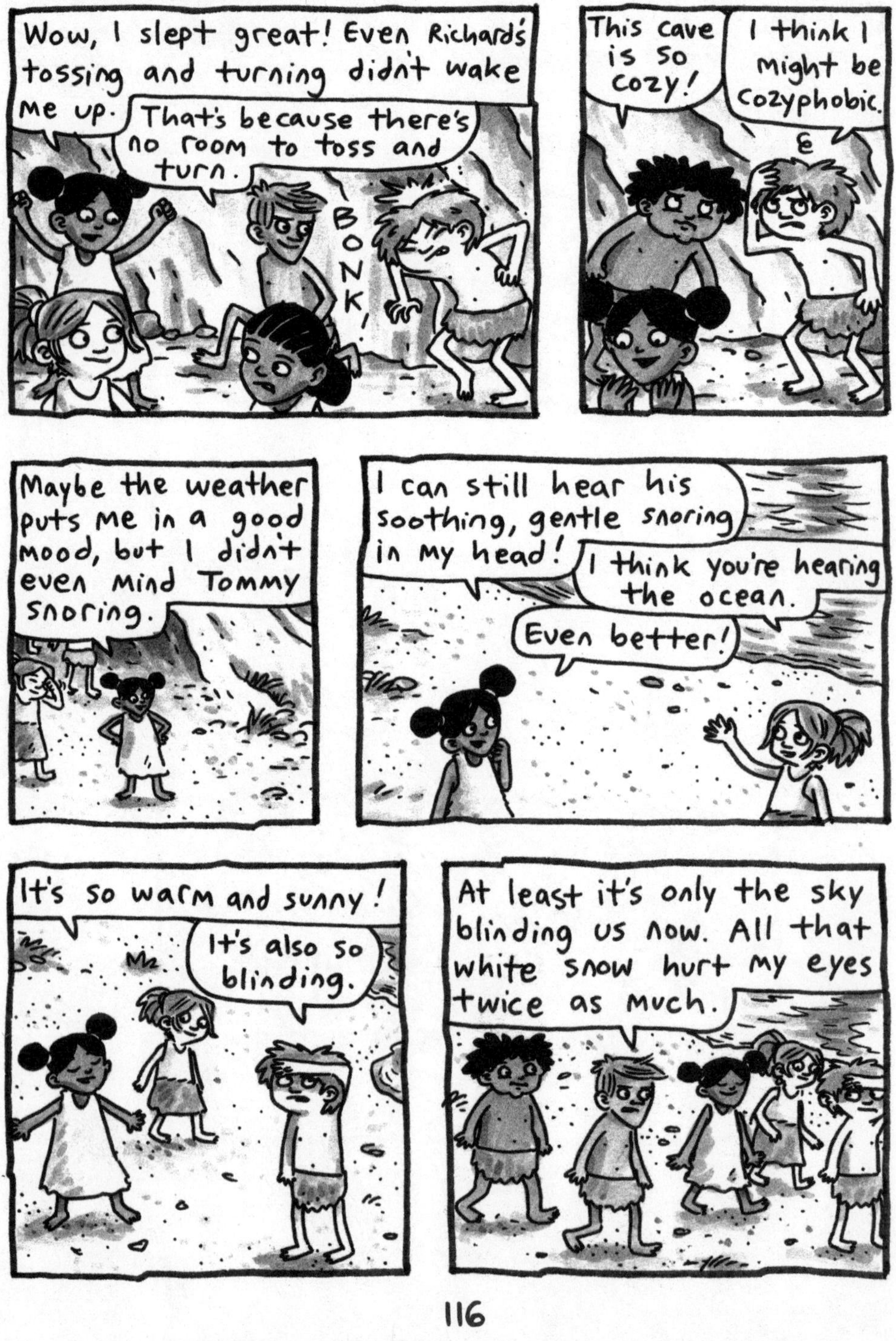
Wow, I slept great! Even Richard's tossing and turning didn't wake me up.
That's because there's no room to toss and turn.
BONK!
This cave is so cozy!
I think I might be cozyphobic.
Maybe the weather puts me in a good mood, but I didn't even mind Tommy snoring.
I can still hear his soothing, gentle snoring in my head!
I think you're hearing the ocean.
Even better!
It's so warm and sunny!
It's also so blinding.
At least it's only the sky blinding us now. All that white snow hurt my eyes twice as much.

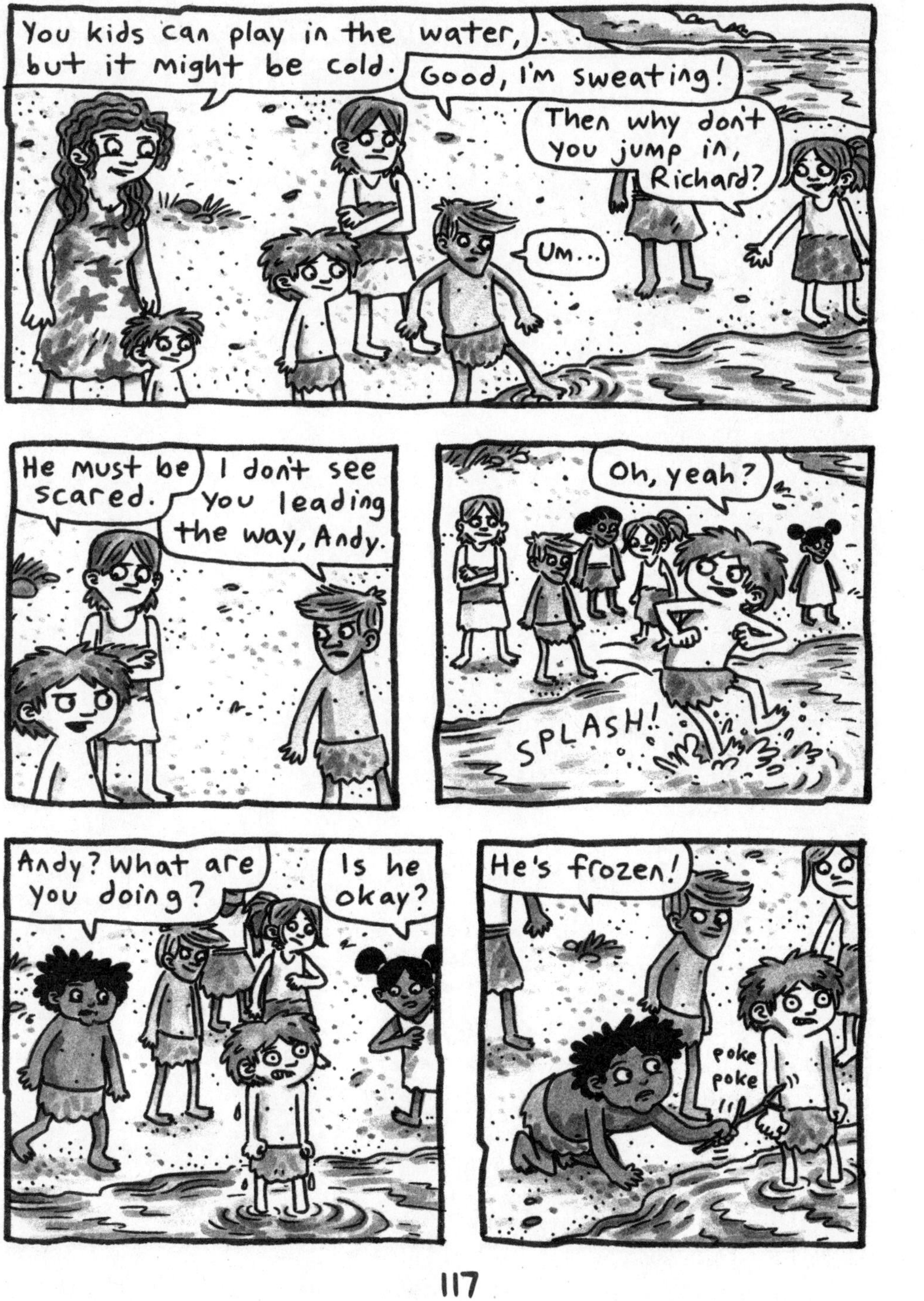
You kids can play in the water, but it might be cold.
Good, I'm sweating!
Then why don't you jump in, Richard?
Um...
He must be scared.
I don't see you leading the way, Andy.
Oh, yeah?
SPLASH!
Andy? What are you doing?
Is he okay?
He's frozen!
poke poke

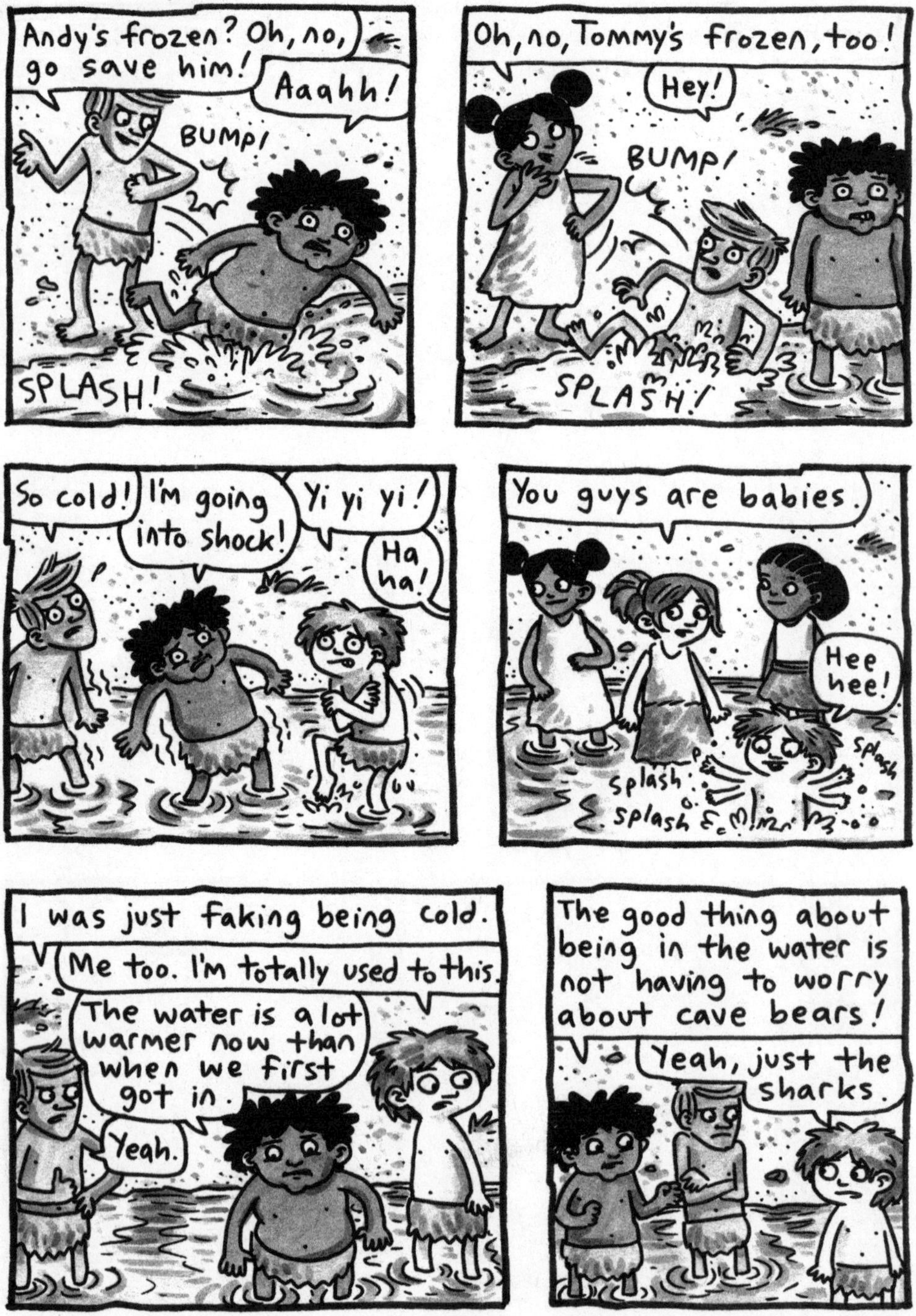
Andy's frozen? Oh, no, go save him!
Aaahh!
BUMP!
SPLASH!
Oh, no, Tommy's frozen, too!
Hey!
BUMP!
SPLASH!
So cold!
I'm going into shock!
Yi yi yi!
Ha ha!
You guys are babies.
Hee hee!
splash
splash
Splash
I was just faking being cold.
Me too. I'm totally used to this.
The water is a lot warmer now than when we first got in.
Yeah.
The good thing about being in the water is not having to worry about cave bears!
Yeah, just the sharks.

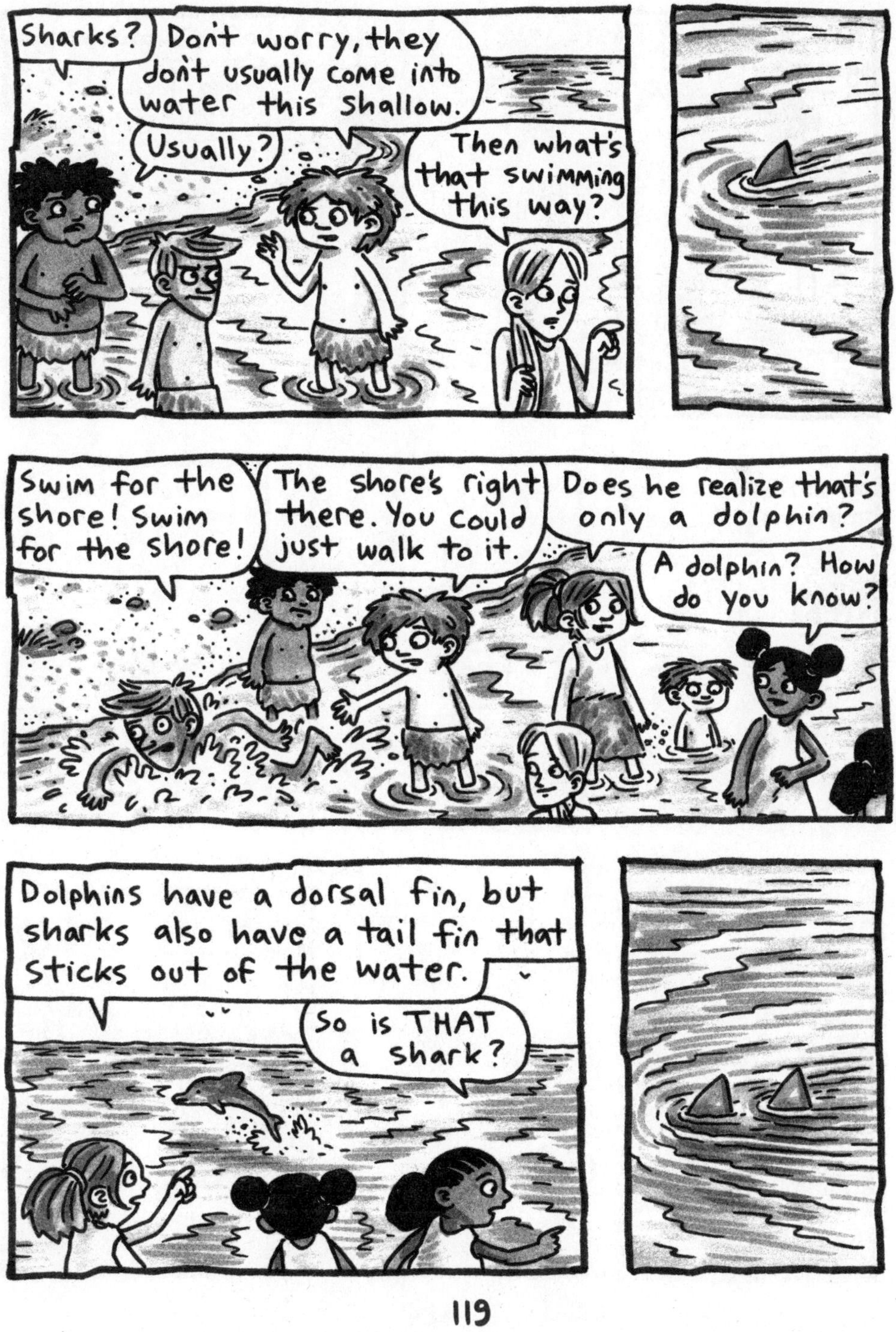
Sharks?
Don't worry, they don't usually come into water this shallow.
Usually?
Then what's that swimming this way?
Swim for the shore! Swim for the shore!
The shore's right there. You could just walk to it.
Does he realize that's only a dolphin?
A dolphin? How do you know?
Dolphins have a dorsal fin, but sharks also have a tail fin that sticks out of the water.
So is THAT a shark?

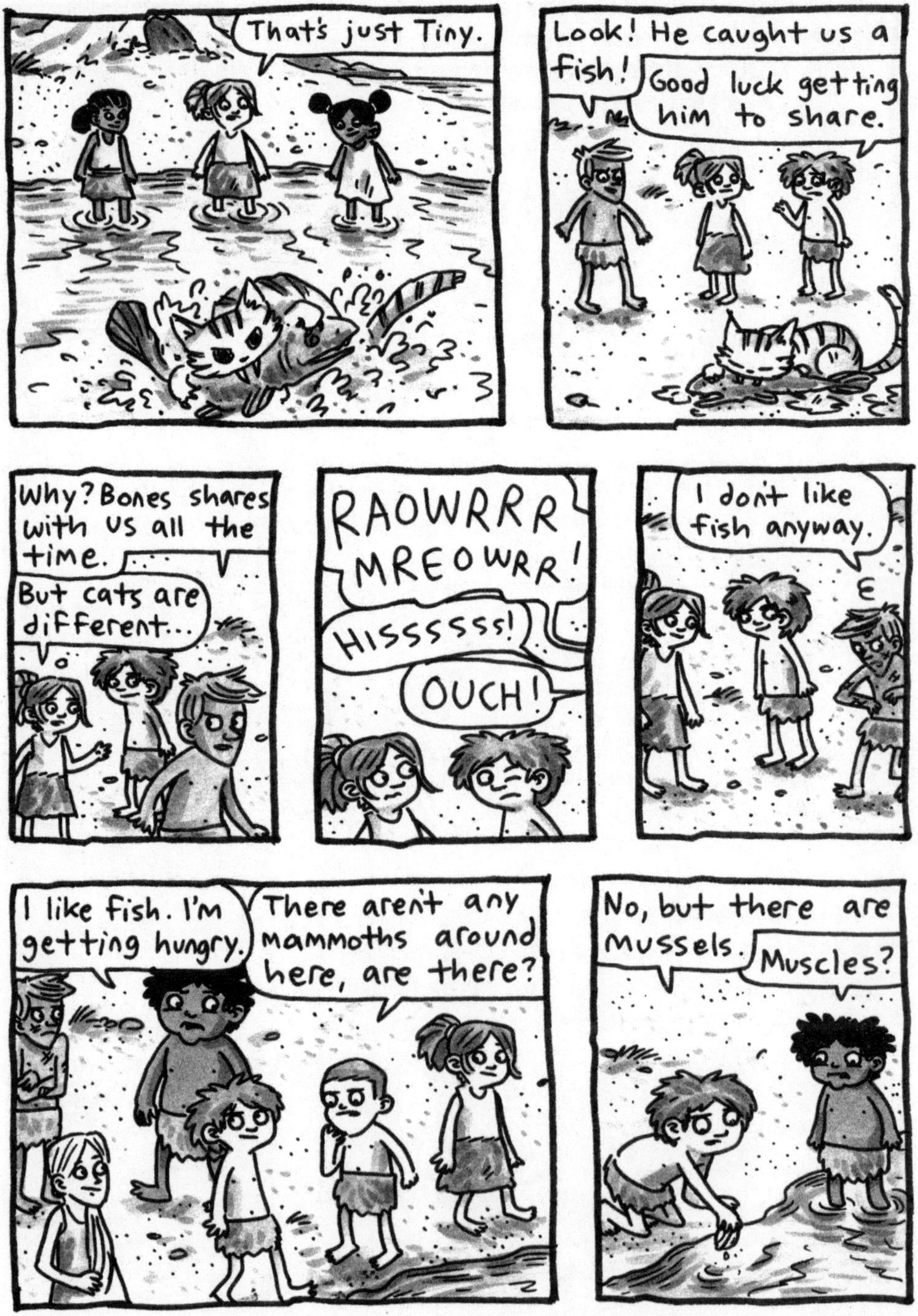
That's just Tiny.
Look! He caught us a fish!
Good luck getting him to share.
Why? Bones shares with us all the time.
But cats are different...
RAOWRRR MREOWRR!
HISSSSSS!
OUCH!
I don't like fish anyway.
I like fish. I'm getting hungry.
There aren't any mammoths around here, are there?
No, but there are mussels.
Muscles?

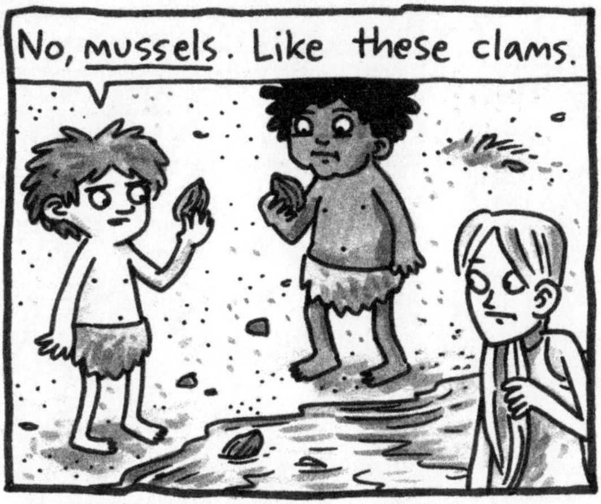
No, mussels. Like these clams.

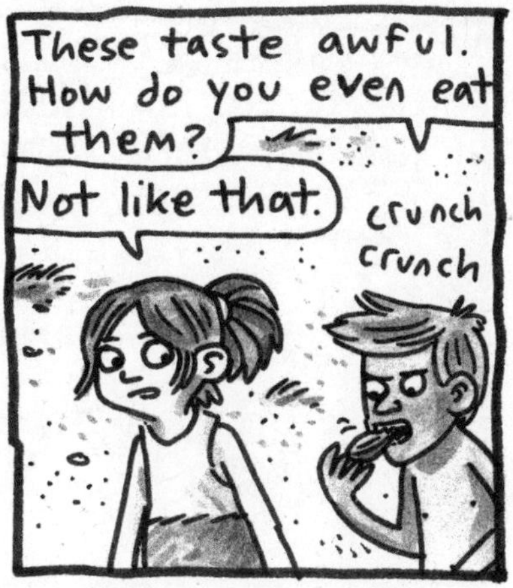
These taste awful. How do you even eat them?
Not like that.
crunch crunch

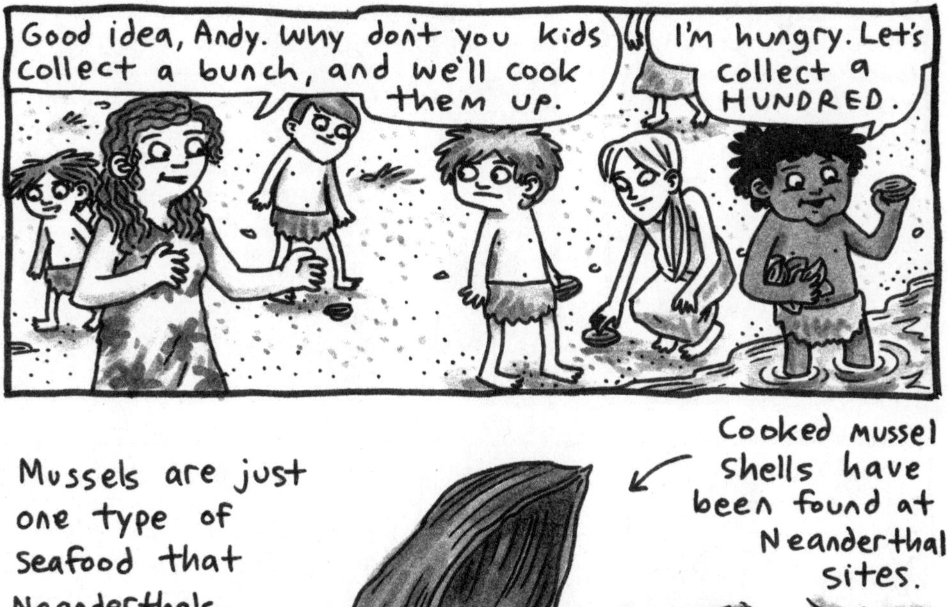
Good idea, Andy. Why don't you kids collect a bunch, and we'll cook them up.
I'm hungry. Let's collect a HUNDRED.

Mussels are just one type of seafood that Neanderthals ate!

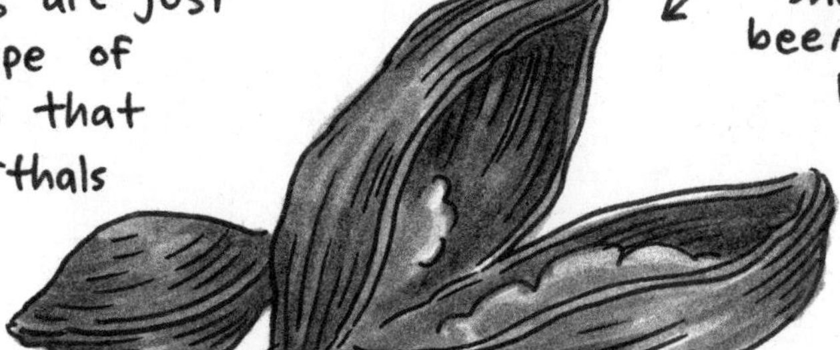

Cooked mussel shells have been found at Neanderthal sites.

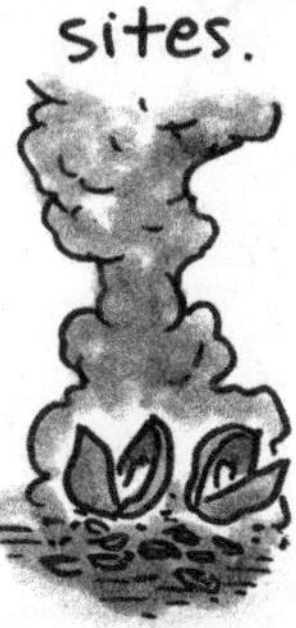

Mussels were placed on embers of fires to open them up for eating.

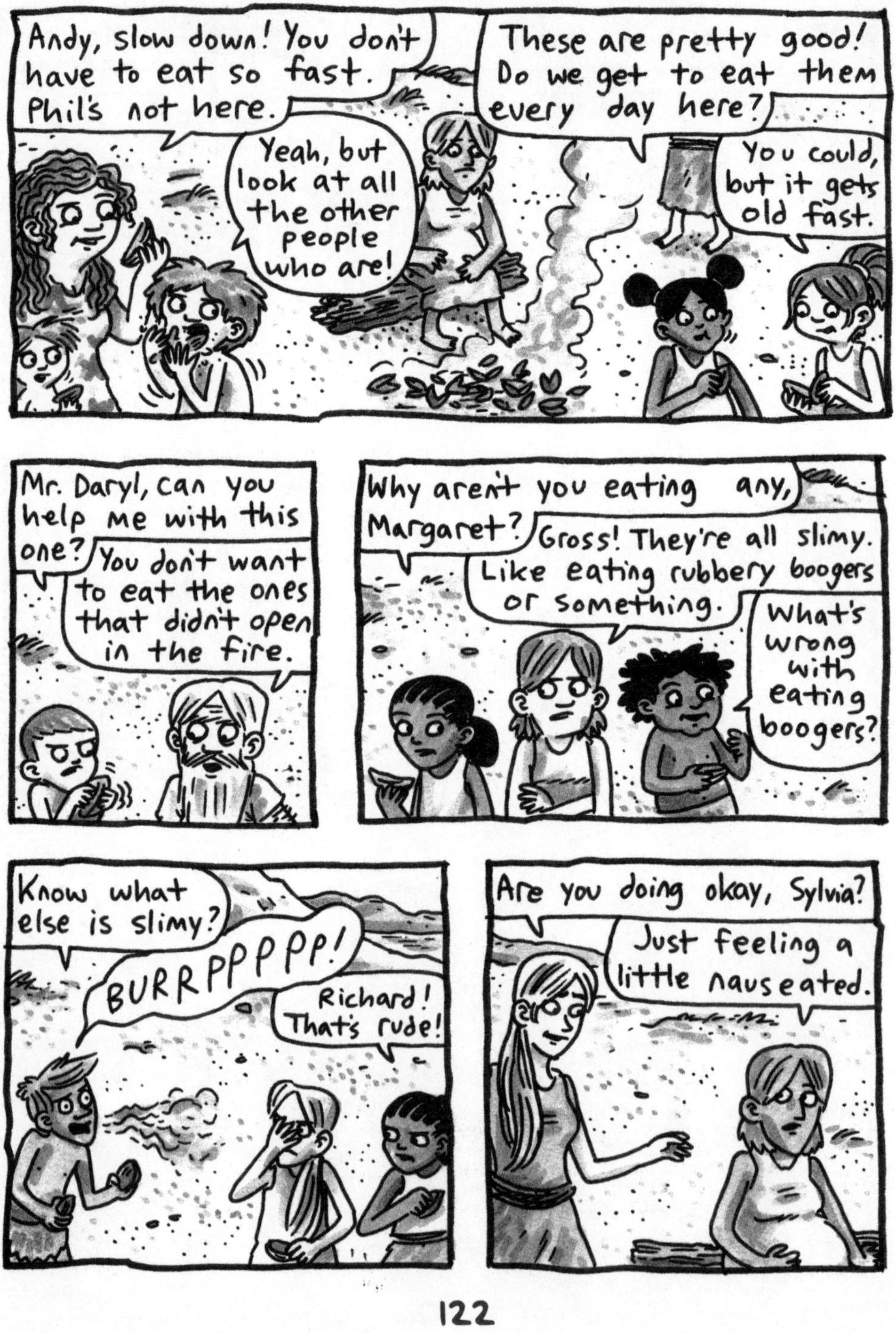
Andy, slow down! You don't have to eat so fast. Phil's not here.
Yeah, but look at all the other people who are!
These are pretty good! Do we get to eat them every day here?
You could, but it gets old fast.
Mr. Daryl, can you help me with this one?
You don't want to eat the ones that didn't open in the fire.
Why aren't you eating any, Margaret?
Gross! They're all slimy. Like eating rubbery boogers or something.
What's wrong with eating boogers?
Know what else is slimy?
BURRPPPPP!
Richard! That's rude!
Are you doing okay, Sylvia?
Just feeling a little nauseated.

I'm so huge and uncomfortable.
And hot.
I have a backache.
And a headache.
And an ache-ache.
I wonder why.
Stop kicking sand on me.
Ouch!
Look, Danny is throwing up!
Hey!
Oops!
Okay, kids, lunch is over. Go play!
But we ARE playing.
Farther!
Where do they want us to play, out in the water?
What are we going to do, anyway?

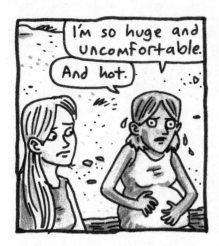

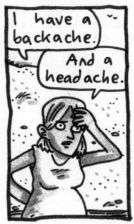

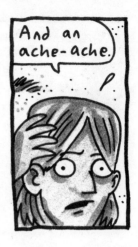

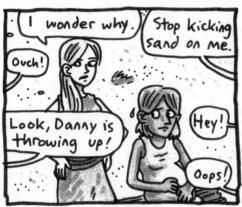

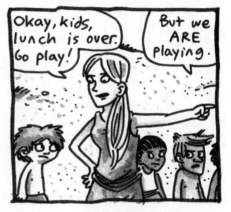

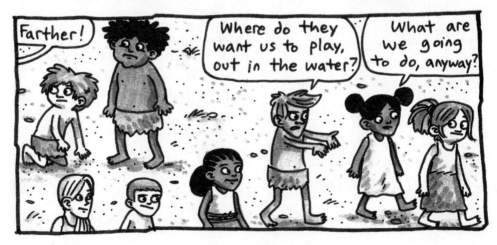

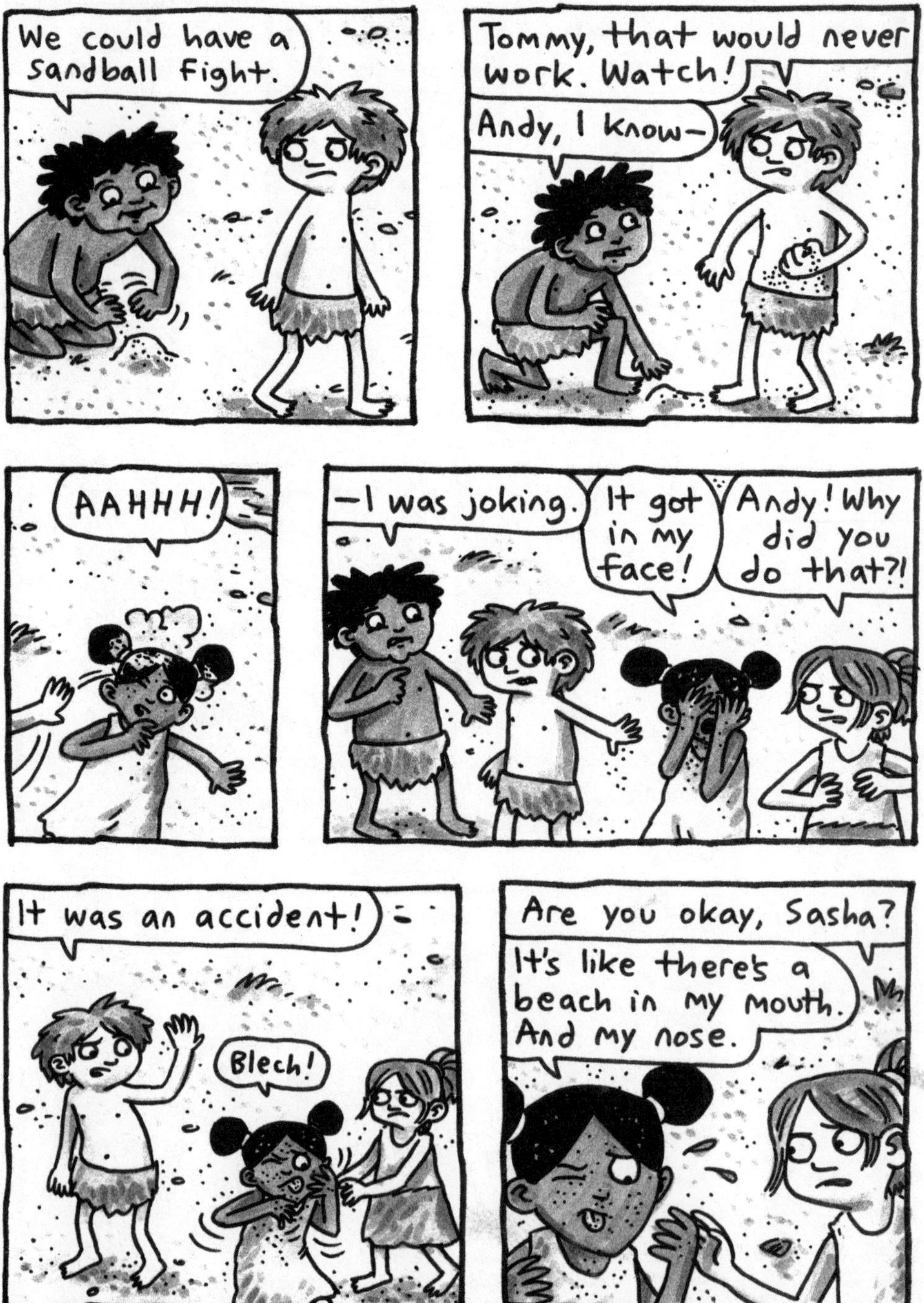
We could have a sandball fight.
Tommy, that would never work. Watch!
Andy, I know—
AAHHH!
—I was joking.
It got in my face!
Andy! Why did you do that?!
It was an accident!
Blech!
Are you okay, Sasha?
It's like there's a beach in my mouth. And my nose.

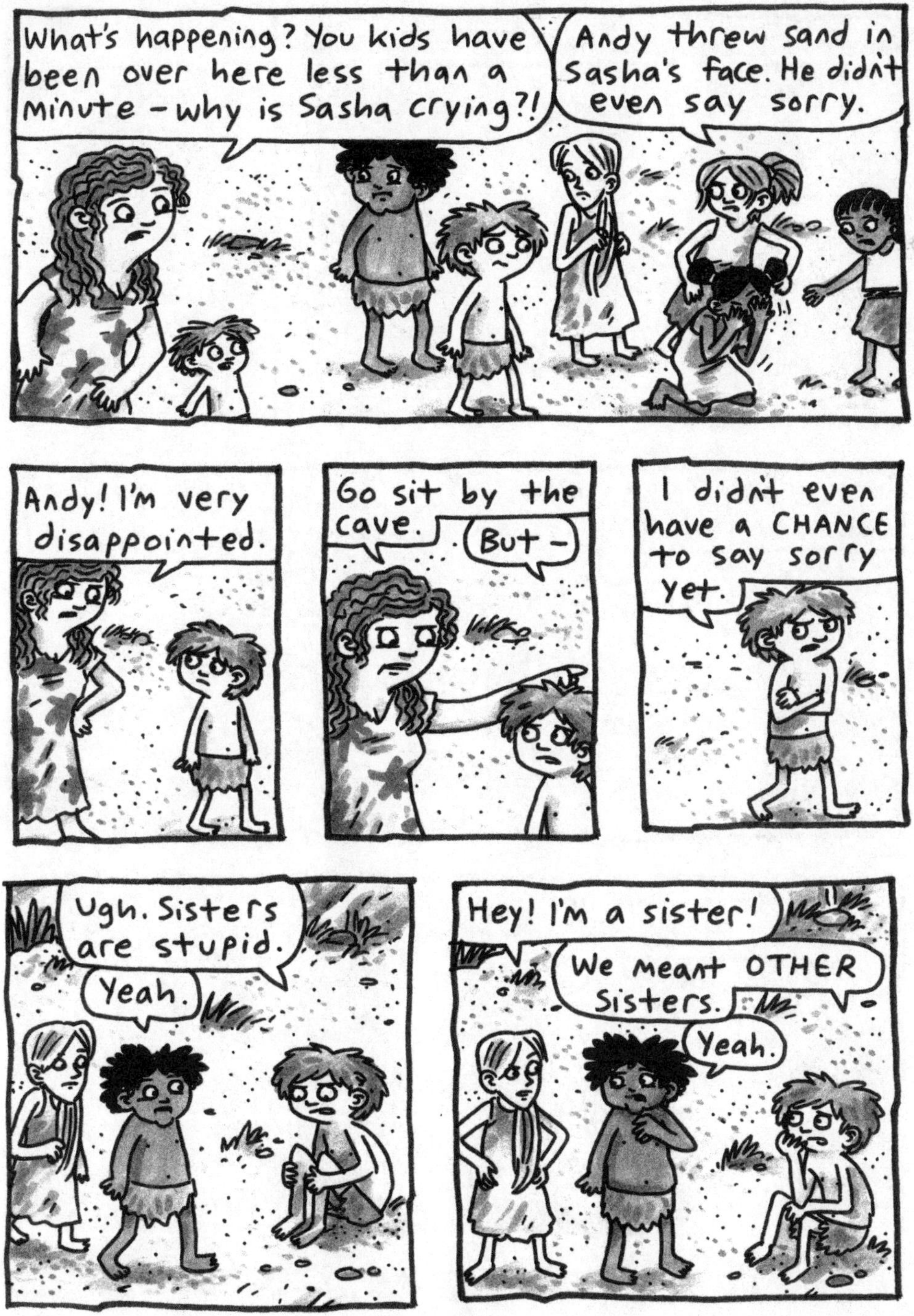
What's happening? You kids have been over here less than a minute - why is Sasha crying?!
Andy threw sand in Sasha's face. He didn't even say sorry.
Andy! I'm very disappointed.
Go sit by the cave.
But -
I didn't even have a CHANCE to say sorry yet.
Ugh. Sisters are stupid.
Yeah.
Hey! I'm a sister!
We meant OTHER sisters.
Yeah.

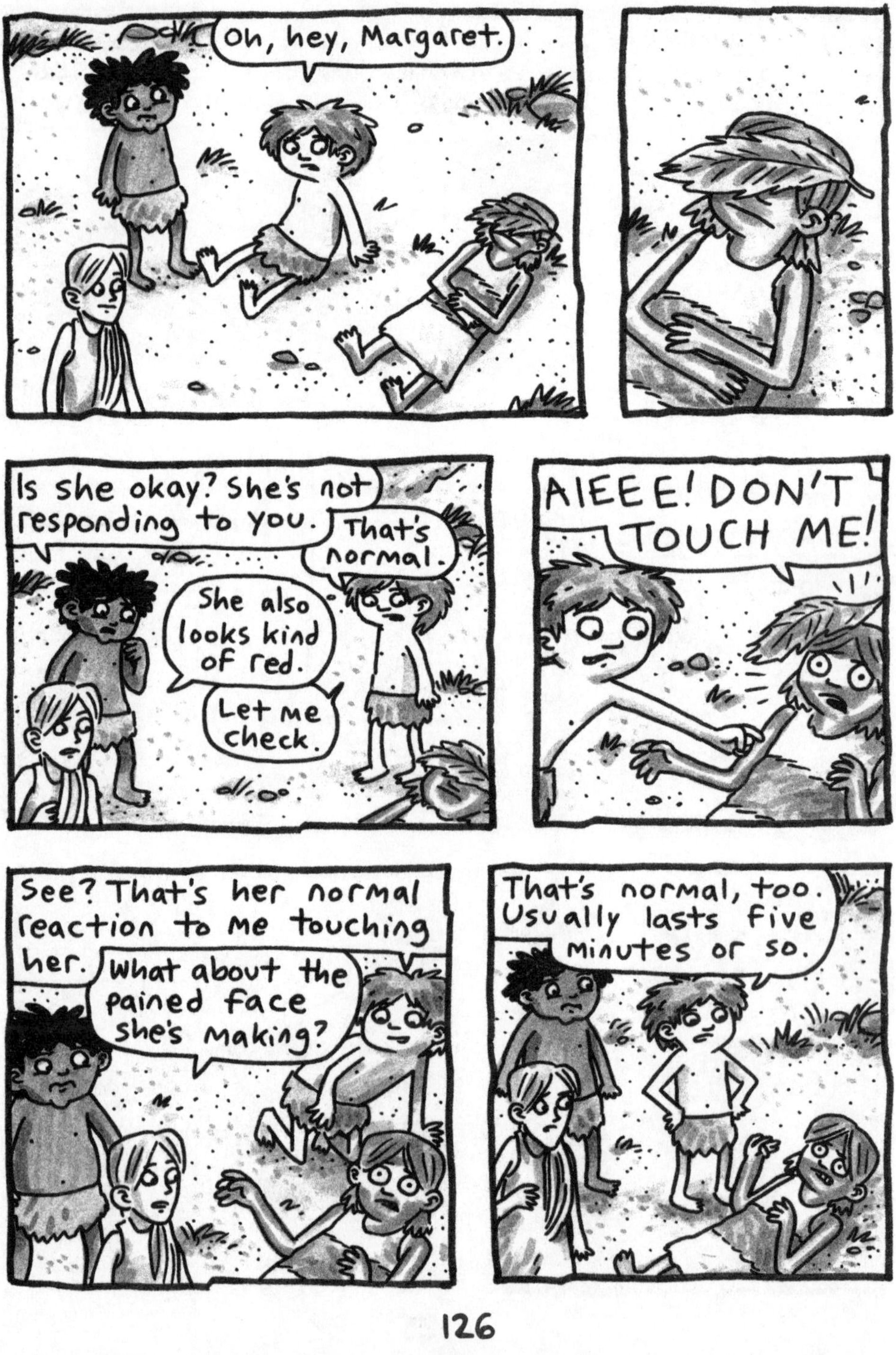
Oh, hey, Margaret.
Is she okay? She's not responding to you.
That's normal.
She also looks kind of red.
Let me check.
AIEEE! DON'T TOUCH ME!
See? That's her normal reaction to me touching her.
What about the pained face she's making?
That's normal, too. Usually lasts five minutes or so.

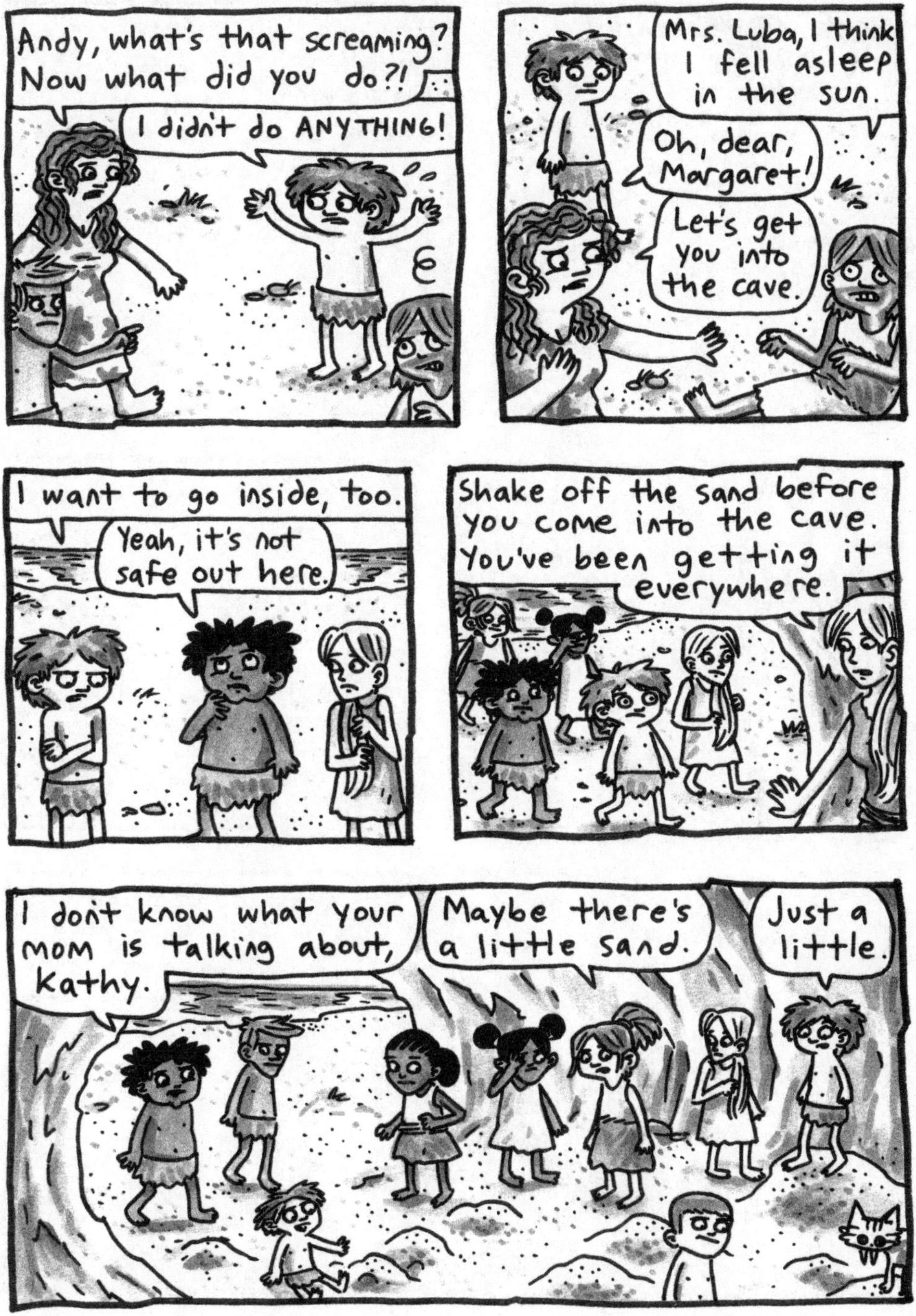
Andy, what's that screaming? Now what did you do?!
I didn't do ANYTHING!
Mrs. Luba, I think I fell asleep in the sun.
Oh, dear, Margaret!
Let's get you into the cave.
I want to go inside, too.
Yeah, it's not safe out here.
Shake off the sand before you come into the cave. You've been getting it everywhere.
I don't know what your mom is talking about, Kathy.
Maybe there's a little sand.
Just a little.

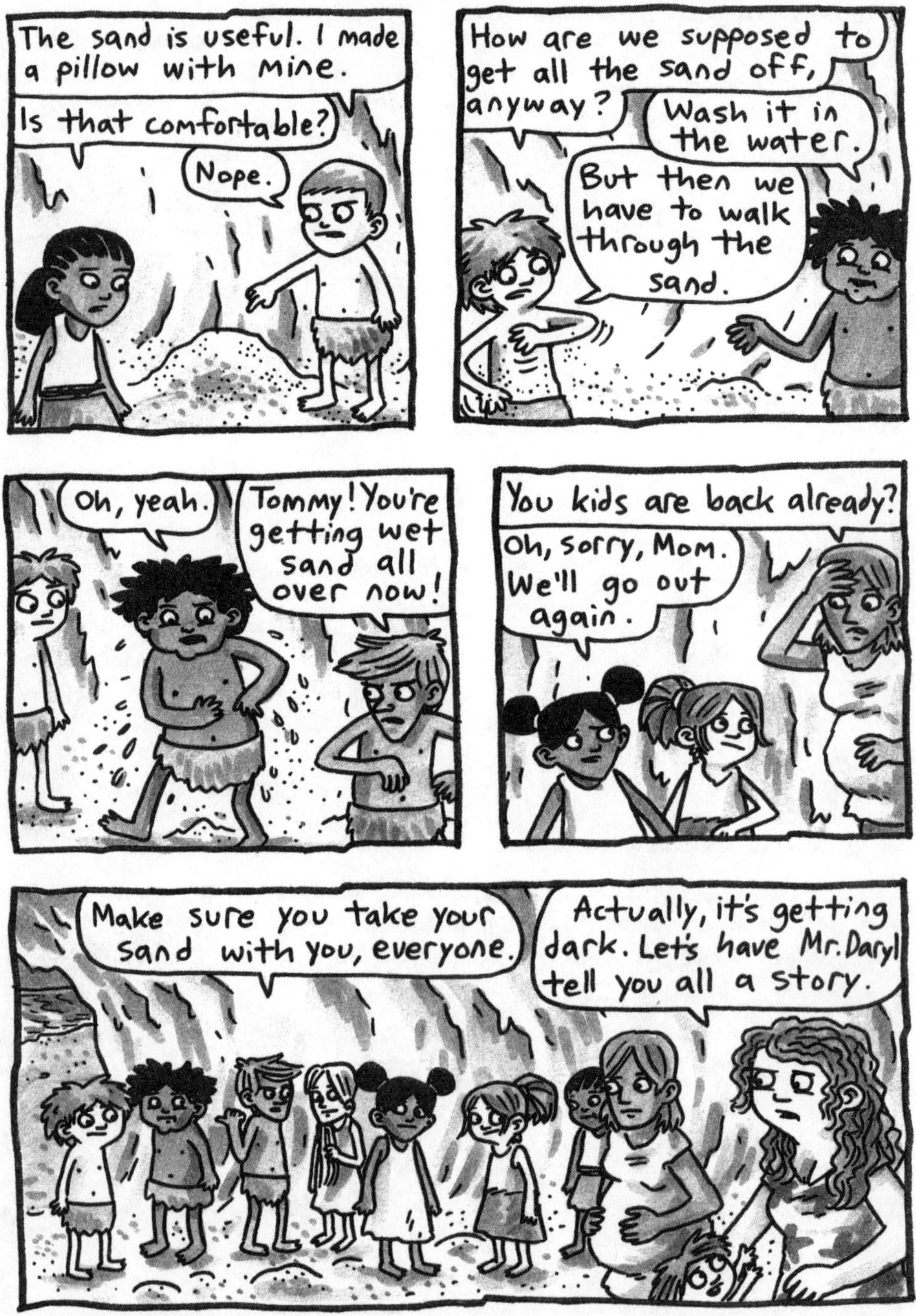
The sand is useful. I made a pillow with mine.
Is that comfortable?
Nope.
How are we supposed to get all the sand off, anyway?
Wash it in the water.
But then we have to walk through the sand.
Oh, yeah.
Tommy! You're getting wet sand all over now!
You kids are back already?
Oh, sorry, Mom. We'll go out again.
Make sure you take your sand with you, everyone.
Actually, it's getting dark. Let's have Mr. Daryl tell you all a story.

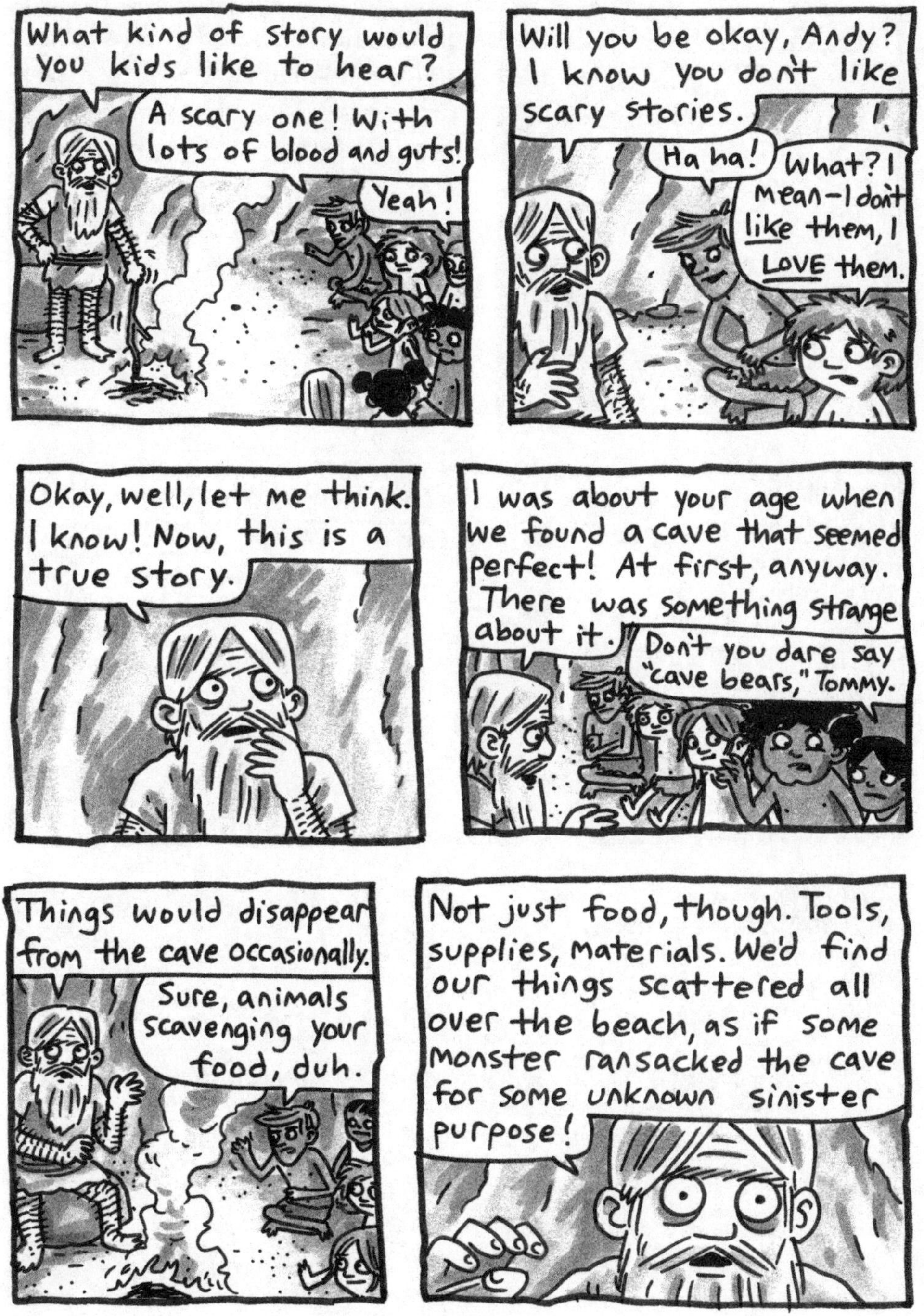
What kind of story would you kids like to hear?
A scary one! With lots of blood and guts!
Yeah!
Will you be okay, Andy? I know you don't like scary stories.
Ha ha!
What?! I mean—I don't like them, I LOVE them.
Okay, well, let me think. I know! Now, this is a true story.
I was about your age when we found a cave that seemed perfect! At first, anyway. There was something strange about it.
Don't you dare say "cave bears," Tommy.
Things would disappear from the cave occasionally.
Sure, animals scavenging your food, duh.
Not just food, though. Tools, supplies, materials. We'd find our things scattered all over the beach, as if some monster ransacked the cave for some unknown sinister purpose!

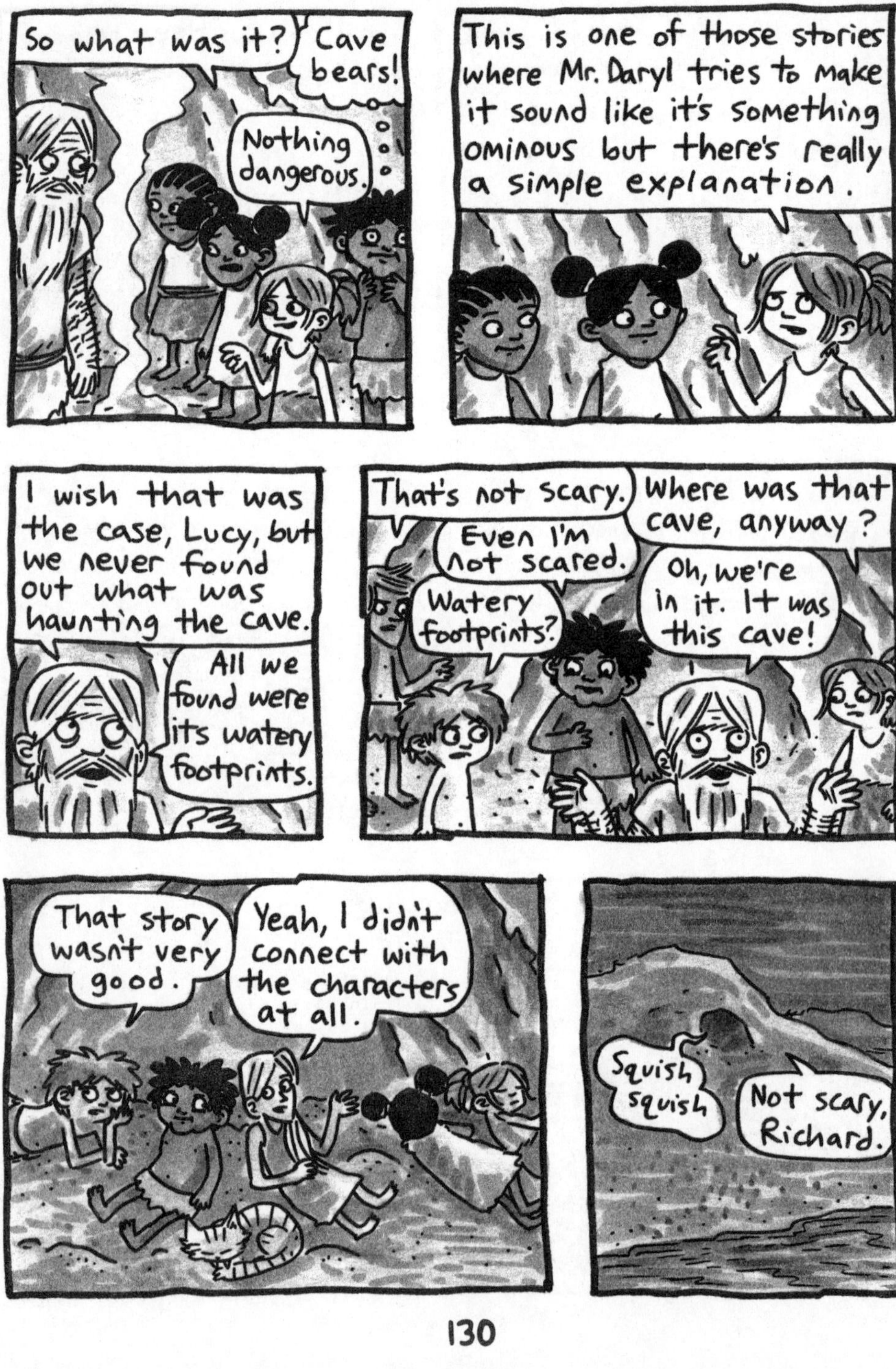
So what was it?
Cave bears!
Nothing dangerous.
This is one of those stories where Mr. Daryl tries to make it sound like it's something ominous but there's really a simple explanation.
I wish that was the case, Lucy, but we never found out what was haunting the cave.
All we found were its watery footprints.
That's not scary.
Even I'm not scared.
Watery footprints?
Where was that cave, anyway?
Oh, we're in it. It was this cave!
That story wasn't very good.
Yeah, I didn't connect with the characters at all.
Squish squish
Not scary, Richard.

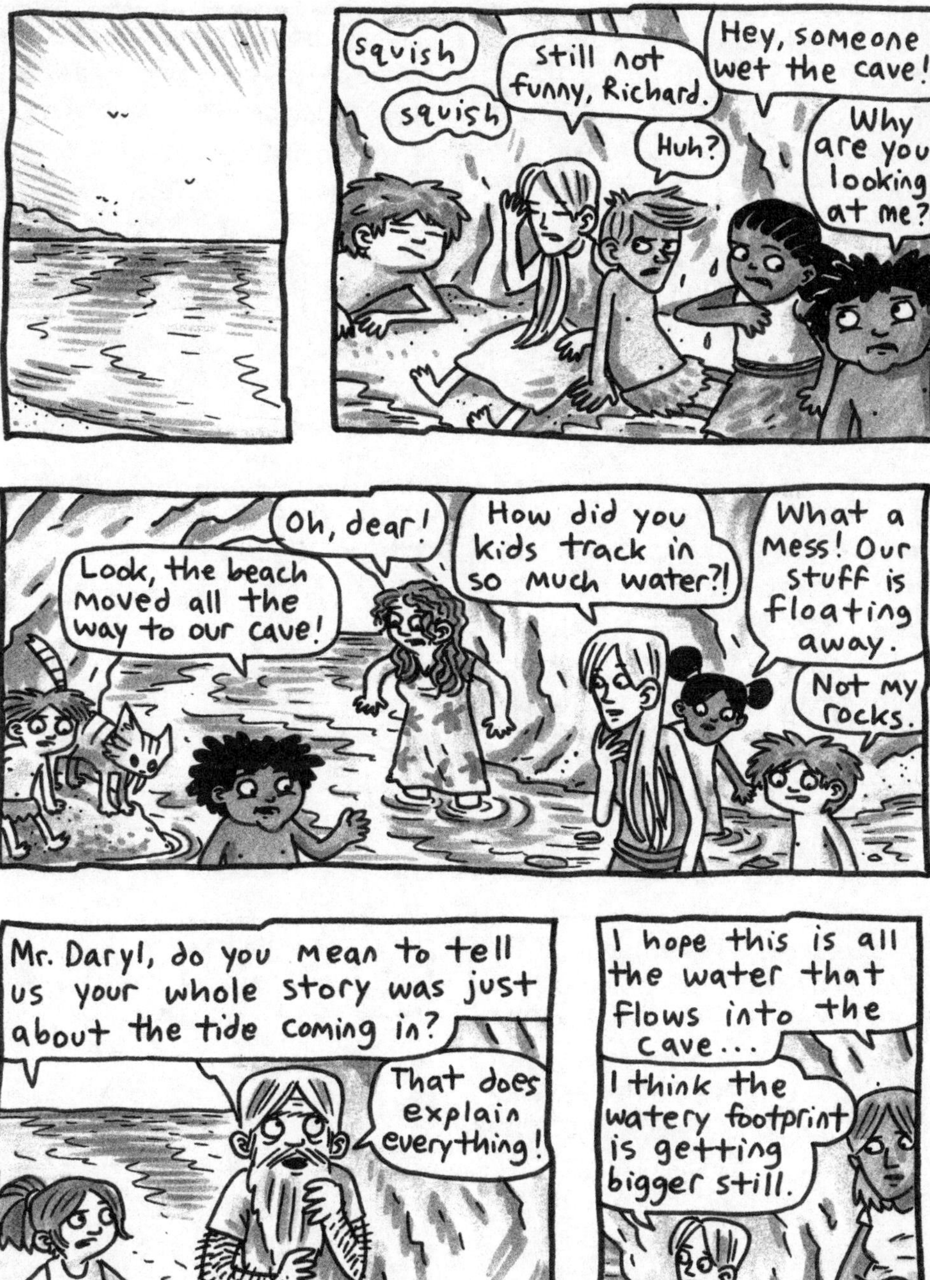
squish
squish
Still not funny, Richard.
Hey, someone wet the cave!
Huh?
Why are you looking at me?
Look, the beach moved all the way to our cave!
Oh, dear!
How did you kids track in so much water?!
What a mess! Our stuff is floating away.
Not my rocks.
Mr. Daryl, do you mean to tell us your whole story was just about the tide coming in?
That does explain everything!
I hope this is all the water that flows into the cave...
I think the watery footprint is getting bigger still.

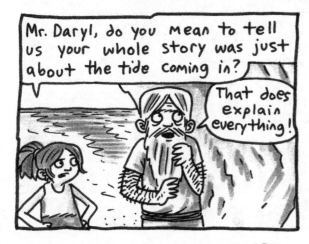

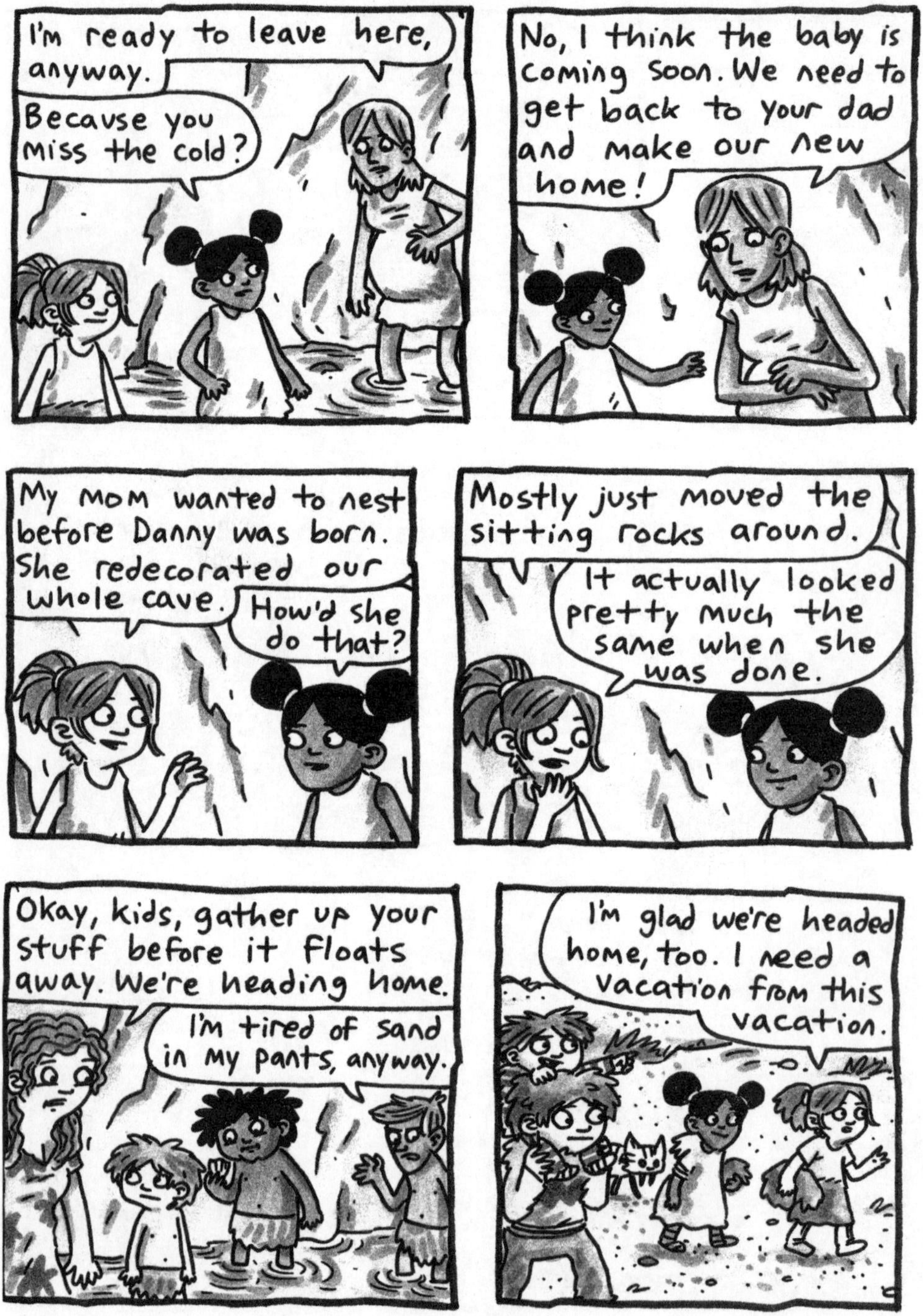
I'm ready to leave here, anyway.
Because you miss the cold?
No, I think the baby is coming soon. We need to get back to your dad and make our new home!
My mom wanted to nest before Danny was born. She redecorated our whole cave.
How'd she do that?
Mostly just moved the sitting rocks around.
It actually looked pretty much the same when she was done.
Okay, kids, gather up your stuff before it floats away. We're heading home.
I'm tired of sand in my pants, anyway.
I'm glad we're headed home, too. I need a vacation from this vacation.

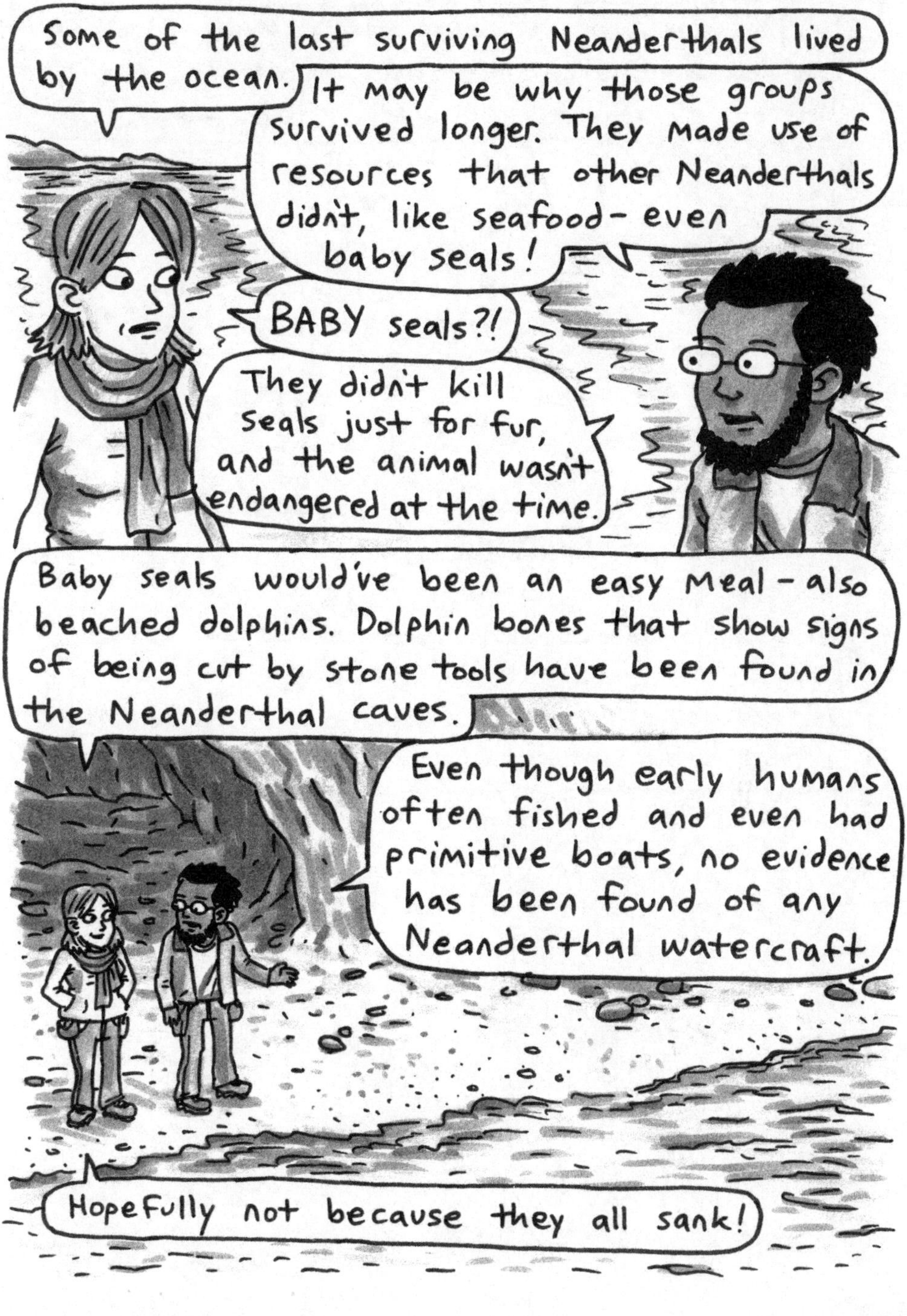
Some of the last surviving Neanderthals lived by the ocean.
It may be why those groups survived longer. They made use of resources that other Neanderthals didn't, like seafood- even baby seals!
BABY seals?!
They didn't kill seals just for fur, and the animal wasn't endangered at the time.
Baby seals would've been an easy meal - also beached dolphins. Dolphin bones that show signs of being cut by stone tools have been found in the Neanderthal caves.
Even though early humans often fished and even had primitive boats, no evidence has been found of any Neanderthal watercraft.
Hopefully not because they all sank!

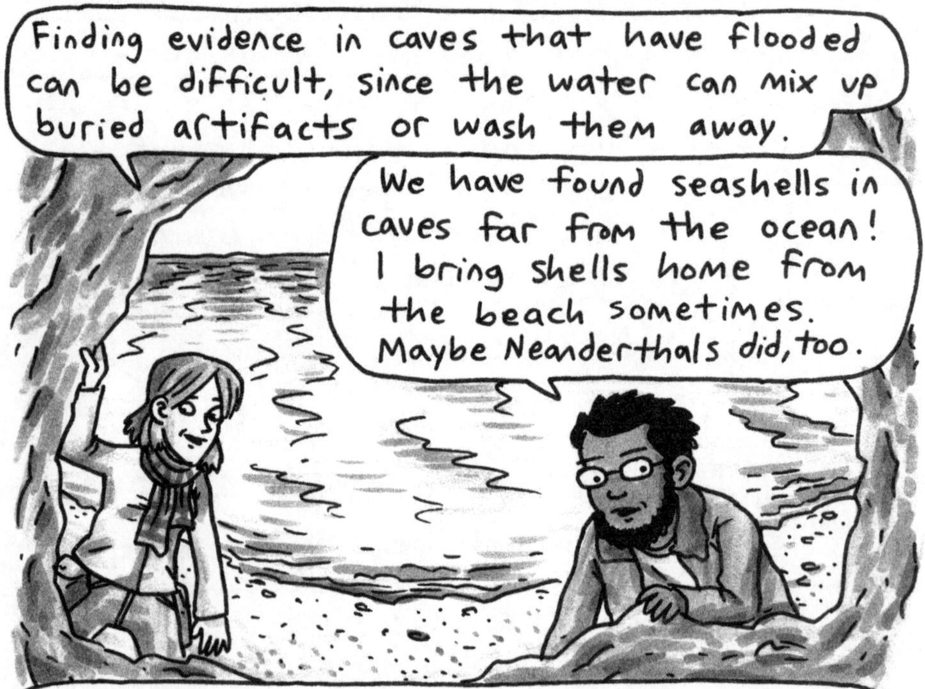
Finding evidence in caves that have flooded can be difficult, since the water can mix up buried artifacts or wash them away.
We have found seashells in caves far from the ocean! I bring shells home from the beach sometimes. Maybe Neanderthals did, too.

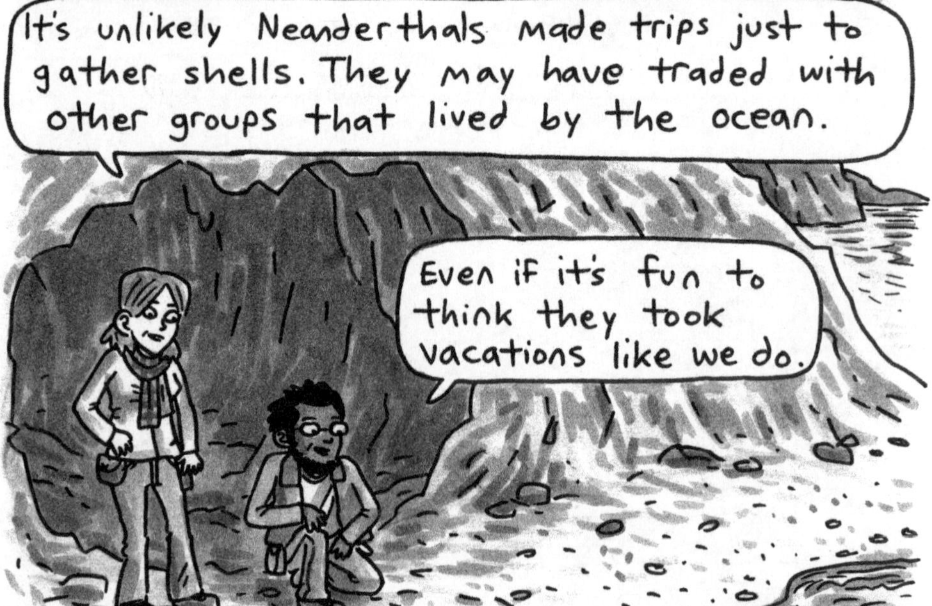
It's unlikely Neanderthals made trips just to gather shells. They may have traded with other groups that lived by the ocean.
Even if it's fun to think they took vacations like we do.

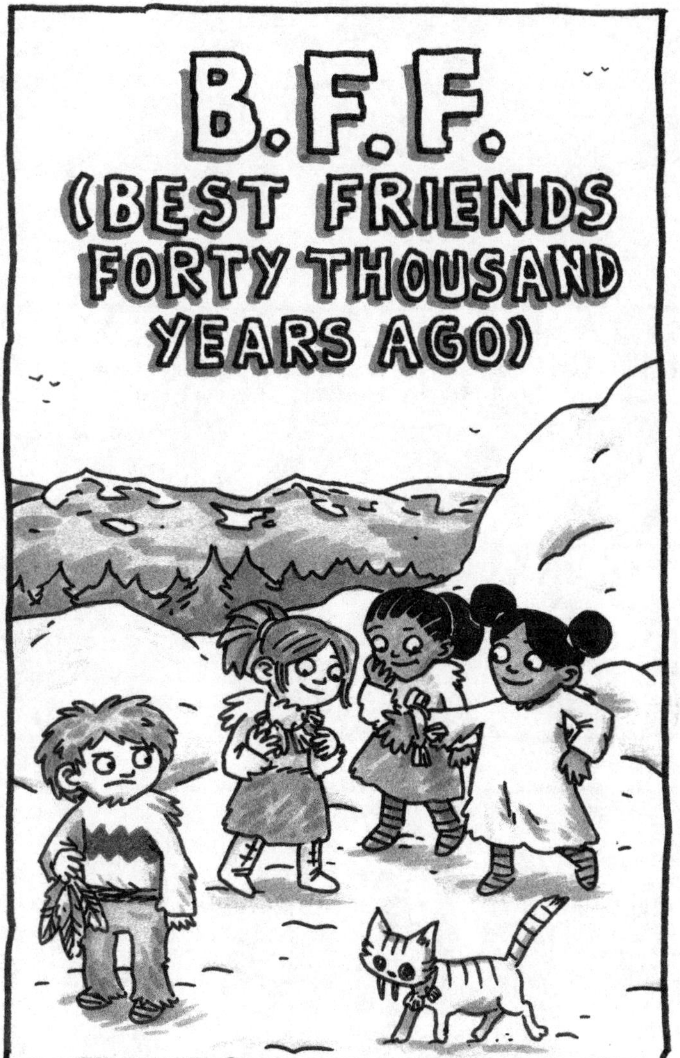
B.F.F.
(BEST FRIENDS
FORTY THOUSAND
YEARS AGO)

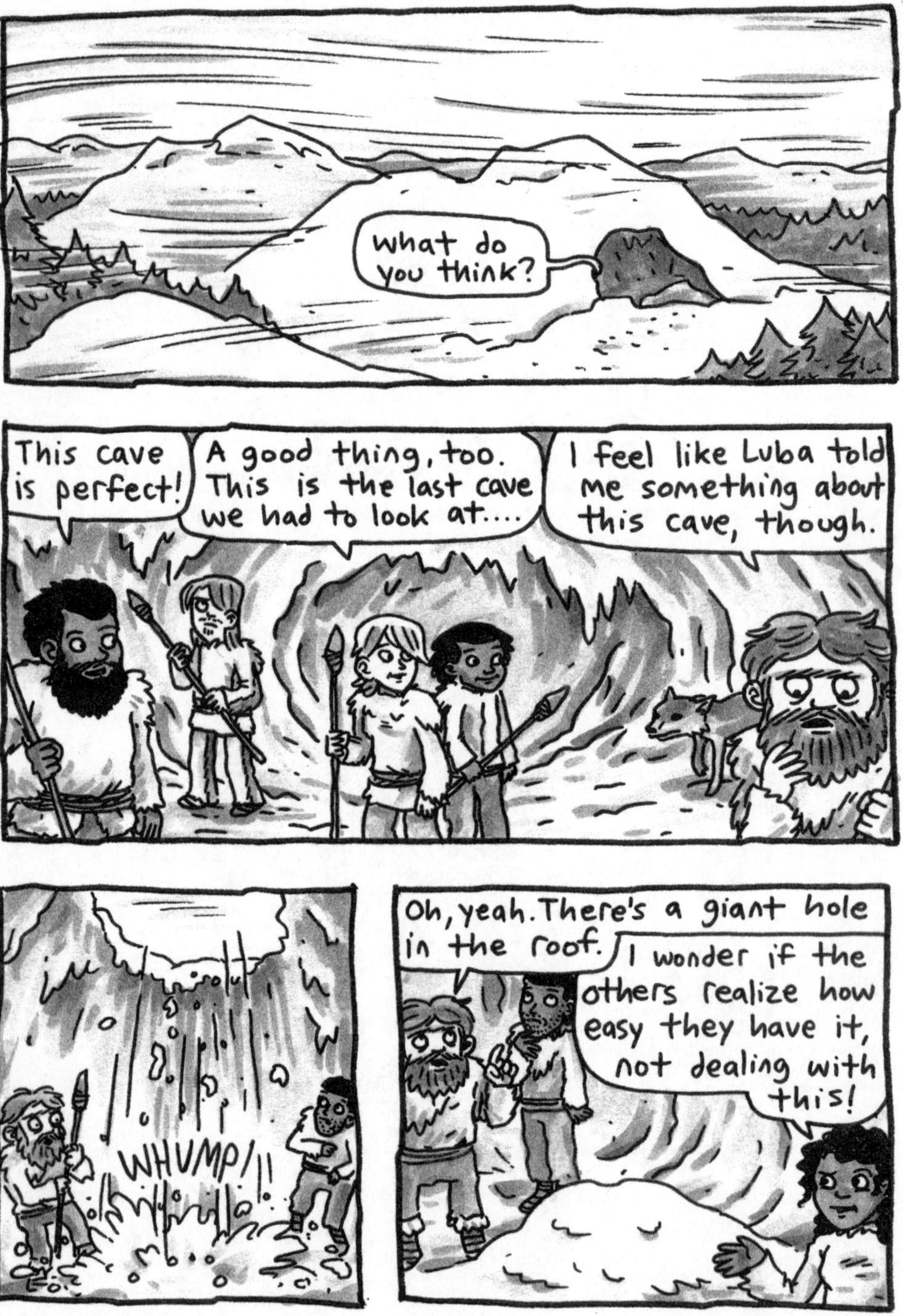
what do you think?
This cave is perfect!
A good thing, too. This is the last cave we had to look at....
I feel like Luba told me something about this cave, though.
WHUMP!!
Oh, yeah. There's a giant hole in the roof.
I wonder if the others realize how easy they have it, not dealing with this!

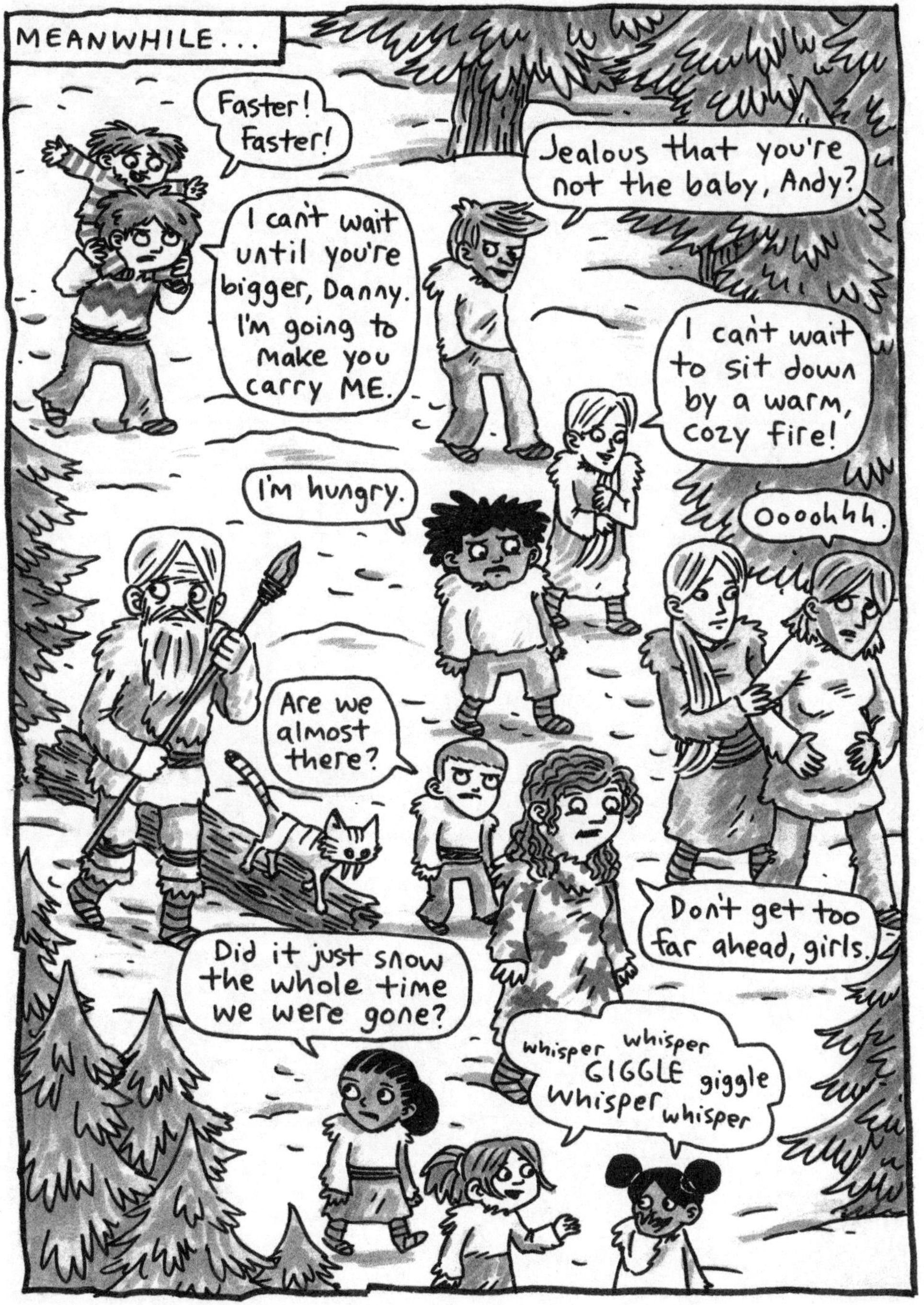
MEANWHILE...
Faster! Faster!
I can't wait until you're bigger, Danny. I'm going to make you carry ME.
Jealous that you're not the baby, Andy?
I can't wait to sit down by a warm, cozy fire!
I'm hungry.
Ooooh h h.
Are we almost there?
Don't get too far ahead, girls.
Did it just snow the whole time we were gone?
whisper whisper GIGGLE giggle whisper whisper

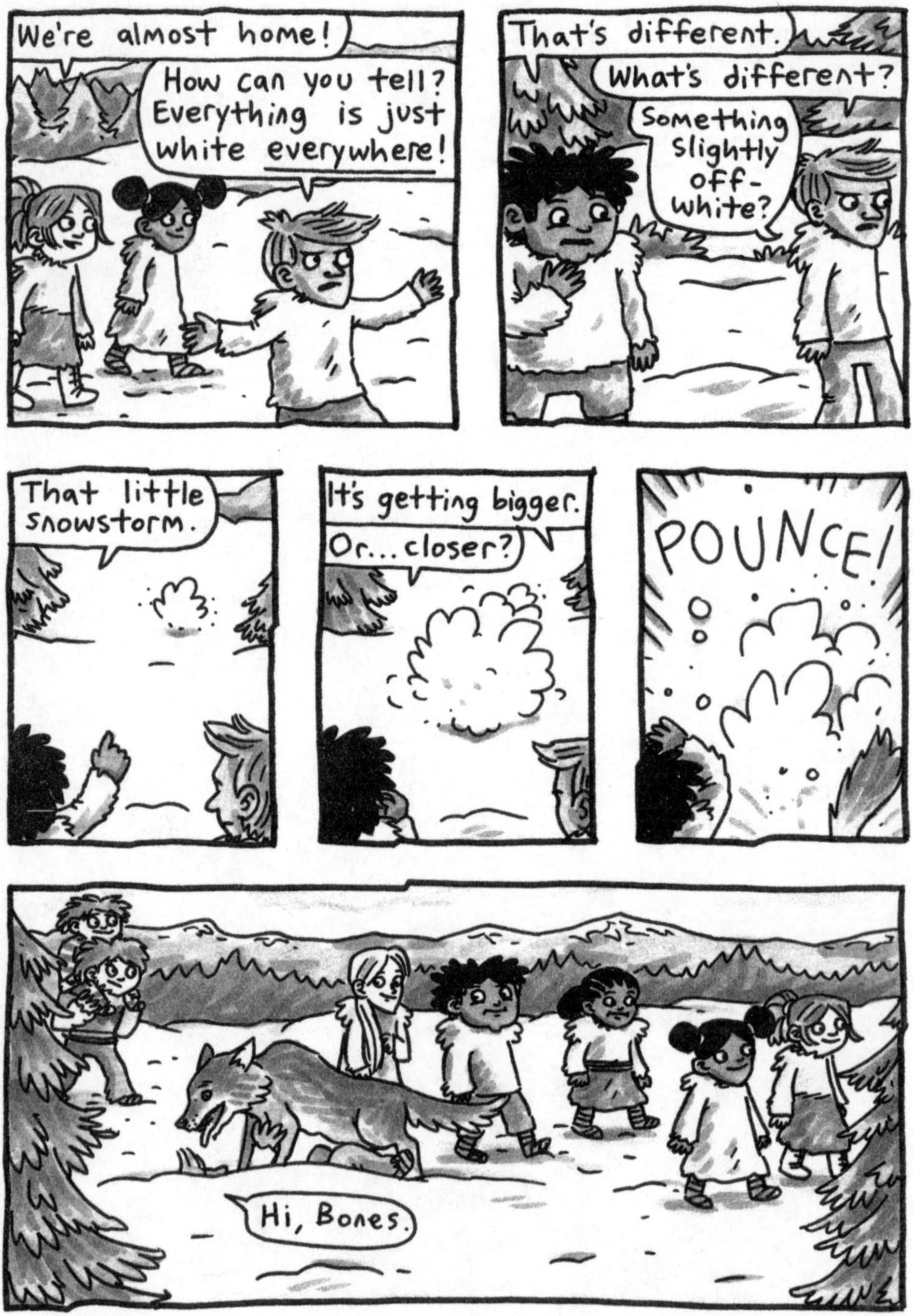
We're almost home!
How can you tell? Everything is just white everywhere!
That's different.
What's different?
Something slightly off-white?
That little snowstorm.
It's getting bigger.
Or... closer?
POUNCE!
Hi, Bones.

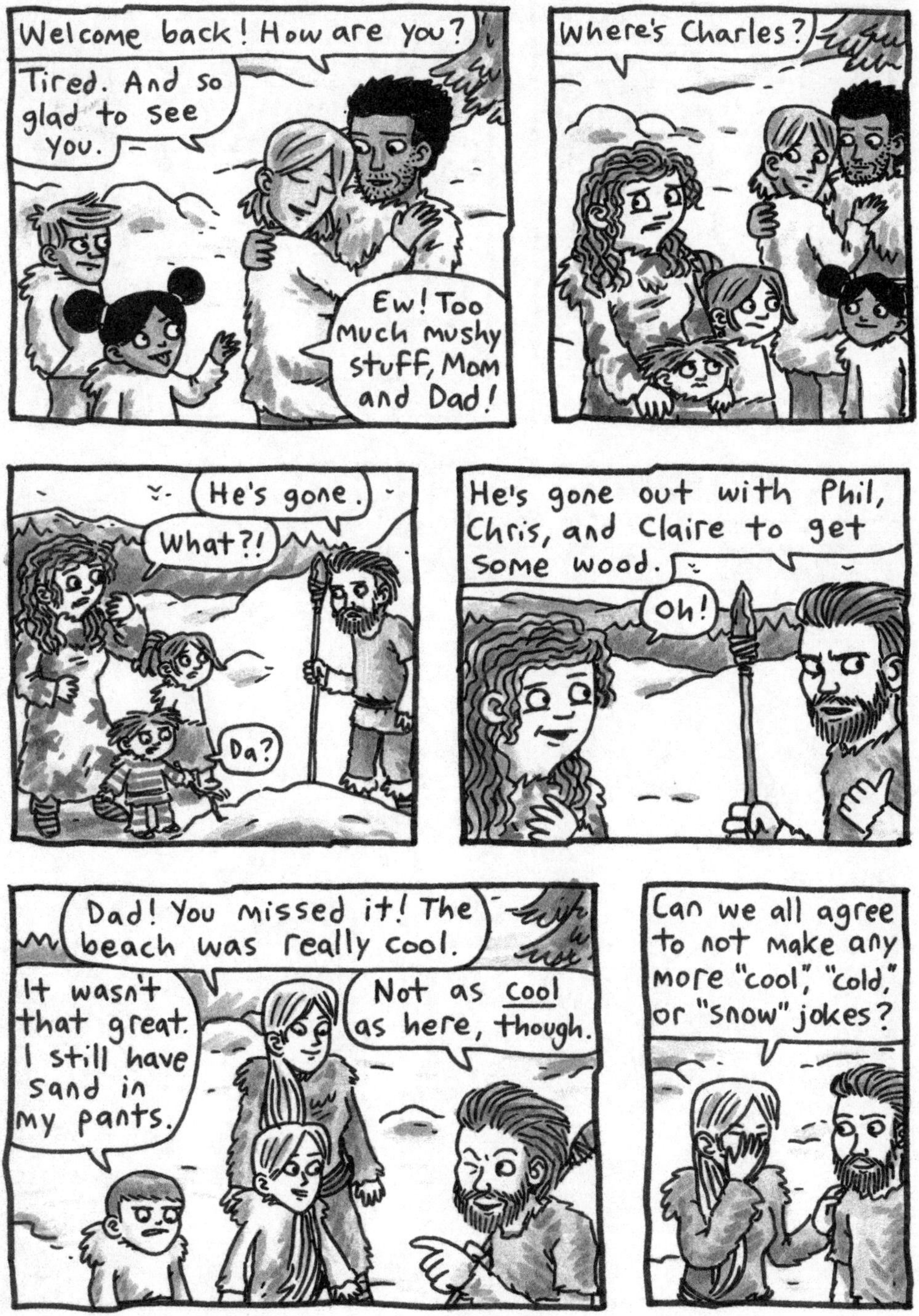
Welcome back! How are you?
Tired. And so glad to see you.
Ew! Too much mushy stuff, Mom and Dad!
Where's Charles?
He's gone.
What?!
Da?
He's gone out with Phil, Chris, and Claire to get some wood.
Oh!
Dad! You missed it! The beach was really cool.
It wasn't that great. I still have sand in my pants.
Not as cool as here, though.
Can we all agree to not make any more "cool," "cold," or "snow" jokes?

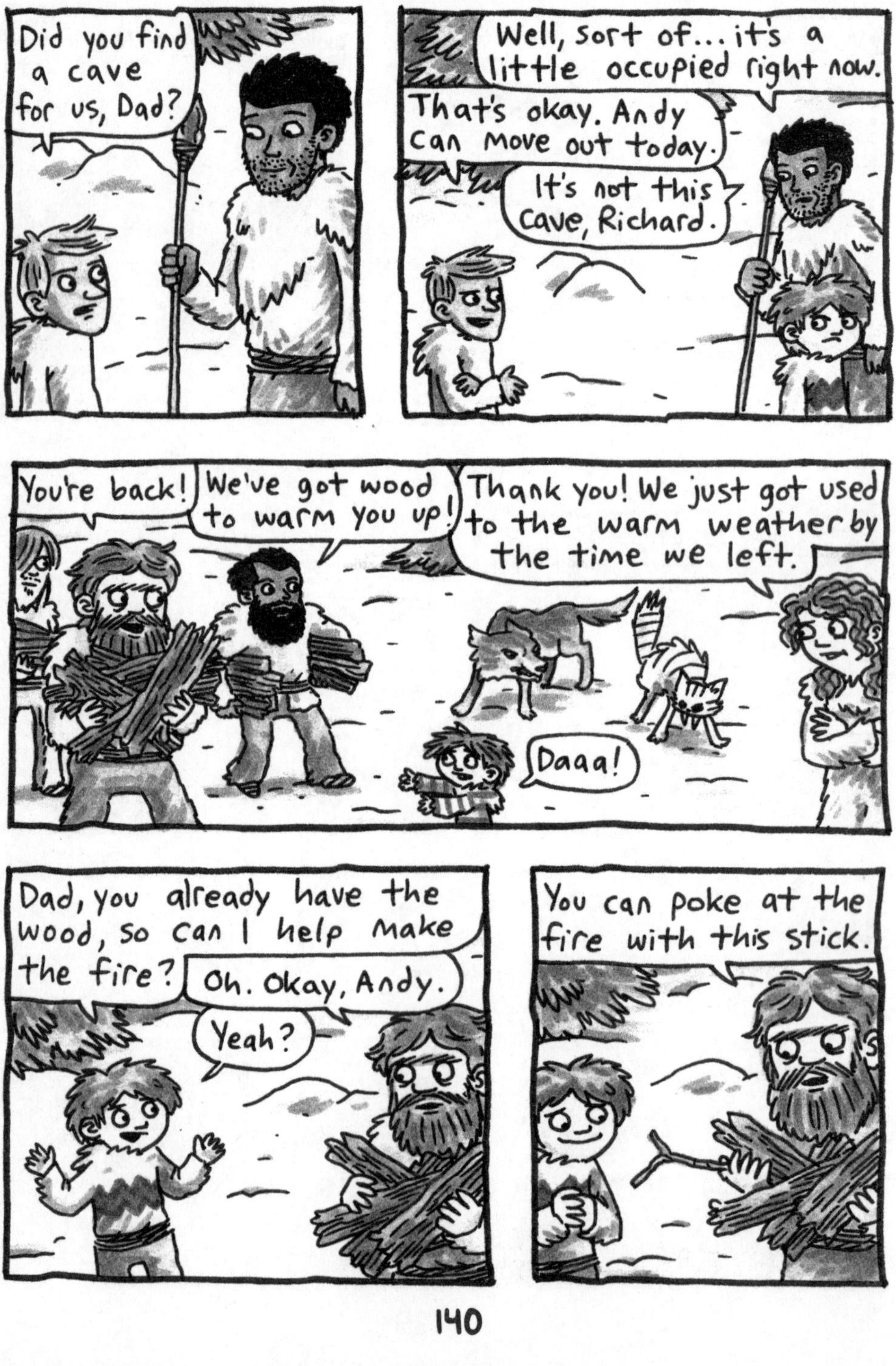
Did you find a cave for us, Dad?
Well, sort of... it's a little occupied right now.
That's okay. Andy can move out today.
It's not this cave, Richard.
You're back!
We've got wood to warm you up!
Thank you! We just got used to the warm weather by the time we left.
Daaa!
Dad, you already have the wood, so can I help make the fire?
Oh. Okay, Andy.
Yeah?
You can poke at the fire with this stick.

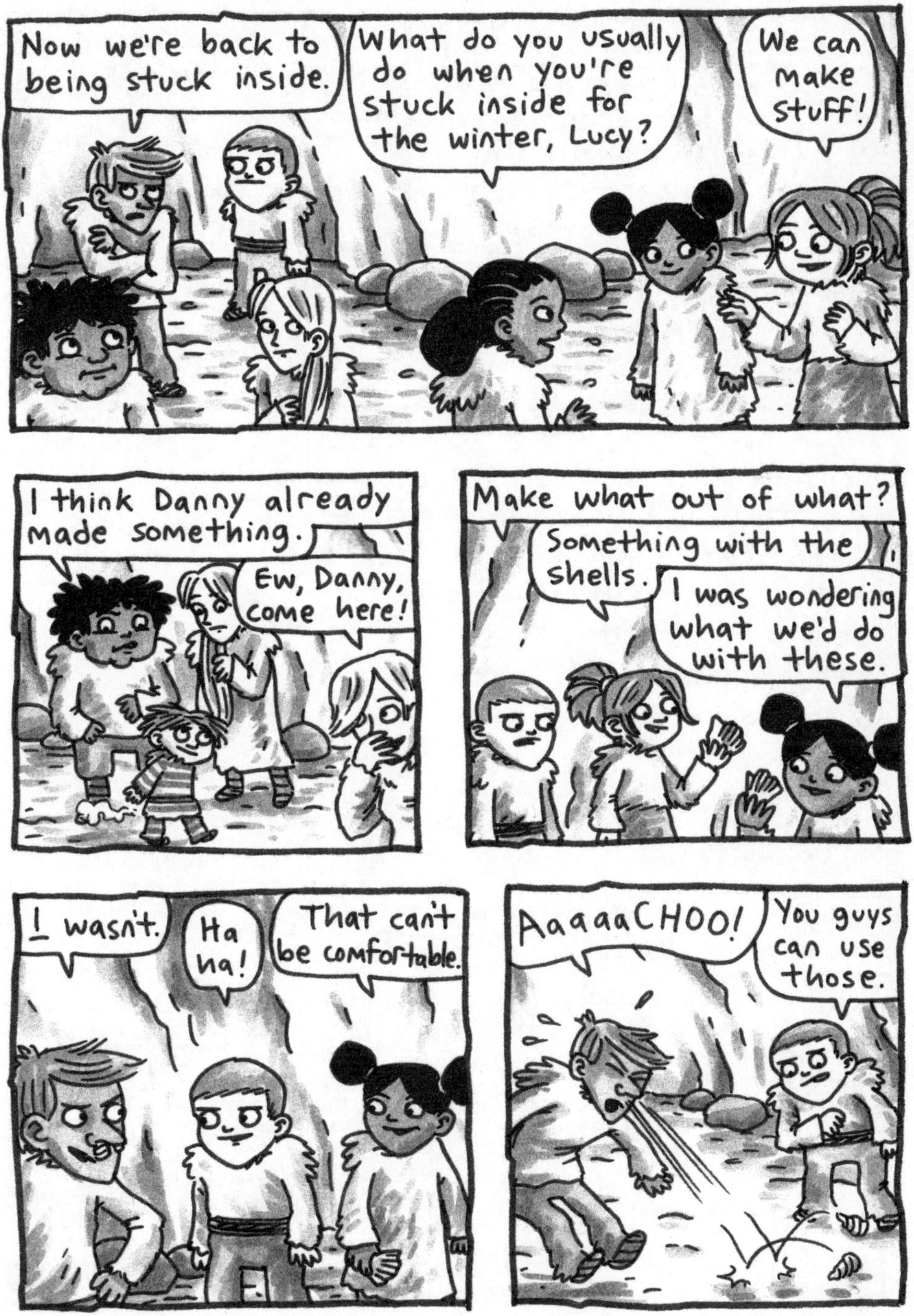
Now we're back to being stuck inside.
What do you usually do when you're stuck inside for the winter, Lucy?
We can make stuff!
I think Danny already made something.
Ew, Danny, come here!
Make what out of what?
Something with the shells.
I was wondering what we'd do with these.
I wasn't.
Ha ha!
That can't be comfortable.
AaaaaCHOO!
You guys can use those.

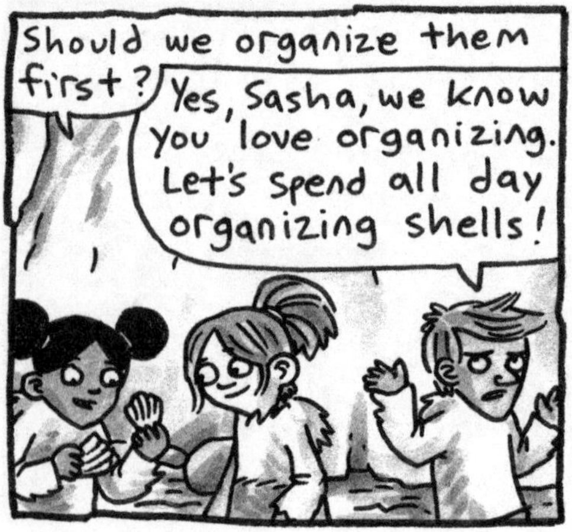
Should we organize them first?
Yes, Sasha, we know you love organizing. Let's spend all day organizing shells!

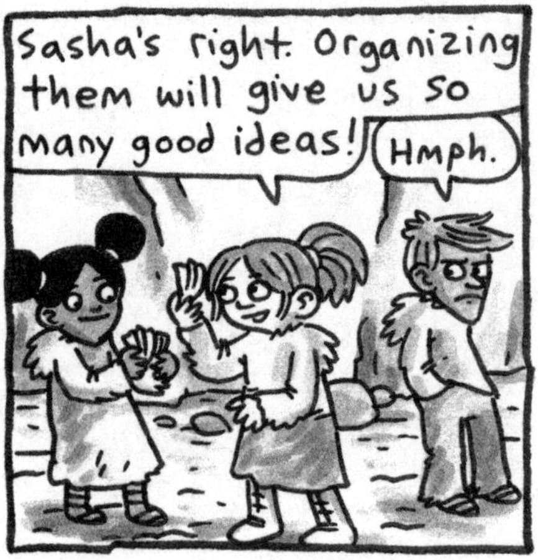
Sasha's right. Organizing them will give us so many good ideas!
Hmph.

Shells found in Neanderthal caves have holes that had been drilled by snails. There wasn't anything left in the shells to eat, but the holes were all the same size, making them just right to string on a necklace.

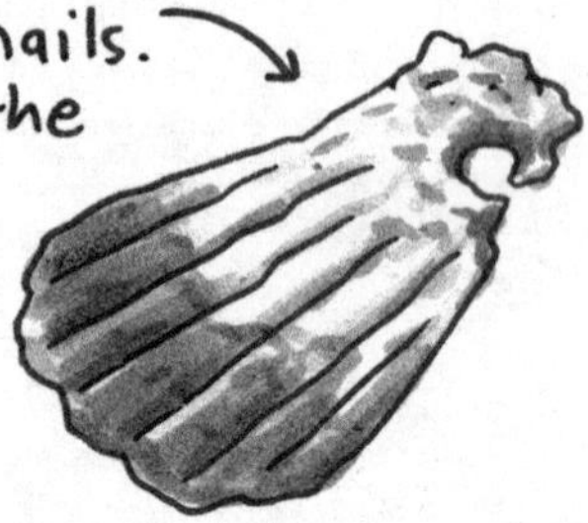

Some shells have colored pigment on them, indicating those were picked specifically for decoration.

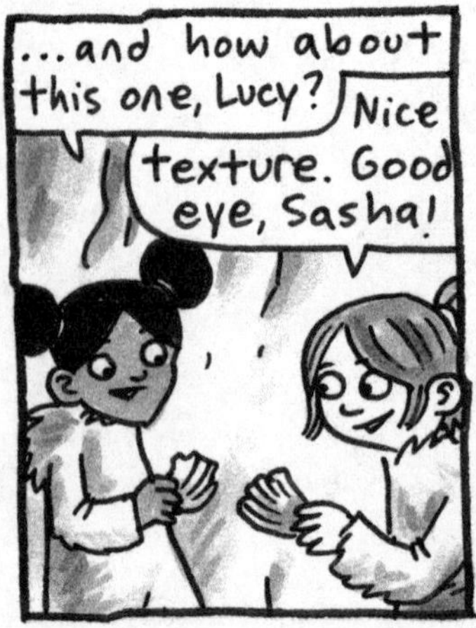
...and how about this one, Lucy?
Nice texture. Good eye, Sasha!

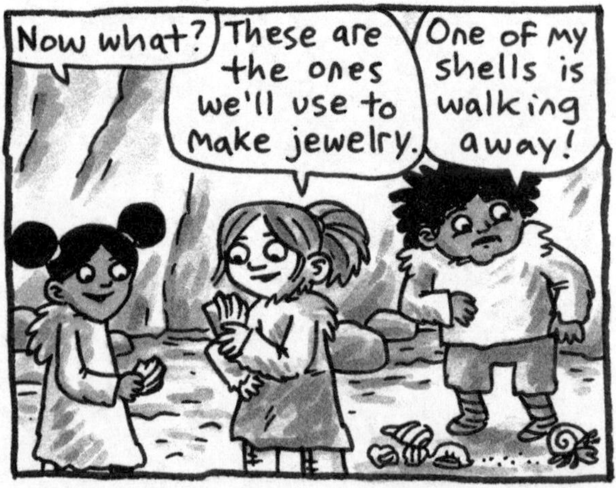
Now what?
These are the ones we'll use to make jewelry.
One of my shells is walking away!

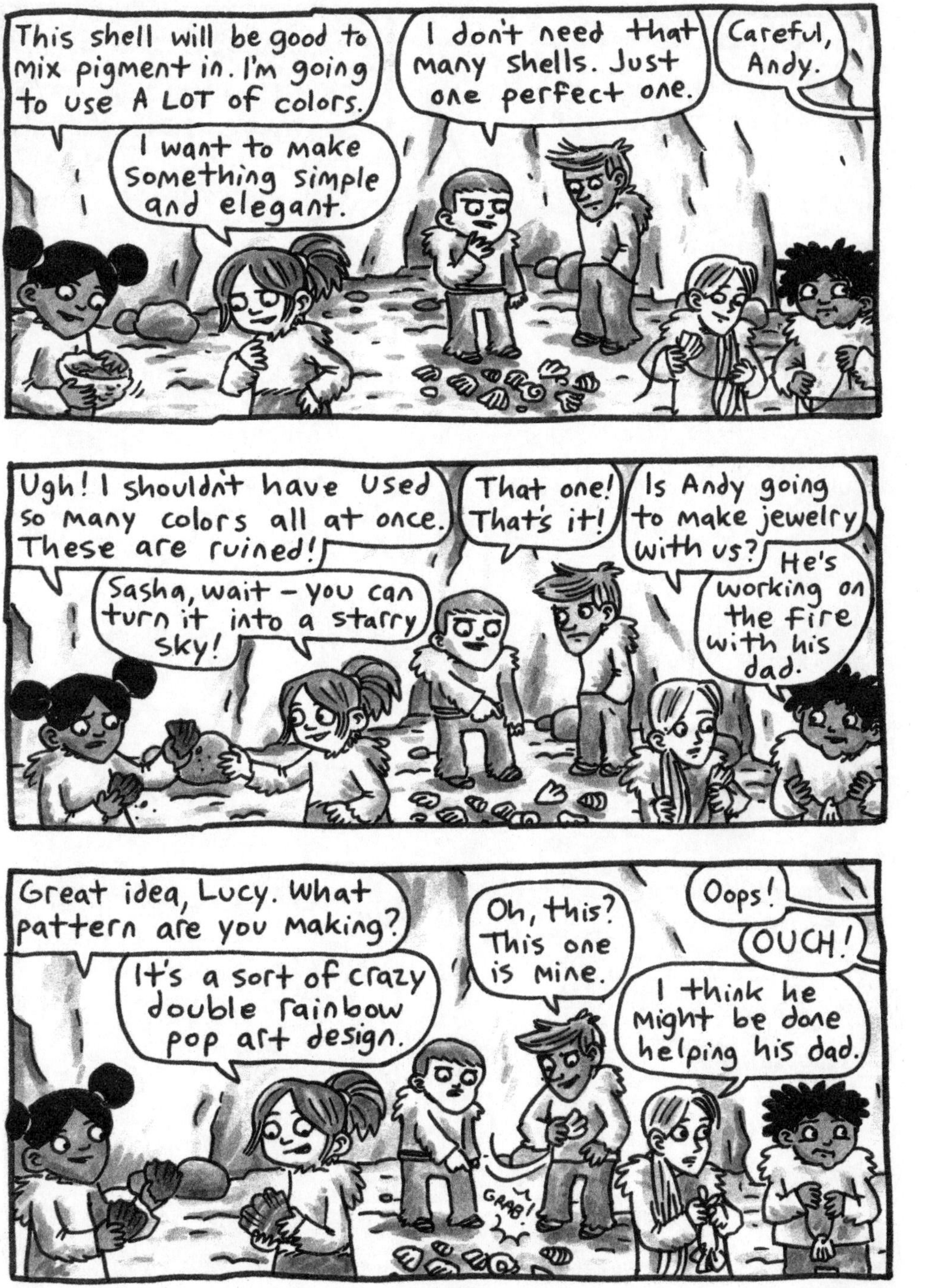
This shell will be good to mix pigment in. I'm going to use A LOT of colors.
I want to make something simple and elegant.
I don't need that many shells. Just one perfect one.
Careful, Andy.
Ugh! I shouldn't have used so many colors all at once. These are ruined!
Sasha, wait - you can turn it into a starry sky!
That one! That's it!
Is Andy going to make jewelry with us?
He's working on the fire with his dad.
Great idea, Lucy. What pattern are you making?
It's a sort of crazy double rainbow pop art design.
Oh, this? This one is mine.
GRAB!
Oops!
OUCH!
I think he might be done helping his dad.

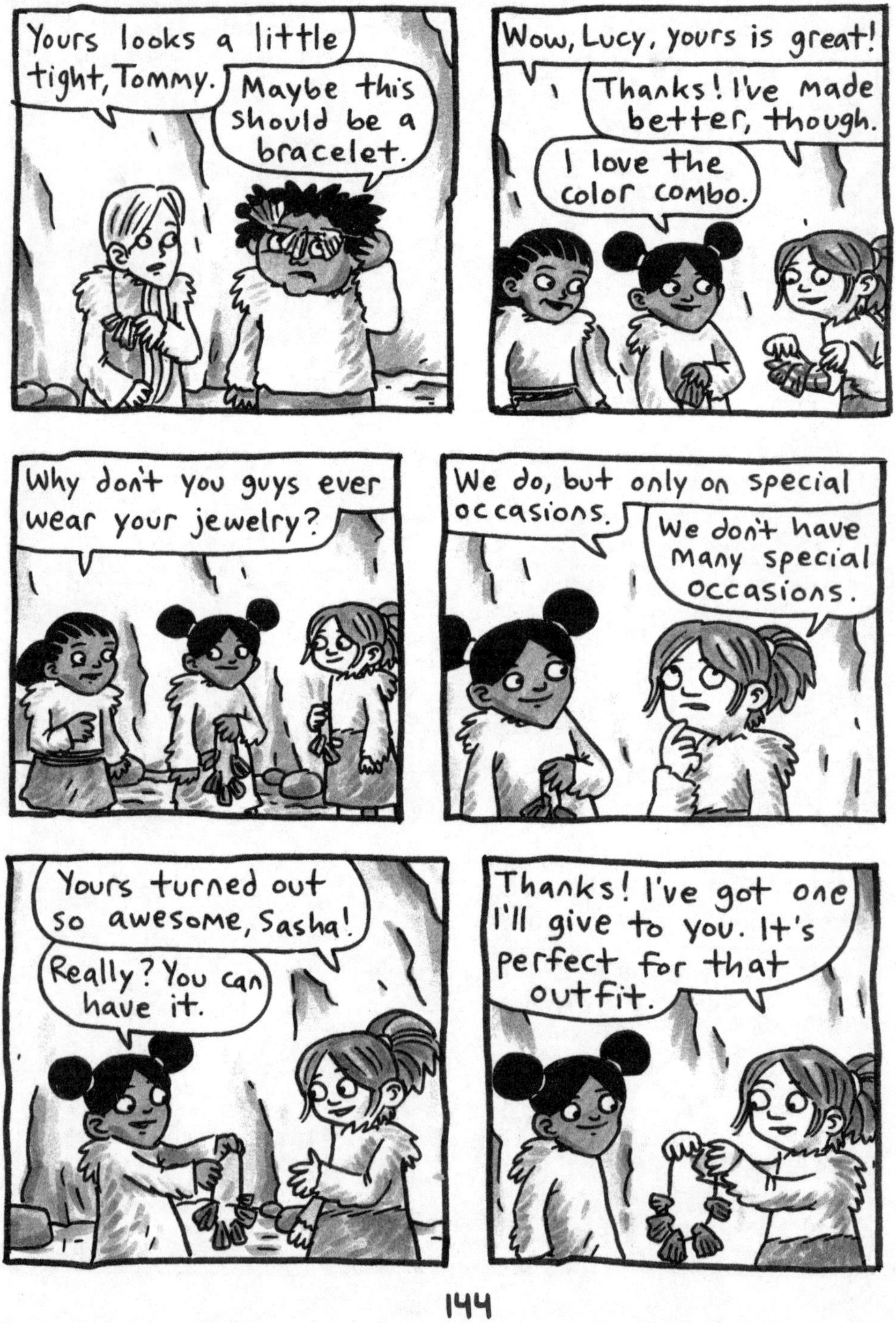
Yours looks a little tight, Tommy.
Maybe this should be a bracelet.
Wow, Lucy, yours is great!
Thanks! I've made better, though.
I love the color combo.
Why don't you guys ever wear your jewelry?
We do, but only on special occasions.
We don't have many special occasions.
Yours turned out so awesome, Sasha!
Really? You can have it.
Thanks! I've got one I'll give to you. It's perfect for that outfit.

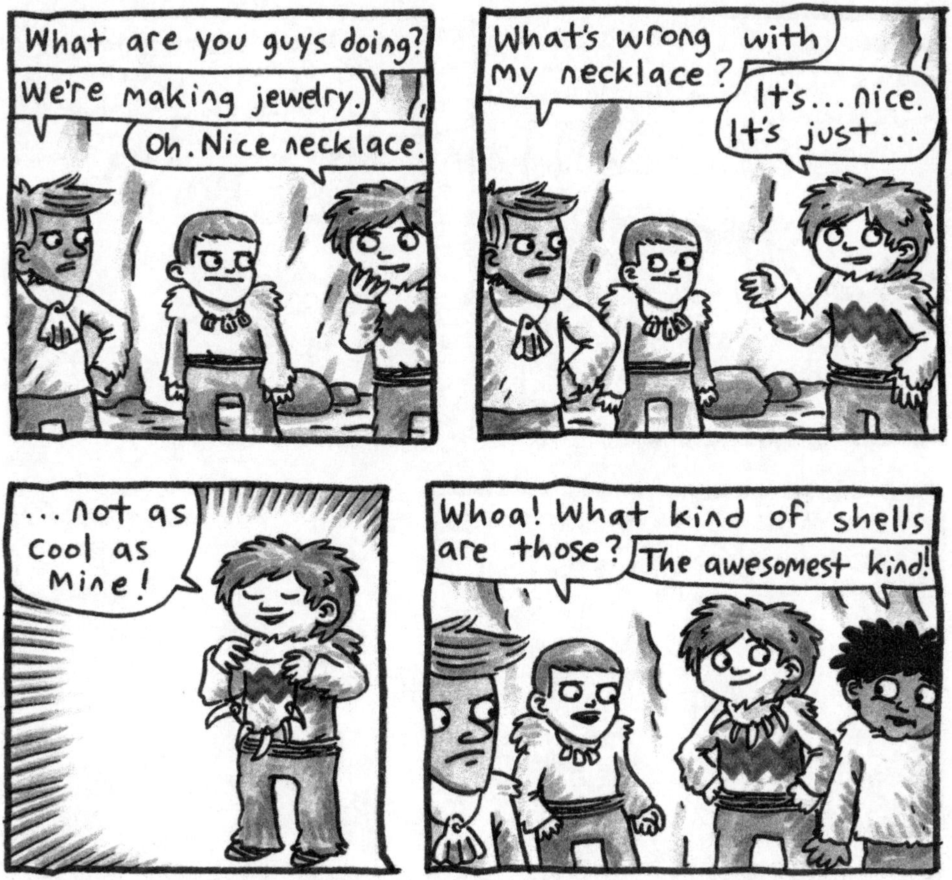
What are you guys doing?
We're making jewelry.
Oh. Nice necklace.
What's wrong with my necklace?
It's... nice. It's just...
...not as cool as mine!
Whoa! What kind of shells are those?
The awesomest kind!

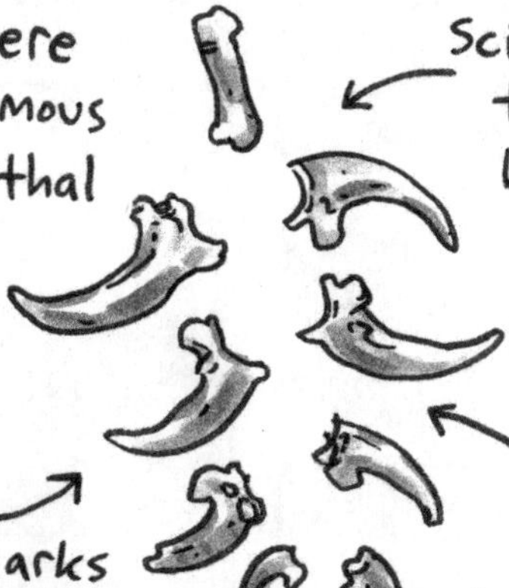
Eagle talons were found at the famous Krapina Neanderthal site!
Scientists think the talons may have been used to make necklaces or bracelets.
Some of the talons show marks from stone tools.
There are also signs that the talons were polished.

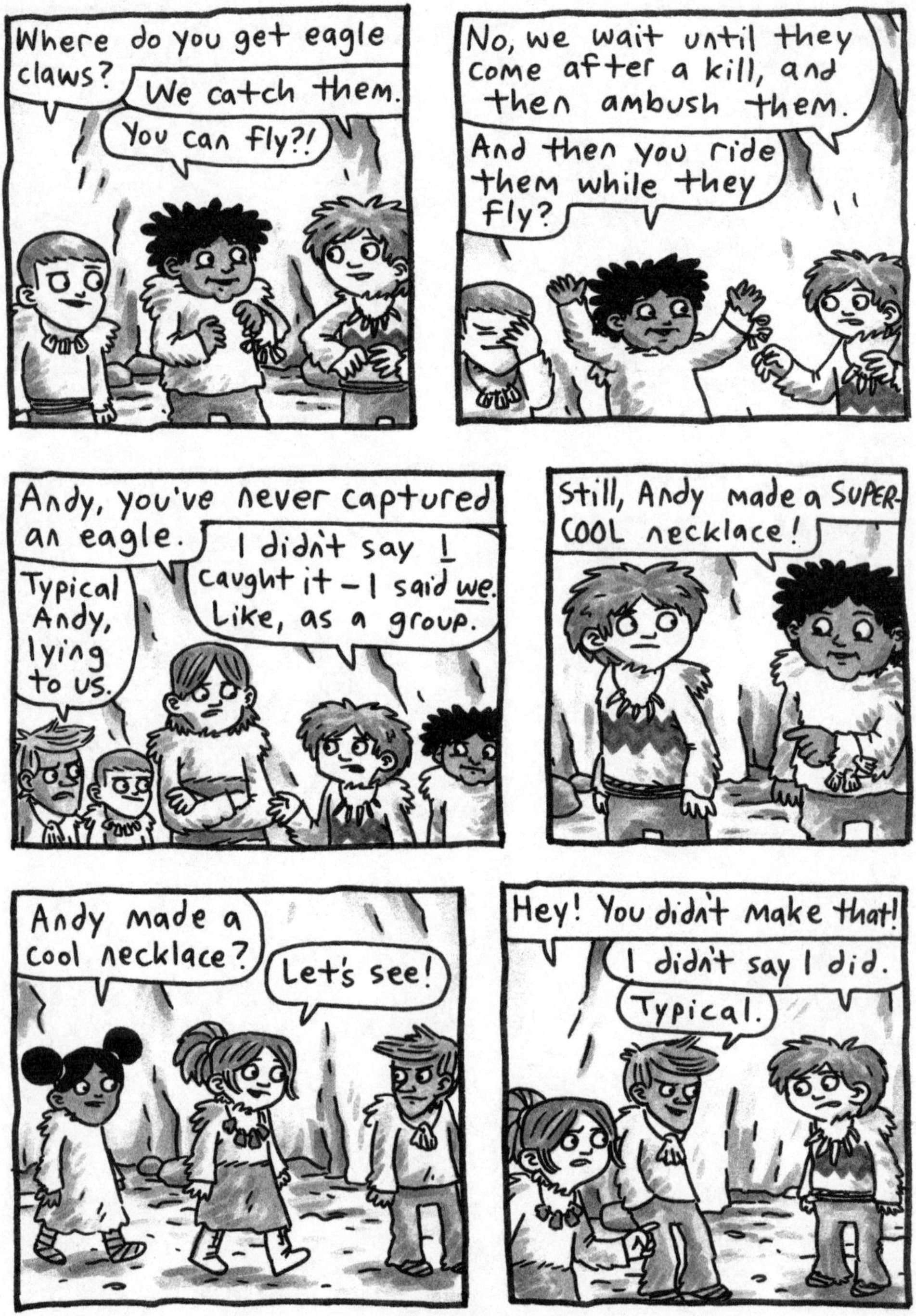
Where do you get eagle claws?
We catch them.
You can fly?!
No, we wait until they come after a kill, and then ambush them.
And then you ride them while they fly?
Andy, you've never captured an eagle.
Typical Andy, lying to us.
I didn't say I caught it — I said we. Like, as a group.
Still, Andy made a SUPER-COOL necklace!
Andy made a cool necklace?
Let's see!
Hey! You didn't make that!
I didn't say I did.
Typical.

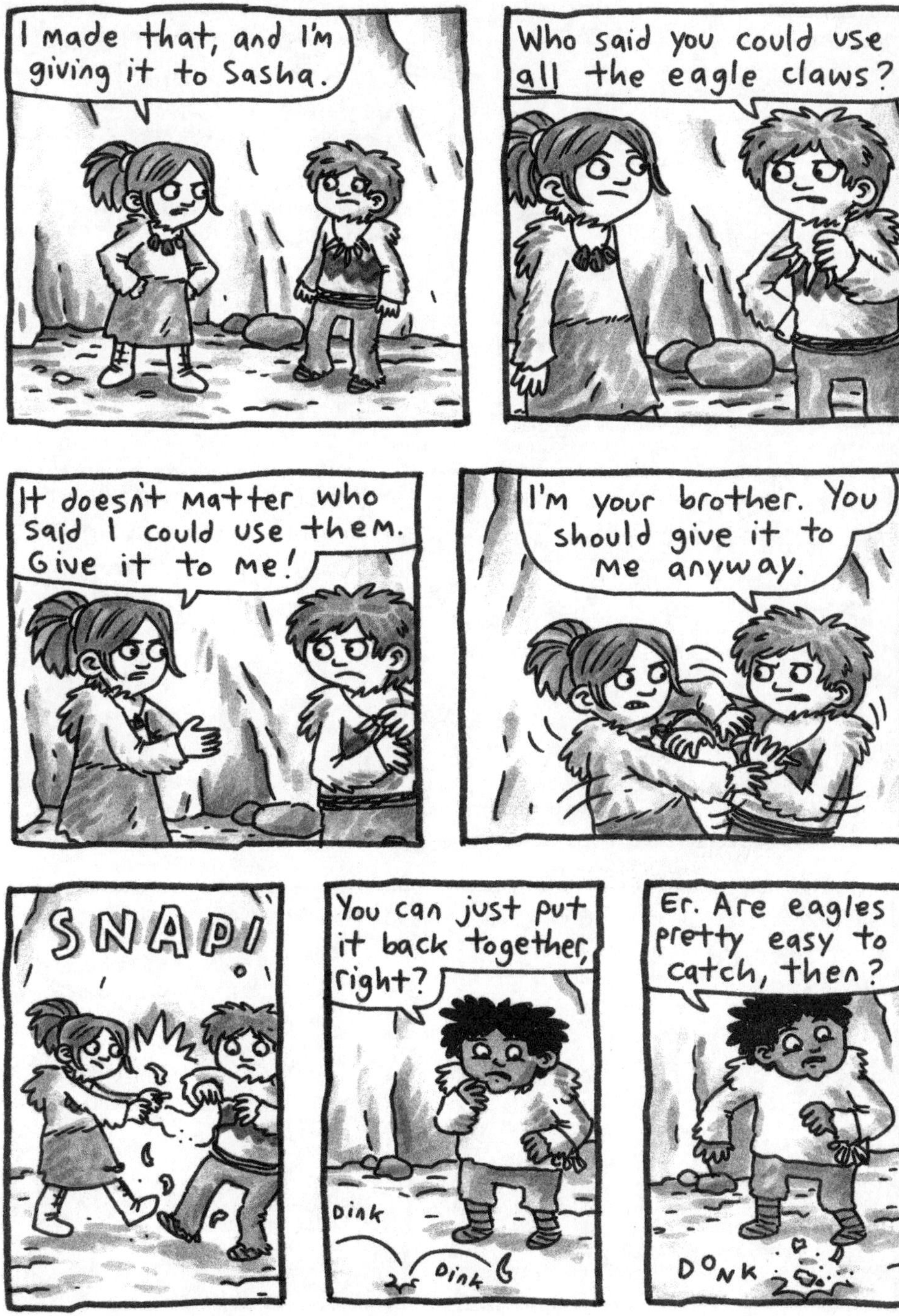
I made that, and I'm giving it to Sasha.
Who said you could use all the eagle claws?
It doesn't matter who said I could use them. Give it to me!
I'm your brother. You should give it to me anyway.
SNAP!
You can just put it back together, right?
DINK
DINK
Er. Are eagles pretty easy to catch, then?
DONK

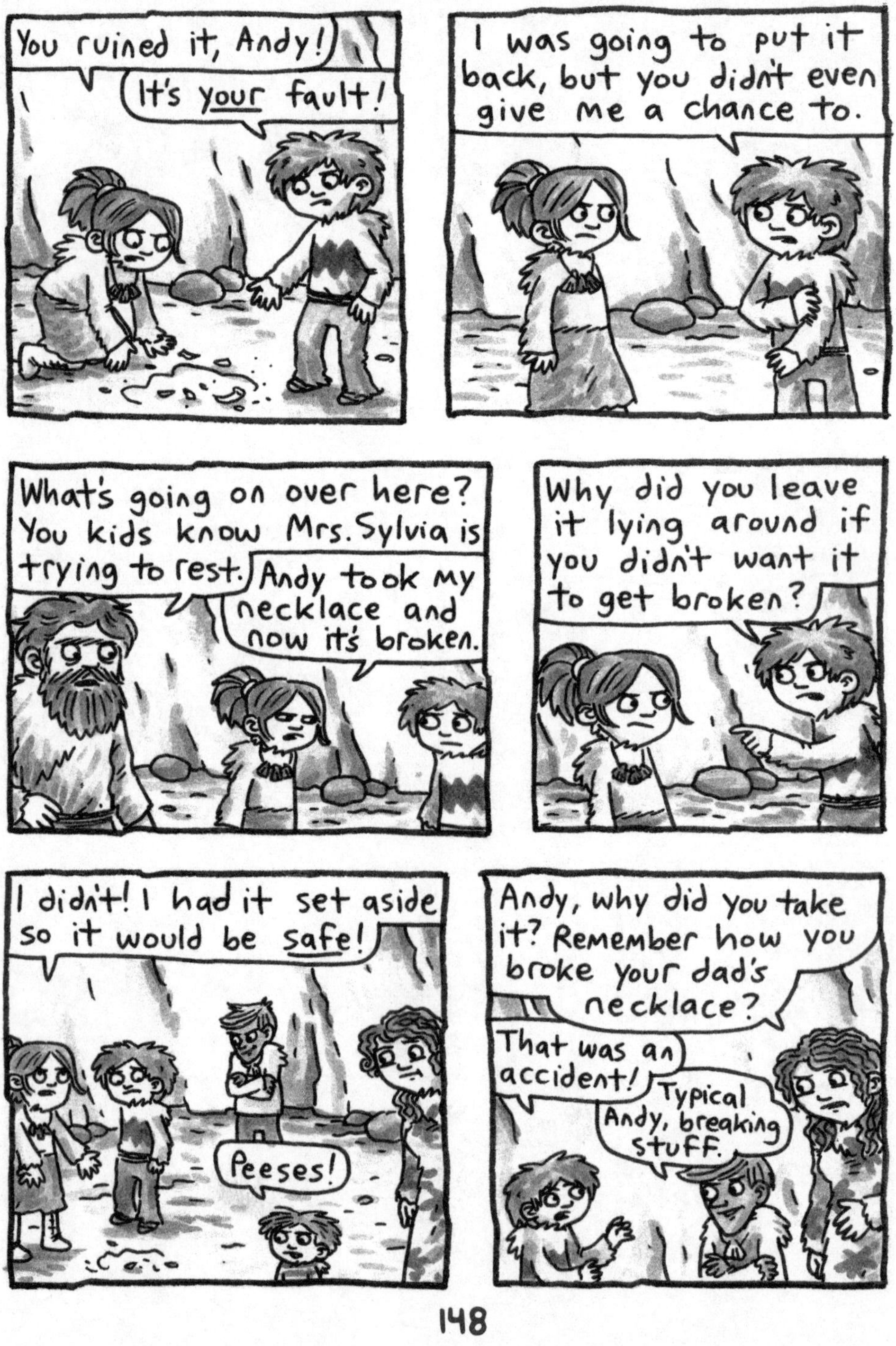
You ruined it, Andy!
It's your fault!
I was going to put it back, but you didn't even give me a chance to.
What's going on over here? You kids know Mrs. Sylvia is trying to rest.
Andy took my necklace and now it's broken.
Why did you leave it lying around if you didn't want it to get broken?
I didn't! I had it set aside so it would be safe!
Peeses!
Andy, why did you take it? Remember how you broke your dad's necklace?
That was an accident!
Typical Andy, breaking stuff.

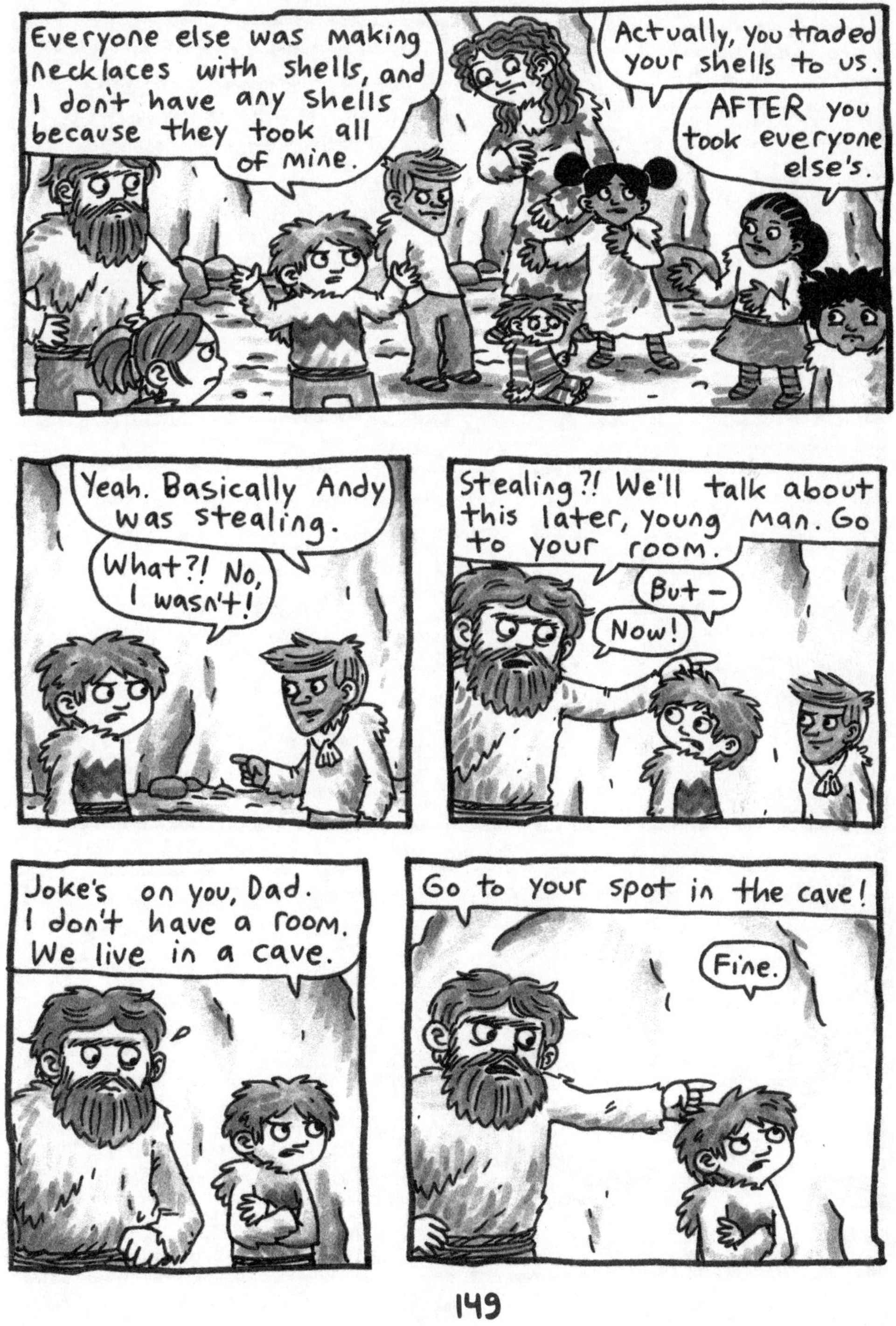
Everyone else was making necklaces with shells, and I don't have any shells because they took all of mine.
Actually, you traded your shells to us.
AFTER you took everyone else's.
Yeah. Basically Andy was stealing.
What?! No, I wasn't!
Stealing?! We'll talk about this later, young man. Go to your room.
But -
Now!
Joke's on you, Dad. I don't have a room. We live in a cave.
Go to your spot in the cave!
Fine.

Too bad you're stuck with such a bratty brother, Lucy.
What a loser.
You know I can hear you. I keep telling you this cave isn't that big.
Andy, I'm sorry I got mad at you. Actually, I'm glad you broke the necklace.
Huh?
Now Sasha and I can make a new one— together!
Yeah! I just got another idea!
Andy, will you help me fix my necklace?
Uh. Sure!

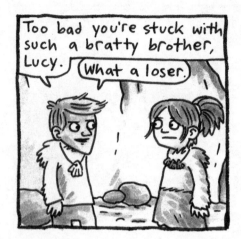

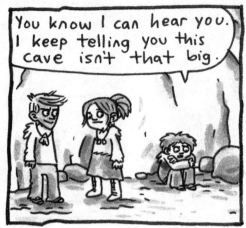

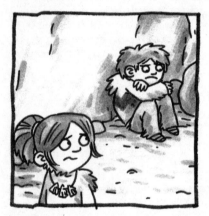

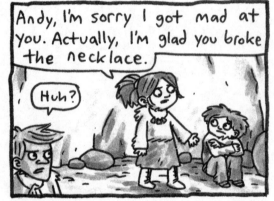

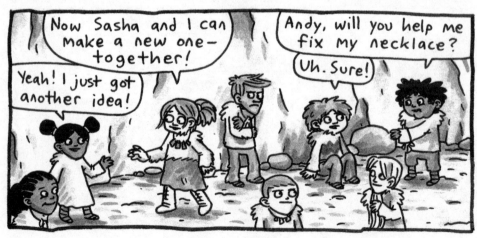

It's pretty amazing to think that humans were wearing jewelry 40,000 years ago.

And Neanderthals!

They could've been copying the idea of jewelry from humans, though.

Actually, evidence indicates that Neanderthal jewelry was made <u>before</u> early humans arrived in their territory.

Neanderthals didn't have metal, like gold or silver, so they used other materials to adorn themselves. Like more recent primitive cultures, Neanderthals used feathers.

The feathers and claws we've found are from a number of different eagles, which aren't a common bird in the fossil record.

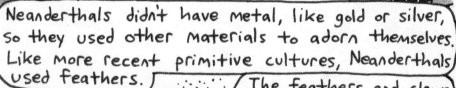

That means the Neanderthals must have captured the eagles, since randomly finding a dead one would've been extremely unlikely.

Those claws were rare and special, even if they weren't made of gold!

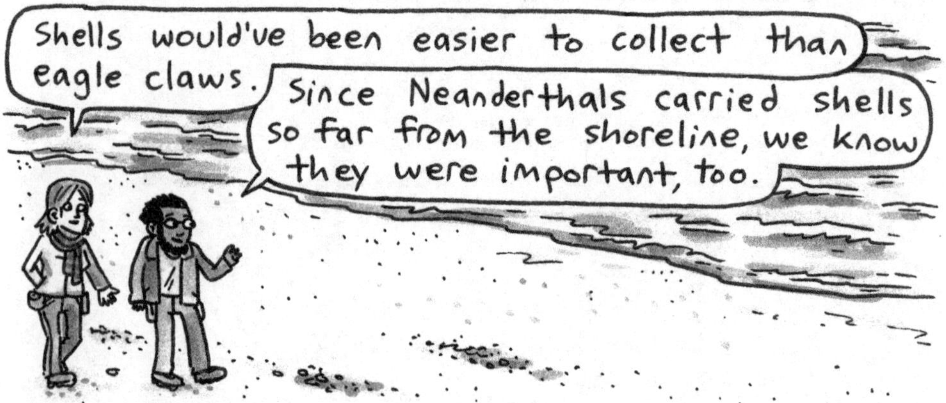
Shells would've been easier to collect than eagle claws.
Since Neanderthals carried shells so far from the shoreline, we know they were important, too.

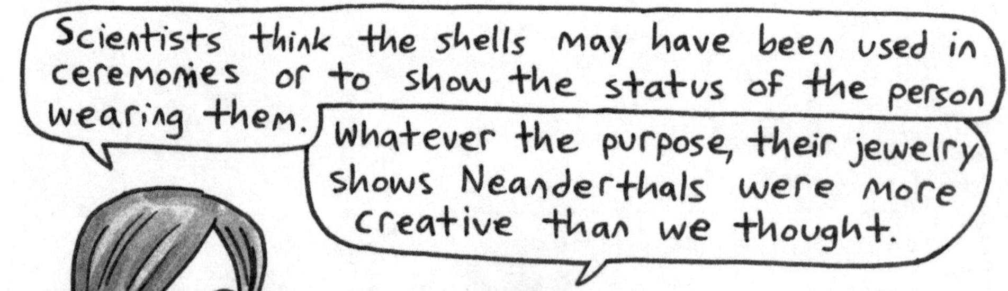
Scientists think the shells may have been used in ceremonies or to show the status of the person wearing them.
Whatever the purpose, their jewelry shows Neanderthals were more creative than we thought.

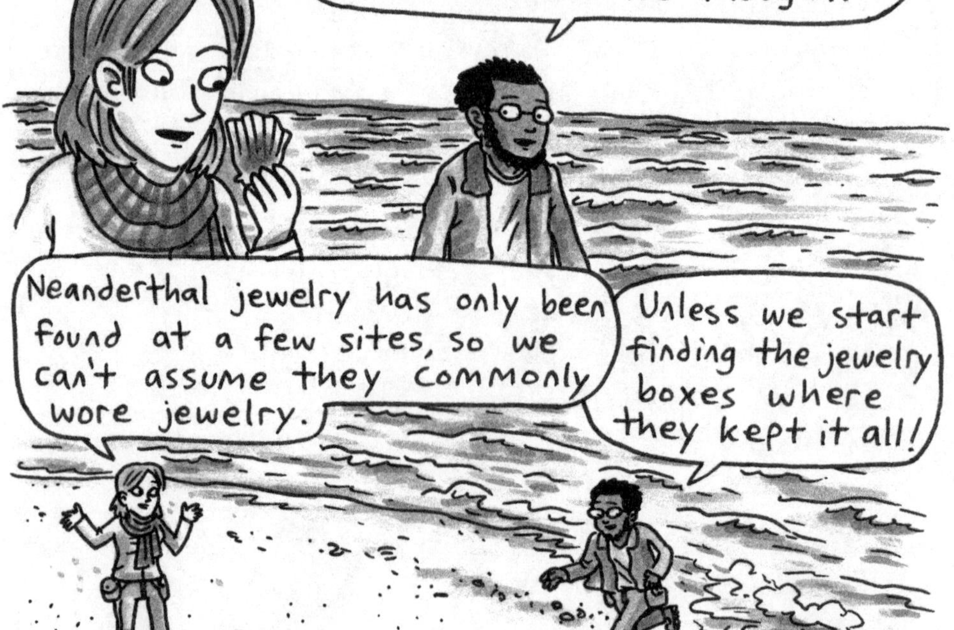
Neanderthal jewelry has only been found at a few sites, so we can't assume they commonly wore jewelry.
Unless we start finding the jewelry boxes where they kept it all!

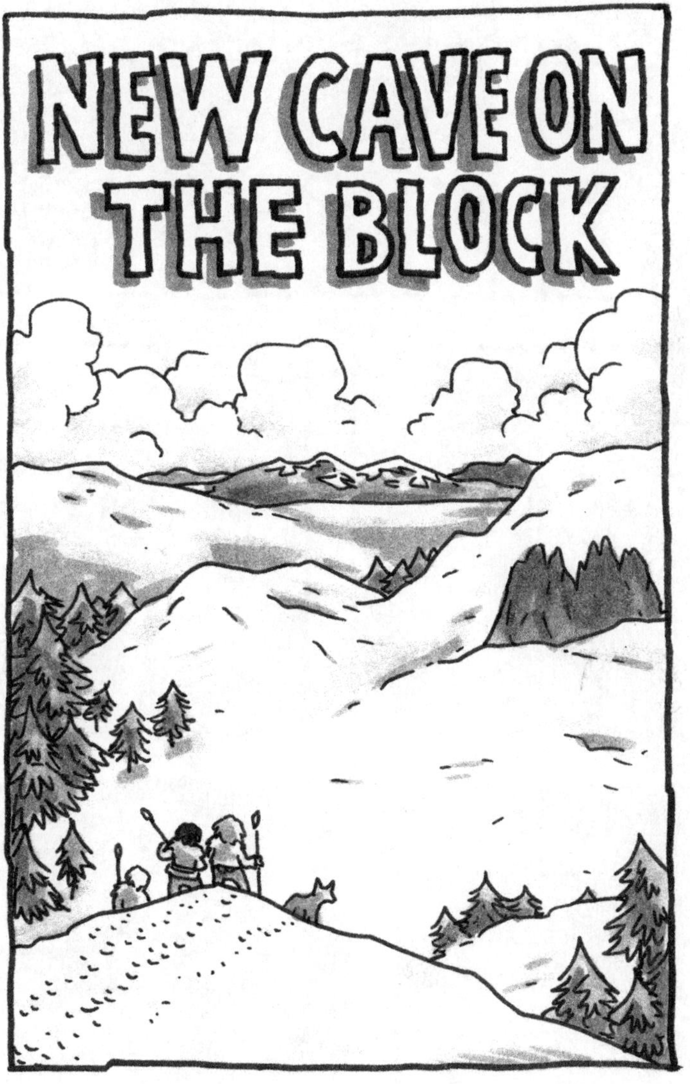
NEW CAVE ON THE BLOCK

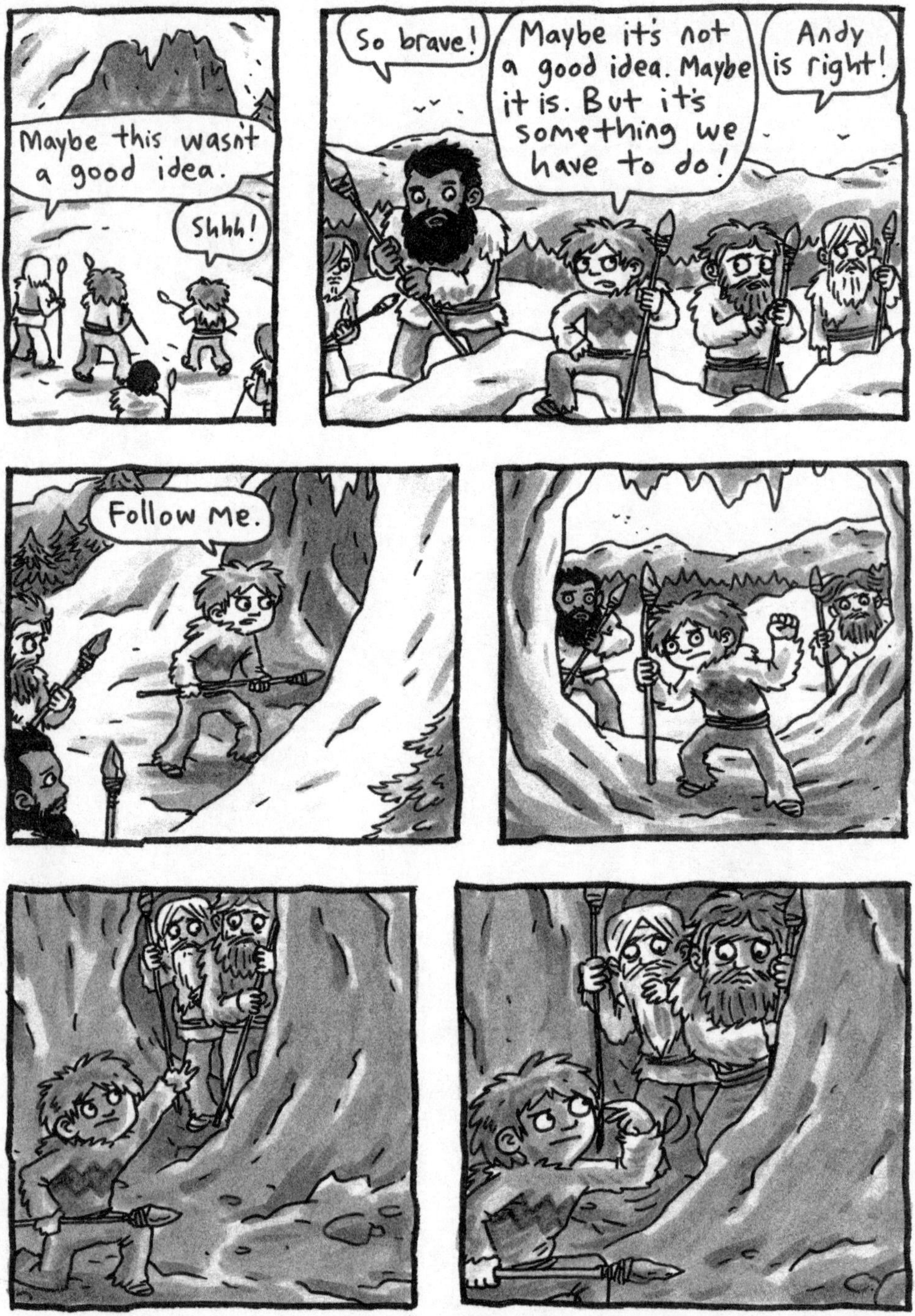
Maybe this wasn't a good idea.
Shhh!
So brave!
Maybe it's not a good idea. Maybe it is. But it's something we have to do!
Andy is right!
Follow me.

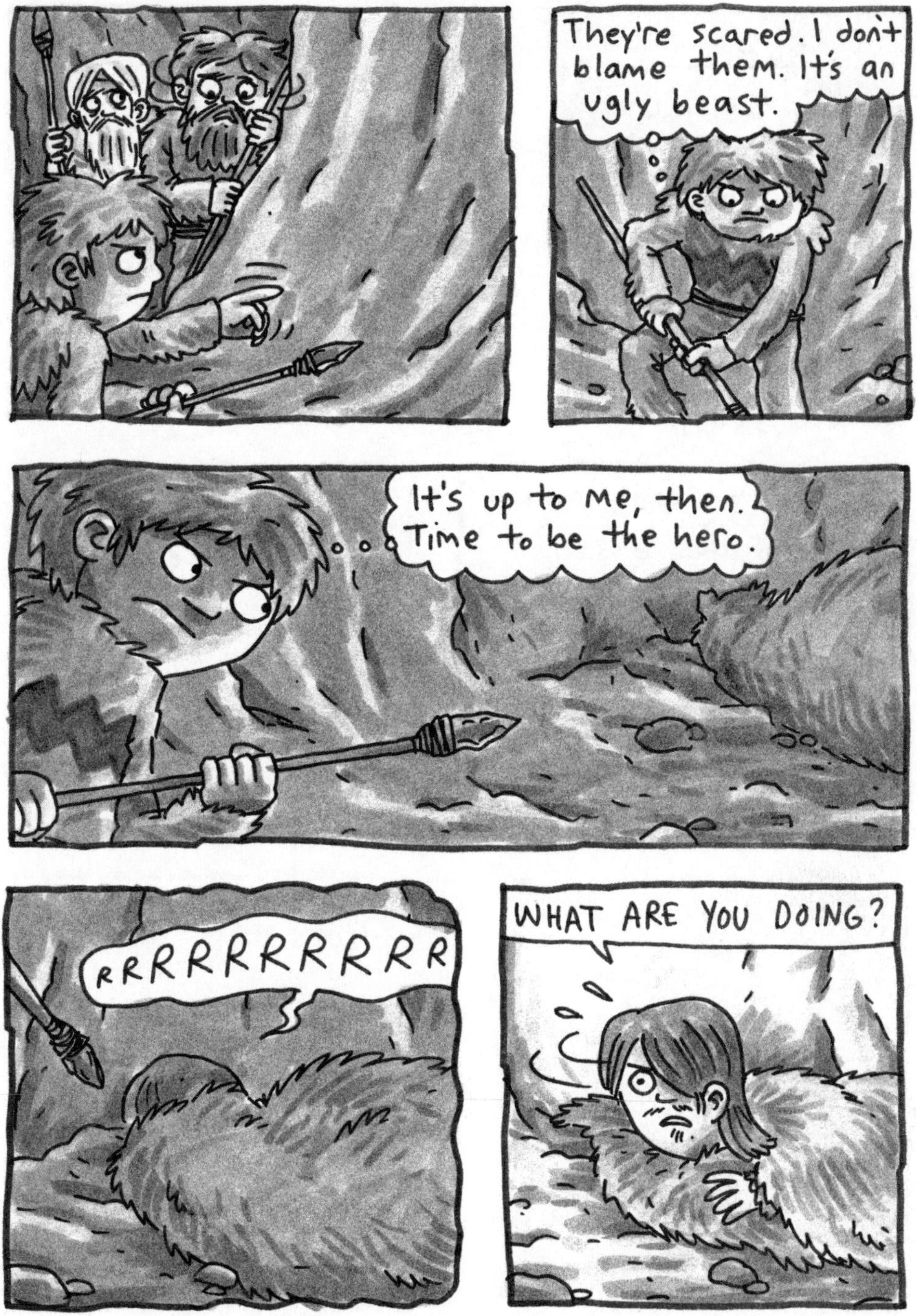
They're scared. I don't blame them. It's an ugly beast.
It's up to me, then. Time to be the hero.
rRRRRRRRRRR
WHAT ARE YOU DOING?

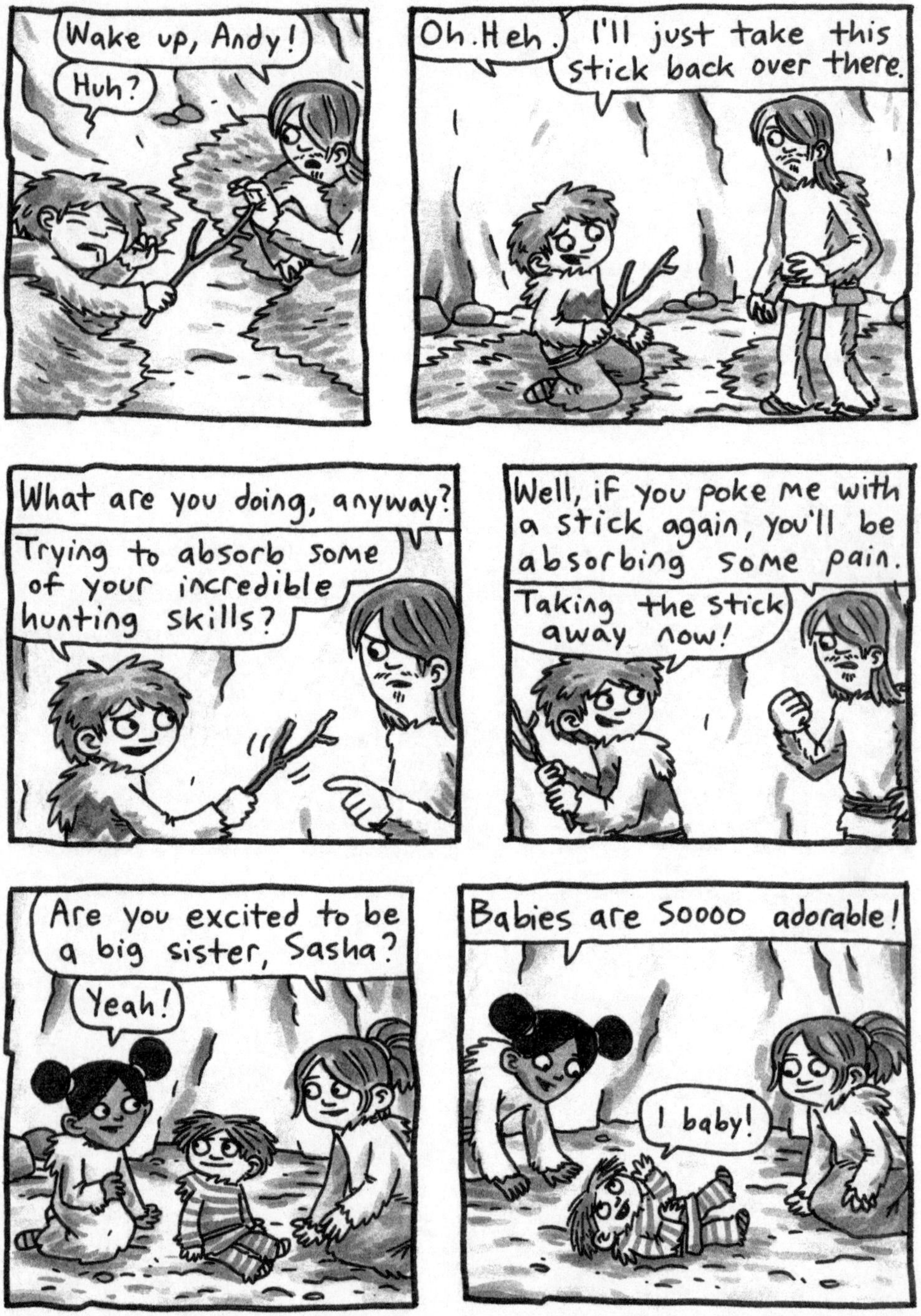
Wake up, Andy!
Huh?
Oh. Heh.
I'll just take this stick back over there.
What are you doing, anyway?
Trying to absorb some of your incredible hunting skills?
Well, if you poke me with a stick again, you'll be absorbing some pain.
Taking the stick away now!
Are you excited to be a big sister, Sasha?
Yeah!
Babies are Soooo adorable!
I baby!

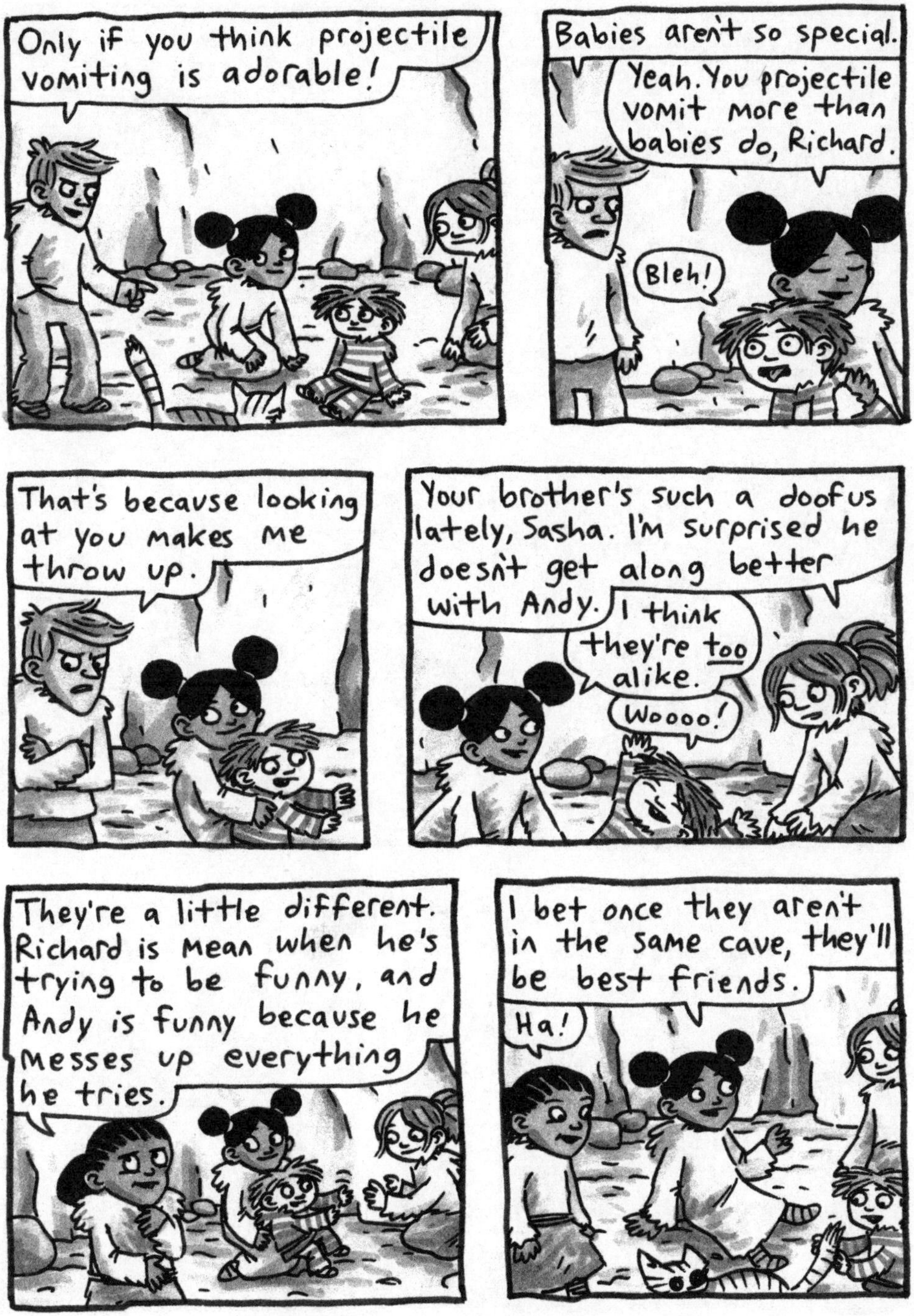
Only if you think projectile vomiting is adorable!
Babies aren't so special.
Yeah. You projectile vomit more than babies do, Richard.
Bleh!
That's because looking at you makes me throw up.
Your brother's such a doofus lately, Sasha. I'm surprised he doesn't get along better with Andy.
I think they're too alike.
Woooo!
They're a little different. Richard is mean when he's trying to be funny, and Andy is funny because he messes up everything he tries.
I bet once they aren't in the same cave, they'll be best friends.
Ha!

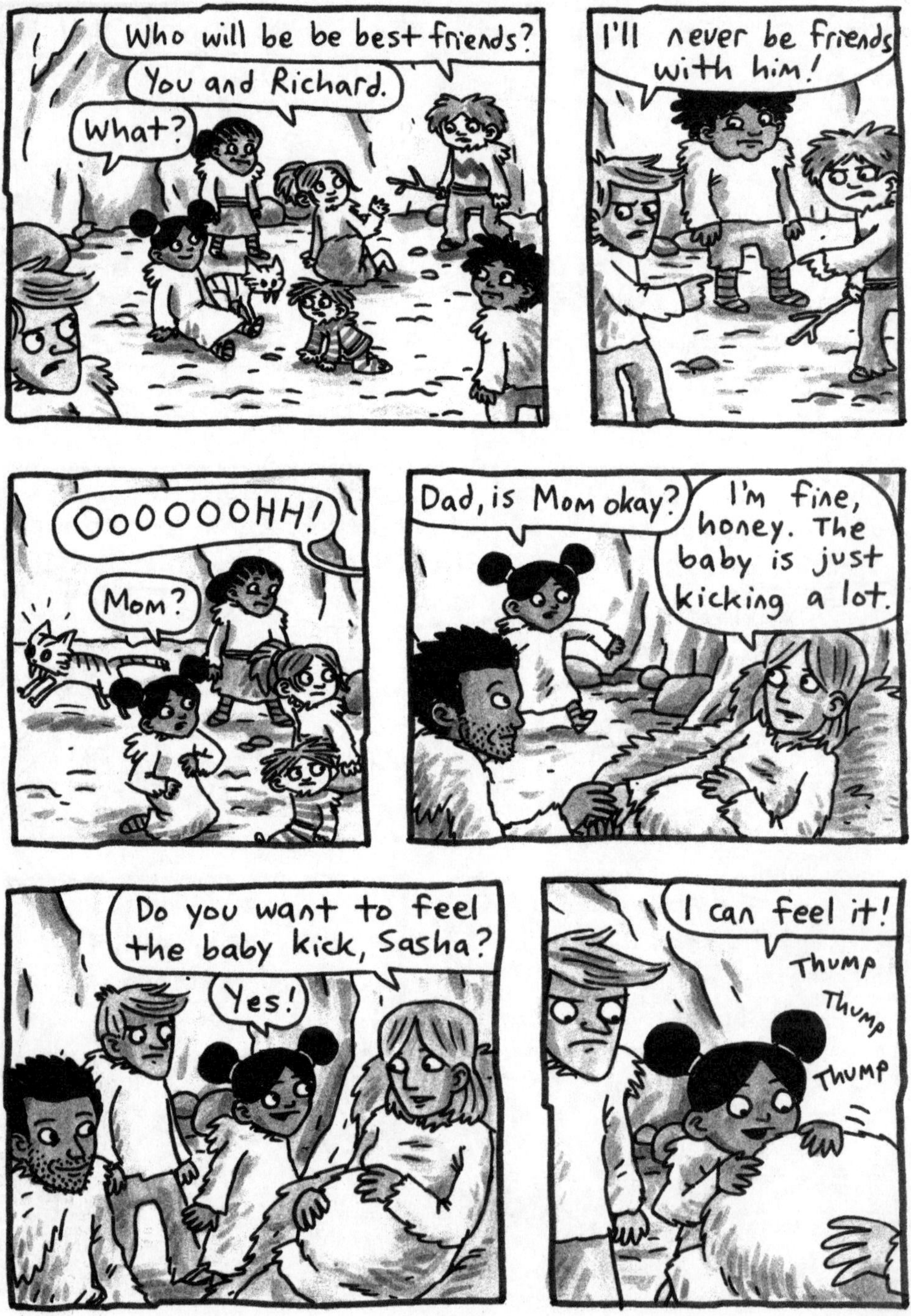
Who will be be best friends?
You and Richard.
What?
I'll never be friends with him!
OOOOOOHH!
Mom?
Dad, is Mom okay?
I'm fine, honey. The baby is just kicking a lot.
Do you want to feel the baby kick, Sasha?
Yes!
I can feel it!
THUMP
THUMP
THUMP

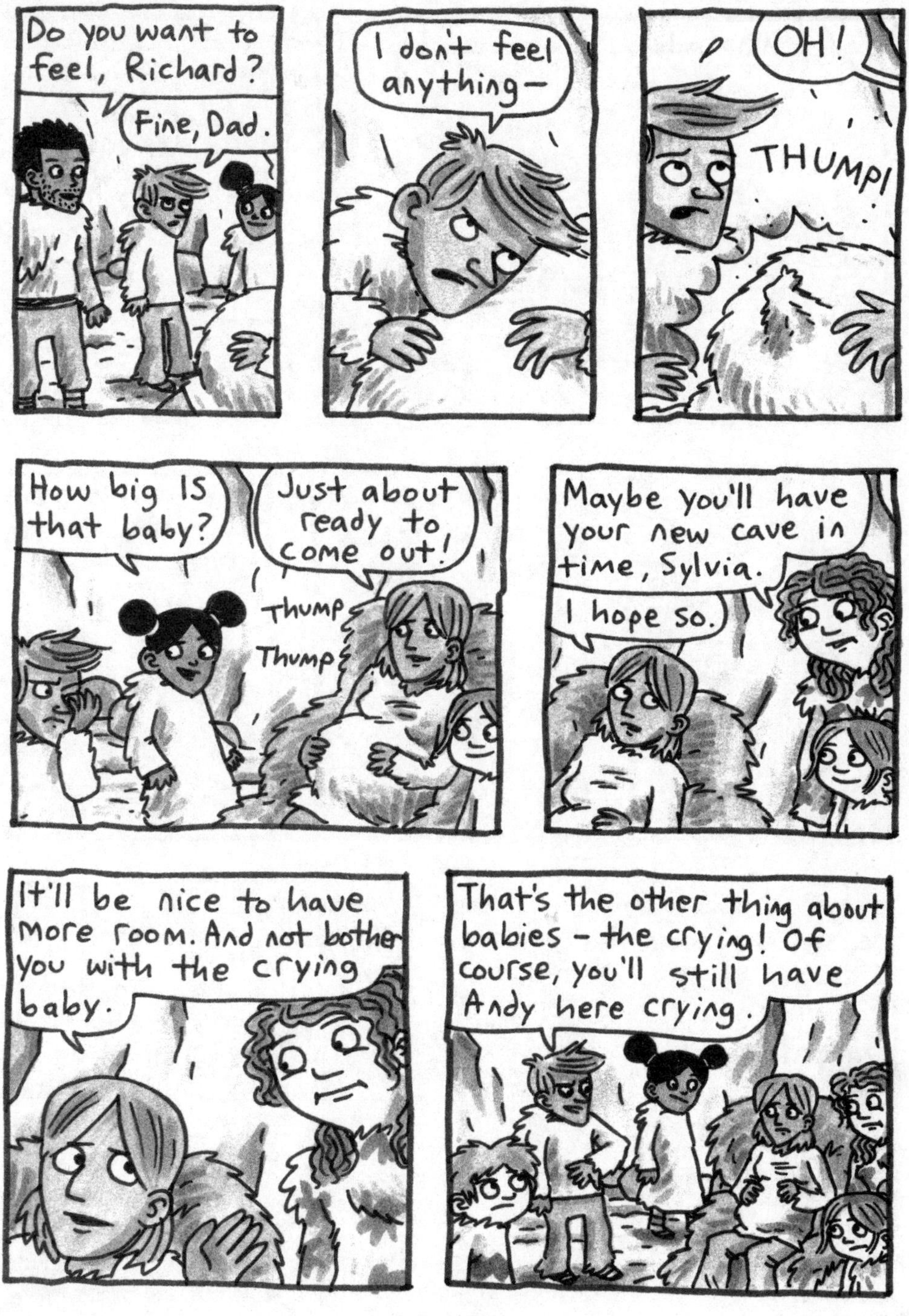
Do you want to feel, Richard?
Fine, Dad.
I don't feel anything—
OH!
THUMP!
How big IS that baby?
Just about ready to come out!
Thump
Thump
Maybe you'll have your new cave in time, Sylvia.
I hope so.
It'll be nice to have more room. And not bother you with the crying baby.
That's the other thing about babies – the crying! Of course, you'll still have Andy here crying.

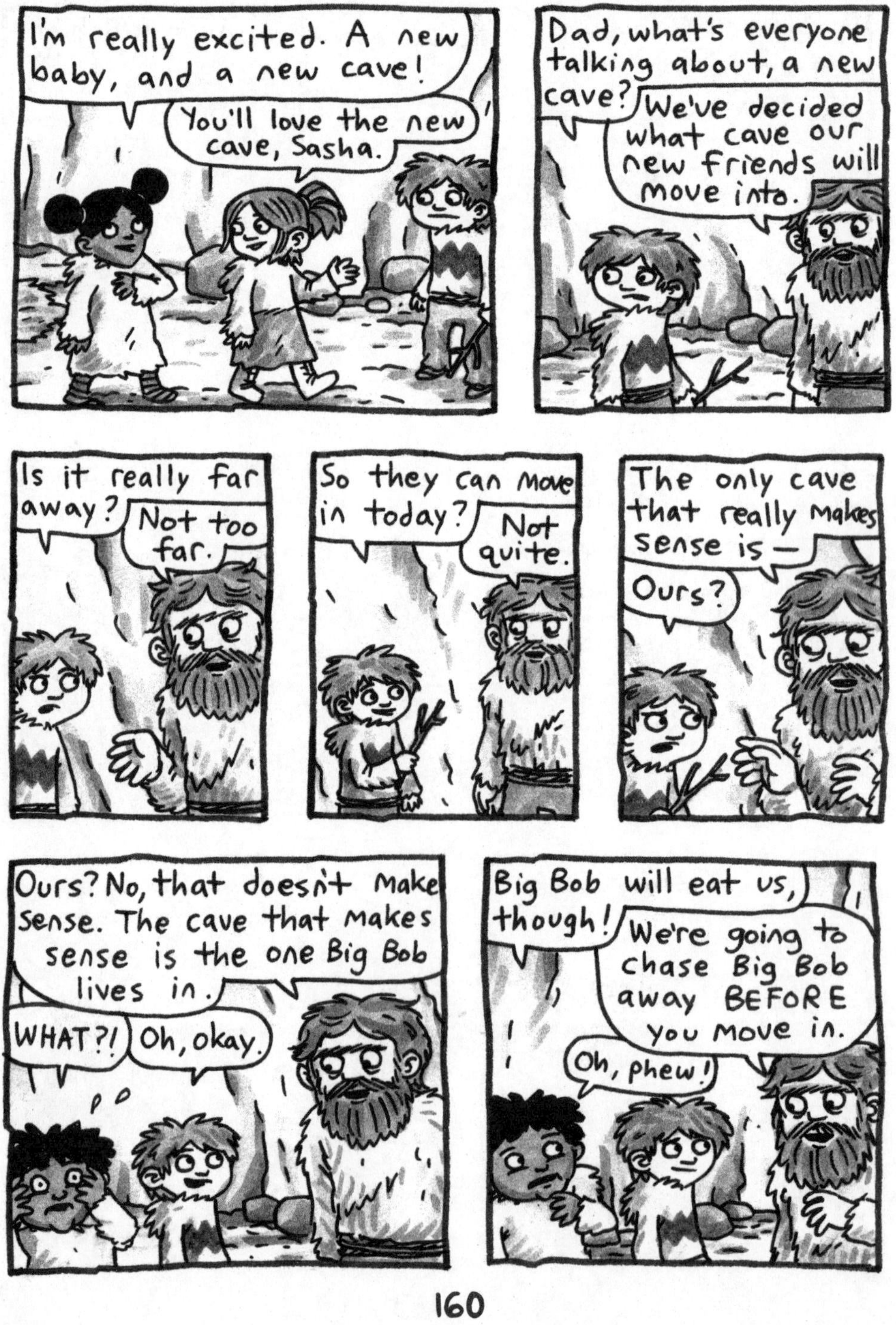
I'm really excited. A new baby, and a new cave!
You'll love the new cave, Sasha.
Dad, what's everyone talking about, a new cave?
We've decided what cave our new friends will move into.
Is it really far away?
Not too far.
So they can move in today?
Not quite.
The only cave that really makes sense is—
Ours?
Ours? No, that doesn't make sense. The cave that makes sense is the one Big Bob lives in.
WHAT?!
Oh, okay.
Big Bob will eat us, though!
We're going to chase Big Bob away BEFORE you move in.
Oh, phew!

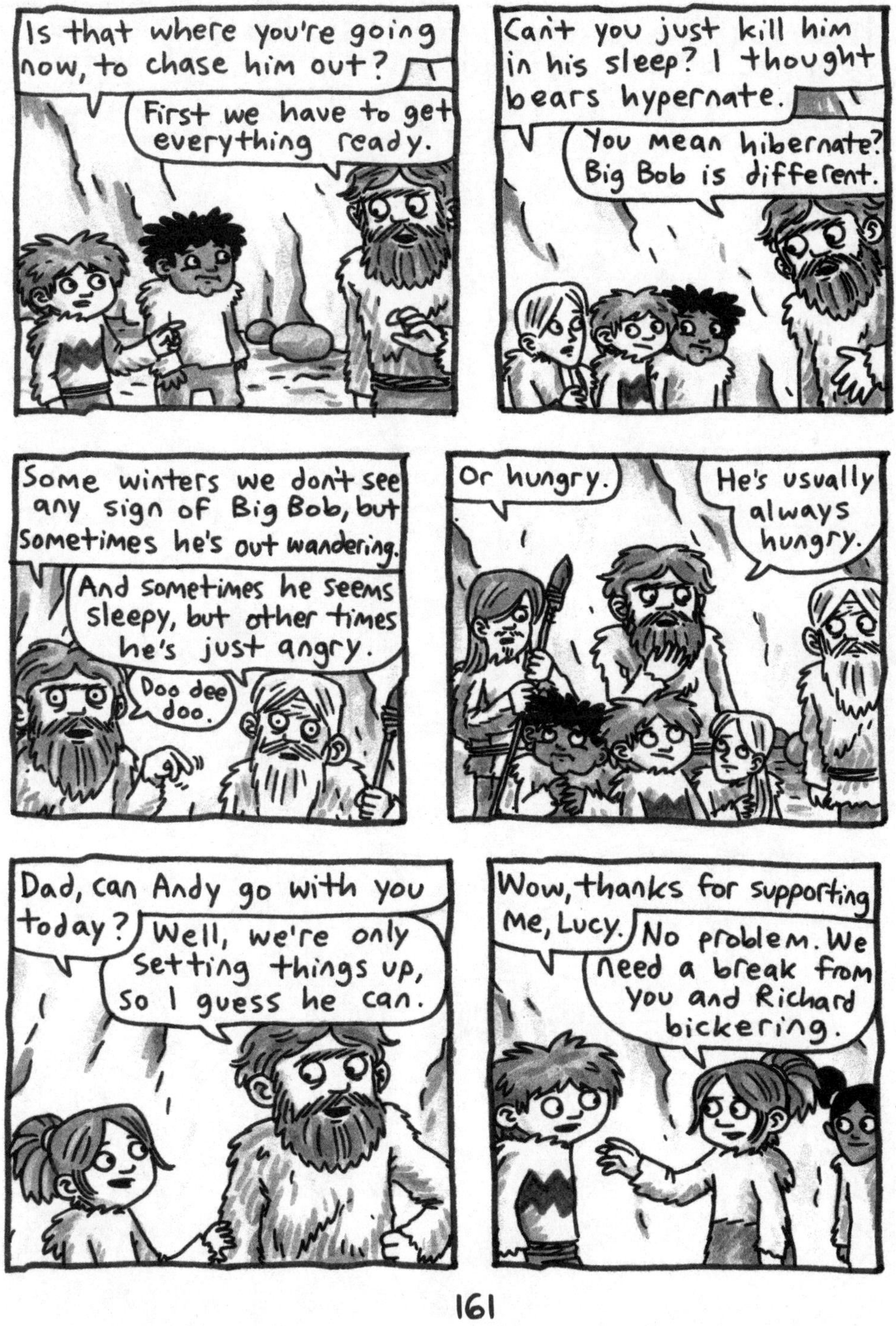
Is that where you're going now, to chase him out?
First we have to get everything ready.
Can't you just kill him in his sleep? I thought bears hypernate.
You mean hibernate? Big Bob is different.
Some winters we don't see any sign of Big Bob, but sometimes he's out wandering.
And sometimes he seems sleepy, but other times he's just angry.
Doo dee doo.
Or hungry.
He's usually always hungry.
Dad, can Andy go with you today?
Well, we're only setting things up, so I guess he can.
Wow, thanks for supporting me, Lucy.
No problem. We need a break from you and Richard bickering.

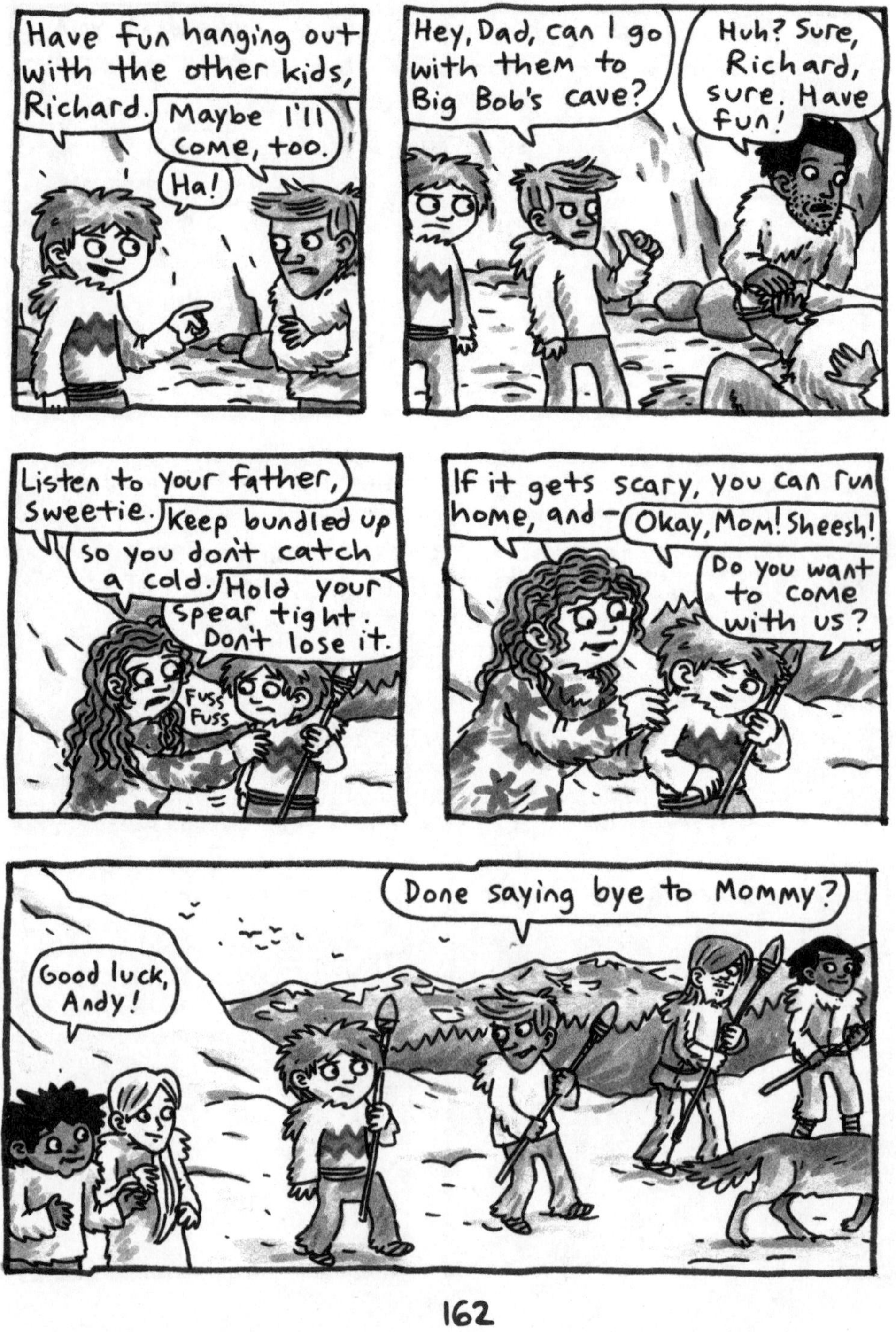
Have fun hanging out with the other kids, Richard.
Maybe I'll come, too.
Ha!
Hey, Dad, can I go with them to Big Bob's cave?
Huh? Sure, Richard, sure. Have fun!
Listen to your father, Sweetie.
Keep bundled up so you don't catch a cold.
Hold your spear tight. Don't lose it.
Fuss Fuss
If it gets scary, you can run home, and—
Okay, Mom! Sheesh!
Do you want to come with us?
Good luck, Andy!
Done saying bye to Mommy?

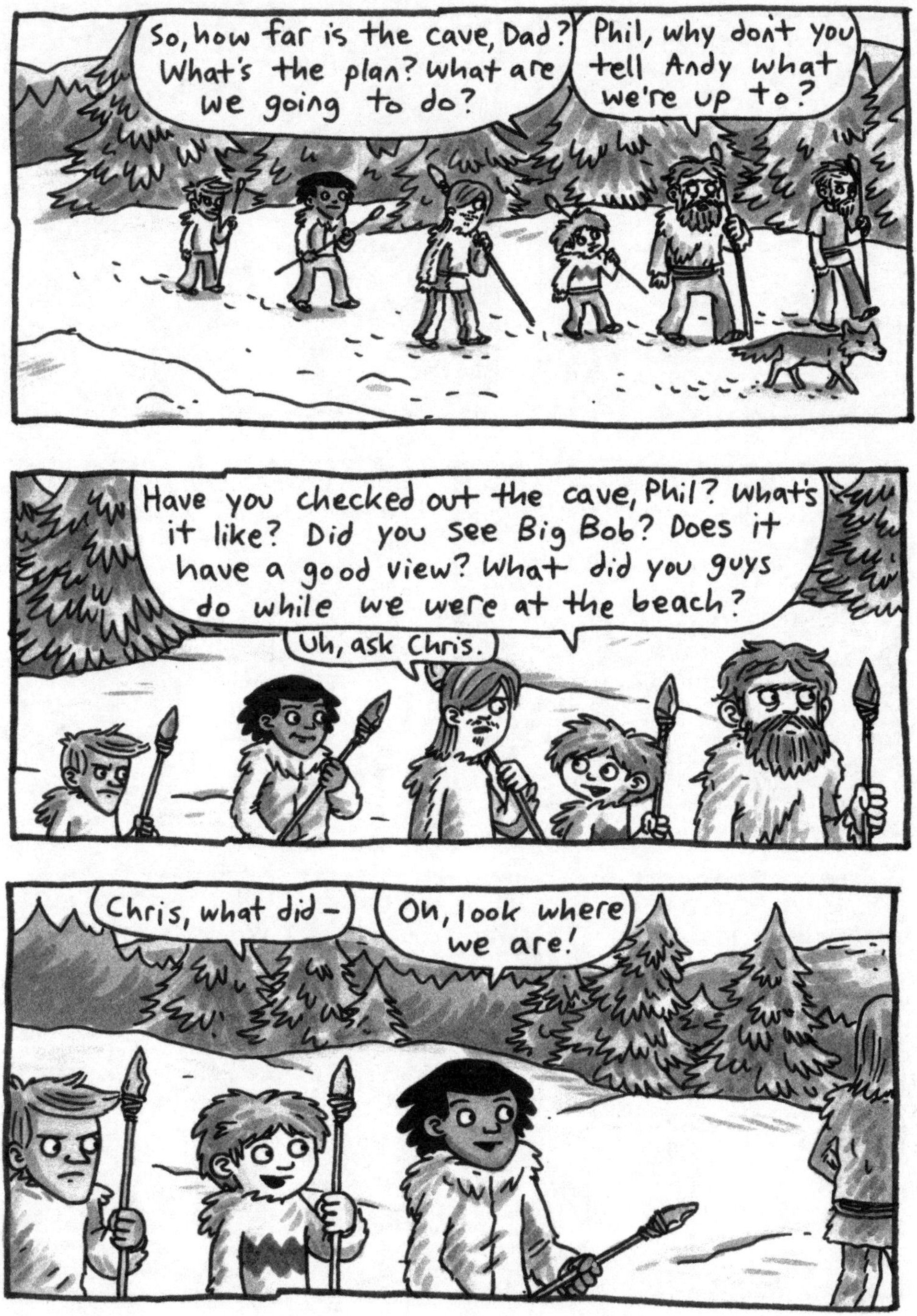

So, how far is the cave, Dad? What's the plan? What are we going to do?
Phil, why don't you tell Andy what we're up to?
Have you checked out the cave, Phil? What's it like? Did you see Big Bob? Does it have a good view? What did you guys do while we were at the beach?
Uh, ask Chris.
Chris, what did—
Oh, look where we are!

Now we go see if Big Bob is in there, right?

He is.

How do you know?

Bones knows. He can smell the cave bear.

I don't smell anything.

RRRRRRR

That's because your own odor covers other bad smells.

Mr. Daryl says Big Bob sleeps in a spot way deep in the cave. Let me guess. I wait out here while you all go in.

Actually, we need your help, Andy!

I'm ready! Let's go!

Okay!

Start gathering up firewood and bring it back here!

All right!

Wait, what?!

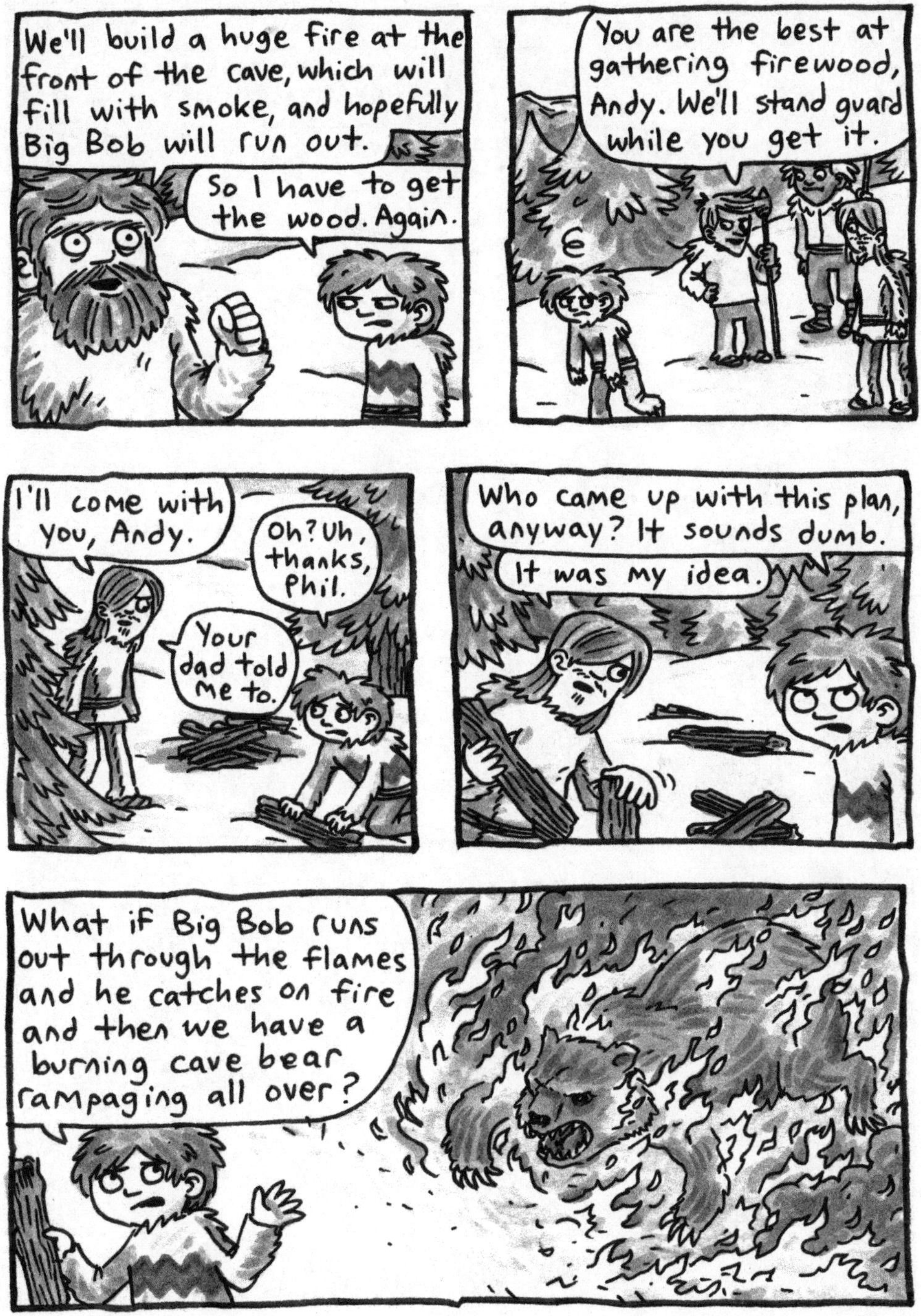
We'll build a huge fire at the front of the cave, which will fill with smoke, and hopefully Big Bob will run out.
So I have to get the wood. Again.
You are the best at gathering firewood, Andy. We'll stand guard while you get it.
I'll come with you, Andy.
Oh? Uh, thanks, Phil.
Your dad told me to.
Who came up with this plan, anyway? It sounds dumb.
It was my idea.
What if Big Bob runs out through the flames and he catches on fire and then we have a burning cave bear rampaging all over?

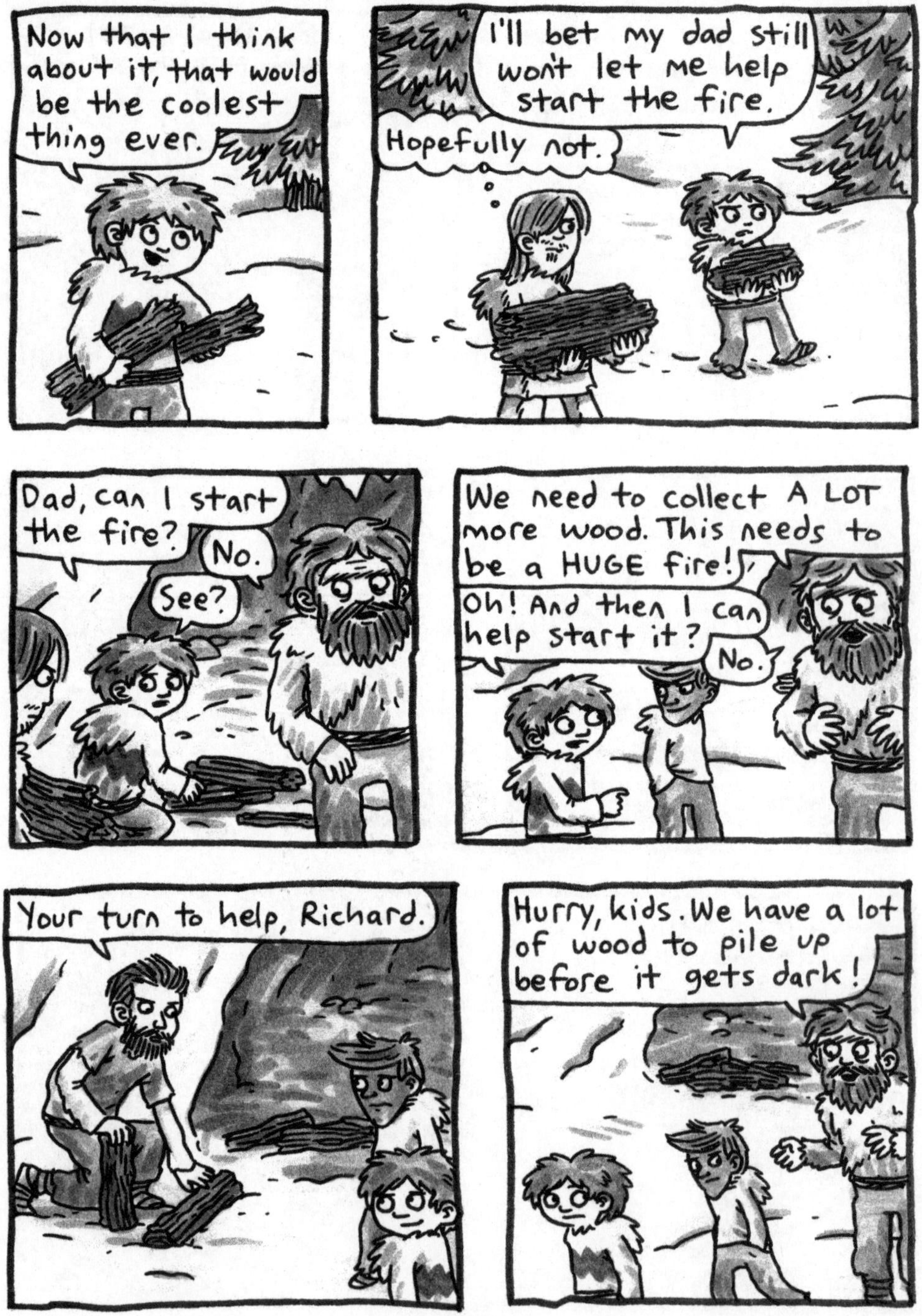

Now that I think about it, that would be the coolest thing ever.
I'll bet my dad still won't let me help start the fire.
Hopefully not.
Dad, can I start the fire?
No.
See?
We need to collect A LOT more wood. This needs to be a HUGE fire!
Oh! And then I can help start it?
No.
Your turn to help, Richard.
Hurry, kids. We have a lot of wood to pile up before it gets dark!

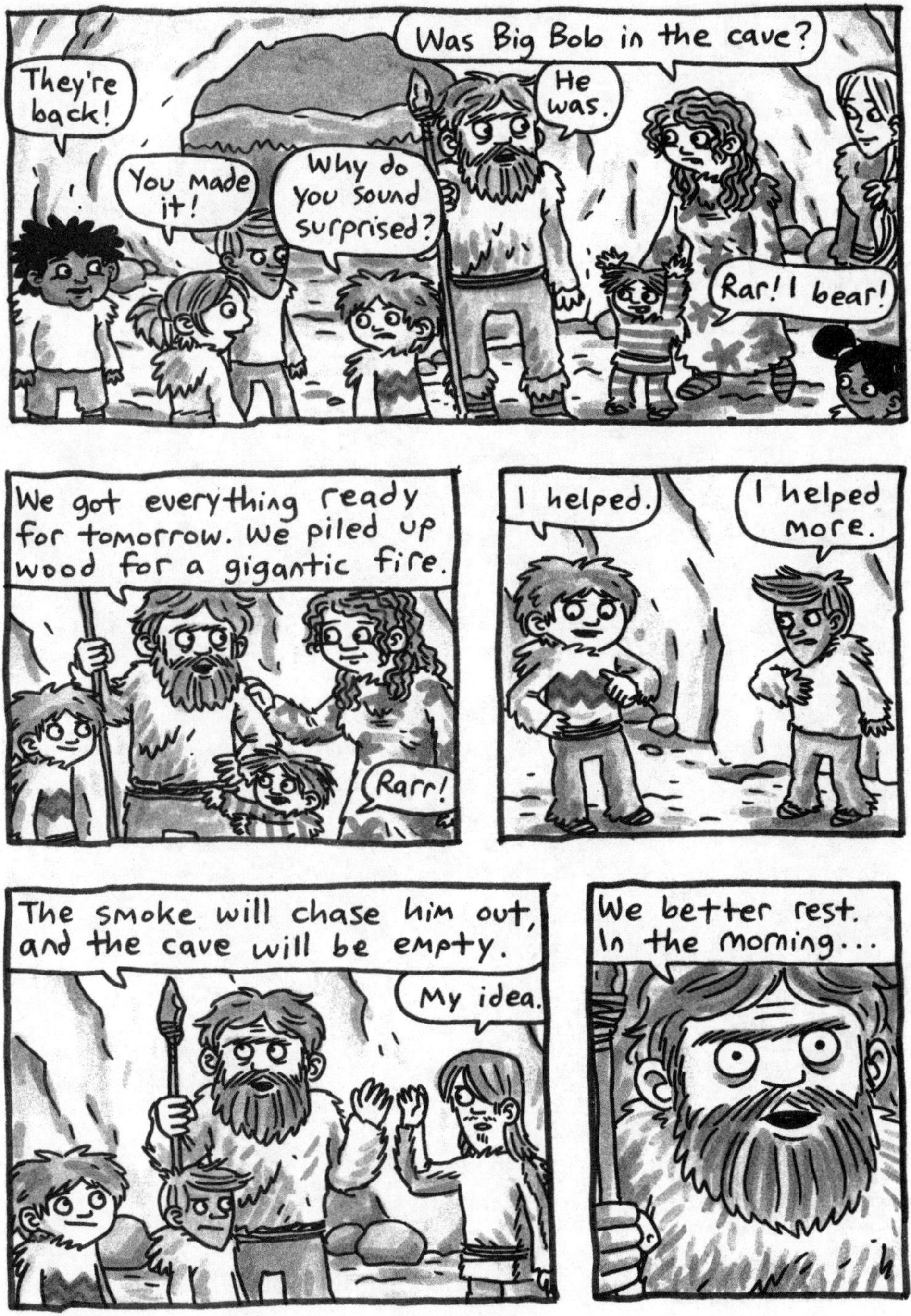
They're back!
You made it!
Why do you sound surprised?
Was Big Bob in the cave?
He was.
Rar! I bear!
We got everything ready for tomorrow. We piled up wood for a gigantic fire.
Rarr!
I helped.
I helped more.
The smoke will chase him out, and the cave will be empty.
My idea.
We better rest. In the morning...

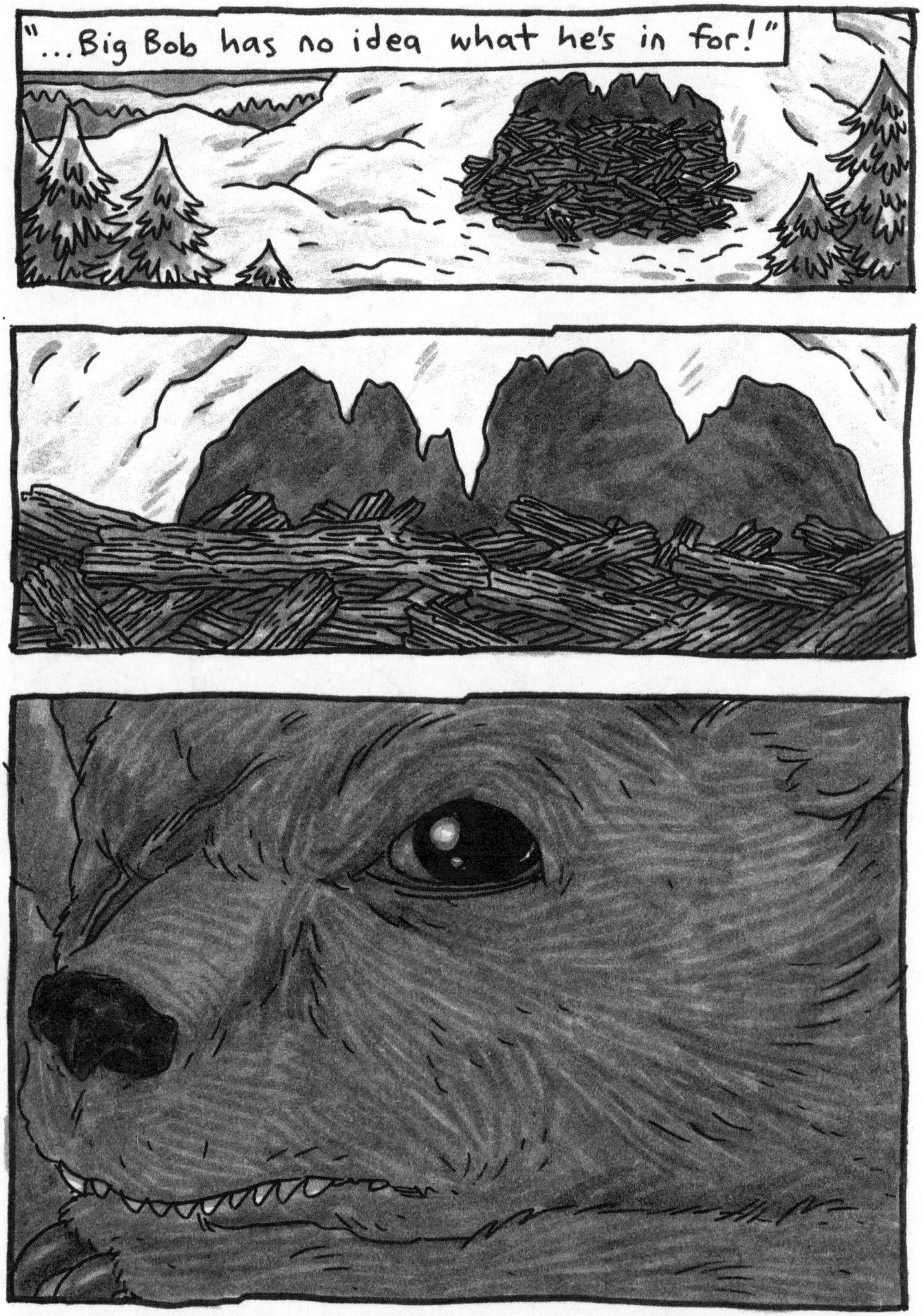
"...Big Bob has no idea what he's in for!"

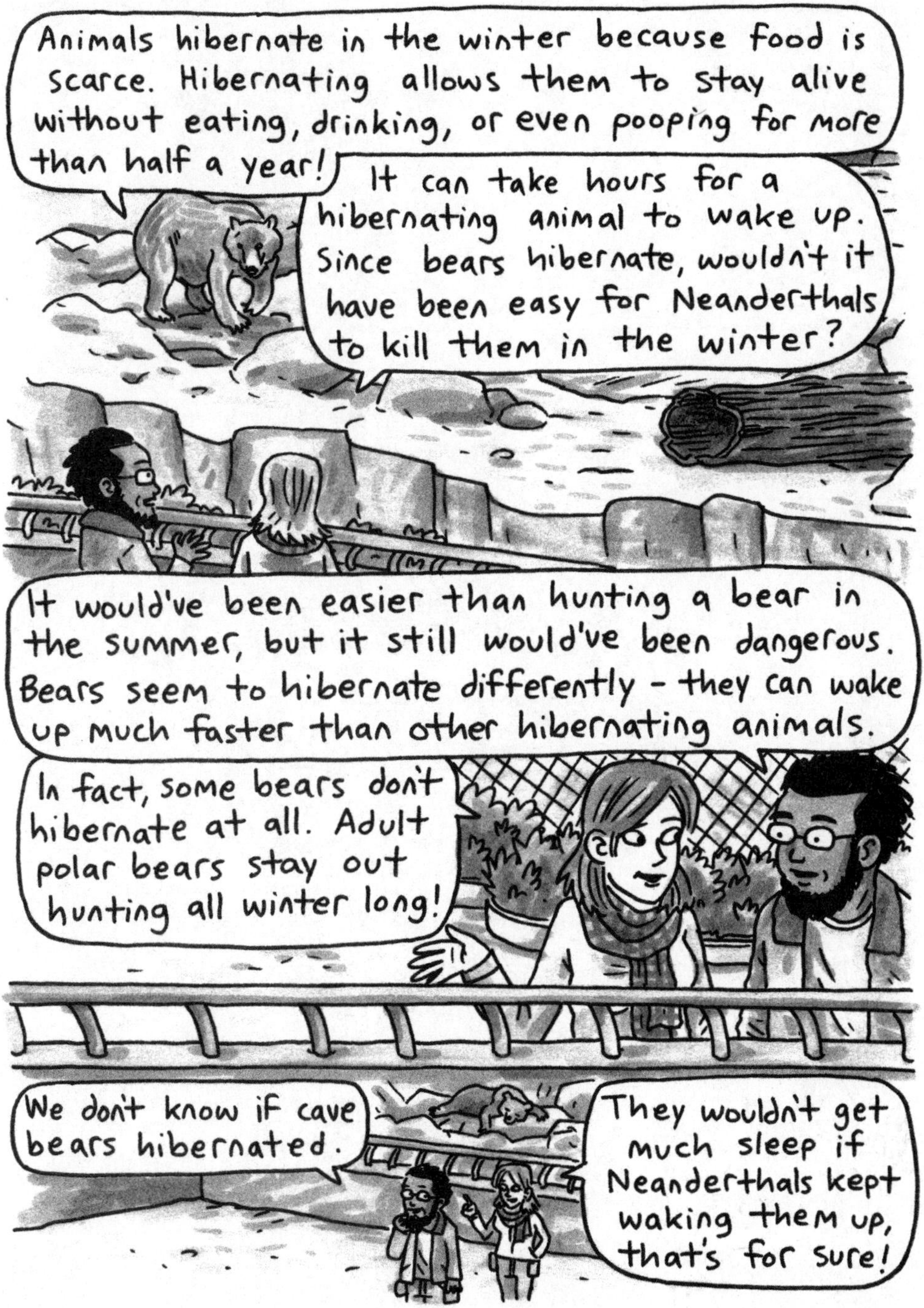
Animals hibernate in the winter because food is scarce. Hibernating allows them to stay alive without eating, drinking, or even pooping for more than half a year!
It can take hours for a hibernating animal to wake up. Since bears hibernate, wouldn't it have been easy for Neanderthals to kill them in the winter?
It would've been easier than hunting a bear in the summer, but it still would've been dangerous. Bears seem to hibernate differently - they can wake up much faster than other hibernating animals.
In fact, some bears don't hibernate at all. Adult polar bears stay out hunting all winter long!
We don't know if cave bears hibernated.
They wouldn't get much sleep if Neanderthals kept waking them up, that's for sure!

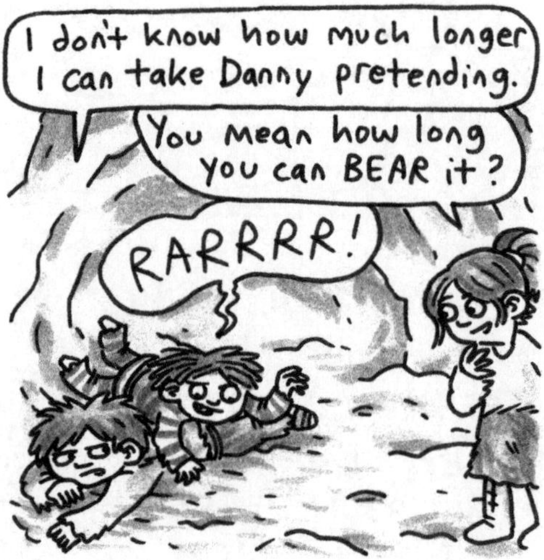
I don't know how much longer I can take Danny pretending.
You mean how long you can BEAR it?
RARRRR!

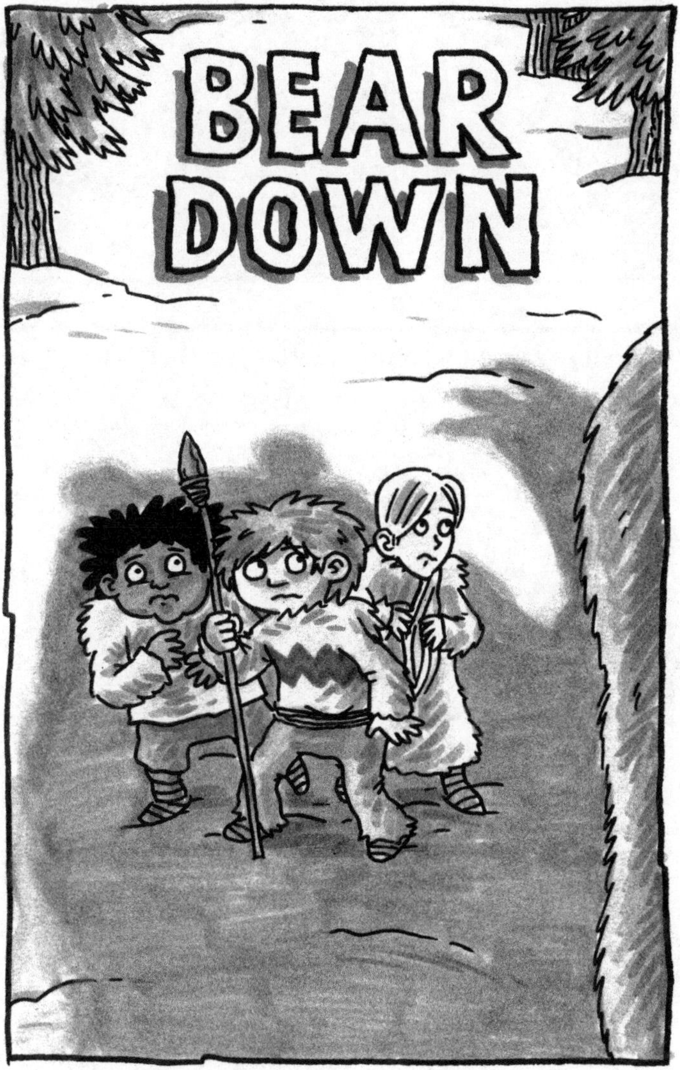
BEAR DOWN

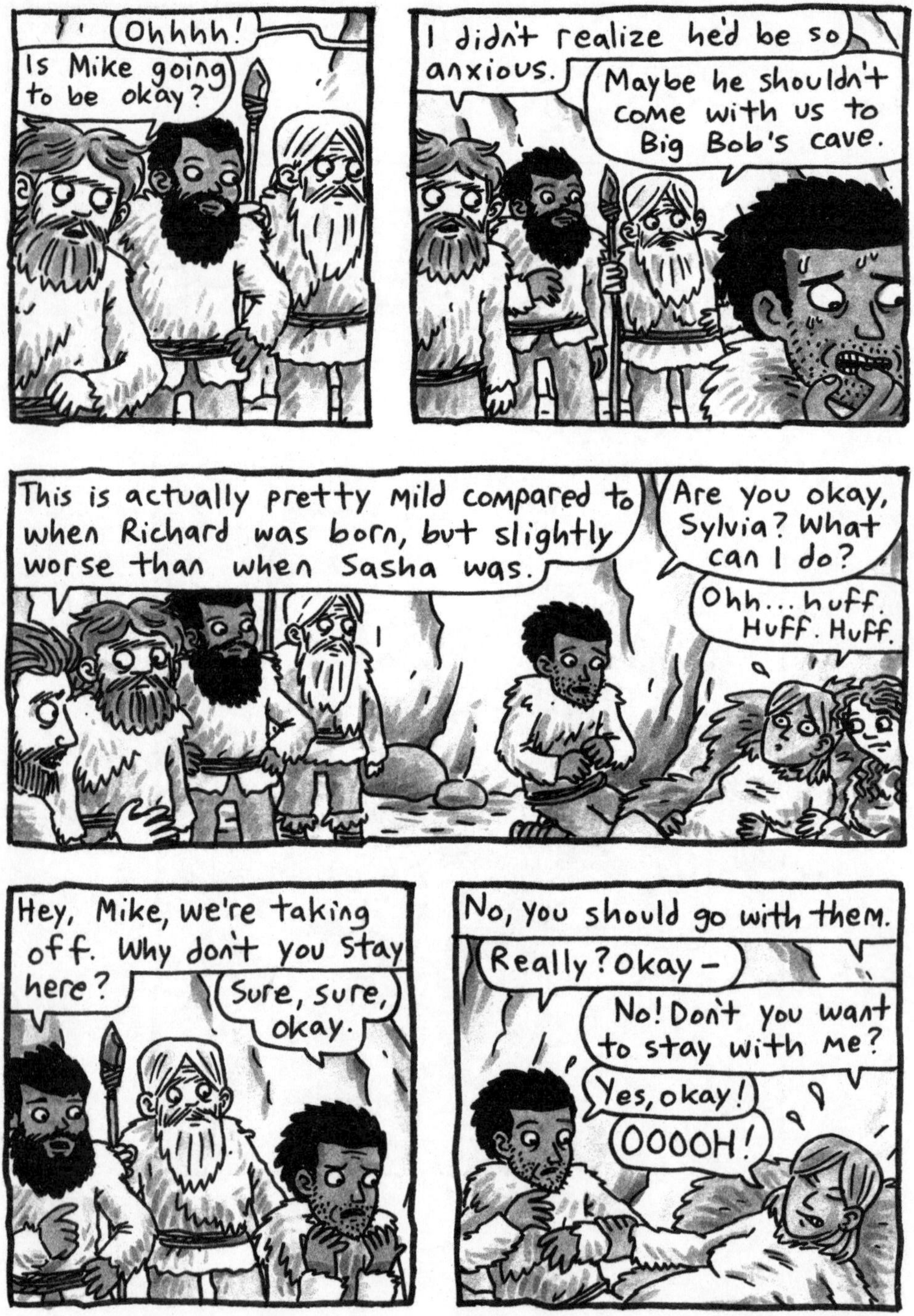
Ohhhh!
Is Mike going to be okay?
I didn't realize he'd be so anxious.
Maybe he shouldn't come with us to Big Bob's cave.
This is actually pretty mild compared to when Richard was born, but slightly worse than when Sasha was.
Are you okay, Sylvia? What can I do?
Ohh... huff. Huff. Huff.
Hey, Mike, we're taking off. Why don't you stay here?
Sure, sure, okay.
No, you should go with them.
Really? Okay –
No! Don't you want to stay with me?
Yes, okay!
OOOOH!

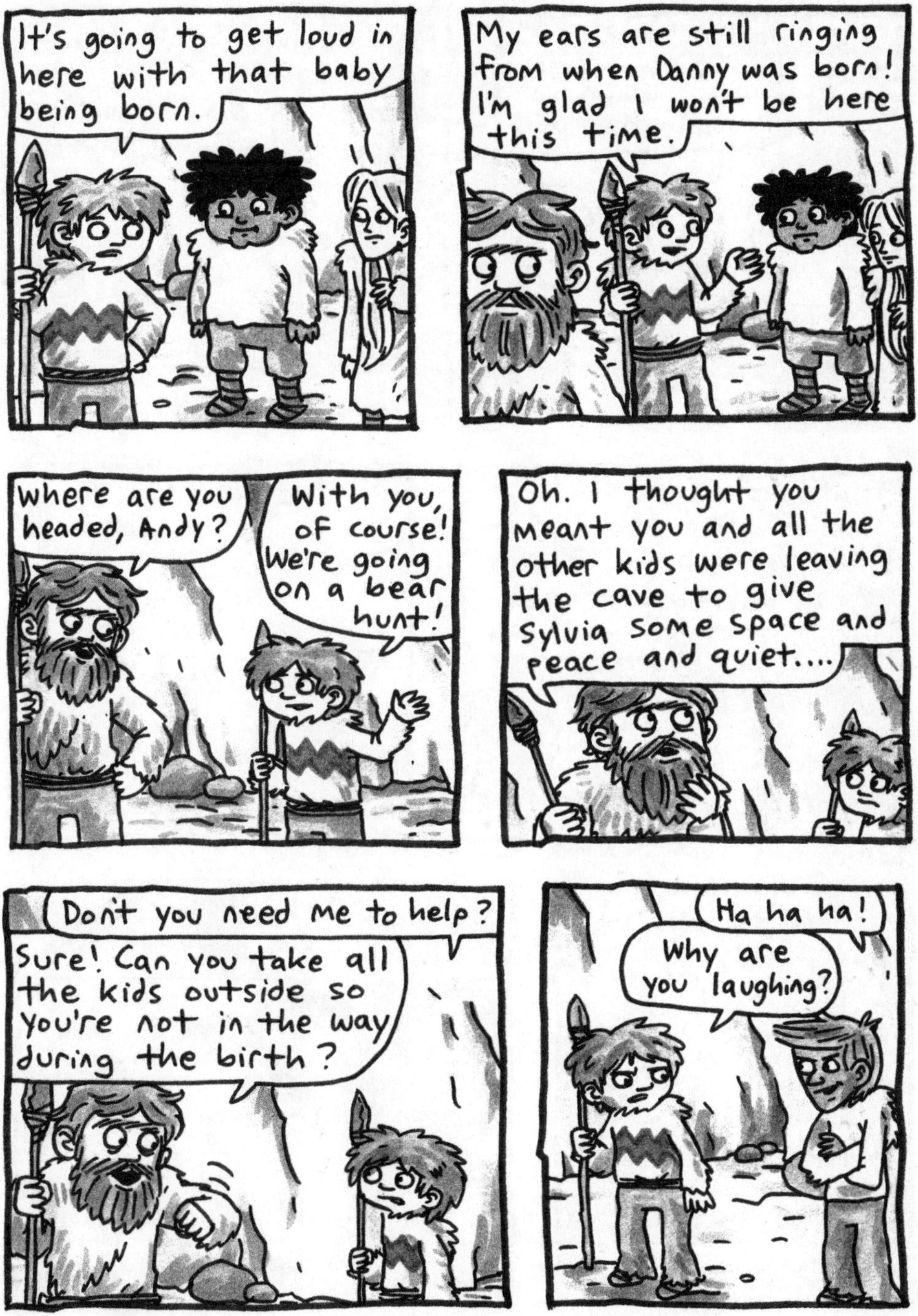
It's going to get loud in here with that baby being born.
My ears are still ringing from when Danny was born! I'm glad I won't be here this time.
Where are you headed, Andy?
With you, of course! We're going on a bear hunt!
Oh. I thought you meant you and all the other kids were leaving the cave to give Sylvia some space and peace and quiet....
Don't you need me to help?
Sure! Can you take all the kids outside so you're not in the way during the birth?
Ha ha ha!
Why are you laughing?

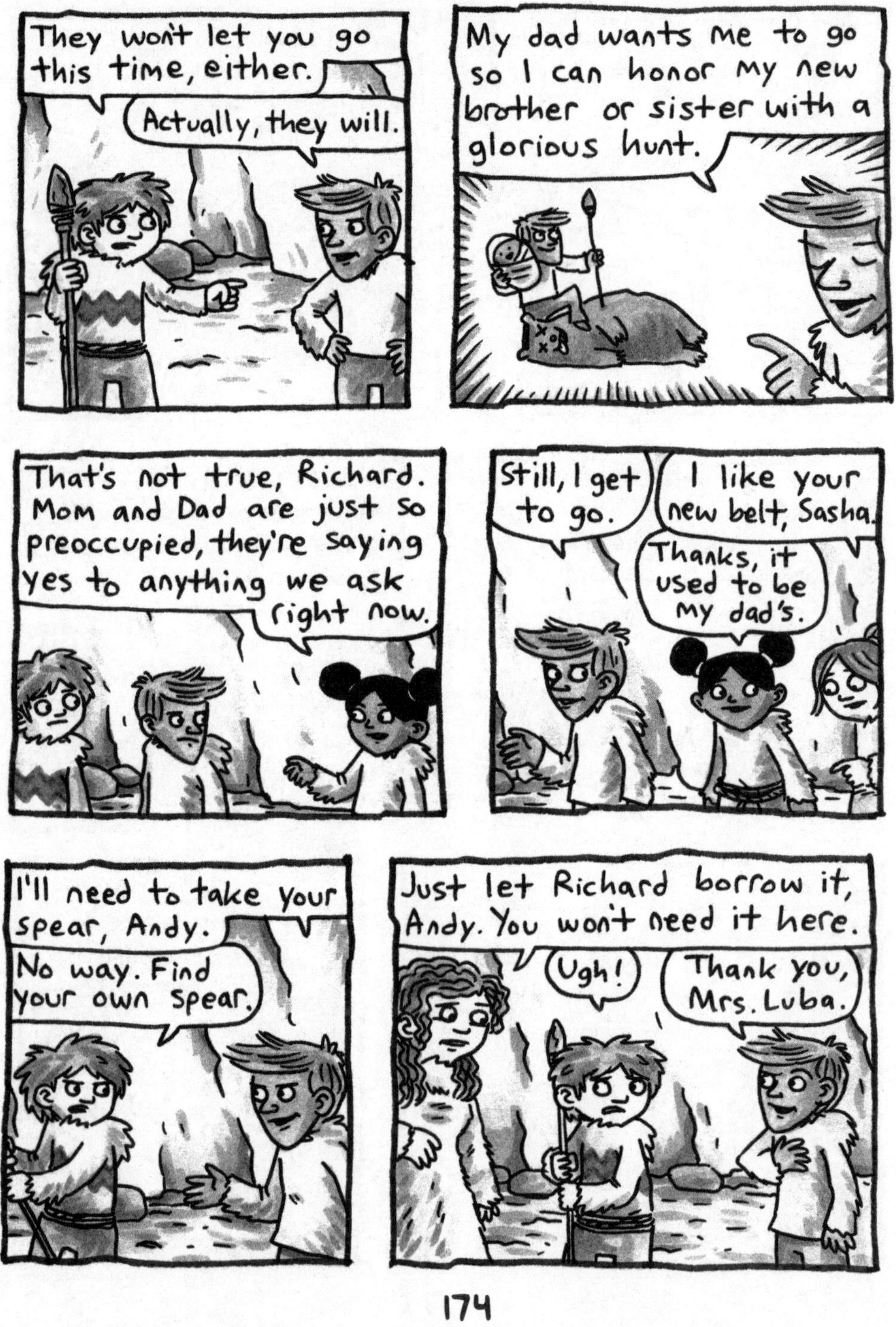
They won't let you go this time, either.
Actually, they will.
My dad wants me to go so I can honor my new brother or sister with a glorious hunt.
That's not true, Richard. Mom and Dad are just so preoccupied, they're saying yes to anything we ask right now.
Still, I get to go.
I like your new belt, Sasha.
Thanks, it used to be my dad's.
I'll need to take your spear, Andy.
No way. Find your own spear.
Just let Richard borrow it, Andy. You won't need it here.
Ugh!
Thank you, Mrs. Luba.

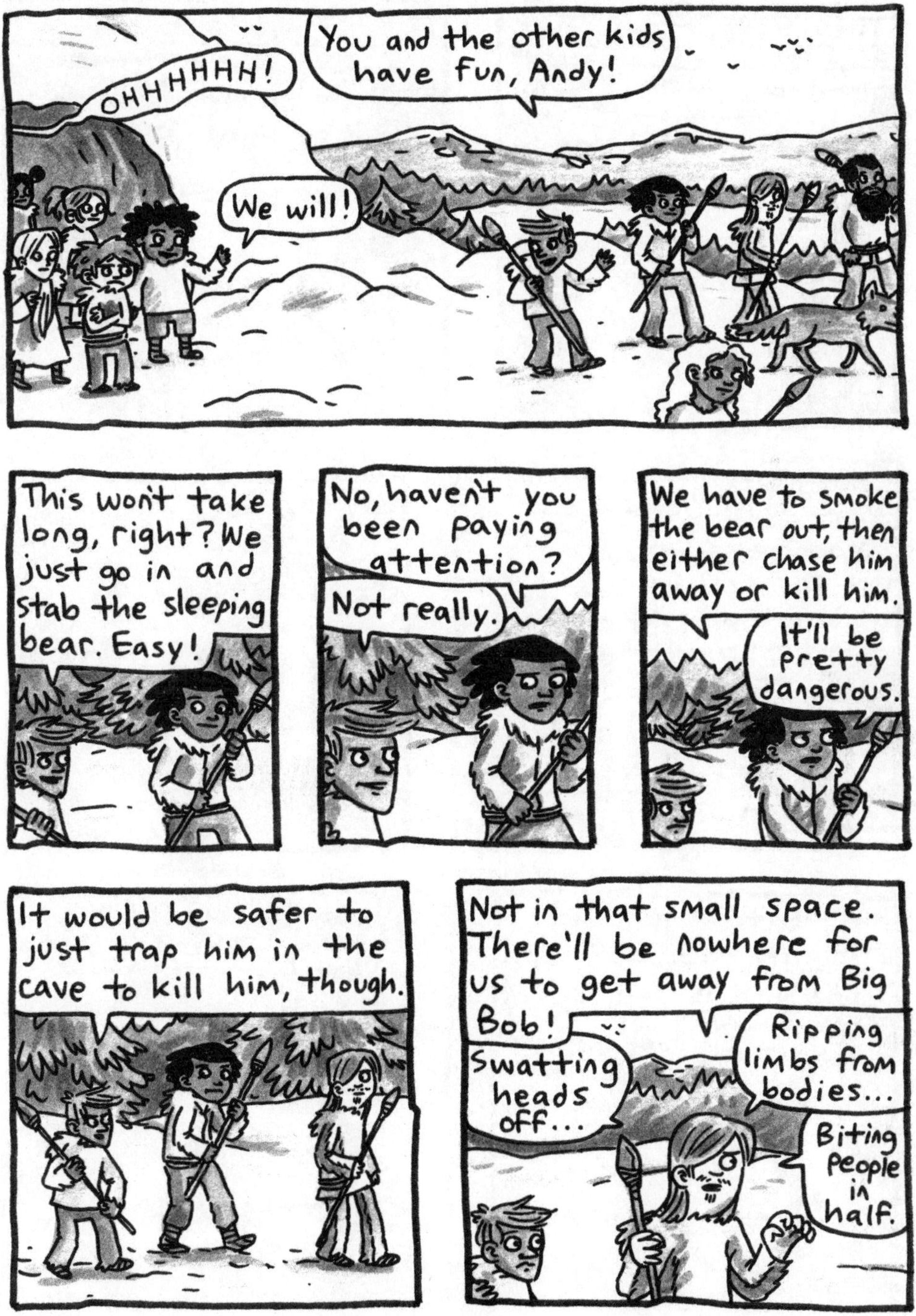
OHHHHHH!
You and the other kids have fun, Andy!
We will!
This won't take long, right? We just go in and stab the sleeping bear. Easy!
No, haven't you been paying attention?
Not really.
We have to smoke the bear out, then either chase him away or kill him.
It'll be pretty dangerous.
It would be safer to just trap him in the cave to kill him, though.
Not in that small space. There'll be nowhere for us to get away from Big Bob!
Swatting heads off...
Ripping limbs from bodies...
Biting people in half.

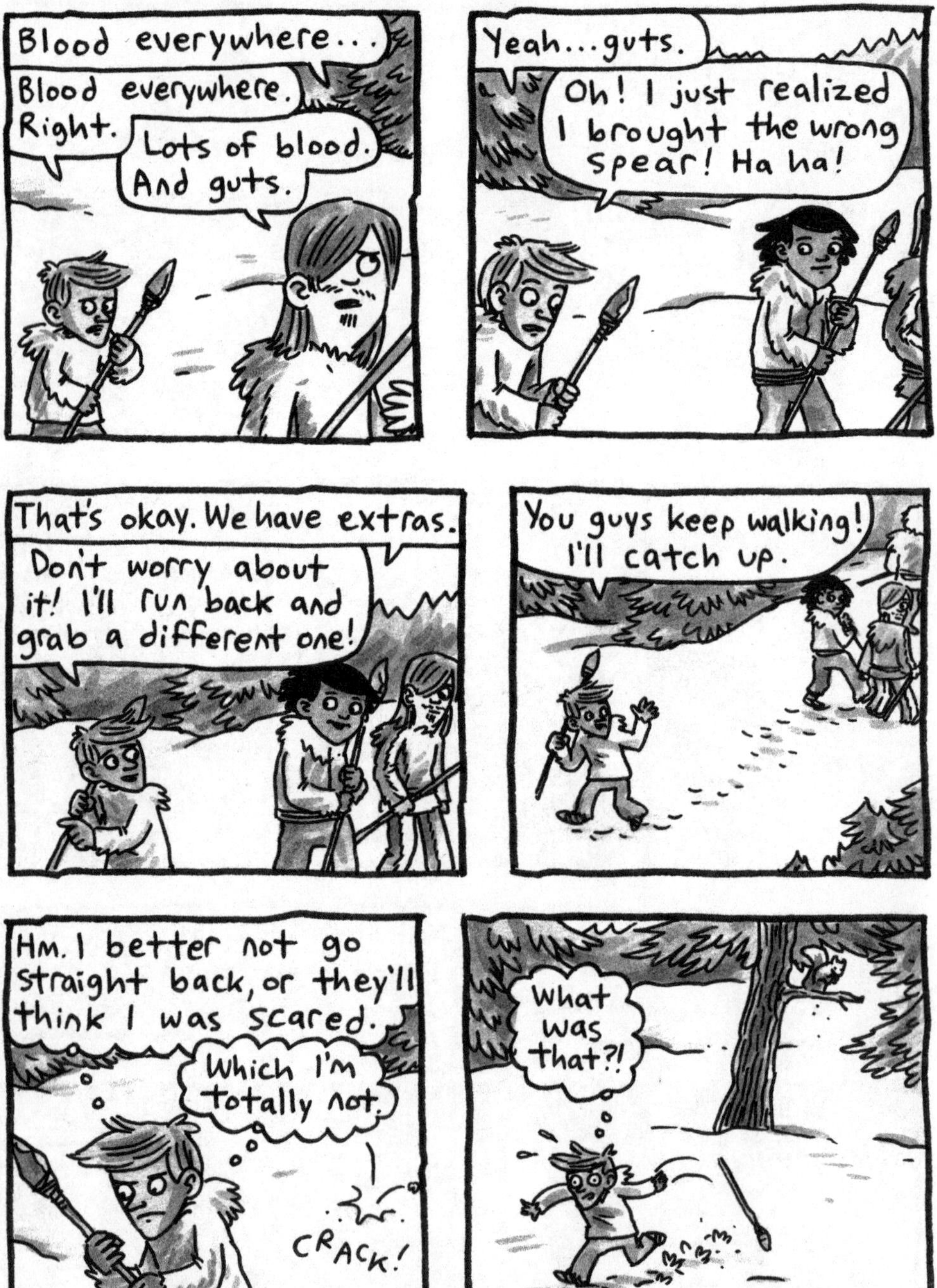
Blood everywhere...
Blood everywhere. Right.
Lots of blood. And guts.
Yeah...guts.
Oh! I just realized I brought the wrong spear! Ha ha!
That's okay. We have extras.
Don't worry about it! I'll run back and grab a different one!
You guys keep walking! I'll catch up.
Hm. I better not go straight back, or they'll think I was scared.
Which I'm totally not.
CRACK!
What was that?!

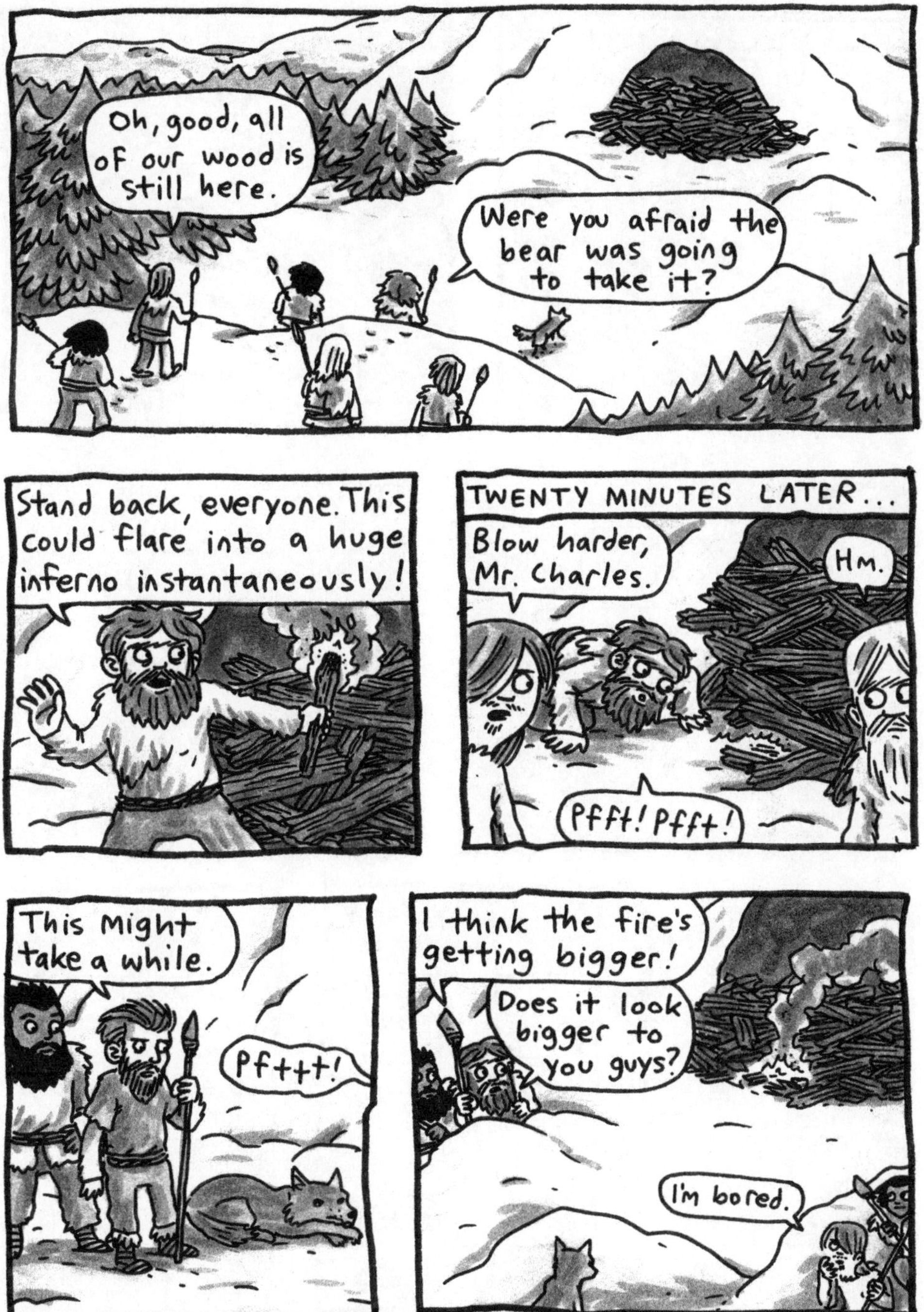
Oh, good, all of our wood is still here.
Were you afraid the bear was going to take it?
Stand back, everyone. This could flare into a huge inferno instantaneously!
TWENTY MINUTES LATER...
Blow harder, Mr. Charles.
Hm.
Pfft! Pfft!
This Might take a while.
Pfttt!
I think the fire's getting bigger!
Does it look bigger to you guys?
I'm bored.

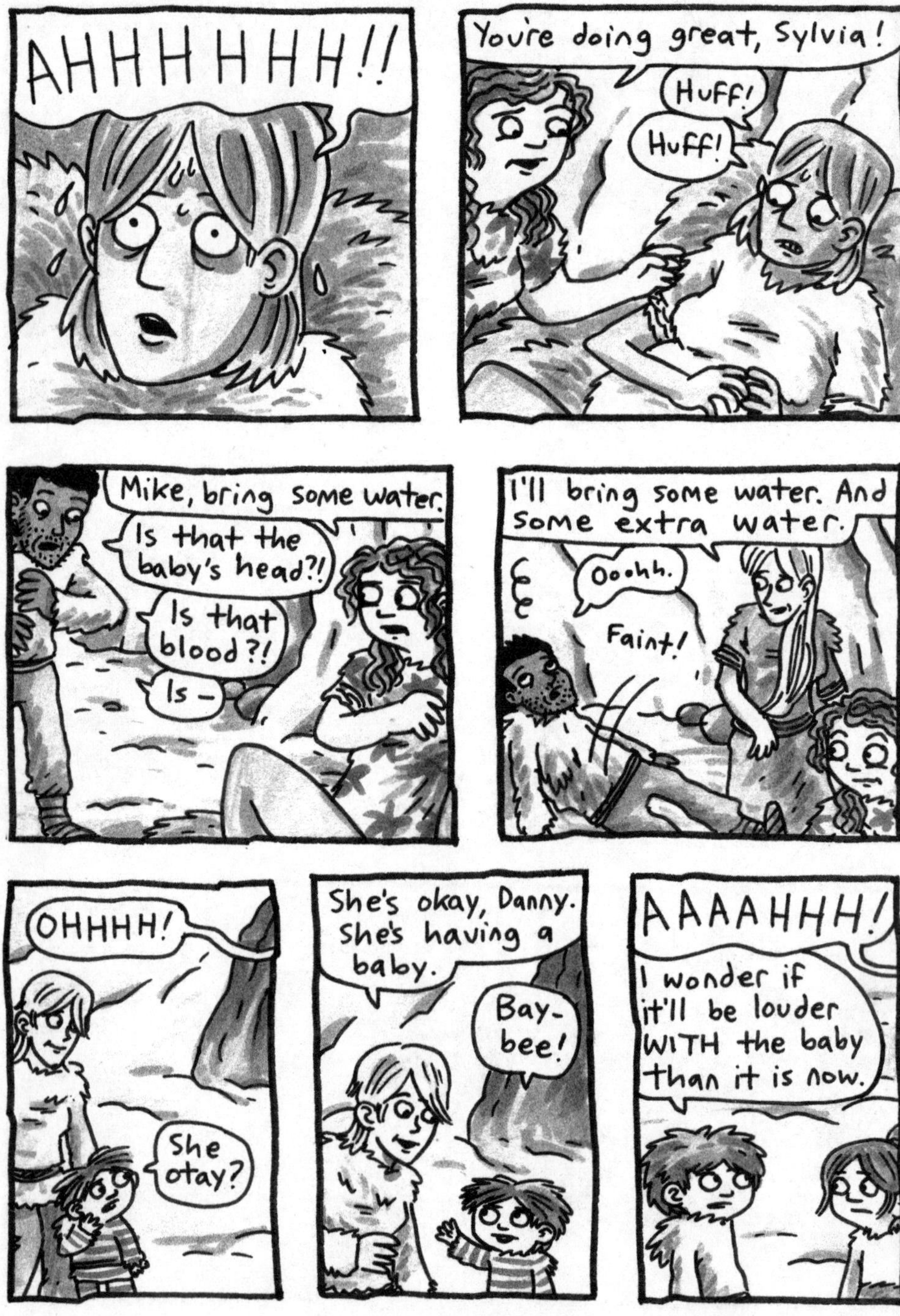
AHHHHHHH!!
You're doing great, Sylvia!
Huff!
Huff!
Mike, bring some water.
Is that the baby's head?!
Is that blood?!
Is –
I'll bring some water. And some extra water.
Ooohh.
Faint!
OHHHH!
She otay?
She's okay, Danny. She's having a baby.
Bay-bee!
AAAAHHH!
I wonder if it'll be louder WITH the baby than it is now.

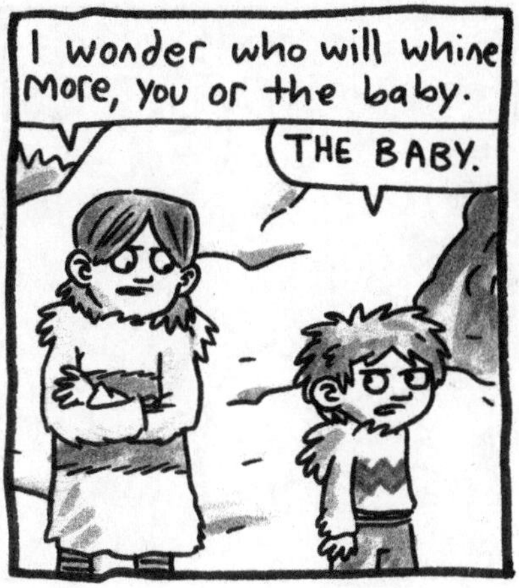
I wonder who will whine more, you or the baby.
THE BABY.

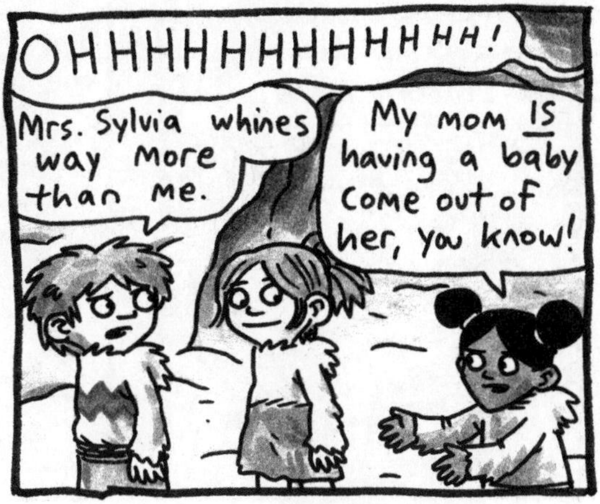
OHHHHHHHHHHHHH!
Mrs. Sylvia whines way more than me.
My mom IS having a baby come out of her, you know!

Neanderthal bones were denser, and scientists think they may have been less flexible at birth!

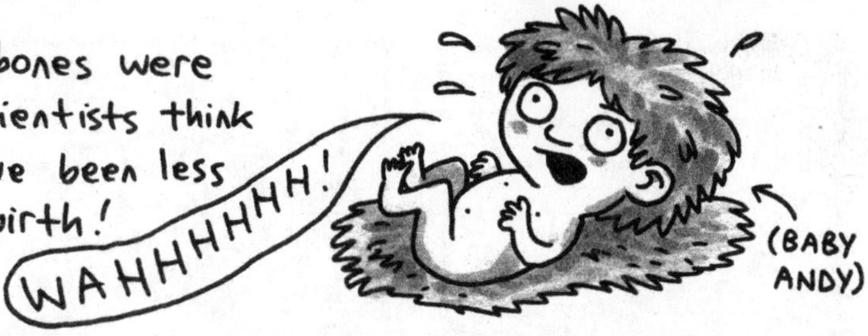
WAHHHHHHH!
(BABY ANDY)

Despite differences in anatomy like the wider hips of Neanderthals, their babies were probably similar in size to early human babies at birth.

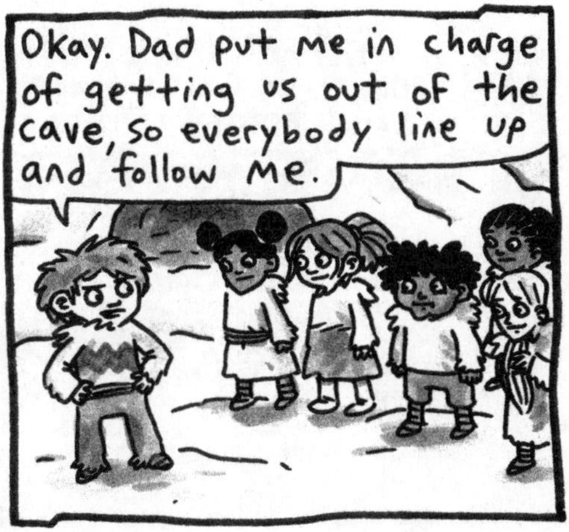
Okay. Dad put me in charge of getting us out of the cave, so everybody line up and follow me.

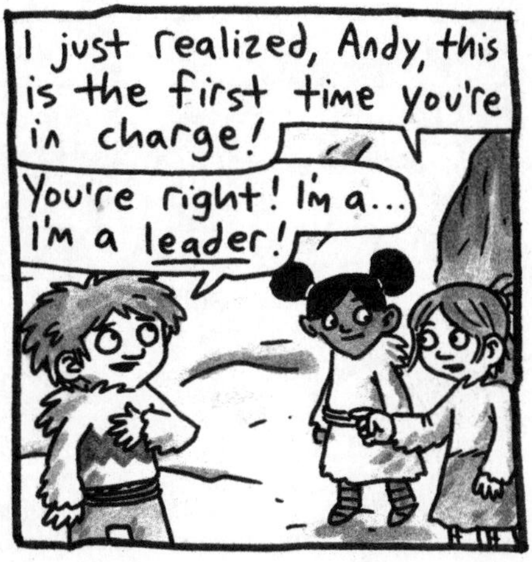
I just realized, Andy, this is the first time you're in charge!
You're right! I'm a... I'm a leader!

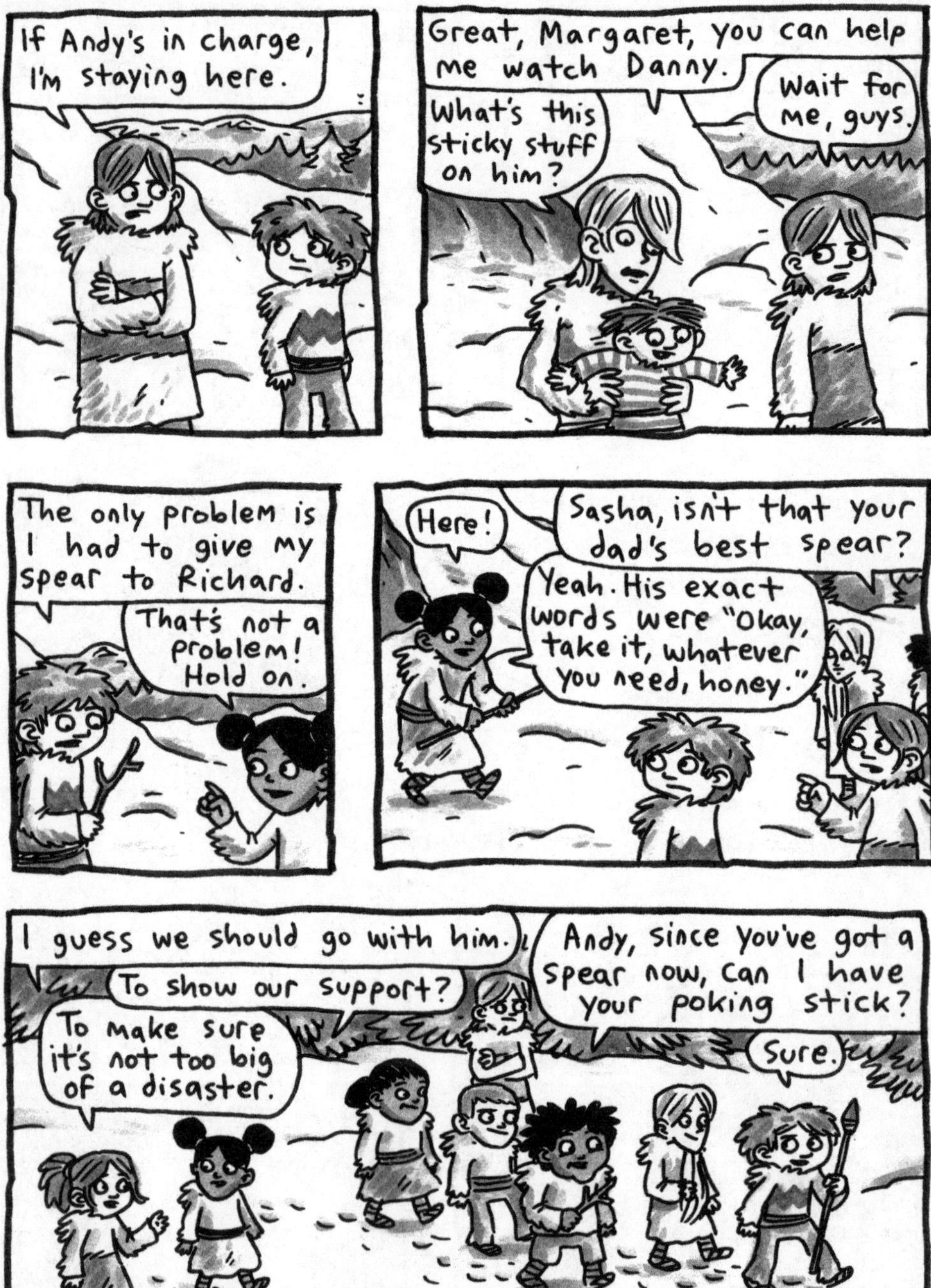

If Andy's in charge, I'm staying here.
Great, Margaret, you can help me watch Danny.
What's this sticky stuff on him?
Wait for me, guys.
The only problem is I had to give my spear to Richard.
That's not a problem! Hold on.
Here!
Sasha, isn't that your dad's best spear?
Yeah. His exact words were "Okay, take it, whatever you need, honey."
I guess we should go with him.
To show our support?
To make sure it's not too big of a disaster.
Andy, since you've got a spear now, can I have your poking stick?
Sure.

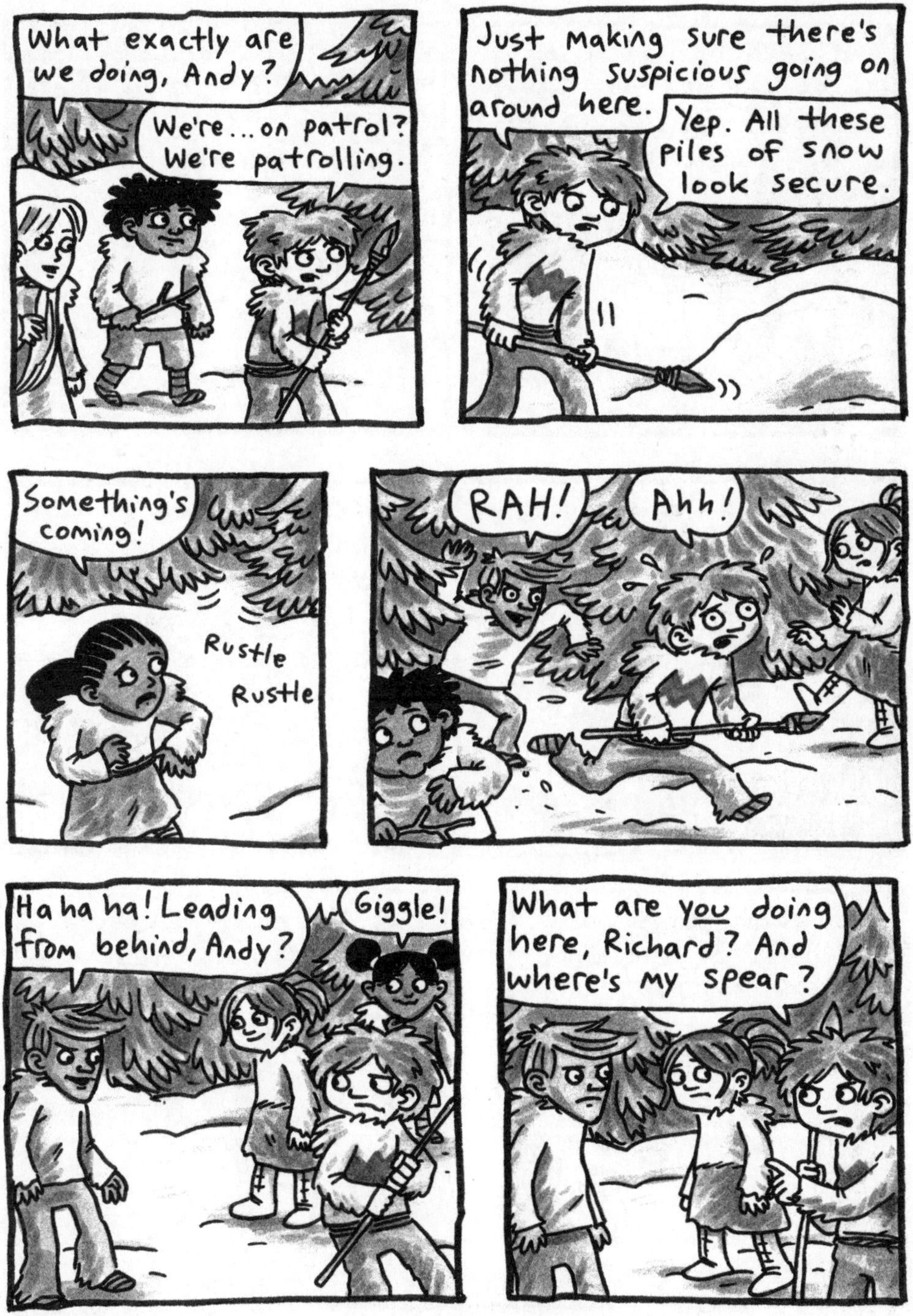
What exactly are we doing, Andy?
We're... on patrol? We're patrolling.
Just making sure there's nothing suspicious going on around here.
Yep. All these piles of snow look secure.
Something's coming!
Rustle
Rustle
RAH!
Ahh!
Ha ha ha! Leading from behind, Andy?
Giggle!
What are you doing here, Richard? And where's my spear?

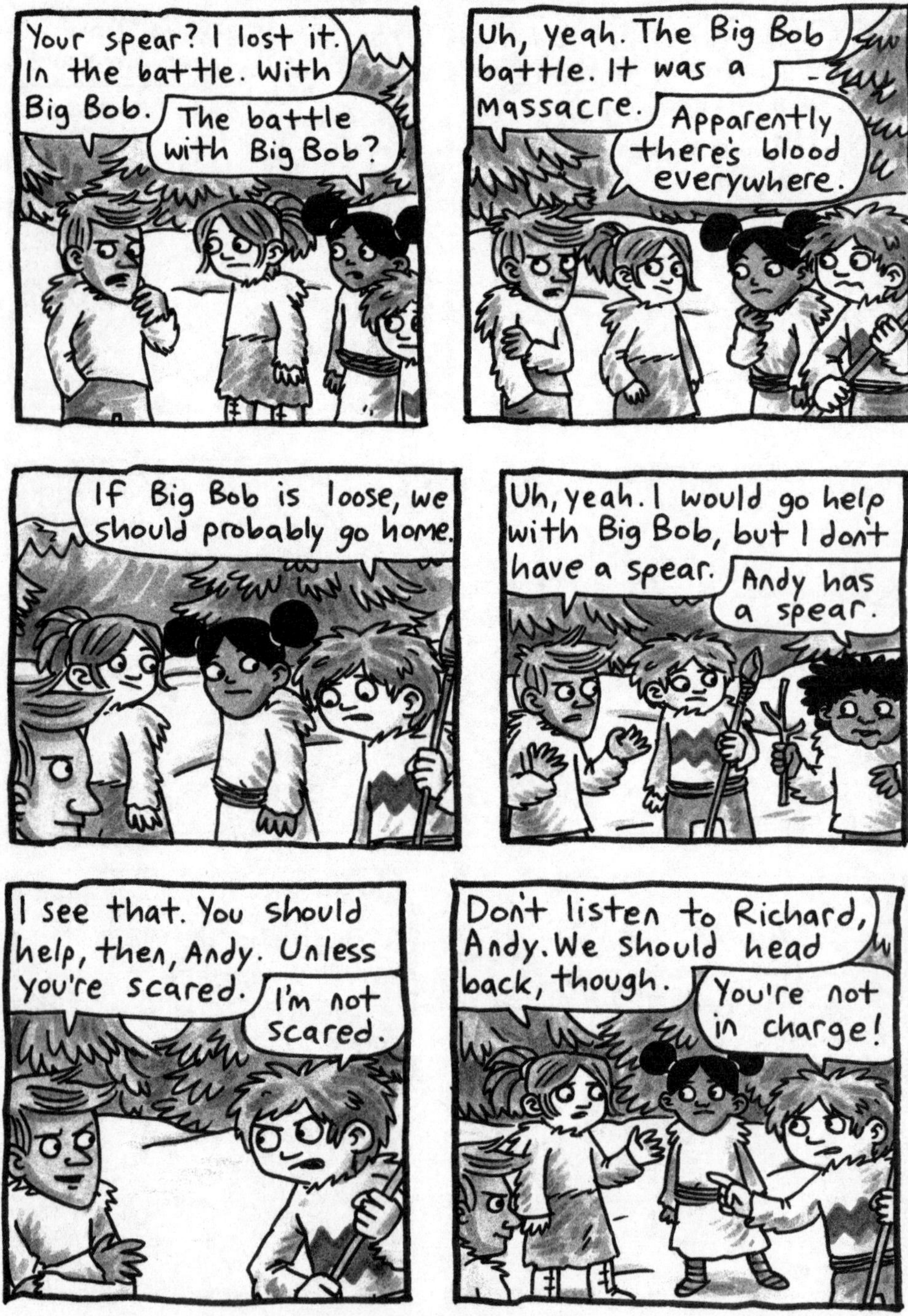
Your spear? I lost it. In the battle. With Big Bob.
The battle with Big Bob?
Uh, yeah. The Big Bob battle. It was a massacre.
Apparently there's blood everywhere.
If Big Bob is loose, we should probably go home.
Uh, yeah. I would go help with Big Bob, but I don't have a spear.
Andy has a spear.
I see that. You should help, then, Andy. Unless you're scared.
I'm not scared.
Don't listen to Richard, Andy. We should head back, though.
You're not in charge!

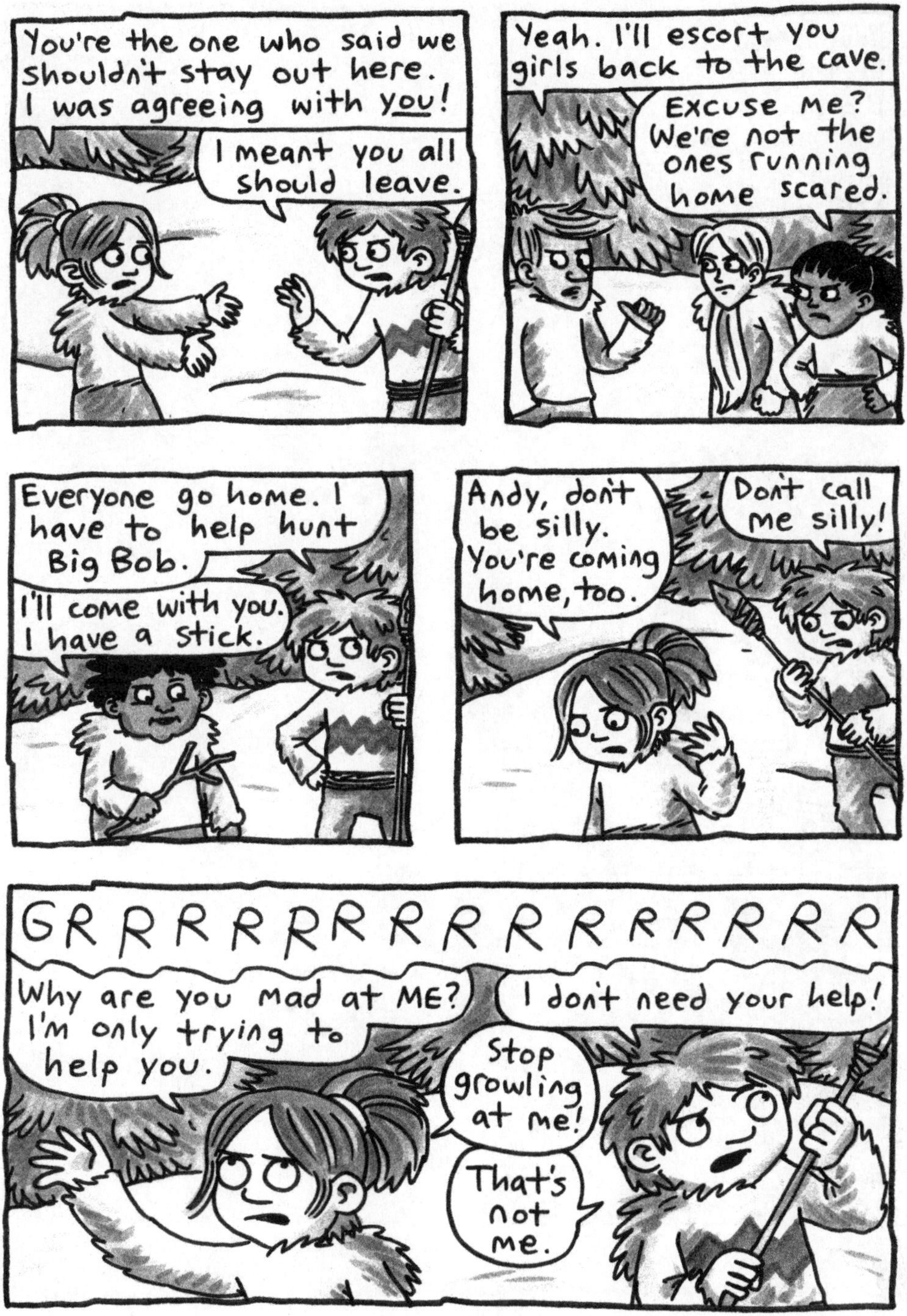
You're the one who said we shouldn't stay out here. I was agreeing with you!
I meant you all should leave.
Yeah. I'll escort you girls back to the cave.
Excuse me? We're not the ones running home scared.
Everyone go home. I have to help hunt Big Bob.
I'll come with you. I have a stick.
Andy, don't be silly. You're coming home, too.
Don't call me silly!
GRRRRRRRRRRRRR
Why are you mad at ME? I'm only trying to help you.
I don't need your help!
Stop growling at me!
That's not me.

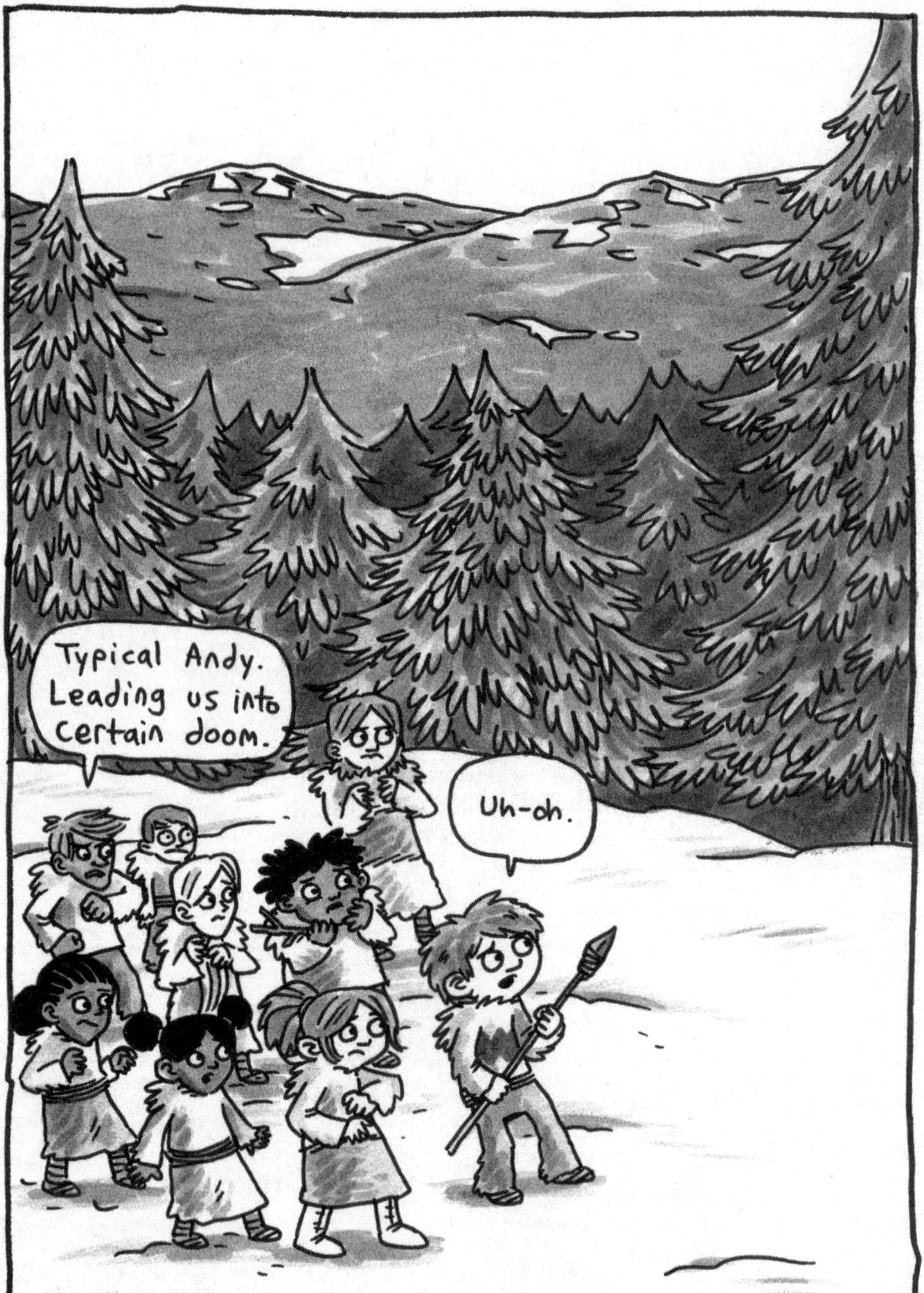
Typical Andy. Leading us into certain doom.
Uh-oh.

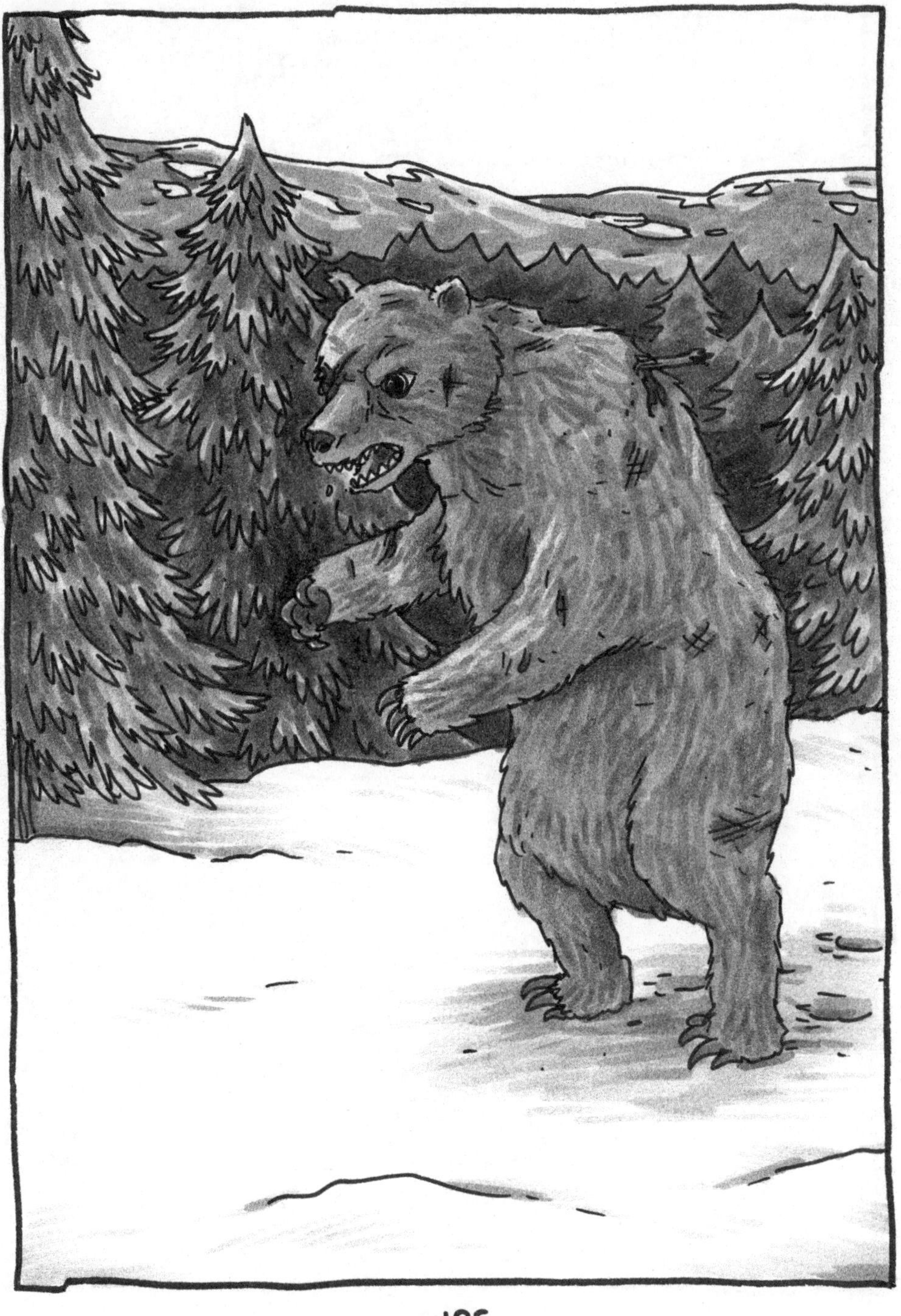

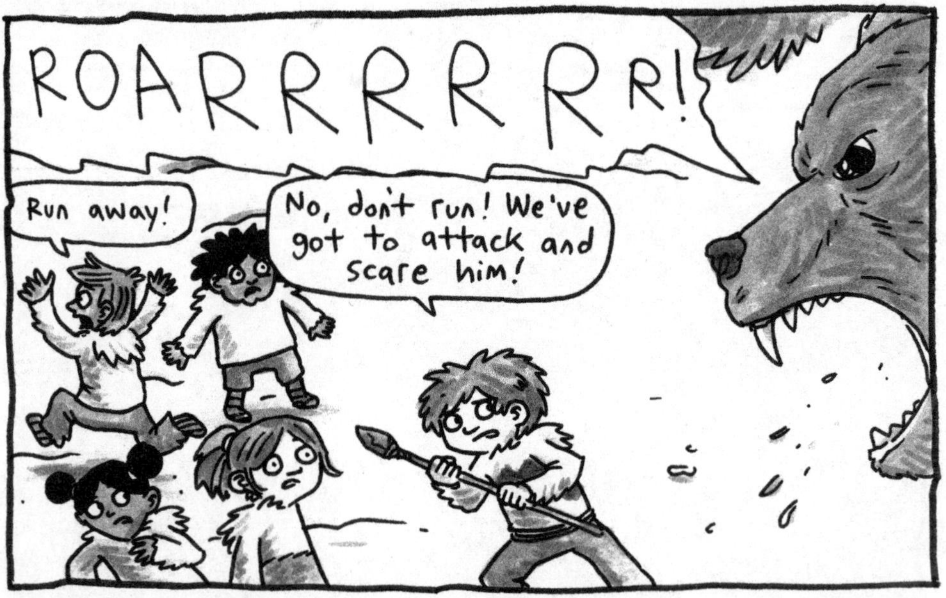
ROARRRRRRR!
Run away!
No, don't run! We've got to attack and scare him!

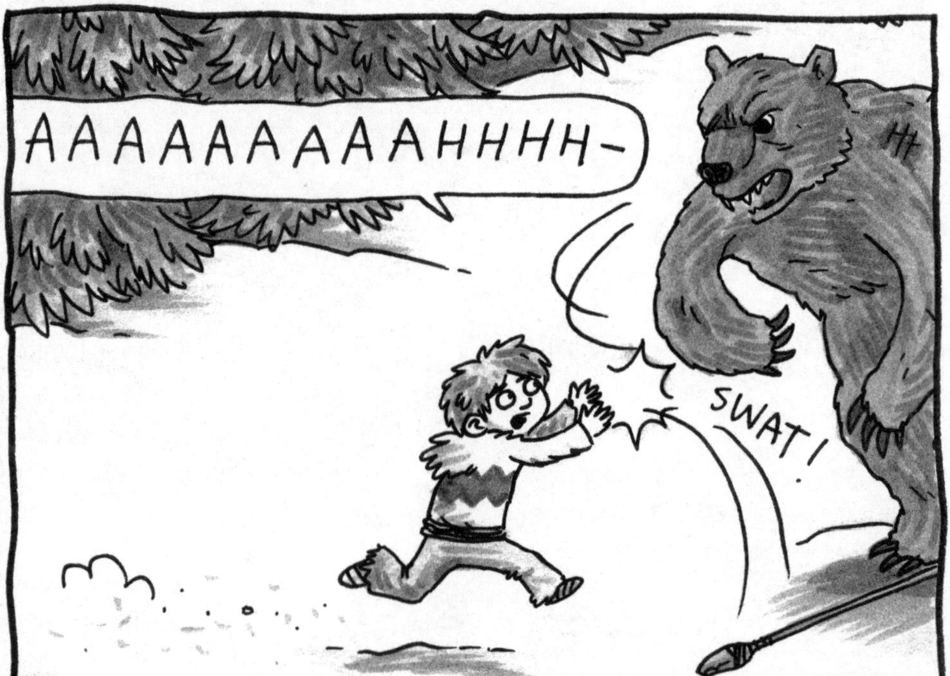
AAAAAAAAAHHHH-
SWAT!

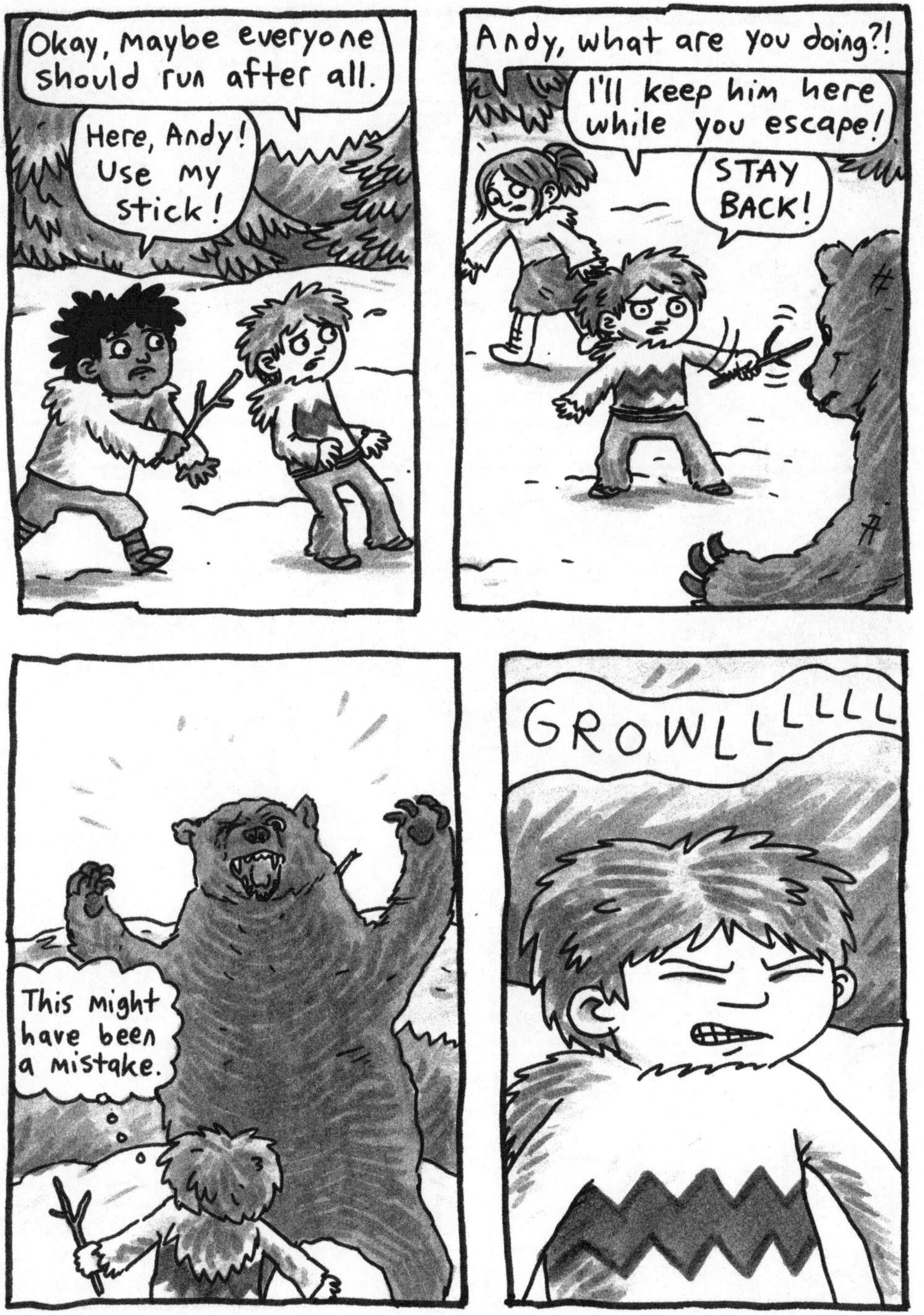
Okay, maybe everyone should run after all.
Here, Andy! Use my stick!
Andy, what are you doing?!
I'll keep him here while you escape!
STAY BACK!
This might have been a mistake.
GROWLLLLLL

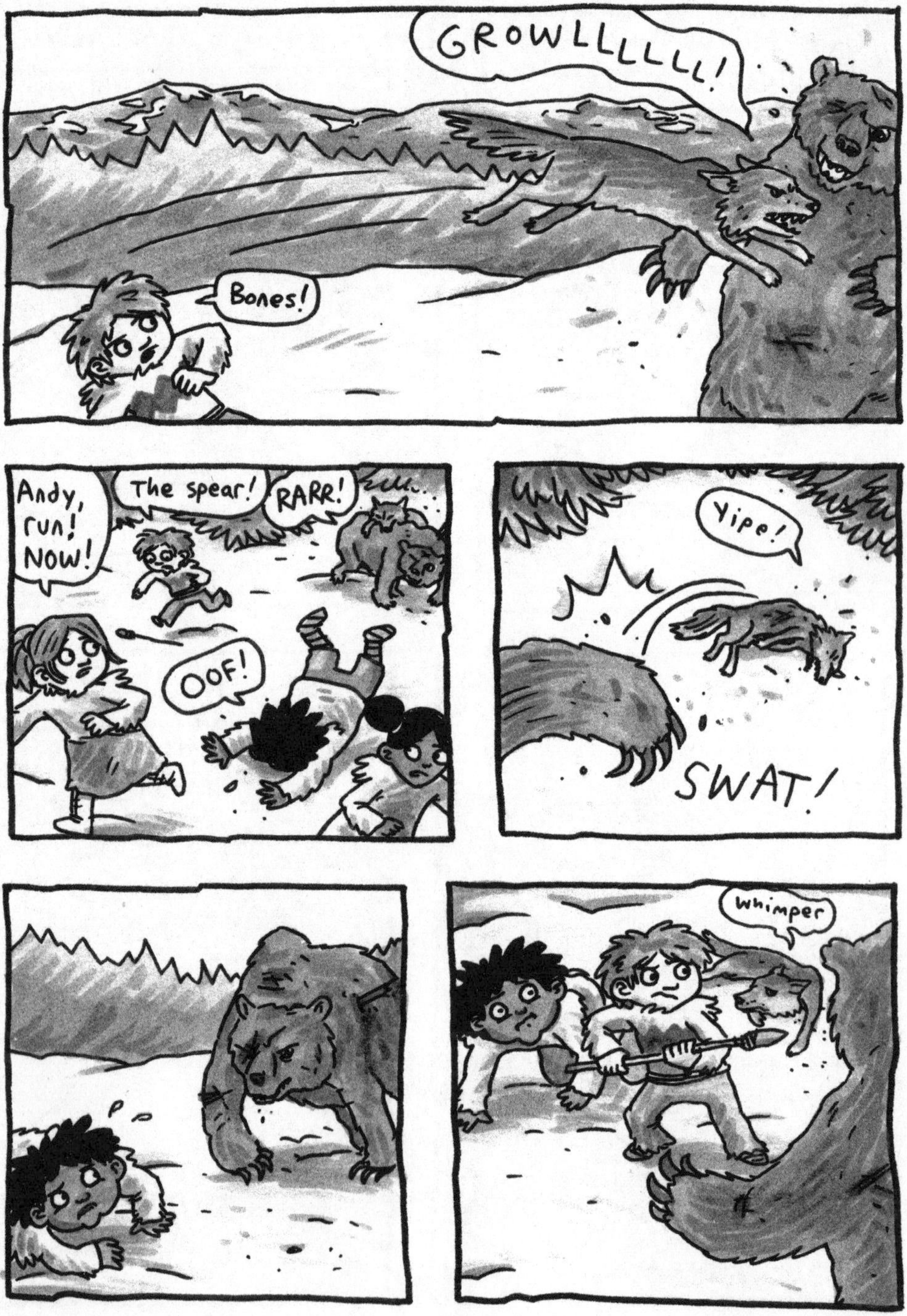
GROWLLLLLL!
Bones!
Andy, run! NOW!
The spear!
RARR!
OOF!
Yipe!
SWAT!
whimper

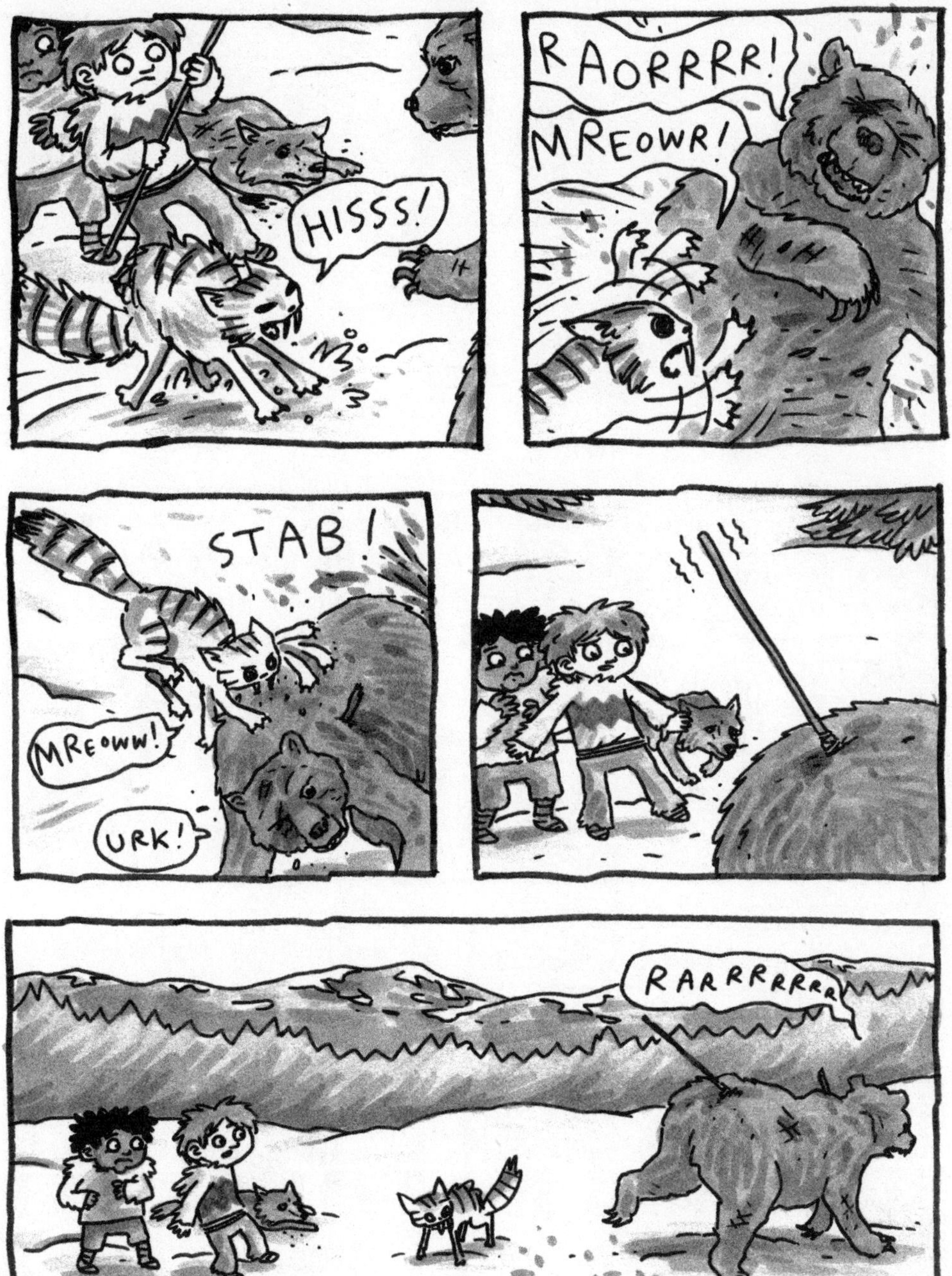
HISSS!
RAORRRR!
MREOWR!
STAB!
MREOWW!
URK!
RARRRRRRR

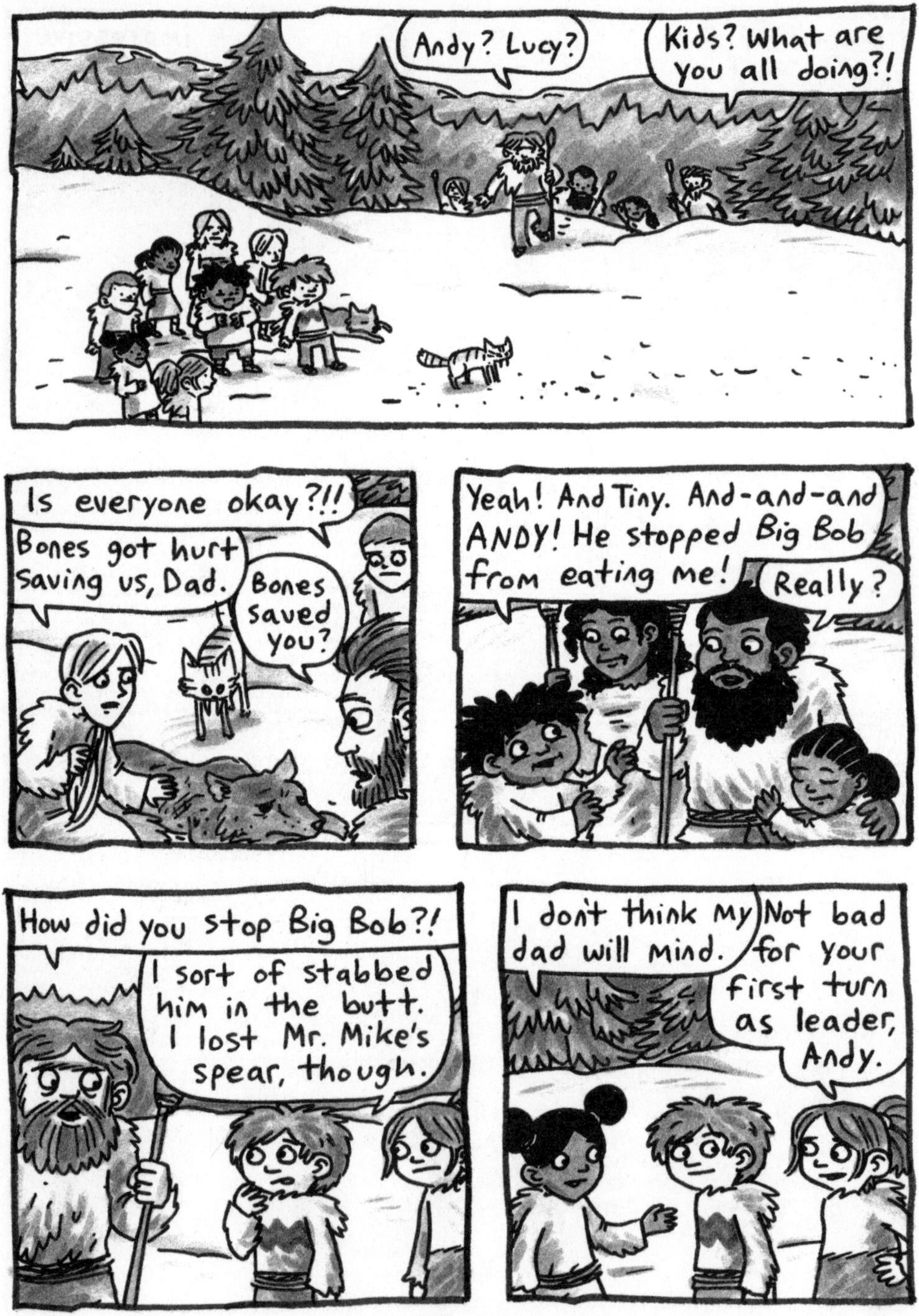
Andy? Lucy?
Kids? What are you all doing?!
Is everyone okay?!!
Bones got hurt saving us, Dad.
Bones saved you?
Yeah! And Tiny. And-and-and ANDY! He stopped Big Bob from eating me!
Really?
How did you stop Big Bob?!
I sort of stabbed him in the butt. I lost Mr. Mike's spear, though.
I don't think my dad will mind.
Not bad for your first turn as leader, Andy.

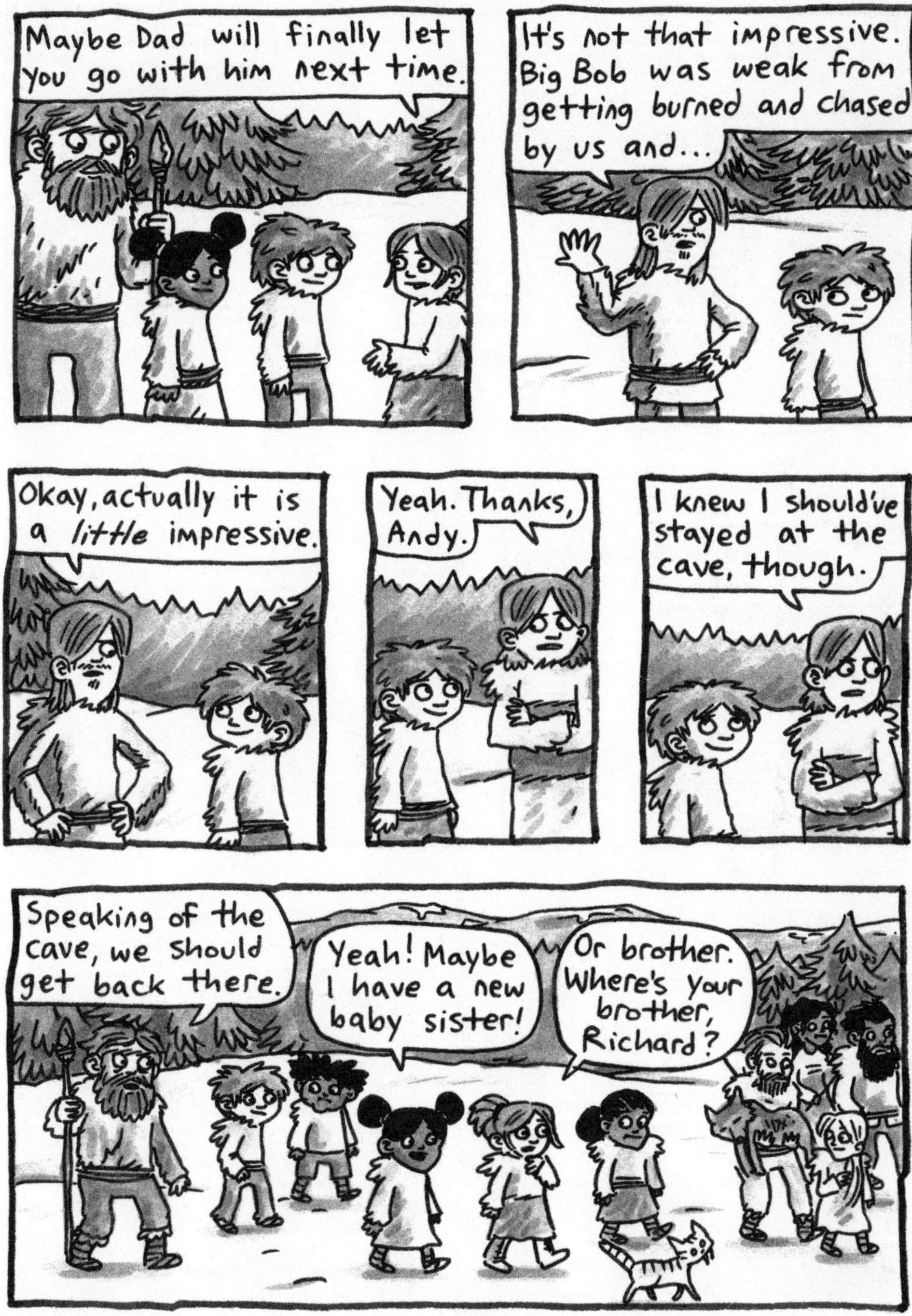
Maybe Dad will finally let you go with him next time.
It's not that impressive. Big Bob was weak from getting burned and chased by us and...
Okay, actually it is a *little* impressive.
Yeah. Thanks, Andy.
I knew I should've stayed at the cave, though.
Speaking of the cave, we should get back there.
Yeah! Maybe I have a new baby sister!
Or brother. Where's your brother, Richard?

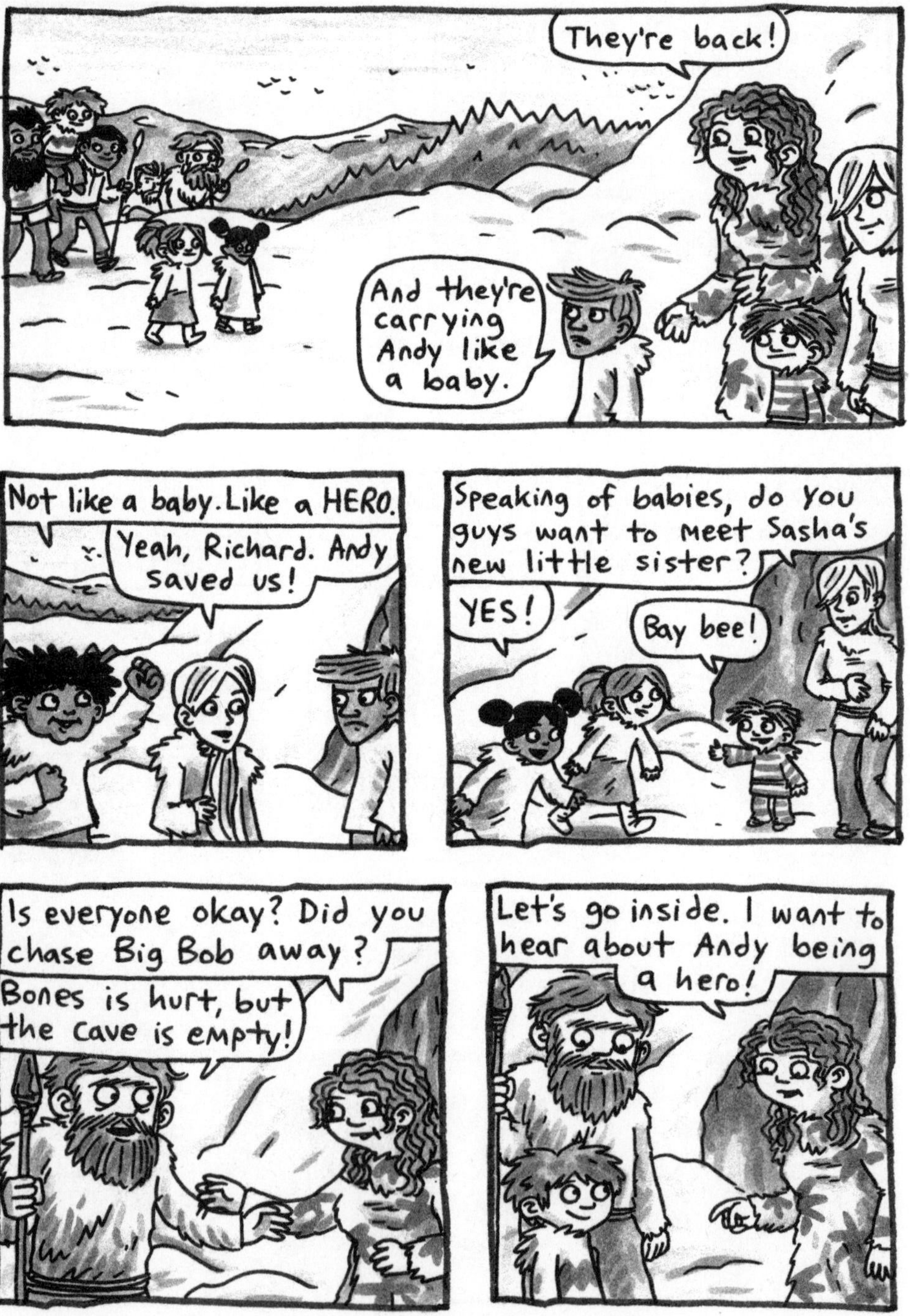
They're back!
And they're carrying Andy like a baby.
Not like a baby. Like a HERO.
Yeah, Richard. Andy saved us!
Speaking of babies, do you guys want to meet Sasha's new little sister?
YES!
Bay bee!
Is everyone okay? Did you chase Big Bob away?
Bones is hurt, but the cave is empty!
Let's go inside. I want to hear about Andy being a hero!

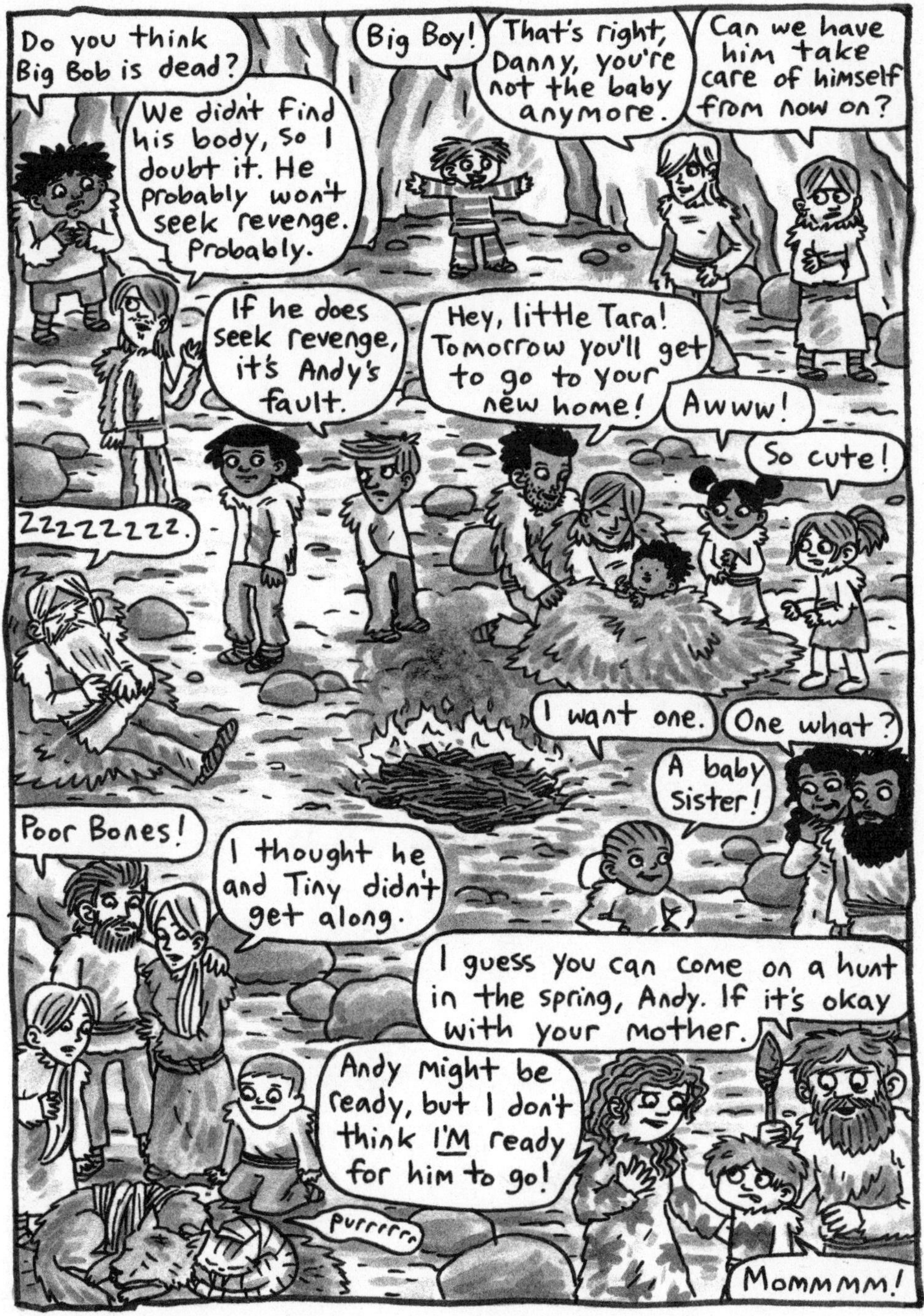
Do you think Big Bob is dead?
We didn't find his body, so I doubt it. He probably won't seek revenge. Probably.
Big Boy!
That's right, Danny, you're not the baby anymore.
Can we have him take care of himself from now on?
If he does seek revenge, it's Andy's fault.
Hey, little Tara! Tomorrow you'll get to go to your new home!
Awww!
So cute!
ZZZZZZZZ.
I want one.
One what?
A baby sister!
Poor Bones!
I thought he and Tiny didn't get along.
I guess you can come on a hunt in the spring, Andy. If it's okay with your mother.
Andy might be ready, but I don't think I'M ready for him to go!
purrrrrr
MOMMMM!

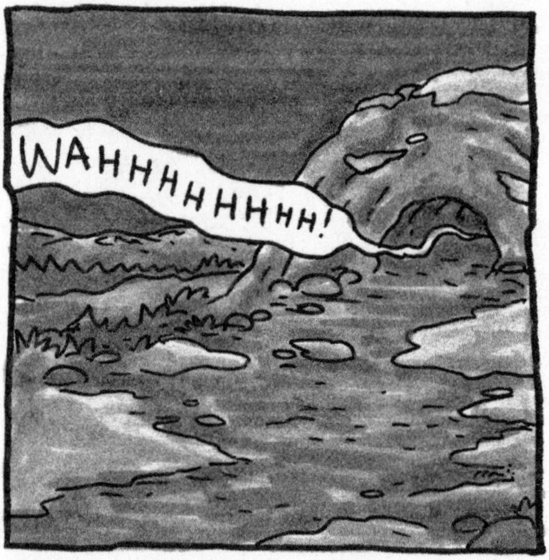
WAHHHHHHHHH!

THE END

...OF WINTER
(AND A GOOD NIGHT'S REST)!

FORTY THOUSAND YEARS LATER... (TODAY)

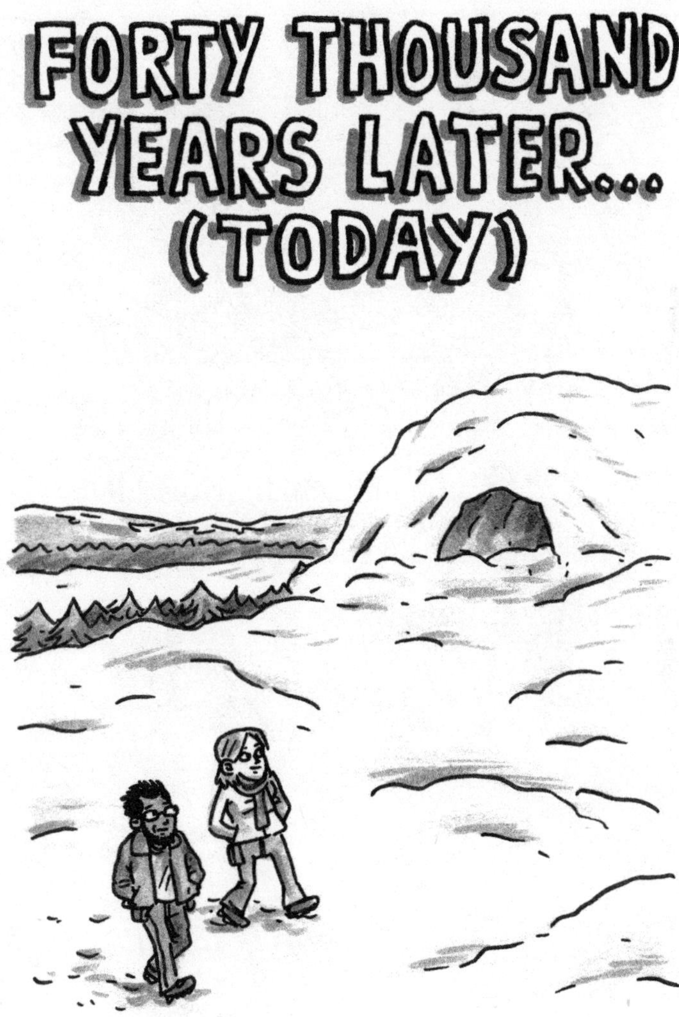

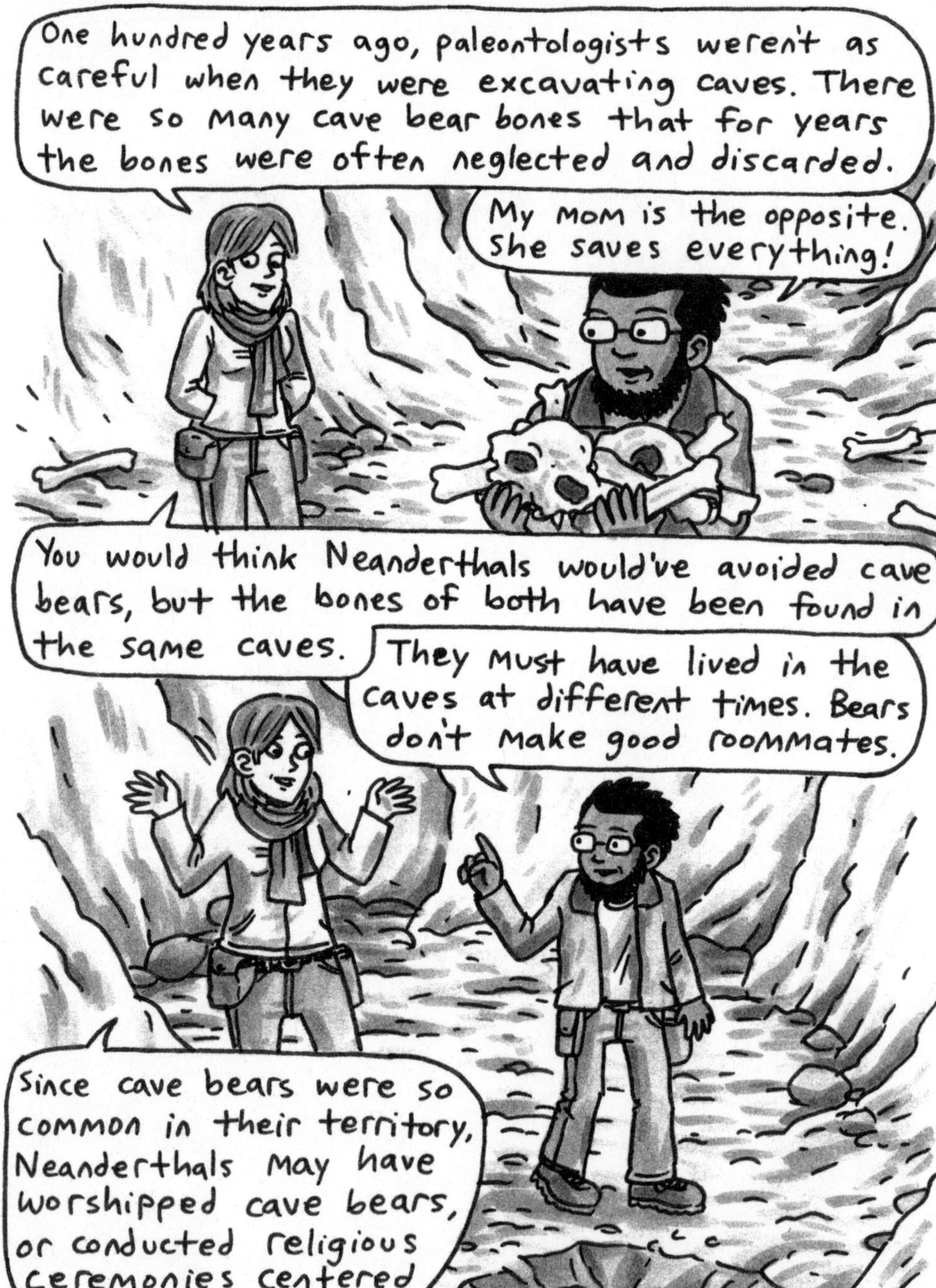
One hundred years ago, paleontologists weren't as careful when they were excavating caves. There were so many cave bear bones that for years the bones were often neglected and discarded.
My mom is the opposite. She saves everything!
You would think Neanderthals would've avoided cave bears, but the bones of both have been found in the same caves.
They must have lived in the caves at different times. Bears don't make good roommates.
Since cave bears were so common in their territory, Neanderthals may have worshipped cave bears, or conducted religious ceremonies centered on the animal.

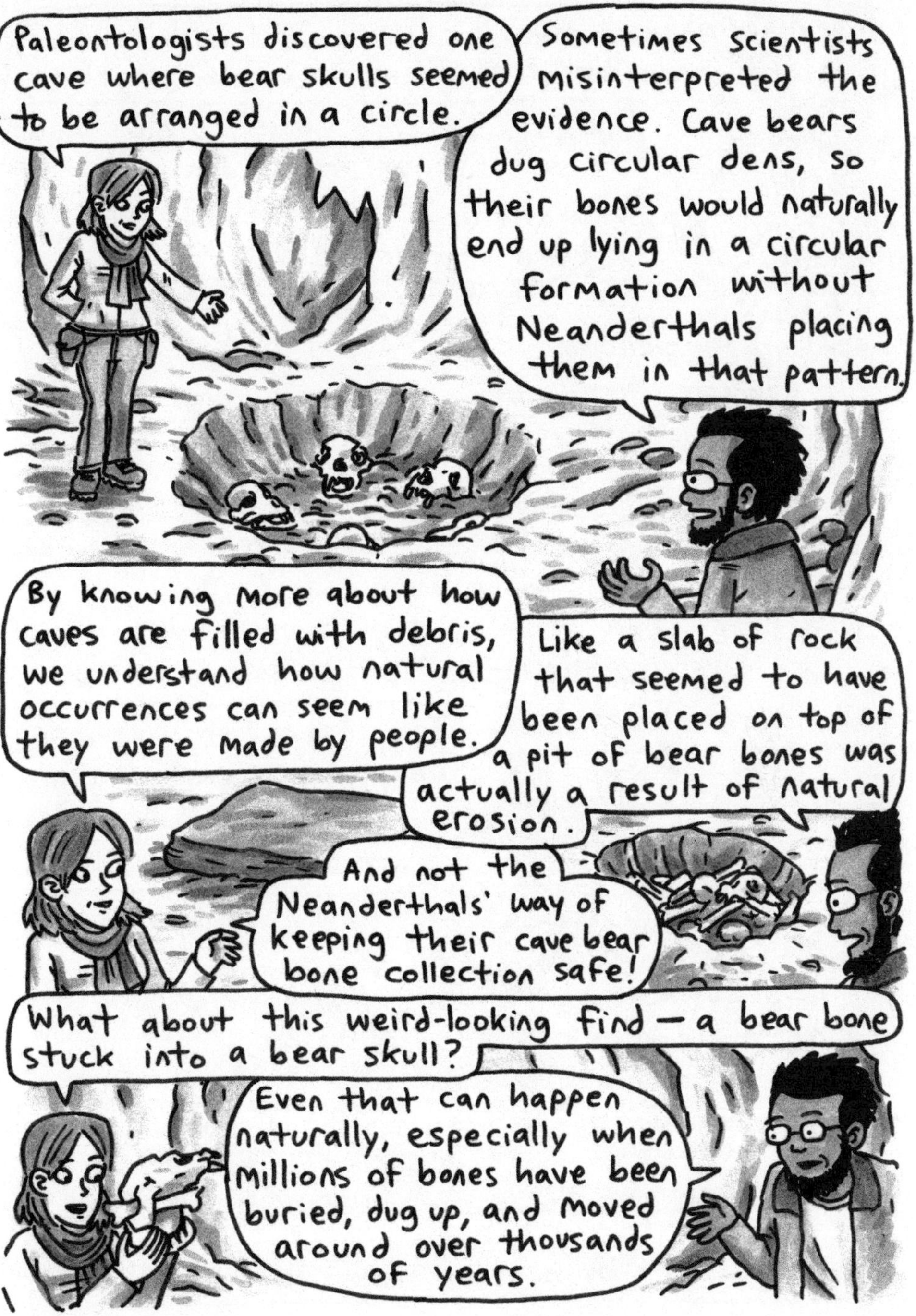
Paleontologists discovered one cave where bear skulls seemed to be arranged in a circle.
Sometimes scientists misinterpreted the evidence. Cave bears dug circular dens, so their bones would naturally end up lying in a circular formation without Neanderthals placing them in that pattern.
By knowing more about how caves are filled with debris, we understand how natural occurrences can seem like they were made by people.
Like a slab of rock that seemed to have been placed on top of a pit of bear bones was actually a result of natural erosion.
And not the Neanderthals' way of keeping their cave bear bone collection safe!
What about this weird-looking find—a bear bone stuck into a bear skull?
Even that can happen naturally, especially when millions of bones have been buried, dug up, and moved around over thousands of years.

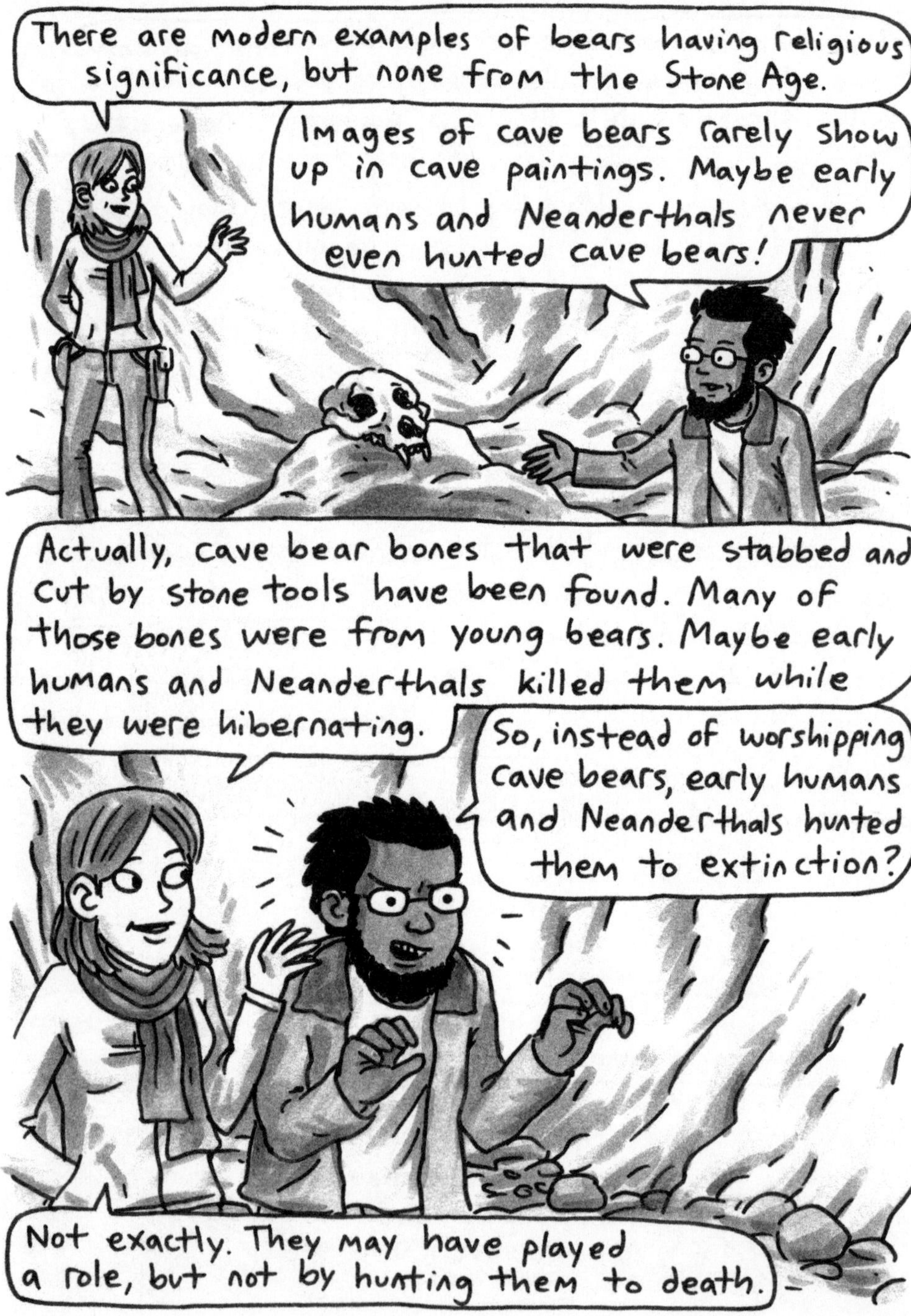
There are modern examples of bears having religious significance, but none from the Stone Age.
Images of cave bears rarely show up in cave paintings. Maybe early humans and Neanderthals never even hunted cave bears!
Actually, cave bear bones that were stabbed and cut by stone tools have been found. Many of those bones were from young bears. Maybe early humans and Neanderthals killed them while they were hibernating.
So, instead of worshipping cave bears, early humans and Neanderthals hunted them to extinction?
Not exactly. They may have played a role, but not by hunting them to death.

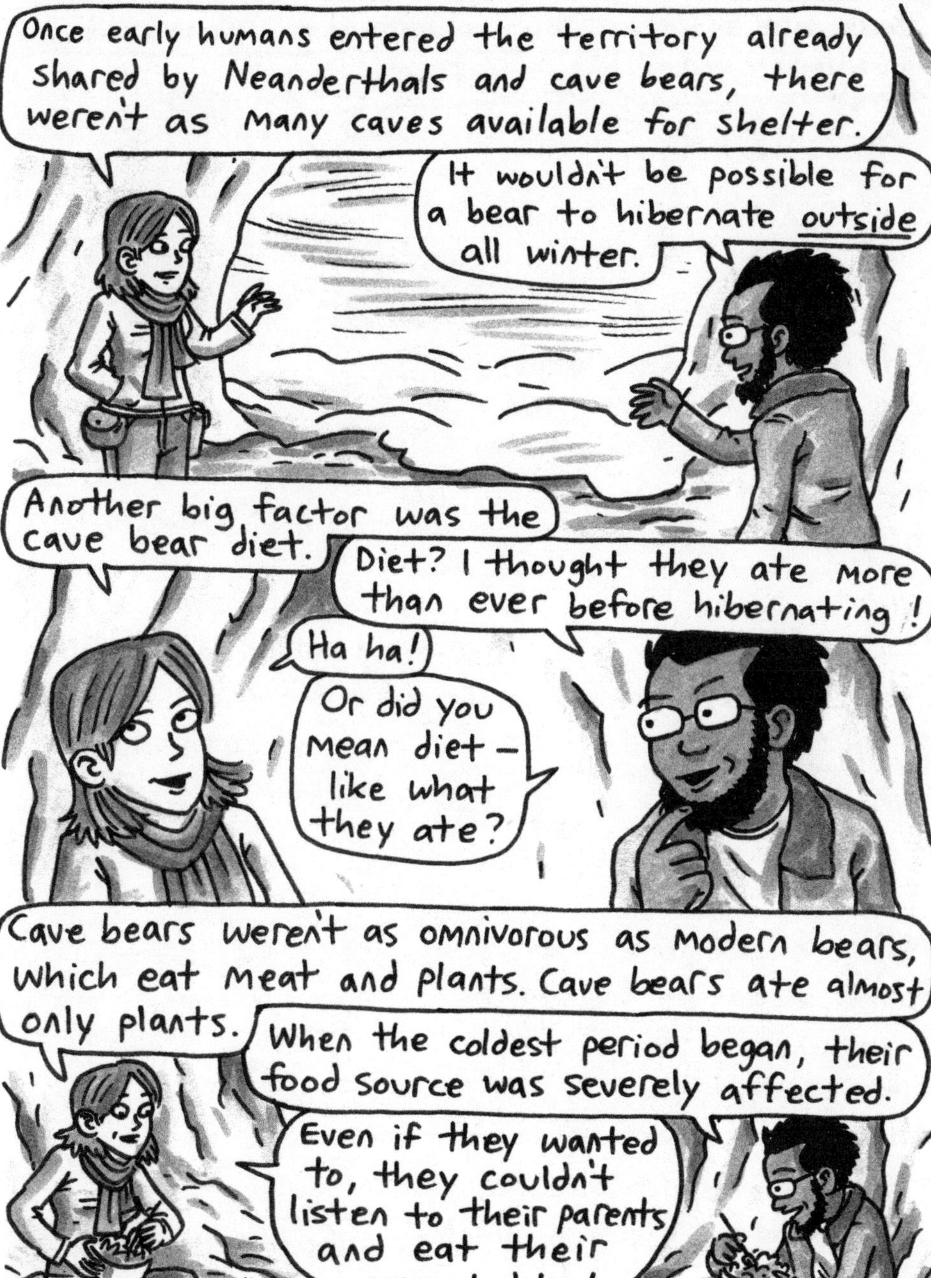
Once early humans entered the territory already shared by Neanderthals and cave bears, there weren't as many caves available for shelter.
It wouldn't be possible for a bear to hibernate outside all winter.
Another big factor was the cave bear diet.
Diet? I thought they ate more than ever before hibernating!
Ha ha!
Or did you mean diet — like what they ate?
Cave bears weren't as omnivorous as modern bears, which eat meat and plants. Cave bears ate almost only plants.
When the coldest period began, their food source was severely affected.
Even if they wanted to, they couldn't listen to their parents and eat their vegetables!

How do we know how cold it was thousands of years ago?

Lots of ways!

The effects of glaciers on the landscape and soil deposits show how much land was covered by ice in the past.

Tree rings show how climate changed over time. Narrow rings can indicate drought or extreme cold.

Microscopic pollen can be found alongside bones and other artifacts. Since different plants thrive in different climates, the type of pollen found can be studied to learn what the climate was like at different times.

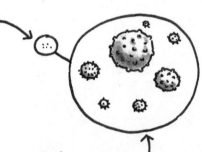

Can't tell how much this pollen made Neanderthals sneeze, though.

Ice core samples contain layers of ice going back thousands of years. The composition of the ice, as well as the dust and debris found in each layer, reflect the conditions on Earth at the time the layer formed.

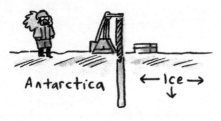

Antarctica ←Ice→

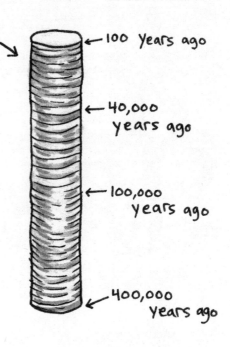

← 100 years ago

← 40,000 years ago

← 100,000 years ago

← 400,000 years ago

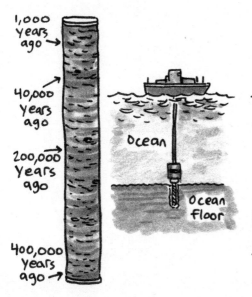

1,000 years ago →

40,000 years ago →

200,000 years ago →

400,000 years ago →

Ocean

Ocean floor

A special drill is used to take ocean core samples from the bottom of the sea. The samples contain thousands of years' worth of sediment deposits that have built up on the ocean floor. Scientists study the remains of plankton and other organisms in each layer to determine the climates of different time periods.

We know that ice ages come and go on Earth. What causes that?
There are lots of factors, but the main explanation is the Milankovitch Cycles, named for the scientist who came up with the theory.

The Milankovitch Cycles involve three key concepts.

ECCENTRICITY

The Earth orbits the sun in an ellipse, not a circle. This orbital ellipse changes slowly over time, so about every 100,000 years, the Earth spends more time farther away from the sun. This cools the Earth.

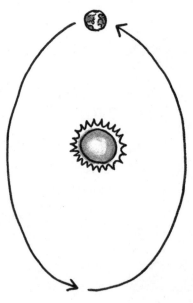

TILT

The end of the Earth that's tilted toward the sun changes every 40,000 years. When the Northern Hemisphere is tilted away from the sun, our summers are cooler.

N

S

WOBBLE

The Earth's axis – an imaginary line through the center of the Earth – wobbles as the planet spins. Every 26,000 years, this cycle affects the seasons.

The ways these three cycles overlap through time can alter the Earth's climate in significant ways!

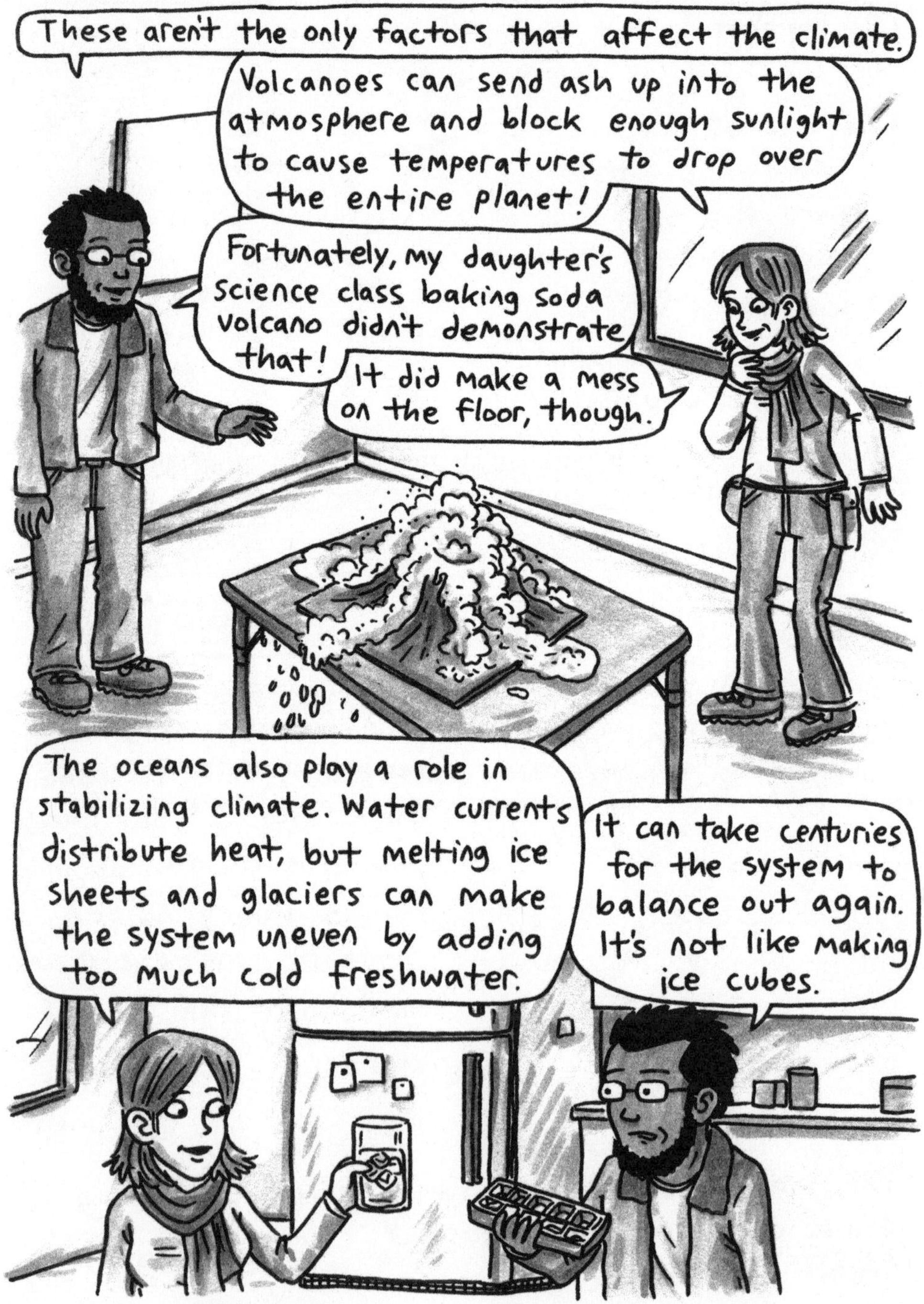
These aren't the only factors that affect the climate.
Volcanoes can send ash up into the atmosphere and block enough sunlight to cause temperatures to drop over the entire planet!
Fortunately, my daughter's science class baking soda volcano didn't demonstrate that!
It did make a mess on the floor, though.
The oceans also play a role in stabilizing climate. Water currents distribute heat, but melting ice sheets and glaciers can make the system uneven by adding too much cold freshwater.
It can take centuries for the system to balance out again. It's not like making ice cubes.

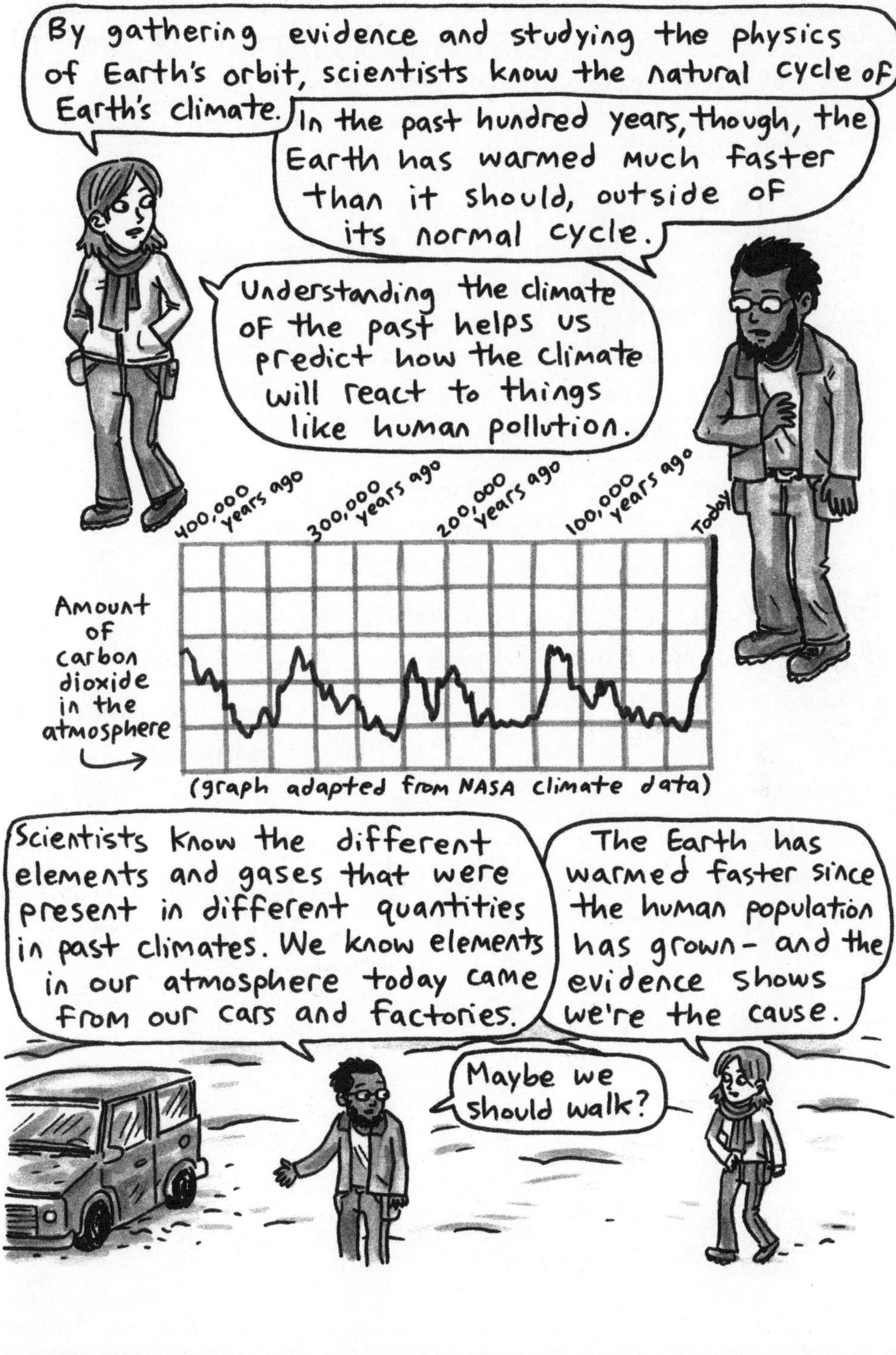
By gathering evidence and studying the physics of Earth's orbit, scientists know the natural cycle of Earth's climate.
In the past hundred years, though, the Earth has warmed much faster than it should, outside of its normal cycle.
Understanding the climate of the past helps us predict how the climate will react to things like human pollution.
400,000 years ago
300,000 years ago
200,000 years ago
100,000 years ago
Today
Amount of carbon dioxide in the atmosphere
(graph adapted from NASA climate data)
Scientists know the different elements and gases that were present in different quantities in past climates. We know elements in our atmosphere today came from our cars and factories.
The Earth has warmed faster since the human population has grown– and the evidence shows we're the cause.
Maybe we should walk?

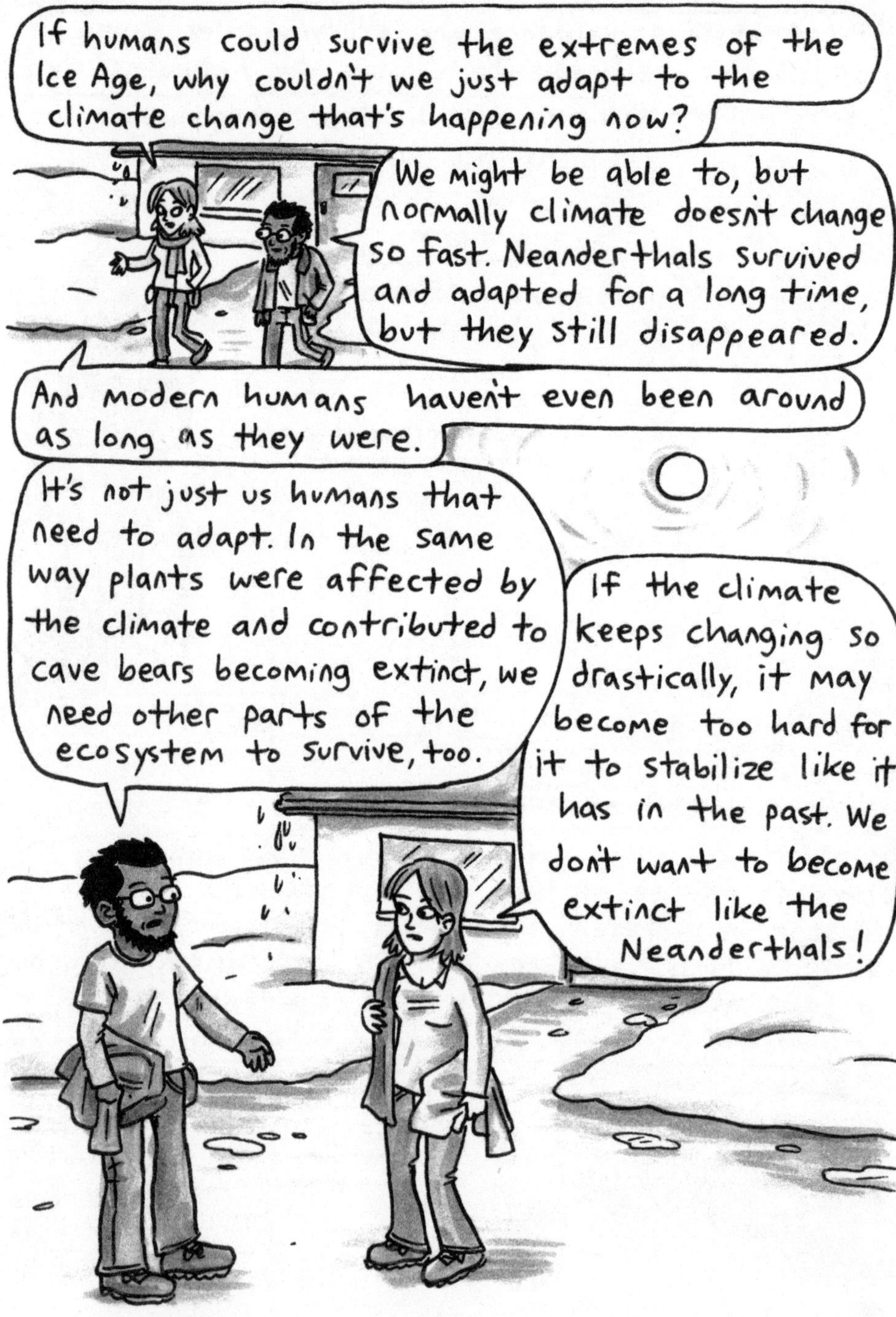
If humans could survive the extremes of the Ice Age, why couldn't we just adapt to the climate change that's happening now?
We might be able to, but normally climate doesn't change so fast. Neanderthals survived and adapted for a long time, but they still disappeared.
And modern humans haven't even been around as long as they were.
It's not just us humans that need to adapt. In the same way plants were affected by the climate and contributed to cave bears becoming extinct, we need other parts of the ecosystem to survive, too.
If the climate keeps changing so drastically, it may become too hard for it to stabilize like it has in the past. We don't want to become extinct like the Neanderthals!

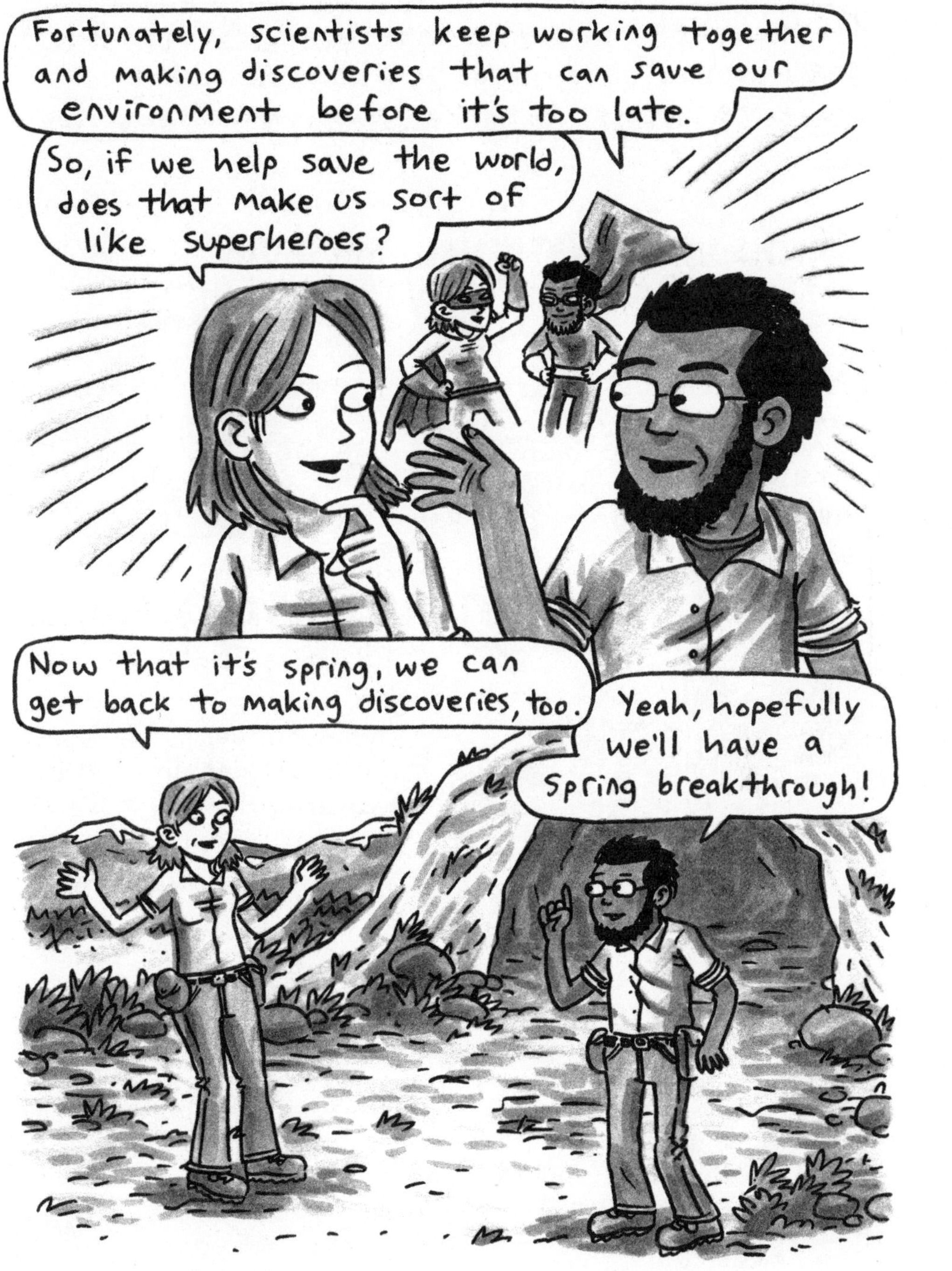
Fortunately, scientists keep working together and making discoveries that can save our environment before it's too late.
So, if we help save the world, does that make us sort of like superheroes?
Now that it's spring, we can get back to making discoveries, too.
Yeah, hopefully we'll have a Spring breakthrough!

Do you want to learn more about Neanderthals, early humans, and cave bears? You can visit these museums to make your own discoveries!

SMITHSONIAN NATIONAL MUSEUM OF NATURAL HISTORY

Washington, D.C., USA

See ancient mammal skeletons and fossils.

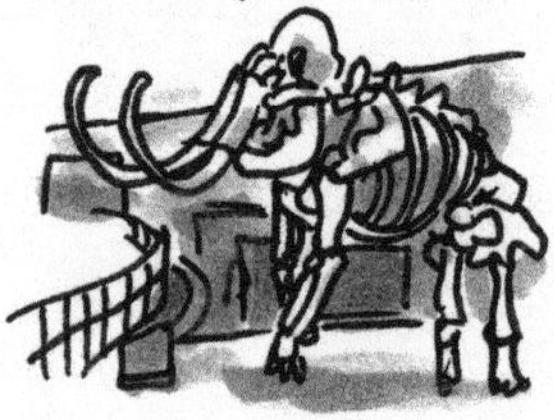

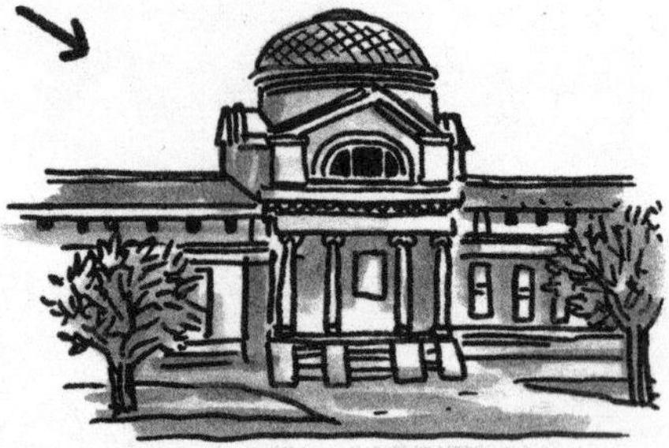

NATURAL HISTORY MUSEUM

London, England

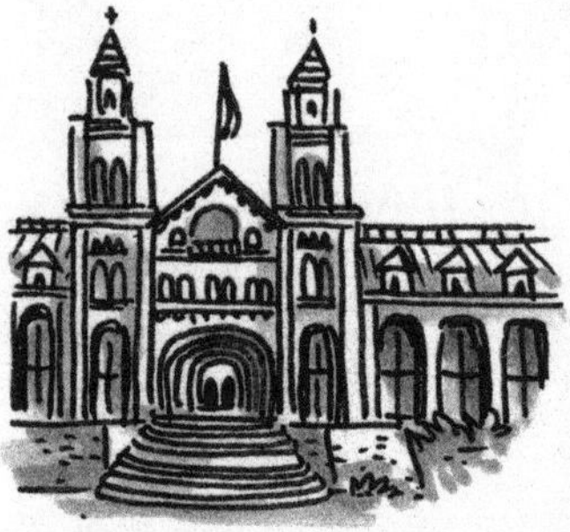

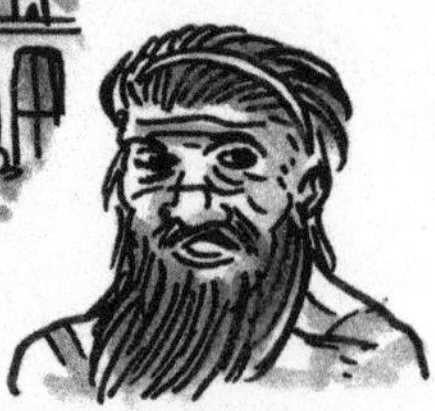

Check museums for special exhibitions like the Natural History Museum's "Britain: One Million Years of the Human Story."

KRAPINA NEANDERTHAL MUSEUM

Krapina, Croatia

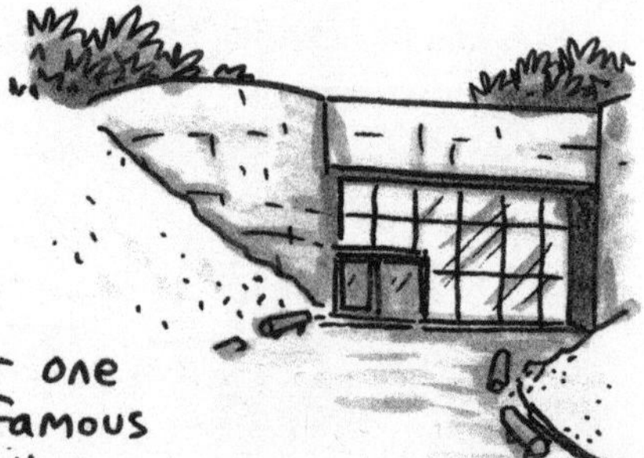

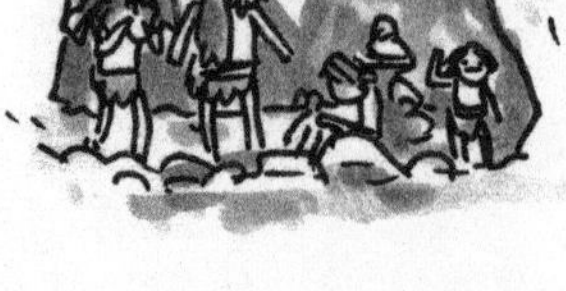

Located near one of the most famous Neanderthal sites.

A TIMELINE OF KEY* NEANDERTHAL DISCOVERIES

*Discoveries may become less important and not key due to future, more spectacular discoveries.

1829 & 1848: First Neanderthal bones are found, but no one knows what they are.

"We'll figure it out later."

"Let's just stick them in a drawer for now."

1856: Neanderthal bones found in Germany.

"This seems important."

1864: Bones found in Germany give name to new fossil species Neanderthals.

"They were found in the Neander Valley, so let's call them Neanderthals."

1886: Two nearly complete Neanderthal skeletons are discovered in Belgium.

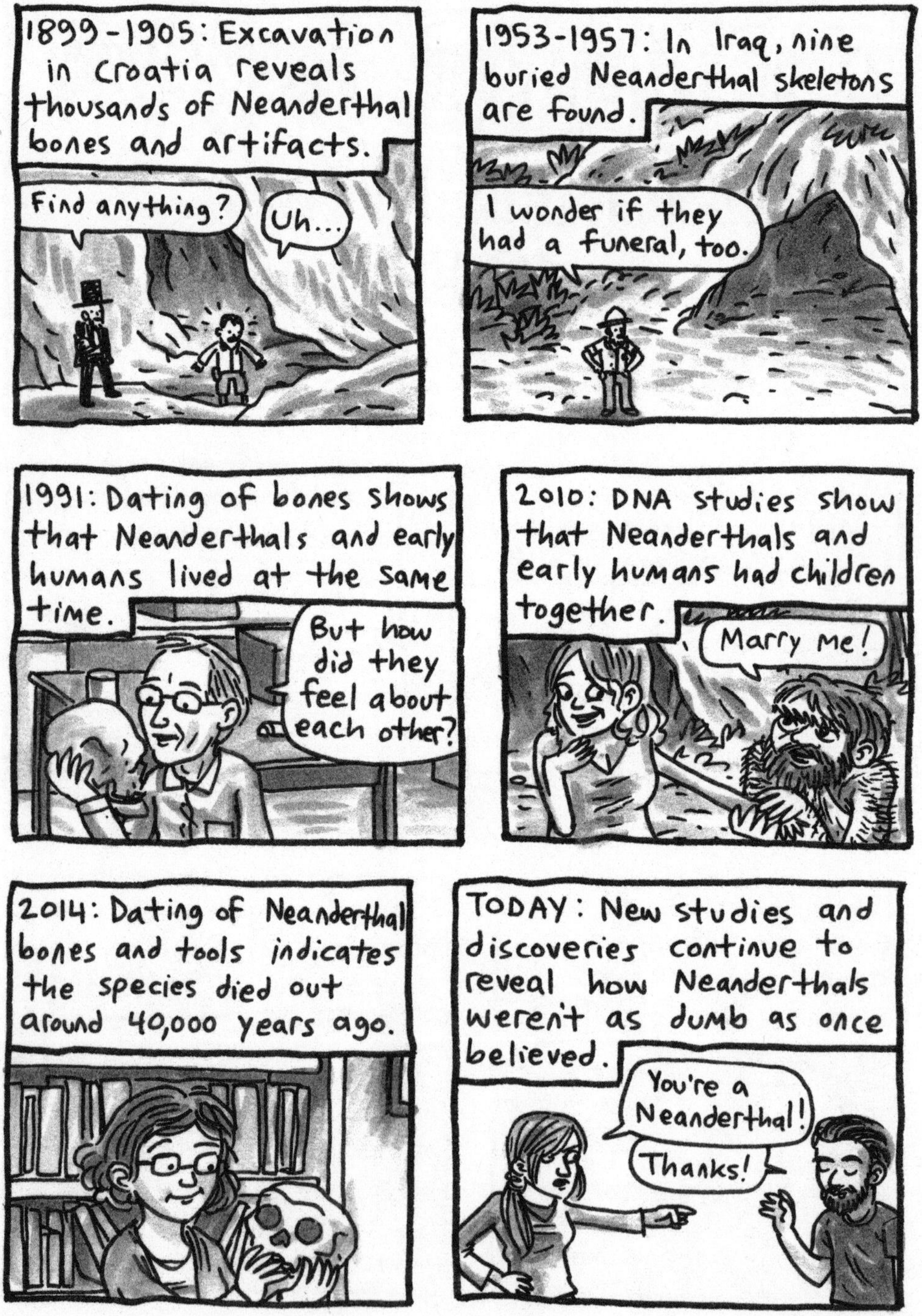
1899-1905: Excavation in Croatia reveals thousands of Neanderthal bones and artifacts.
Find anything?
Uh...
1953-1957: In Iraq, nine buried Neanderthal skeletons are found.
I wonder if they had a funeral, too.
1991: Dating of bones shows that Neanderthals and early humans lived at the same time.
But how did they feel about each other?
2010: DNA studies show that Neanderthals and early humans had children together.
Marry me!
2014: Dating of Neanderthal bones and tools indicates the species died out around 40,000 years ago.
TODAY: New studies and discoveries continue to reveal how Neanderthals weren't as dumb as once believed.
You're a Neanderthal!
Thanks!

FICTION VS. FACT

What's true in Lucy and Andy's story based on what scientists have learned, and what's stretching the truth? Read on!

WHAT DID NEANDERTHALS KNOW ABOUT BEAR SAFETY? Neanderthals most likely knew how to deal with cave bears. For bear safety today, check out information from a trusted source like the National Park Service (not Phil!).

COULD NEANDERTHALS OUTRUN EARLY HUMANS? The body type of Neanderthals wasn't as good for running, so early humans would have been faster. Neither group should have been running on slippery ice, though!

DID NEANDERTHALS HAVE WINTER COATS AND PARKAS? Because bones of animals like the wolverine have been found in their caves along with bone needles, scientists know early humans made warm garments. No conclusive evidence has been found to show Neanderthal winter clothing was as advanced.

DID NEANDERTHALS TAKE VACATIONS?
Neanderthals may have occupied different territories for different seasons, but travel was far more difficult, so they wouldn't have made weekend trips just for fun.

DID NEANDERTHALS GIVE GIFTS?
Neanderthals may have given gifts on certain occasions, or to cement relationships. They probably didn't have birthday parties. Especially since they didn't have cake!

WERE THERE PETS 40,000 YEARS AGO?
There were no domesticated animals or pets in the time of Neanderthals. Too bad, but at least pets weren't ruining the furniture! Of course, there was no furniture, either.

DID NEANDERTHALS HAVE FIRES INSIDE THEIR CAVES?
Evidence of smoke pollution and fires has been found inside Neanderthal caves. They didn't have chimneys, but caves could have high ceilings and extra openings so people wouldn't breathe in too much smoke.

SILLY CAVEMAN MYTHS

CAVEMAN RIDING A T. REX

If a caveman did meet a T. rex, he'd get eaten! Fortunately, dinosaurs died out 65 million years before Neanderthals or humans first lived!

CAVEMAN INVENTING THE WHEEL

The first wheels weren't invented until almost 6,000 years ago.

CAVEMEN BONKED CAVEWOMEN ON THE HEAD AND DRAGGED THEM BY THE HAIR

Don't even think about it.

This myth was popularized after appearing in many 1920s comic strips. There is no evidence of this ever happening, and there's no good reason cavemen would have behaved this way. Not only is it dangerous, it's not very attractive!

CAVEMEN HAD HORRIBLE POSTURE

Because one of the first Neanderthal skeletons had a spine curved by disease, people at first depicted all cavemen with an overly hunched back.

CAVEMEN WERE REALLY, REALLY HAIRY

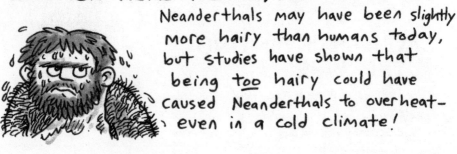

Neanderthals may have been slightly more hairy than humans today, but studies have shown that being too hairy could have caused Neanderthals to overheat- even in a cold climate!

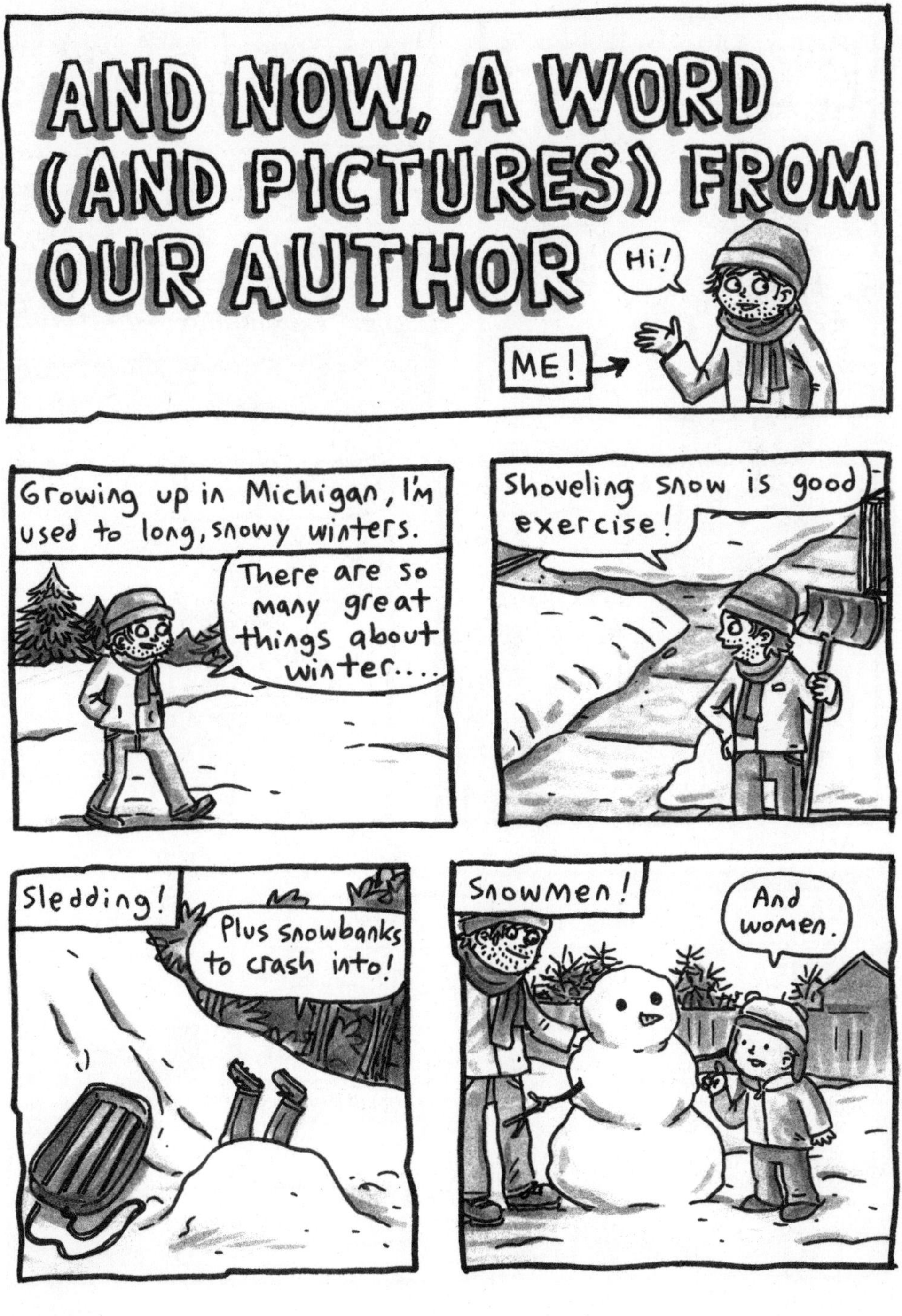
AND NOW, A WORD (AND PICTURES) FROM OUR AUTHOR
Hi!
ME!
Growing up in Michigan, I'm used to long, snowy winters.
There are so many great things about winter...
Shoveling snow is good exercise!
Sledding!
Plus snowbanks to crash into!
Snowmen!
And women.

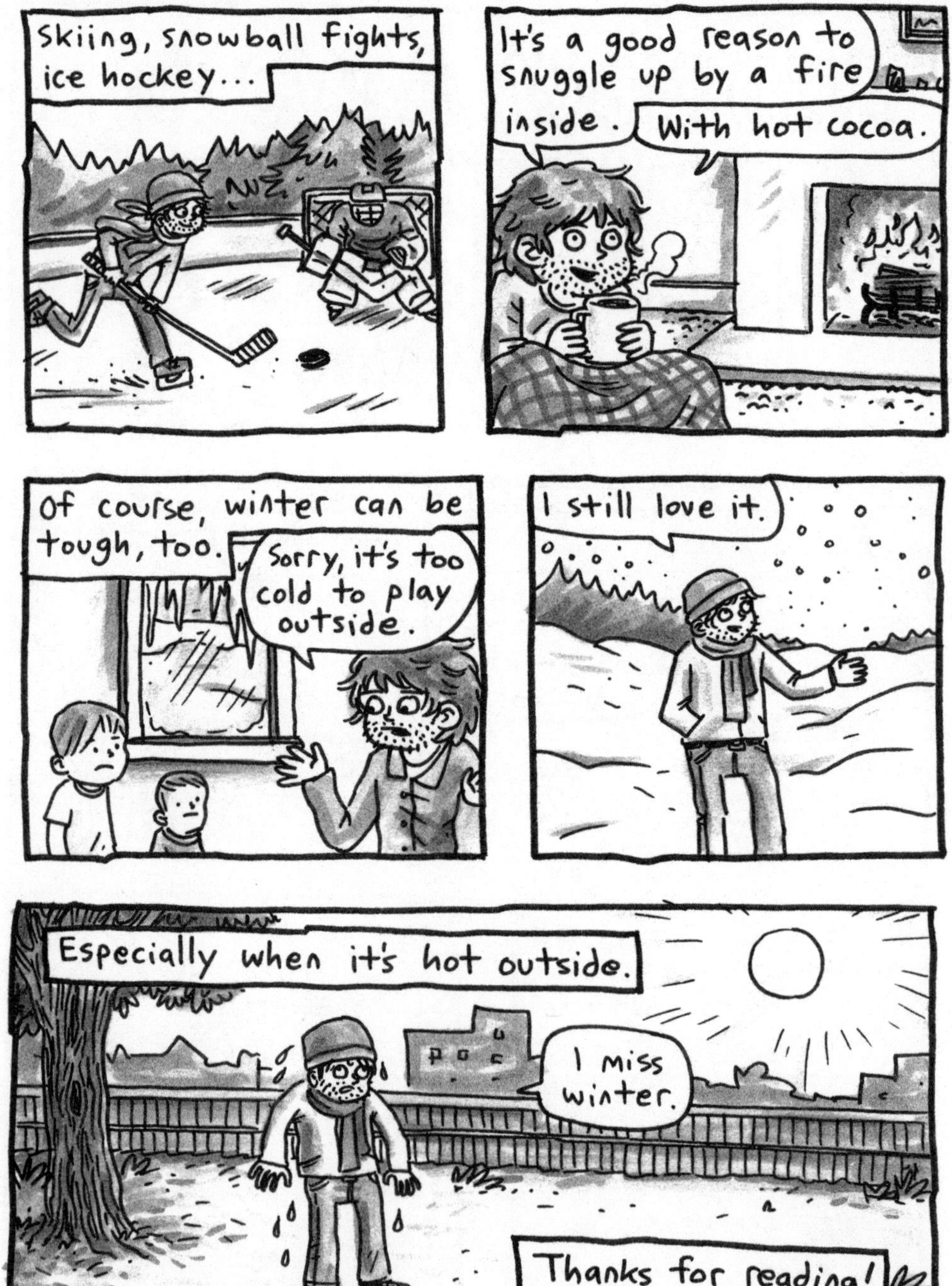
Skiing, snowball fights, ice hockey...
It's a good reason to snuggle up by a fire inside.
With hot cocoa.
Of course, winter can be tough, too.
Sorry, it's too cold to play outside.
I still love it.
Especially when it's hot outside.
I miss winter.
Thanks for reading!

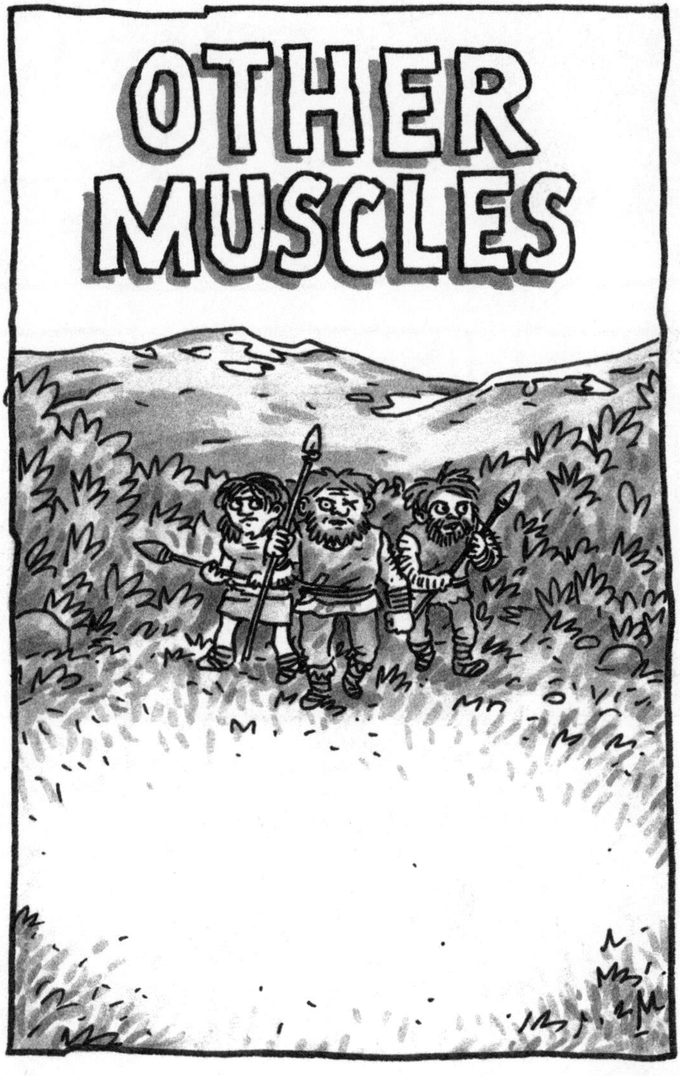
OTHER
MUSCLES

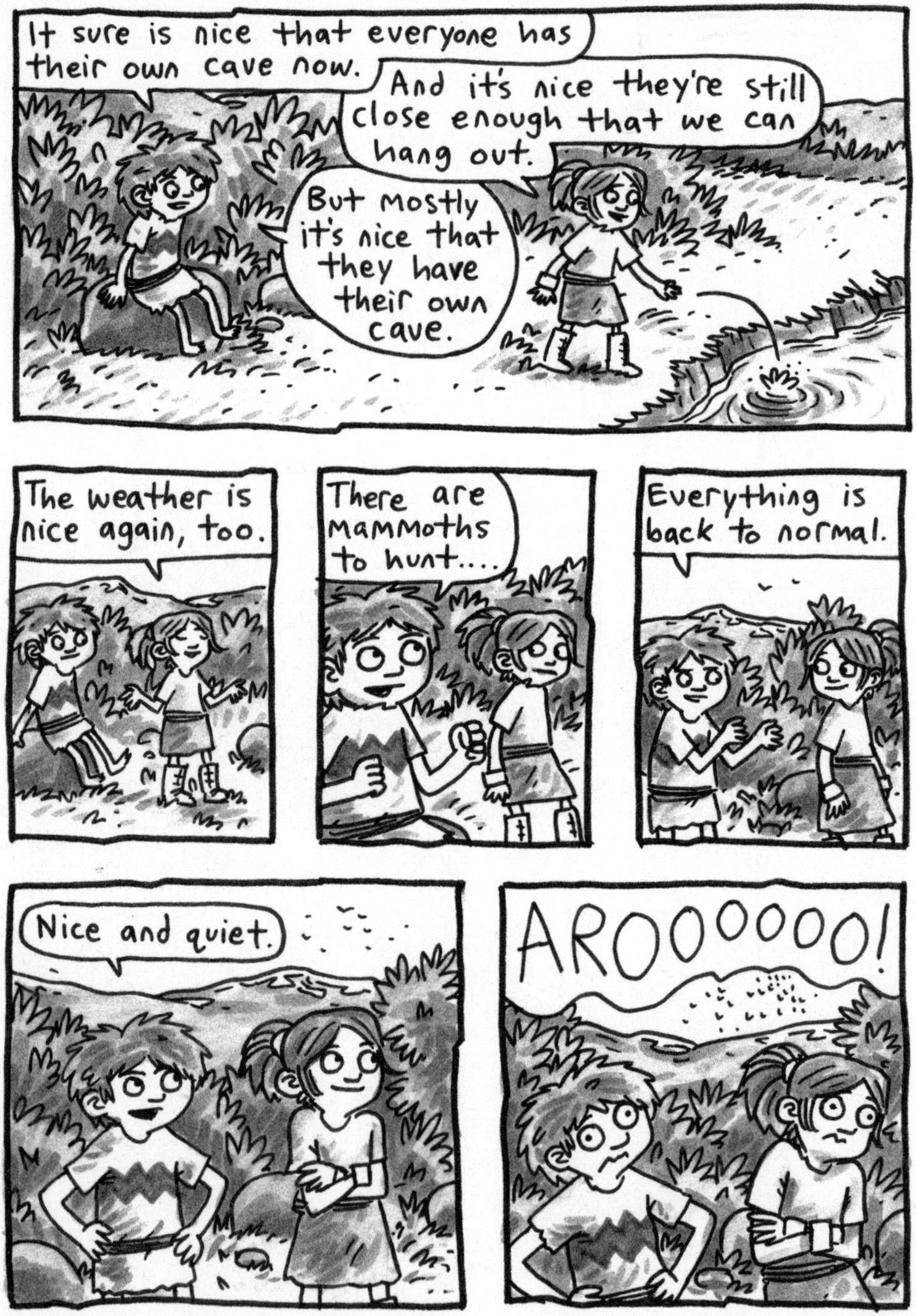
It sure is nice that everyone has their own cave now.
And it's nice they're still close enough that we can hang out.
But mostly it's nice that they have their own cave.
The weather is nice again, too.
There are mammoths to hunt....
Everything is back to normal.
Nice and quiet.
AROOOOOO!

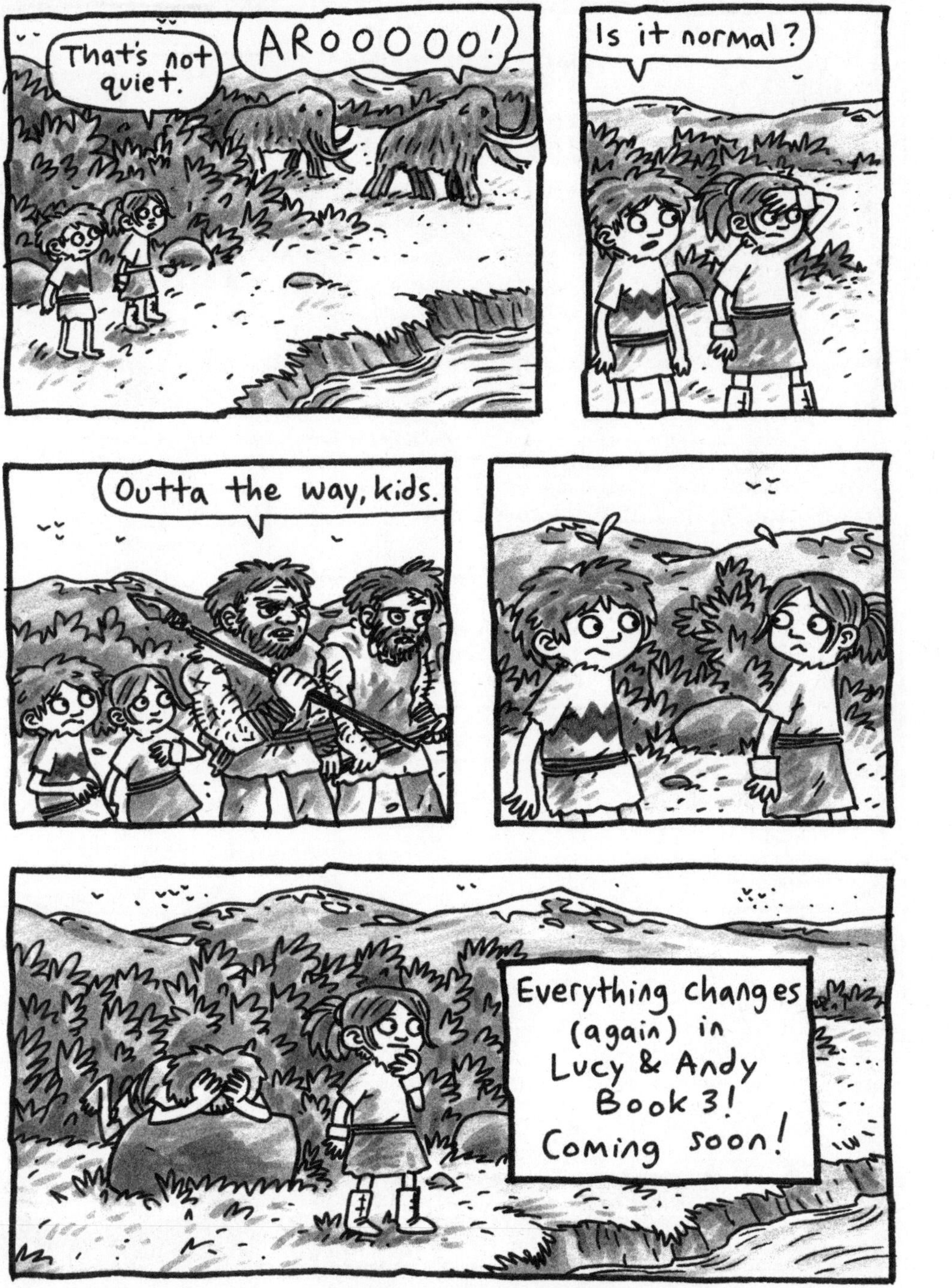
That's not quiet.
AROOOOO!
Is it normal?
Outta the way, kids.
Everything changes (again) in Lucy & Andy Book 3! Coming soon!

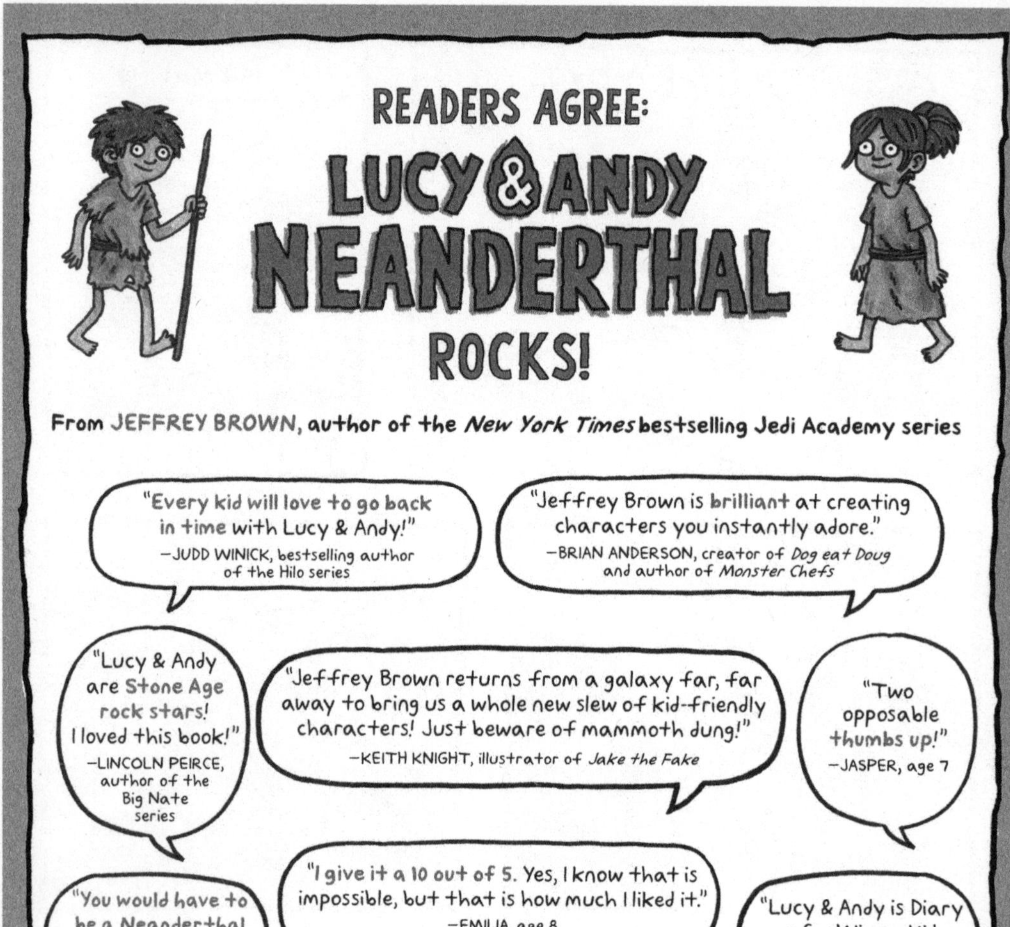
READERS AGREE:
LUCY & ANDY NEANDERTHAL
ROCKS!
From JEFFREY BROWN, author of the New York Times bestselling Jedi Academy series
"Every kid will love to go back in time with Lucy & Andy!" —JUDD WINICK, bestselling author of the Hilo series
"Jeffrey Brown is brilliant at creating characters you instantly adore." —BRIAN ANDERSON, creator of Dog eat Doug and author of Monster Chefs
"Lucy & Andy are Stone Age rock stars! I loved this book!" —LINCOLN PEIRCE, author of the Big Nate series
"Jeffrey Brown returns from a galaxy far, far away to bring us a whole new slew of kid-friendly characters! Just beware of mammoth dung!" —KEITH KNIGHT, illustrator of Jake the Fake
"Two opposable thumbs up!" —JASPER, age 7
"You would have to be a Neanderthal not to like it." —JOSH, age 8
"I give it a 10 out of 5. Yes, I know that is impossible, but that is how much I liked it." —EMILIA, age 8
"Lucy & Andy is Diary of a Wimpy Kid for the Stone Age" —EMERSON, age 10
Check out the first book!
Yeah, I was pretty great in it.
LUCY & ANDY NEANDERTHAL
Jeffrey Brown
LUCY & ANDY NEANDERTHAL
THE STONE COLD AGE
Jeffrey Brown
Art © 2016 Jeffrey Brown
JeffreyBrownComics.com
CROWN